"What are you afraid of, Paige?"

"That's a complicated question," she whispered because that was all she could manage. Her lungs squeezed. She couldn't tell him the truth. She was afraid once he saw past everything, he wouldn't like what he found. Just like everyone else.

But he didn't back off. He didn't move away. He stared at her until the world fell silent, until his gaze fell to her lips. She knew he would kiss her before his lips pressed into hers. She knew, but she didn't back away, either. Her heart pounded so hard it ached and when his lips were finally on hers, she kissed him back, letting her knees go weak, letting herself sink into him, letting go.

SOMETHING LIKE LOVE

SOMETHING LIKE LOVE

A Heart of the Rockies Novel

SARA RICHARDSON

FOREVER

NEW YORK   BOSTON

Copyright © 2015 by Sara Richardson
Excerpt from *More Than a Feeling* copyright © 2015 by Sara Richardson

Forever
Hachette Book Group
1290 Avenue of the Americas
New York, NY 10104

www.HachetteBookGroup.com

Printed in the United States of America

First Edition: October 2015
10 9 8 7 6 5 4 3 2 1

OPM

Forever is an imprint of Grand Central Publishing.
The Forever name and logo are trademarks of Hachette Book Group, Inc.

The Hachette Speakers Bureau provides a wide range of authors for speaking events. To find out more, go to www.hachettespeakersbureau.com or call (866) 376-6591.

The publisher is not responsible for websites (or their content) that are not owned by the publisher.

To my sweet mom, Emy Lou: Thank you for recognizing the gift long before I did.

Acknowledgments

I am so blessed to have a whole cast of incredible characters who make this writing dream possible. Thank you Megha Parekh, editor extraordinaire, for always knowing exactly what a story needs. To the whole team at Forever—I am beyond grateful for all of the work you put into proofreading, producing, marketing, and selling my books. You don't get nearly enough credit for what you do.

Thank you, Langdon Adams of Elk Mountain Expeditions in Aspen, for patiently answering my questions about rafting the Roaring Fork. Any mistakes, inaccuracies, or misrepresentations are all mine.

A huge thank you to Matt Crocker of Omega Consulting Group for working so hard on my behalf. Your marketing expertise has been invaluable in planning for the release of this series.

Erin Romero, my sister and best friend, thank you for

working so hard to get people excited about my books and for helping me form the best street team in the world.

Will, AJ, and Kaleb, thank you for never complaining about the messy house, the lack of creative meals, or the hours I spend in my imaginary world. Thank you for loving me so well and for giving me the freedom to pursue my heart. I know I don't deserve you!

SOMETHING LIKE LOVE

CHAPTER ONE

Smile. Always smile. A smile communicates something positive in any language.

Paige recited the adage the perky instructor had indoctrinated into her during the daylong customer service torture—training—her boss had strongly encouraged her to attend.

Everyone is beautiful when they smile. Smiling can defuse even the tensest situation and soften even the worst temper.

Except she'd tried smiling all morning and it had gotten her nowhere.

Paige ground her trusty hiking boots to a stop on the side of the trail and glanced back to evaluate her latest group of "customers," which consisted of an overweight insurance salesman from Oklahoma, along with his painfully polite and heavily made-up wife and three teenaged boys who had zero ability to look any farther north than Paige's chest. Yes, she happened to be well-endowed (thanks for that, Gramma Lou), but she was also wearing a sports bra that happened to be the equivalent of one of those 1800s girdles, so what was that about?

Clomp, clomp, clomp. The group plodded up the trail a good quarter mile behind her, their cowboy boots scraping the packed dirt, metallic belt buckles glistening in the early morning sun. Not exactly ideal attire for scaling the side of a mountain to have a picnic at a lake.

Stifling the groan that thundered somewhere far beneath her ribcage, she studied the western horizon. The granite spikes of Castle Peak loomed high above, glaciers glinting with sunlit sparkles. Against the mind-blowing blue sky, those cliffs presided over the entire valley, presided over her. Lower, the cragged slopes gave way to the forested valley, which was crowded with towering green pine and plumes of aspen groves. Where the sunlight cut through the pine needles and leaves, bright green grass sprouted like tufts of a baby's hair, new and shiny and soft. Wildflowers of all colors carpeted the valley floor—the red Indian paintbrush, the purple asters, the yellow alpine buttercups and, her favorite, the blue columbines. Paige inhaled the calming scent of the mountain air—that perfect blend of honeysuckle and evergreen and sun-ripened dirt. The vast wilderness that stretched out on all sides of her had become her refuge. It was both terrifying and beautiful, dangerous and yet the only place she felt safe enough to be true to herself.

Only, she wasn't by herself. Her gaze settled back on the spectacle behind her. She'd lucked out by being the only Walker Mountain Ranch guide available to lead the *Howdy Doody* cast up a mountain.

Be nice, Paige. She was trying. God, was she trying. She'd even carried Hal's pack for most of the trip, but...

A quick glance at her Timex sent her pulse into overdrive. Their opportunity to make it to the lake in clear weather ticked away with each second they dragged their boots on that packed trail.

"Hot diggity!" Hal called behind her. "Looks like it's time for a break," he wheezed.

She turned. *Smile, damn it. Smile.* "Um, Hal...we've had quite a few breaks. Don't you think?" Her boots scuffed closer to his. "Why don't you take a sip of water and we'll keep going? Every time we stop we're allowing the lactic acid in our muscles to—"

"Gals like you are a hell of a lot prettier when they're quiet." The man laughed. He actually laughed like he thought belittling women was some kind of joke.

His wife, Brenda, fashioned her freshly slathered red lips into an apologetic smile, a silent *I know, I know. He's hopeless.*

Disgust rippled Paige's mouth into what her mother called a sour expression. *Those faces will give you wrinkles, Paige.* Who cared about wrinkles? This man was about to give her an aneurysm. Not only was he insulting her, they'd also been on the trail for about two hours and had maybe gone one mile. Seeing as how the entire trail up to the lake was only three and a half miles, it should've been a cakewalk, but Hal might as well have been scaling Mount Everest. About every tenth of a mile, he'd stop and double over and guzzle about a quart of water and Paige would have to wander away a couple steps before she blurted out the question that hammered her brain. Why had he booked a hiking trip when he could've taken the damn shuttle to the lake?

Miss Customer Service Trainer would definitely not approve.

It is never, ever, under any circumstances okay to curse in front of a customer.

Who the hell was that lady kidding? They were in the

wilderness, for Mona Lisa's sake! There were no "customers" out here. Only survivors. There was a reason she barked out orders and pushed her clients to the edges of their physical limits. Not because she enjoyed being a drill sergeant. When she met these people, when she shook their hands and looked at the eager faces, into their bright, expectant eyes, she made them a silent promise. *I will keep you safe.* She added their well-being to the weight stuffed in her pack. Things out here could change in the shift of the wind, in the slip of a boot. She knew that better than anyone.

So, while she had agreed to cut back on the whole swearing thing, she had a job to do. Like it or not, she had to lead the Funkleman family to their destination, whatever it took.

And she had to do it soon.

Paige shifted a wary gaze back to the horizon where a hearty thunderhead, swollen and black, encroached on Castle Peak, merely a few miles away. They had maybe another two hours before the clouds built and unleashed hell right on top of them. Thunderstorms above tree line brewed horror stories. No protection. Nowhere to hide. Just you and the millions of volts of electricity zinging across the sky. One cloud-to-ground current could take out an entire group.

What about that, Miss Customer Service Trainer? What would you say to that?

"Woo hoo!" Hal dumped half of his third water bottle over his head and shook like a drenched dog, jowls swaying and everything.

Oh no he didn't. She plowed toward him, steam clouds rising from her mouth. "What did I tell you about wasting water, Hal?"

"Can't help it. I'm parched." He eyed her with a sheepish grin. "You got plenty more in your pack, Miss Paige. Am I right?"

It is inappropriate to argue with a customer. If they say something you don't agree with, find a way to redirect them instead of firing back.

Redirect. Redirect.... She had to redirect before she sucker-punched the man. He was so not worth getting fired over.

"All right, guys!" Pivoting, she shifted back into cheerleader mode. "We need to hustle. Gotta get up there before noon." Which meant... "No more breaks. We're gonna keep moving."

Sweat slicked Hal's sideburns against his ruddy skin. He doubled over and peered up at her. "I ain't movin'. I can't. I might bust a lung."

Every client said that at least once during a climb. She studied the others behind him. Brenda, his lovely wife, gasped like a beached trout. Surprisingly, her teased blond hair still stood about eight inches above her forehead, though her Mary Kay makeup had melted. The three boys, whom she liked to think of as Larry, Curly, and Moe, plodded behind their mother in typical sullen teenager fashion.

Okay. So. Cheerleader mode wasn't working. It was time to level with this guy. She had never failed on a mission to get a client up a mountain, and not even Hal Funkleman would stop her from showing this family how it felt to stand up there and look out over the vastness of an endless beauty. It was power. It was fear. It was the reward. That moment made every step, every aching muscle worth it.

Assume the stance. She posted her hands on her hips exactly like a drill sergeant would and stomped over to Hal. "Stand up. We're going."

His jaw dropped and exposed four silver fillings.

Pretending not to notice the ice in his stare, she gestured to Brenda and the Three Stooges. "Come on. This way.

Step around him and keep hiking." One by one, his family obeyed, casting apologetic glances at the head of their household. Apparently, they feared her more than him. That was a good thing.

Hal pushed off his knees and stood at full height, his grizzly-bear-like body towering over her. "Are you crazy, lady? I can hardly breathe up here. You're gonna kill me."

"This will so not kill you." She smiled. "It's good for you. Just take deep breaths and walk slowly. As long as you keep moving, you'll be fine." She'd taken three-hundred-pound clients up to the lake, and nearly cried at the look of accomplishment on their faces when they saw the view.

The man faked a hacking cough.

Brenda glanced back with worry furrowed into her forehead, but Paige swept her hand through the air in a silent command for her to turn around. *That's right, Brenda. Keep on movin'. Nothin' to see here.* She'd take care of Hal, no problem. He might be a big guy, but how tough could he be?

Let's find out. She stepped up until they stood toe-to-toe, like two cowboys about to duel. Except she didn't have the belt buckle or the boots or the stubble on her chin. But that'd never stopped her before. She'd held her own with plenty of Hal Funklemans. If she could handle Shooter, she could handle Hal.

"I'm not goin' nowhere." He glared down at her, cheeks splotched, lips crusted with spit, eyes crazy with the stress of physical exertion. "No, sir. I don't take orders from people like you."

"People like me." Women. He meant he didn't take orders from women. *That's it.* For two hours, she'd babied him, smiled, and encouraged him. *You're doing great, Hal! Looking good! Keep it up!* She'd given the customer service method her best effort—for Bryce and Avery—and it didn't work. No amount of customer service training could change the fact that she was responsible for what happened out here. Screw being nice. She'd have to resort to what she did best: tough love.

Paige pushed up the sleeves of her thermal. "See those clouds over there?" She pointed above Hal's head. "Those are called thunderheads."

He assessed the clouds with a shrug. "Yeah. So?"

"Have you ever stood above tree line during a lightning storm, Hal?"

"Sure haven't." He tugged on his belt as it seemed to have slipped, exposing the fact that his flannel shirt had been tucked into plaid boxer shorts.

She averted her eyes back to his. "Let me tell you something about lightning. One cloud-to-ground strike at this altitude could fry your body like a piece of bacon."

At the mention of bacon, Hal's eyes lit.

Okay. Bad idea distracting the man with pork. She tried again. "I mean, it'll stop your heart instantly, burn your skin to a crisp."

"Like bacon." Hal nodded, his eyes gleaming with a frightening hunger. "You know what? I got some jerky in my pack. Seems like a good time to stop for lunch, don't it?"

If you feel yourself losing your temper with a customer, be sure to stop, smile politely, and count silently to ten. Refrain from lashing out.

Was she starting to lose her temper? *Yes.* The answer flashed in the heat of her cheeks like a glowing neon sign. Inhaling a cleansing breath, she tried it out. *One, two, three...oh screw it.* They were engaged in some kind of weird chauvinistic power struggle, and he couldn't win. Not out here. "What I'm trying to say is, we don't have time for jerky, Hal. We're not stopping."

His chin tipped upward in defiant child fashion. "That's not your call." He shimmied out of his backpack straps and let the thing fall to the ground with a thud. "I believe we're the ones payin' for this here hike."

"And I believe I'm here to make sure everyone gets to the lake alive." Her jaw ground out the words. "That means we have to bag this thing by ten. Get off the trail by noon. Before we get struck by lightning. Got it?"

Hal's eyes searched the sky above her head. "Don't look too bad to me." As if proving he wasn't the least bit concerned, he plopped down. Well, as much as a heavy-set man can plop. It was more like a grimacing collapse that ended in a wince. "A little rain never hurt nobody." He pawed through his pack. When he pulled out the bag of jerky Paige could've sworn she saw tears of joy in his eyes.

Wow. This guy was unbelievable.

If a disagreement arises, gently sway the customer using positive tactics. Listen first, then reiterate your point of view.

Yeah. Right. Maybe that worked with reasonable people. She had half a mind to swipe that bag of jerky out of his greedy hand and tie it to a stick so she could lure him up the mountain like a carrot leading a donkey. "I'm not talking about a little rain, Hal," she spat. "I'm talking about an electrical storm." Memories shivered through her. "Trust me. I've been there. Lightning so close you can hear it zing in the air. The hair on your head and arms standing straight up—"

"And you didn't get struck down, didya?" Obvious disappointment tugged at the corners of his mouth.

If all else fails and you feel you can no longer serve the customer, remove yourself from the situation for a moment. Gain some perspective and go back to the customer when you're ready.

Paige grinned. Now that she could do. At least the training day hadn't been a total waste. "You know what, Hal? Forget it." She spun away. "You go ahead and take a long lunch break. We'll see you in a few hours."

"You can't leave me by myself! What if I see a bear? A mountain lion?"

She glanced over her shoulder. *Smile politely.* "If I were you, I'd make sure my hands didn't smell like jerky."

And with that, she blazed up the trail to join the others.

CHAPTER TWO

How'd this happen? How the hell did this happen?" Benjamin Hunter Noble III clicked off the big screen and bolted across his bachelor kitchen—all streamlined stone and dark wood—and poured himself a glass of whiskey. Swirling the ice, he edged to the bay window and gazed out into the dimming light of the evening sun at the thousands of acres that made up his sprawling ranch. That land—his land—stretched all the way to the horizon.

Damn. He'd give his left testicle to be out there, galloping across that Texas prairie land on Keg's back, wind in his face, the thud of hooves in his ears, life-altering disgraces left in the dust.

"I told you she was trouble." Gracie Hunter Noble, whom he'd called "Mother" until he graduated from college and she insisted he start using her first name, followed on his heels in the regal stance she'd perfected as a senator's wife.

"I knew it the moment I laid eyes on that girl. She couldn't be trusted."

"Are you kidding? You practically picked out china for the two of them!" This from his sweet sister, Julia, who steered her wheelchair close enough to run over their mother's toes. "She had you eating out of her hand." J clutched her hands under her chin and batted her thick eyelashes. "Oh, Mrs. Noble, I just love your dress, your hair, your lovely makeup. Why, I'd happily wipe your prim bottom, if you asked me to," she purred like a southern belle.

He busted out a laugh. He couldn't help it. J never missed an opportunity to poke fun at their tightly wound mother. She'd always gotten away with a hell of a lot more than him.

Gracie's lips puckered into a disapproving frown. "Don't be vulgar, Julia. It's not ladylike."

Ha. They all knew Julia had given up on the ladylike thing a long time ago. Though his sister was the image of their mother with those movie-star cheekbones, pouting lips, and thick, shoulder-length chestnut hair—which his mother had to pay a fortune to maintain—the two of them were complete opposites in every way. It always made for interesting family gatherings.

"Forget who's to blame." Kevin Mackey, his senatorial campaign guru, clicked the television back on, mouth pulled into that grim look he always wore. With his dark slicked-back hair, pale skin, and pointed chin, Kev looked like he could've fit right in with the Addams Family.

"What matters is how we handle it." His eyeballs scrolled back and forth as if he was reading the news ticker that ran across the bottom of the screen.

Ben took another shot of whiskey and welcomed the sting. He didn't need to look up to know what the news outlets were saying.

Famous catalog model—there was an oxymoron if he'd ever heard one—*Valentina Giovanni, girlfriend of senatorial candidate Benjamin Hunter Noble III*—make that former girlfriend—*exposes his blatant mistreatment of the cattle and land on the Noble ranch in a series of shocking photos she captured on her cell phone.*

Then came the sound bite. "I loved Ben very much, but when I realized what he was doing, how he was treating these innocent animals, how he was raping the land, I couldn't stay silent. I couldn't live with myself if I didn't speak out."

Yeah right. Her speaking out had nothing to do with a bribe from the Democratic Party. He should've known something was up when she'd suddenly traded in her small two-bedroom apartment for a swanky downtown loft. Not that he'd been able to find any proof, but he knew how these things worked.

Nausea thundered through him. He peeked up at the television screen. Sure enough, the pictures were there. Pictures she had to have doctored because he'd never once in his life taken a shovel to a steer's head. Crazy as it was, he loved his cattle like they were his kids, even gave a couple of 'em names. But somehow she'd managed to make him look like a monster. Damn Photoshop.

"That's bullshit!" Julia growled, waving an arm at the screen.

"This is defamation!" Gracie cried. "Slander!" She spun to him. "How could you let her do this to us? To this family? To our name?" When her hands clutched at her chest, he couldn't take it anymore.

"Simmer down, Gracie." Her overreactions always made him feel like they were on some shitty primetime sitcom. As his late father had been fond of saying, she'd missed her calling as a low-budget actress.

Steering his eyes clear of the television, he cruised to the sectional and sank into the leather. "How the hell could I have known she worked for the Democratic Party?" Those bastards had gotten desperate. After a successful stint in Congress, Ben's popularity had skyrocketed. The opposition knew he'd be elected, and they weren't about to let that happen. So they'd found Valentina somewhere and set him up.

He'd met her at a fund-raiser for the Paralympics. She was a gorgeous woman, no doubt about it, but she also seemed genuinely interested in his desire to increase state funding for people with disabilities. People like Julia.

Pushing that legislation was the reason he'd entered the race. Actually, it wasn't all his idea. After being a congressman for two years, he was burned-out on the whole thing. But Granddad wouldn't let it go. He was the one who'd talked him into it. *It's what your father would've wanted, Ben. You owe it to the family. Yada yada yada. Besides, it'll be good publicity. God knows the family needs it. You can show the world we're not a bunch of rednecked Republicans who don't know horseshit from cow dung.*

He'd smiled, then, when all this was still just an idea. *But we are a bunch of rednecks,* he'd reminded Granddad. Always had been, always would be, and he couldn't give a damn what anyone thought about it. He lived for the ranch, lived for the expanse of space, the manual labor, the freedom the land gave him. Still, the man had a point. Ben owed it to the family. To Julia, mostly. This was his chance to do something for her. Once he was in the Senate, he could introduce the bill Julia had been helping him write. It was one of his campaign platforms. Most accident victims in her situation didn't have access to the same therapies and rehabilitation opportunities she'd had. Their parents spent hundreds of thousands of dollars pursuing every therapy available. It killed J to see people who couldn't afford it being sent away while she continued to improve and regain movement in her legs.

The bill had become their project together. It'd given her purpose, brought them closer. They both knew that helping other victims would make what happened to her count for something. He wasn't naïve enough to believe it would atone for the past, but he had to make sure the accident wasn't for nothing.

He'd never forget the truth. Wasn't for him, she never would've been in that accident. Her legs never would've been crushed beyond recognition. She'd be walking and jogging and riding and living the party life of every other twenty-seven-year-old. Instead she was confined to a chair.

And that made him crave another drink. He stood and sauntered across the room to get a refill.

"We have to go on the offensive." His mother nodded once, her mind made up. "That's what we'll do. We'll dig until we find something in that tramp's past. Then we'll prove she's a liar and a fraud and no one will believe a word she says."

Ha. She'd been living in her semi-royalty fairy-tale land too long. The damage was done. It would be her word against his. He couldn't prove she'd fabricated those pictures. To the rest of the world, she'd been his adoring girlfriend, and it "broke her heart to have to do this." No one would believe that she was really a conniving backstabber with ties to his opponent. Hell, Gracie had her checked out by a private detective and everything about her seemed squeaky clean.

"Attacking her is *not* our best move." Kev joined him at the bar and leaned close enough that Ben caught whiff of that strange scent that always hazed around him. Smelled like some kind of BBQ rub—cumin, brown sugar, garlic. It'd sure be good on a rib eye.

"His image is already bad enough. An attack would make him look desperate." He filled a Mason jar glass to the brim with whiskey. "Besides, if we get pulled into an all-out war, who knows what she'll dig up on him." Those pointy eyebrows raised in a warning. Ben got his meaning.

They might start asking more questions about Julia's accident.

Dad was a senator when it'd happened. Every detail about the crash was carefully guarded, altered. His PR people had spun it into a senseless tragedy, a result of a rainy back road. But they all knew what the world didn't. Ben could've prevented that accident. If he would've been a better man, he would've prevented the accident. All the whiskey in the world couldn't change that fact.

Maybe that was why he'd liked Valentina. She couldn't have cared less about his past. Never even asked him what happened to his sister. Apparently, the whole time she'd only been interested in ruining his political career. God, he was a fool. Truth was, he should've seen it coming. The woman hailed from Dallas, which wasn't exactly ranch country. More like fake everything country—hair color, breast implants, acrylic nails. Well now he'd learned his lesson. He'd had enough fake. His next woman had to be real. He didn't want be with someone who kept a strict regimen of spa treatments and cleanses and Pilates. He wanted someone who could hang with him when he felt like surfing in Australia or paragliding in the Andes or skiing the Matterhorn...

Kev dug his phone out of pocket and started to type. "I'll have Carla release a statement citing the accusations as false.

And I'm sure there'll be some kind of investigation. But in the meantime, we have to improve your image. In a big way. A visible way."

"We'll make another donation to the zoo." Gracie walked briskly to her purse as though she planned to write out the check right there. "A million. They can build a new habitat or something."

"The zoo?" Ben shot her his best are-you-kidding-me look. "We've already made three donations to the zoo. Hell, the damn conservatory is named after Granddad."

"Stop swearing, Benjamin. Really." She frowned, but dropped her purse back to the counter.

"What about one of those reality shows where they dump people out in the wild so they can survive the elements?" J's voice sounded a little too innocent, a little too sincere.

Sure enough, a glimmer in her eye clued him in on her intent to shock their mother again. "There's this new one on Discovery Channel. The people run around buck naked! You should see their—"

"Julia Grace Hunter Noble!" The words sailed out in a horrified gasp. "That is disgusting. What kind of trash television—"

"Ben's right." Kev downed the rest of his whiskey. He seemed to drink about ten times more whenever Gracie was around. Come to think of it, they all seemed to drink about ten times more when she was around. "Money's too easy. Everyone knows you've got plenty to go around. It won't carry the impact we need." Kev gave Ben's mother a pointed look. "We have to find something that'll prove he's all about animals and the environment."

"I still say we stick him out in the wilderness," Julia muttered. "Have some cameras follow him around. Maybe he could rescue a wounded rabbit or something." Her eyebrows shot up. "Nothing more appealing to female voters than a naked man saving the planet."

Nice. Ben walked past his sister and ruffled her hair.

Gracie pressed a hand to her forehead like she might faint. He wouldn't put it past her.

"Actually, it's not a bad idea," Kev said.

"Running around naked in the woods?" The guy had lost his mind. He'd completely lost it. But still...he couldn't pass on the opportunity to rile up Gracie. "Guess I could try it. I'd have to hit the tanning booth, first. No doubt about that."

"You will do no such thing, Benjamin!" His mother stalked away from him and perched on the couch in a pout.

Julia cackled.

"I'm not talking about the naked thing." Kev rolled his eyes. "I'm talking about getting you some environmental exposure."

"Indecent exposure." Julia cracked herself up again.

"Really, Julia. I raised you better than this." Gracie delivered her signature line. "After all I've done for you, everything I've taught you, this is how you repay me?"

J smiled sweetly. He had to hand it to her. She seemed to be happy living outside of everyone's expectations. Free. Gracie never seemed to get to her.

Kev, on the other hand, looked like he was about to explode. "I'm talking about inviting the press to see a different side of you. Not the cattle rancher. The environmentalist."

There was one problem with that plan. "I'm *not* an environmentalist."

"But you *do* like the outdoors," Kev pointed out.

"Sure. Yeah." He was outdoorsy. In fact, he'd prefer to be outdoors now. He glanced out the window. Dusk had settled, smothering everything in its colorless haze. Still, if the moon was full, it might be light enough for a midnight ride...

"You still own all that land west of Aspen?"

He turned back to Kev. "Yeah. Why?"

"How many acres?"

"About a thousand, give or take." Granddad had bought it last year. They'd talked about expanding the ranch to Colorado, but he was still trying to figure out how to deal with the harsh winters.

"That's what you'll donate." He whipped out his phone.

"Donate?" Who the hell would want a bunch of land out in the middle of nowhere?

"I still think we should go after that hussy." Gracie glared at the television. "We can't let her get away with this."

Kev waved her off. "The investigation will exonerate him. In the meantime, you can donate the land as a wildlife refuge. Get a huge tax write-off. We'll travel up there. Make it a big thing with the press. Set up a ceremony. The whole deal."

"We can stay at Bryce's place!" Much to Ben's disapproval, J had always had a crush on his old college roommate. "It'll be perfect! We haven't been up there since they opened the pool! Can't wait to see that man in a swimsuit."

"He's married," Ben growled, even though Julia knew that full well.

"I know but he's one fine piece of man. I can still look, right?"

No. No man he'd ever met deserved her, could take care of her, was worthy of her. To him, she'd stopped aging when she was fifteen. But J's lust for Bryce wasn't the only reason he hesitated. Something told him not everyone at the Walker Mountain Ranch would be happy to see him. Especially a certain guide . . .

"The Walker Mountain Ranch would be the perfect place to stay." Kev's eyes were lit with the possibilities. "Your land is right on the Roaring Fork River, right? We could set up a rafting trip, deliver you right to the ceremony in style."

Hmmm. In style and sitting right next to the Walker Mountain Ranch's best rafting guide, Paige Harper. Memories stoked the embers of their quick romance and delivered a punch of heat right to his gut. God, he'd wanted that woman...if only he hadn't gone and screwed everything up.

Wasn't his fault, exactly. But when Avery'd thrown a gala to save Bryce's ranch last year, he and Paige had hooked up. Well, almost. They were headed up to his room when the woman he'd hooked up with at the bar the night before saw him and threw her martini right in his face.

After that, Paige bolted. Said he was a player and she didn't date guys like him. But how the hell was he supposed to know he'd meet someone like her the next night? He'd tried to get in touch with her for a few months after but she never returned any of his calls.

"So what'dya think, big brother?" J tugged on his pant leg like she'd done ever since she was old enough to follow him around.

He grinned. She wanted to know what he thought?

Well...he thought this just might be his second chance with a woman he couldn't seem to forget.

He turned to Kev. "You're right. It's a good idea. I'll talk it over with Granddad." If he was on board, Ben would call Bryce and set it up.

"Perfect. I'll start making the arrangements." Kev punched some numbers into his phone and held it up to his ear.

"If you're going up there, I'm coming with you." Gracie posted her hands on her hips.

Great. Last thing he needed was his overbearing momma tagging along on a publicity mission. "I don't think—"

"I'm coming along." She stuck out her chin like a debu-tante and he knew there was no point in arguing.

"Fine. But you have to promise not to say a word about Valentina to the media." Kev was right. Going after her would be a bad idea.

"Of course I won't."

Uh-huh. She was about as believable as a spooked lawyer. He crossed the kitchen and opened the back door. "I'm gonna ride over to Granddad's. Make sure he's on board." Then he'd take a good long ride up to the ridge and back.

Maybe that'd ease the tension in his neck and give him time to figure out how to win back the girl he'd lost.

CHAPTER THREE

Here we go. Paige's heart launched into a tumbling routine that could've rivaled Gabby Douglas's Olympic gold performance. She eased her Subaru into a parking spot outside the Walker Mountain Ranch office and cut the engine. Being summoned to the office was never a good sign. Didn't matter if you were in high school or at a Catholic church camp, the words, *Can I see you in my office?* infused a sense of dread into your bloodstream. Especially when it came in the form of a voice mail from your boss.

Not that Bryce Walker scared her. No, it wasn't about fear. She hated disappointing him, that was all. She'd been a disappointment her whole life, as nearly every member of her family liked to remind her. But when she'd started working for the Walkers in high school, they'd treated her more like a person instead of a pest and now she hated to let Bryce down.

She obviously had, somehow. His voice mail had an unmistakable undertone of disappointment. She should know. She'd heard that tone her whole life.

The parking lot sat empty, as it typically did in the middle of the week. Most of their outfitting clients came in on a Thursday or Friday and left on a Monday or Tuesday. Wednesday was their day off. Not that she minded coming in. She spent most of her free time around there, anyway, helping groom the horses or mucking out the stables or chatting with Elsie and doing whatever else needed to be done. The Walker Mountain Ranch always hummed with life, with people coming and going, sharing a meal, laughing and chatting. It was the one place she fit.

Besides all of that, if she spent time at the ranch she wouldn't risk one of her siblings stopping by her apartment to ask when she planned to stop being so selfish and come work at the café so Dad and Mom didn't have to work so much. That happened at least once a week.

A foreign sense of dread pulsed through her as she shuffled up the porch steps. Once a one-room dungeon, Bryce and Avery had transformed the Walker Mountain Ranch lobby into a palace with three offices, one for Avery, who did most of the marketing, one for Bryce, who handled all of the facilities and trip planning, and one for Kaylee, who'd once been married to Bryce's cousin, Sawyer. Before she'd cheated on the poor man, she took care of the booking and finances.

There was also a gorgeous waiting area for clients who were checking in or out, complete with a grand stone fireplace, heavy pub tables, and leather seating. Oh, and who could forget the espresso machine and freshly baked goods case that Elsie kept stocked with every temptation known to mankind? Paige never missed a chance to stop by and check out the day's selections, but for once her stomach didn't tempt her.

Usually pushing open the solid pine door made her grin, but now she plowed through with her head down, the apprehensions about the impending meeting knotting up her neck.

"Woof!" Moose, Bryce and Avery's massive Bernese mountain dog, charged her.

"Good doggie." She braced herself for impact and scrubbed the dog's ears until his hind leg twitched.

"Hey, Paige."

She looked up.

Bryce stood behind the check-in counter, changing the light bulb in a stained glass lamp.

As usual, he was dressed in his khaki Carhartts and a short-sleeved blue button-up shirt with a monogrammed Walker Mountain Ranch logo on the pocket.

"Hi," she replied, trying to sound chipper, but her tone had gone flat. Normally when she saw Bryce, she'd bound right up to him and punch his shoulder, give him a noogie, or maybe tease him about how short Avery made him keep his hair now. A pang of sadness drew her gaze back to the floor. He was her true big brother, even though she had three others who could claim blood relation. But they'd never looked after her the way Bryce had. They'd never bothered with her at all.

"I'm all set here." He flicked the lamp on and off, as though making sure it worked. "Let's talk in my office."

In the office. Not a casual conversation in the hall . . .

"Okay," she squeaked, and followed him across the lobby sitting room into his office. Moose trotted behind her, rubbing against her legs like he wanted another scratch.

Right outside the door, she stopped.

Bryce's wife, Avery, was lying on his couch, eyes closed, fanning herself with the latest issue of *Backpacker* magazine. Her brand-new baby bump poked out the front of a cute fitted red shirt. Even pregnant, the woman had the best sense of style Paige had ever seen.

"Hey, baby, Paige is here." Bryce sat on the arm of the couch, resting his hand on Avery's belly. It would've been the warmest, cutest scene if Paige hadn't felt so cold. Avery had been called to the meeting, too. And yes, they were friends but Avery was also Bryce's wife, and kind of her boss, too, though no one at the ranch thought of her that way. She was too sweet.

"Hey, Paige," Avery said in that groggy voice she'd grown accustomed to hearing over the last five months.

Bryce slid down next to his wife, kissing her on the cheek and then resting his hand high on her thigh.

Normally, Paige would've made some joke about it, about how they couldn't seem to be in the same room without touching, but this was not a normal day, not a normal meeting, and, for the first time ever, she felt like she didn't fit there.

Moose gave her hand a big ol' sympathetic lick.

Somehow, Avery seemed to sense her trepidation, too. She sat up straighter, smoothing her long, blond hair down over her shoulders while beaming what was probably supposed to be a reassuring smile at Paige.

"Why don't you sit?" She gestured to the chair across from the couch. "I'll make us some lattes." She raised her sculpted brows at Bryce in a secret message.

In response, he reached up and scratched his head.

What the hell were they doing? Baseball signals? Knowing them, probably. The Walker Mountain Ranch baseball team had been the town champions two years running.

"I don't want a latte." Paige had never been good at decoding signals, at politely stepping around issues. "I want to know why I'm here. In your office." She shot Bryce her own coded look. He knew her. He knew she didn't beat around the bush. *If you have something to say, get on with it.*

He acknowledged her with a sigh, obviously getting her meaning.

"Paige...you should sit," Avery insisted, her tone softened into a careful gentleness.

The ache in her stomach twisted into a nauseating whirlpool. No, make that cesspool, churning over and over. She'd heard that tone before. It was the tone a mother would use with a wayward child.

An itch crawled over her skin. Summoning the same courage she always relied on with her own father, she perched on the very edge of the squeaky leather cushion. What had she done wrong? Were they going to fire her? Her mind cataloged back over the last several months. There'd been the time she'd forgotten to log her trip miles, but that was weeks ago...

Seemingly bored with the whole scene, Moose flopped to lie down right on her feet. Because the whole world revolved around him. Shaking her head, Paige leaned over to scratch his belly. But she couldn't miss the pained look Bryce exchanged with his wife. Their carefully guarded expressions communicated things she couldn't understand.

Her eyes heated. The three of them had always been on the same side, ever since Avery had come to the Walker Mountain Ranch, ever since she'd joined the softball team. Paige had been the maid of honor in their wedding, for crying out loud.

Bryce's sharp inhale cut off her thoughts. With a glance and a nod, he seemed to offer the floor to Avery.

"Paige, honey...we've, um, well..." She folded her hands in her lap. "We've gotten some complaints about you. On your guide evaluations."

"Complaints." The fear that swirled in her stomach quieted. That was it? Complaints? Shoot, people might complain about her after the trip, but she never heard any complaints when they stood on top of a mountain or made it through a class four rapid. Sure, her methods might be unconventional but she always delivered. She shot Avery her own smile. "Maybe this is a good time to talk about the customers you keep assigning me. Seriously? Why does Shooter always get to take the fun groups while I'm stuck with people like the Funklemans?"

Neither one of them smiled back. Bryce glared right into her eyes. "Thing is, customers say you're too harsh. You don't listen." His raised his head so he was looking down on her. "Then there was that whole fiasco with the Funklemans."

Heat pierced her, remnants of her mother's Irish temper flaring. "Fiasco? *Fiasco?*" She shot to her feet, pushing Moose aside.

The dog grunted like he was as annoyed as she was.

"I got them up that mountain and back down before the lightning hit. I'd hardly call that a fiasco!" She'd had a feeling Hal would rather follow her up that mountain than sit there by himself. And she was right. He thought he was bear bait. Little did he know, black bears almost always spooked when they even heard a human anywhere in the vicinity.

Bryce swiped at his face, a frustrated gesture she'd seen him make a number of times, but it had never been directed at her.

She sank back to the couch. He wasn't messing around, giving her a flippant reprimand. He was mad.

"Sure, you got them up the mountain. But Mr. Funkleman had plenty to say about *how* you got him up there."

"I did my job. I'm good at my job." She worked harder than anyone to prove herself…

"You are, Paige." Avery leaned over and patted her knee. "You're great. We know that. We appreciate your skills." She nodded in Bryce's direction as if encouraging him to agree.

He didn't. "We need people to like you, too. We need 'em to tell their friends about their great experience. They're getting hung up on your personality."

The comment stung. He'd never had a problem with her personality before. He'd always accepted her, despite her personality. But he of all people had to know why she took her job so seriously, why she was so careful. He'd been a guide once, too.

"I do what I have to do to keep people safe." Because she could never live with herself if something happened to someone out there. That was why she never left without being overly prepared. She carried more weight in emergency supplies than she did in personal items. She kept an eye on the weather. She forced people like Hal to do what she said, even if it meant she had to yell at them.

Bryce and Avery looked at each other, that same coded language firing back and forth between them.

"The thing is..." Avery paused. "We're still trying to establish our brand. Poor customer service won't help."

She stared at her hands. They were weathered for someone her age, chipped nails, cracked, dry skin. In some ways, they matched her personality, hardened by the landscape of her life.

"We can't grow with bad word of mouth." Bryce's gaze drilled into hers until she felt herself start to shrink.

Oh, god. They were going to fire her. What about the program she'd been begging Bryce to start? The therapy program with the horses? Ever since she'd watched MS slowly kill Gramma Lou, she'd wanted to help people with physical challenges experience the peace and solitude of mountains. Bryce kept telling her they'd talk about it as soon as they were more established...

In a swift blink, she saw her dream start to disintegrate. If Bryce fired her, she'd never find another job around here. Everyone would know. She'd never have the chance to start the program.

Moose sat next to the couch and rested his head in her lap as if he felt her pain. She tousled the dog's soft fur, searching for comfort.

"You can't let me go. Please," she begged. "I'll do anything. More customer service training. I'll change. I know I can—"

"Oh, sweetie." Avery's laugh sympathized. "We're not letting you go. We just wanted to have a chat about it."

She snapped up her head and gaped at Avery. They weren't firing her? Her hands clasped together in her lap. "O...kay..."

"We've got an important group coming in." Bryce took over again. "This'll be highly visible, and I need everything to be perfect. Including my guides."

"Of course. No problem." This was the perfect opportunity for her to prove herself, to show them she could handle any client.

Avery and Bryce looked at each other. "Um..." Avery's nose twitched. "The thing is...you kind of already know this guy."

"Really?" That was a good thing, right? It'd make it easier. But if that was the case, then why did Avery look so worried?

"Yeah," Bryce said. "You remember my buddy Ben? Ben Noble?"

Blood surged to her face, then drained too fast, a hot flash that ended in a wintry cold. Ben fuc—bleeping—Noble. *He* was the big client? *He* was the customer she had to take on a rafting trip? She stopped petting Moose, instead fisting her hands at her sides.

The dog nudged her arm once, but then gave up and lay on her feet, again.

"It'll be huge publicity for us," Avery gushed. "He's bringing his whole campaign up here. They're donating the acreage they own west of town to a new land trust."

Shit. Okay, yes, she was trying to cut back on the swearing, but shit. Shit, shit, shit on a stick.

"He wants to do a rafting trip," Bryce said. "All the way down the Fork. His land is just past Enderson Falls, so you can pull over and deliver him right to the signing ceremony."

Bryce went on about how important it was that this went off without a hitch, but all Paige could see, all she could hear, was the scene on the night she'd last seen Ben Noble.

They'd been dancing at a fund-raiser gala that Avery had thrown for Bryce last year, and the man knew his way around a dance floor. Wearing that million-dollar smile, he'd twirled her and dipped her and charmed her all night with that damn smooth voice of his. Then he'd kissed her, brushing his lips against hers until her knees gave and she heard herself agree to go up to his room.

It was a damn good thing that busty blonde had stopped him to throw her drink in his face before she'd made the biggest mistake of her life. It seemed Ben Noble enjoyed the dance but not the morning after, and she didn't do one-night stands. Especially with a guy who'd turned it into an art form. She'd never put herself in that situation again. Not after what Jory had done to her when she was nineteen, convincing her to sleep with him then tossing her aside like a ruined pair of those Nikes he wore.

She'd only been humiliated that way one other time in her entire life, and she'd sworn then she'd never let it happen again.

"Paige?" Avery waved a hand in her face. "Are you okay with this?" she asked, wearing that furrowed frown, girl code for "I know things didn't end well between you two"...Thank god she refrained from saying those words. Bryce had no clue she'd been anywhere near Ben Noble. He'd been too busy kissing Avery that night.

"Because if you're not—"

"Of course I'm okay with it," she said, mentally hiking up her big girl panties and snapping the elastic. This was her chance. If she did this, if she made Ben's trip a success, Bryce couldn't put her off about the therapy program. Not anymore. "It'll be great." She chiseled out a smile. "Ben is *so*...great."

Avery slanted her head and called her out with another look, but she fired up the smile again. "Seriously. I'm fine with it."

Bryce looked back and forth between them. "Why wouldn't she be fine with it?" he demanded.

"No reason," Avery murmured, suddenly appearing very interested in a loose thread on her shirt.

She was so believable.

"It'll be a chance to get us some publicity." Bryce stood and folded his arms, ever and always the worried boss. "I need to know you'll give them—Ben, his campaign guys, the press, *everyone*—a good experience."

"I will." She was vaguely aware that her head nodded too fast but she couldn't seem to slow it down. "I swear. I'll be so sweet you won't even recognize me." It might require a roll of duct tape, but she'd do whatever it took. "You have nothing to worry about," she assured him with a syrupy-sweet smile.

Her, on the other hand? She had plenty to worry about.

The biggest concern? How the hell would she spend a whole week being nice to Benjamin Noble?

CHAPTER FOUR

Okay. So this wasn't exactly the best day to embark on a personality makeover.

Paige shuffled her sandals down the crumbled concrete sidewalk in front of her family's café, careful not to trample the leaning wild daisies that grew in the cracks, and tugged down the green moisture-wicking tank top she'd carefully selected from her closet...as if that could really prepare her for the obscene amount of sweat she'd produce during the next five hours.

Why she'd promised to cover the lunch shift for her sister Penny, she couldn't say. Maybe the guilt of avoiding her family for the last three weeks had gotten to her. Still, just the sight of the faded red brick façade and the green-and-white striped awning stretching over her head worked that familiar tension up her spine until her shoulders tightened like she'd just climbed up the north face of Maroon Peak. She passed by the sign her father had made himself—just one of the many things that made the place *unique*, which was putting it nicely.

THE HIGH ALTITUDE CAFÉ.

WHERE FUN AND MOUNTAINS MEAT.

The hand-painted letters were scrawled in red outdoor paint over an outline of blue hand-drawn mountain peaks. Last year, when Dad had announced he'd decided to redo the sign, she'd naively suggested that maybe he should find a graphic designer to take a look, but because he was an expert in everything, he'd done it himself. Not that it mattered, much. The High Altitude Café wasn't known for an artful appearance. Her family specialized in meat dishes: beef, bison, elk, burgers, steaks. Obviously. But she'd been a vegetarian since she was twelve and even just the greasy smell wafting around her was enough make her stomach queasy.

It would be a long afternoon.

Strategically breathing through her nose, she trudged up the concrete steps to do her penance for being the one Harper who'd "walked away" from the family business. If she'd completely walked away, though, she wouldn't be walking through the door right now, would she? See? Not a total wayward child. She still helped out once in a while. That should count for something. It wouldn't. She already knew that, but it never stopped her from trying.

The bells above the door jangled a sick welcome. They'd dangled there for the last thirty years, ever since her father hung them on opening day. Actually, the whole restaurant hadn't changed much in thirty years. To her it was a baffling place—'50s diner meets truck-stop steakhouse. From the black-and-white linoleum tile floors to the dark wood paneling that decorated the walls to the red vinyl-upholstered booths, the High Altitude Café was embattled in an identity crisis. The locals who flocked there every day said it added to the charm, but to her, it only added to the sense of chaos she felt every time she saw her family. Yet another reminder she didn't fit in.

Deep breath. Brave smile. She paused inside the door to assess the customer situation. Only a couple of the booths were occupied—the Larsens sat in their regular booth and Aspen's elite firefighters sat a few tables away. Quiet now, but give it an hour and there wouldn't be a free seat in the house. The café had been voted the locals' favorite burger joint for fifteen years running.

"Well, look who it is." Her big brother, Pete Junior, appeared from the kitchen and whizzed past her with a full tray of food hoisted over his head. "Can't believe you actually decided to grace us with your presence."

She would've punched his shoulder if it weren't for the tray. "Hey, Petey." Ten years older than her, Pete was her closest sibling. He'd been stuck with all of Mom's Irish genes, fiery red hair, face freckled like a speckled egg. Even though all of the Harper siblings (except her, of course) worked at the café, Petey was really the one who kept things running. He did whatever needed to be done, usually with a smile and a wink. Case in point, today he was apparently the food runner/busboy.

He swung the tray down to rest on an unoccupied table and started to gather the plates of steaming food.

"Need help?" she called. And yes, she was procrastinating going back to the kitchen where Dad and Mom were no doubt stationed at their posts—Dad at the grill and Mom at the food line. When spending time with her family, she usually liked to warm up with Petey. He actually seemed to like her.

He gave her a look that reminded her how many full trays of dishes and food she'd dropped over her illustrious waitressing career. "No thanks, toots. I got it."

"Fine," she said through a sigh. Maybe she shouldn't have come in, after all. They all knew she made a terrible waitress.

"Ma's been waiting for you." His mouth stretched into a grim warning. "Said she read another article about those evil vegetarians. She's worried you're joining a cult or something."

"Why would I do that when I've already escaped from one?" she said snarkily, knowing Petey wouldn't take any offense to the reference about the Harper Family Rules. Years ago, her parents had seriously typed it up on their word processor and posted a printout on their kitchen wall.

1. Family always comes first.
2. Never question thy father and mother (which she was pretty sure was a direct misquote from The Good Book).
3. Always do whatever needs doing and do it with a smile.
4. Always eat your meat.

Legend had it that her father'd added that one with a ballpoint pen two weeks after they'd opened the restaurant.

Unfortunately, she'd inherited Gramma Lou's fierce spirit and had managed to break every single one of those rules during her first three years of life, as her mother loved to remind her.

"Just you wait, Paige..." Petey gave her a conniving look. "We'll suck you back in. You can't hide forever." He gave an evil laugh as he led the way past the bar and through the kitchen doors.

Sure enough, her mother stood at the row of burners stirring something in a saucepan. She wore her typical uniform, sensible black pants with a white button-up shirt. Her long auburn hair, now variegated with thick tracks of gray, had been twisted into a bun on top of her head.

Dad was stationed in his favorite place, flipping burgers over the grill, a spotted white apron tied around his wide girth and the paper chef's hat covering his bald head. None of those fancy chef's coats for him. He liked to keep things old-school.

They both had their backs to her, but Petey slammed down the tray with a loud *thunk.* "Look who's here," he announced.

"Paige!" Her mother's watery mud-puddle eyes always got that wide, bewildered look when she saw her, as if she still couldn't believe she'd had another baby when she was forty-five and "done having kids."

"You look skinny." She dropped the spoon and rushed over. "Have you been eating enough?"

Well, after Bryce and Avery had informed her that Ben was on his way to the ranch, she'd snuck into the kitchen and eaten five freshly baked oatmeal chocolate chip cookies...

Dad snatched a plate off the rack next to the burners and expertly flicked a charred burger right into the middle. He prided himself on his ability to fling burgers and catch them right out of the air. "Time to give up the rabbit food and try one of my burgers."

She pushed away the plate he offered. "Good to see you, too."

"Oh, honey." Mom patted her. "Of course we're happy to see you."

"Wish we'd see more of you," Dad grumbled. "Your mom's hip is buggin' her again."

"Don't be silly, Peter. It's perfectly fine." She set down her spoon and sashayed across the kitchen like she wanted to prove it, except a limp dragged her right foot.

Paige eyed her mother. Had she lost weight? Concern tightened her chest. "Are sure everything's okay?"

"Of course," she snapped. "Anyway, it's not me we should be worried about." She picked up her spoon again and pointed it right at her. "It's you." Red sauce dripped to the floor. "I just read this terrible article," she said, conveniently leaving out the name of the publication. "Did you know most vegetarians are malnourished?"

She deflected her mother's concerned glance with a smile. "I eat great, actually." Elsie made a vegetarian complement to go with every meal at the ranch. "And I'm still wearing the same size I always have." With all the calories she burned as a guide, that alone proved she ate healthier than most people. She definitely wasn't scrawny. She'd inherited Gramma Lou's body along with her personality. It wasn't like she didn't have any curves on her.

"It's not natural. We were made to eat meat," her father insisted as he flipped another burger high in the air.

Her gaze drifted over to the copious amounts of raw meat lumped on the stainless counters. Nausea pulsed up her throat. "What can I say? Not a big fan."

Her mother shook her head. A silent *where did I go wrong? We are not having this conversation again.* "So anyway, I'm covering for Penny today." She snagged a red apron off a hook next to the sink and grimaced at the illustration across the chest. Two cartoon-looking steaks with faces, arms, and legs, staring at each other. Under the picture it read SO WE MEAT AGAIN.

Nice. "I see you got new uniforms."

Her mother chuckled. "Your father has such a sense of humor."

"He sure does." *Aspen Monthly* hadn't dubbed him the King of Bad Puns for nothing.

"Oh." Her mother lifted the pot off the stove and set it next to the plating zone. "Would you go check on the Larsens? They'll be so happy to see you."

"You've got it." She pulled the apron over her head and scurried out the door, tying the strings behind her back.

The Larsens were a sweet elderly couple who'd shown up at the café every day at 10:30 for coffee and a sandwich for the last eighteen years. They even had their own booth, though it wasn't officially labeled. Every member of the Harper family knew and they always kept it open, a silent reservation.

Energy hummed through her as she made her way across the restaurant. This was the perfect way to start her shift, to ease into one of her least favorite activities. The Larsens never complained, never sent food back, never flustered her to the point that she dropped a dish or a tray, even though Mrs. Larsen was known to ask inappropriate questions. But she'd take that over someone complaining any day.

"Paige!" Luke Simms, one of the firemen, who also happened to be her ex, waved at her. "Did you come to see me?"

"You wish." Though he was harmless, Luke had that snide, frat boy look about him—blond spiky hair, piercing blue eyes, and an upper body that looked like it could bench-press five times her weight. They had a lot of time to work out at the firehouse.

She'd dated him last year for all of three months before he'd figured out she wouldn't sleep with him until they were exclusive. Apparently that was too much to ask. Ever since she'd broken things off, he'd been trying to change her mind.

"Come on, Paige. Let me take you out," he called over.

Passing by the table without a glance, she flipped him off.

His fire buddies snorted. "You're right, she's totally into you," one of them mocked.

Totally. She shook her head and veered toward the Larsens' table.

Before she'd even made it to the table, Mrs. Larsen popped off the bench. "Paige!" She hugged her. "How wonderful to see you!"

Though they were about the same height, Mrs. Larsen seemed frail. Paige hugged her back gently, then stood upright. "You, too, Mrs. Larsen." She had a grandmotherly face, full and round with lines where her dimples popped out when she smiled. Her long white hair had been twisted up and knotted on her head.

"My, my, my. You look positively fabulous." She eased back into her seat and eyed her with a curious look Paige knew well. "Do you mind if I ask you a personal question?"

It wouldn't be a normal day if she didn't. "Not at all. Ask away." She started to stack their empty plates and avoided making eye contact.

"Have you ever had work done?" Mrs. Larsen lifted both hands and made circular motions around her chest. "In this area?"

Whoa. She cleared her throat and glanced at Mr. Larsen, who'd gone right back to his crossword puzzle. "I'm sorry? Work?"

"Yes. You know, a boob job?" The woman whispered loudly. "Isn't that what it's called? I mean yours are so perky." She leaned forward and seemed to inspect them. "Aren't they perky, Ed?"

Still decoding the clues of his crossword puzzle, he nodded, but graciously didn't corroborate the gesture with a verbal agreement.

"They look perky to me!" Luke yelled over, earning another laugh from his comrades.

"Dude, you have a death wish," one of them said.

Paige held the pile of stacked plates up to block her cleavage from everyone's probing eyes. "Nope," she informed the room. "Never had any work done." If only she could find tank tops that contained her better. But then she'd be wearing turtlenecks all the time.

"All natural." Luke elbowed the friend on his right. "That's the way I like them."

"From what I hear, you like them any way you can get them," Paige shot back, then turned to Mrs. Larsen.

"Lucky girl!" The woman shook her head sadly. "Mine have been practically dragging on the floor for years now. It might be time. Do you think I should look into it?"

Did she think a seventy-eight-year-old woman should get a boob job? Grinning, she shrugged. "If you want, but a Wonderbra is cheaper."

"A Wonderbra!" Mrs. Larsen heaved her purse, which was large enough to be a duffel bag, onto the table and dug her hand in. She pulled out a pen and a small notebook. "Wonderbra, you said? That might lift them back where they belong?" she asked, squinting up.

"Yes." She laughed, peering into the mugs. "Now can I get you anything besides bra advice?"

"A warm-up on the coffee would be splendid," Mrs. Larsen murmured, still scrawling notes in her notebook.

Head still bowed toward his crossword, Mr. Larsen nodded.

"Coming right up," she called as she hurried past the bar, carefully holding the plates, still smiling. That Mrs. Larsen...you never knew what you were gonna get.

"Excuse me." A woman's cold voice ground her to a stop. Paige spun to the door where the lady stood, hands on hips, eyes glaring. Dressed in an expensive pantsuit, she had that look like once upon a time she'd been a knockout, but years of frowning must've taken their toll because to her, behind the makeup and the shiny hair, the woman looked bitter. No sparkle in her eyes like Mrs. Larsen. They were shark-dull.

Next to her sat a woman about her age in a wheelchair. She had that sweet girlish prettiness about her, long dark hair, brown eyes that beamed like she was keeping the secret to a happy life.

"Hi there." Paige smiled at the girl to avoid looking into the Ice Queen's eyes. "Can I help you?"

"We've been waiting five minutes for someone to seat us," the older woman barked.

"Oh." Paige carefully shifted the stack of empty plates in her hands. "You can seat yourselves. I'll be with you in a few."

"Seat ourselves? You can't be serious." The woman threw up her hands like she was conducting a symphony. "I mean, where are the menus? And my daughter requires special accommodations."

"Don't blame this on me," the dark-haired girl mumbled.

Whoa. All of the warmth she'd gathered from the Larsens dissipated, creating plenty of room for the dread to seep back in. This lady represented everything she despised about the restaurant biz. She didn't even have to wait on her to know nothing would please her. "Okay. Well…" She glanced around for a table that might at satisfy her. "That booth over there by the window would be perfect. You can even see Aspen Mountain." Just a slice of it, but still.

The woman didn't budge. She simply stared, the toe of her overpriced gold heel tapping.

Tension worked its way up her neck, into her jaw. What was this lady's problem?

Before the woman could speak, the door whooshed open.

"Sorry." A guy hustled over to where they stood.

Wait. Her heart squeezed hard then ramped up into over-drive because it wasn't just a guy. It was him. *Him,* him. Ben Noble. She should've averted her eyes to ease the panicked heat that surged through her, but he was even better looking than she remembered. Short, choppy light brown hair, hazel eyes lit with energy and intensity. He wore his jeans tighter than most of the guys she hung out with, but it definitely worked for him. Her gaze lowered to the floor and back up. *Yep.* Definitely worked.

He hadn't seen her, yet. He was too focused on the dark-haired beauty in the wheelchair. "Sorry about that," he drawled. "Had to park clear out in no-man's-land."

The woman directed her sweet smile at him. Well, good, then. Maybe that would make it easier to spend the next week with him. Maybe he'd finally found a woman who was worth a call the next morning...

"Mom was just making a scene." The nice girl in the wheelchair scooted herself closer to him.

Paige let out a breath. So the girl was his sister. And... Mom? The Ice Queen was his mother? Well, that explained a lot. No wonder he had commitment issues...

"Wouldn't be a normal day if she didn't make a scene." He finally looked over in Paige's direction, aiming that funny, spoiled-boy grin at her. But when his eyes met hers, the smile fell off and his face froze in shock. "Paige."

She steeled herself against the way his lazy voice tingled up her spine. *Nuh-huh. No way. Not going there again.*

He sauntered close enough that she could smell the subtle cologne she still remembered from their dance last year, sweet and spicy all at once.

She backed up a step, clutching the ceramic plates against her chest, trying to hold her heart in so it wouldn't leap out of her chest and land right in that man's hands. "Hello, Ben." She cocked her own smile, but it definitely wasn't sweet.

His gaze lowered down her body. "You look good."

She hugged the plates tighter.

"I'm sorry," the Ice Queen broke in. "I wasn't aware you two were acquainted." The woman eyed her with a calculated precision.

Paige volleyed the question to Ben with raised brows. Obviously, he'd never mentioned her. But then again, why would he? He'd probably already found another date five minutes after she left the gala.

"Paige works for Bryce," Ben said, still gazing at her with a determined look fortifying his eyes.

Suddenly, the plates felt too heavy. Or her arms felt too weak…

"Paige, meet my mother." Ben swept out an arm. "Gracie Noble."

She would have said it was a pleasure, but that would've been a bold-faced lie, so she simply nodded.

Finally Ben broke his stare and looked over at his mom. "I hope Gracie wasn't causin' any trouble."

The woman harrumphed and crossed her arms. "I would like to sit, that's all," she drawled. "I've been standing here for ten minutes, waiting."

Ten minutes! Paige tightened her grip on the plates because her arms trembled with the tension building inside of her. Ten minutes ago she was flipping off Luke and chatting with Mrs. Larsen about boob jobs. Ten minutes ago she was smiling and relaxed and her pulse wasn't racing like she was stuck in a runaway train car. Ten minutes ago the memory of hooking up with Ben was still buried as deep as she could stuff it. But now the hot bastard stood too close to her, wreaking havoc on all five of her senses at once.

Dismissing his mother with a roll of those gorgeous eyes, Ben eased closer to her. "All right by you if we find a seat? You're not gonna kick us outta this fine establishment, are you?" His fingertips brushed the hypersensitive skin on the back of her upper arm.

Her muscles went from weak to useless. A loud crash jarred her. Oh no! No, no, no! She'd dropped the plates.

"What the hell?" Dad's voice drifted out from the kitchen.

"Everything's fine!" she called before he lumbered out there to meet the Noble family. That was all she needed. Another contestant on a nightmare version of *Family Feud*.

Mumbling a string of curses that would've made Bryce fire her on the spot, she dropped to her knees to pick up the ceramic shards.

"Here. Let me." Ben knelt to help her.

"No. I've got it." Throwing a solid elbow to block him, she quickly gathered every broken shard before he could touch one, then rose with as much dignity as possible, given the situation. "Please. Go sit in the booth by the window. I'll be right with you." Refusing to look into his eyes, she spun and got the hell away from him.

"We'll need waters right away," the Ice Queen called after her. "I've only been in this town for an hour and I'm already parched."

"Of course," she bit off over her shoulder, then stalked past the bar and finally ducked through the kitchen door where she was safely out of sight.

Blowing the hair out of her eyes, she leaned against the wall and reclaimed the breath that man had stolen from her lungs with just one look.

Yeah. It was going to be a long week.

CHAPTER FIVE

He should go sit.

He should.

Go sit.

But all he could think about was the way his insides imploded when he saw Paige again, as painful as that time a steer had kicked him right under the ribs. Paige. Such a simple name. One syllable. Uncomplicated. Seemed to be her philosophy in life. Not one trace of makeup on her face, but somehow her eyes still stood out. They were an intriguing shade of brown, too dark to be hazel, but too bright to be called chocolate. There was no name for the color of those eyes. Then there was her hair. Long and wavy, auburn but sun-streaked with blond and reddish curls. And don't get him started on her toned body. The way the muscles in her arms pulled the skin taut, the tempting valley between her sculpted breasts...

"Let's go." Gracie tugged his arm like he was five years

old again. "Surely there's a restaurant somewhere in this town that knows how to treat customers. These people obviously don't know what they're doing."

He jerked away from her and glanced toward the kitchen door where Paige had disappeared. "This is the best burger joint in town." Besides that, he couldn't leave now. Not when he knew Paige was there.

"It's a dive is what it is." His mother visibly shivered. "We'll likely end up with E. coli if we eat here, Benjamin."

"Quit yapping, Mother. I want a burger." Julia wheeled away from them and cruised to the booth by the window. With a shrug directed at Gracie, Ben followed his sister. She usually got what she wanted.

"Fine." His mother stalked ahead of him and slid into the booth. He took the other side so they were facing off. Not that different from most days. Even so, he grinned at her. Somethin' about seein' Paige again made him want to smile. "About time you start livin' on the edge, I reckon. Besides, this place knows how to prepare meat."

She held up her hands like she was afraid to touch the table. "That girl can't even do her job. How can I possibly trust them enough to eat their food?"

"Come on, Gracie. Cut her some slack. Maybe she's havin' a bad day." He felt that jolt of appreciation again. She might be havin' a bad day but she looked good. Real good.

"Or maybe she's suffering from the Ben effect," Julia snickered.

"What's that supposed to mean?"

"Oh come on. I've been watching women melt in your presence for years. She was so flustered she dropped the plates!"

"Really?" He couldn't stop another slow smile from creeping across his lips. "You think she likes me?"

"Don't you get any ideas, Benjamin." Disgust curled Gracie's painted lips. "She's a waitress, for heaven's sake!"

"Oh, no, Mother." He grinned. "She's not just a waitress. She works with Bryce. At the Walker Mountain Ranch." Paige was so much more than a waitress.

J's palm smacked her thigh. "Ohmygod! That's the girl you met last summer?" She squirmed around in her chair like she was trying to see back into the kitchen. "She's so pretty!"

A couple of people looked toward their table.

"Damn, Julia. Would you mind keepin' it down?" Last thing he needed was for Paige to hear them all making a fuss. He hadn't told her Paige's name for a reason.

"Why haven't I heard about this Paige?" His mother folded her arms.

"Because he knew you'd act exactly like this," J countered.

Reaching across the table, he shoved a menu into her hands. "Why don't we all give the menu a good look? Before she comes out and hears us talkin' about her."

J didn't seem fazed by his request. She gasped and clapped her hands. "You should go back and talk to her boss. Make sure she doesn't get in trouble for the plates."

"Oh yeah. I'm sure she'd appreciate—"

J's eyes went wide and he instantly shut his trap, turned around.

Paige shot toward them, head down, eyes focused on their table. Damn, she was gorgeous. Even with that pissed-off look on her face.

A tall lanky guy with red hair and a tray of waters followed her.

She stopped at the end of their table and smiled at Julia. Not him. Only Julia.

"I'm so sorry about that." Her formal tone addressed

them like they were strangers, and he had to lock his jaw so he didn't give into the temptation to remind her they weren't strangers. Hell, just last year they'd slow-danced to Barry White's "Love Makin' Music" at Avery's gala.

But if he reminded her about that, she'd also remember the moment when Tiffani from the bar had thrown her martini in his face, and that memory wouldn't exactly help his cause, so he kept his trap shut.

The redhead passed out waters. He leaned down to the table. "Don't worry," he said in a loud whisper. "We've had her checked out at the asylum. She might seem crazy, but she's all good." He winked at J and Ben had an itch to tell him to quit flirting with his baby sister.

J, on the other hand, ate it up with a giggle.

"Best to keep a napkin in your lap, just in case." Red swiped one off the table and shook it out before smoothing it across J's lap, who looked like she might faint with pleasure. "Never know what'll happen when Paige is waiting on you."

Ben glared at him. *Okay, buddy. Move it along.*

"Thank. You. Pete." Paige's jaw had clenched. "That'll be all."

With a bow he made a quick exit. Must've been the look on Paige's face. Fierce. She'd looked at him like that a time or two, and fierce was the only way to describe her.

"Anyway." She held up a pad of paper and a pen and seemed to carefully avoid his eyes. "Have you had a chance to look at the menu?"

"Not yet, I'm afraid." He waited for her to look at him, then pointed at the illustration across the top of her uniform. "I like your apron."

Her face flushed.

"That's funny. 'We meat again.'"

A low groan drifted over from J's direction. He could

hear her silent scolding. She was right. It was a pathetic attempt to start a conversation. Small talk with a pretty lady had never been his strong suit, especially when she looked at him like he was scum. What could he say? Paige left him dumbfounded. Emphasis on the dumb.

"I'll take the mushroom burger." J folded the menu and whacked Ben with it before handing it to Paige with a bright smile. "Extra cheese, please."

"You got it." Paige smiled so easily at his sister. Why wouldn't she smile at him?

Next, her gaze drifted to Gracie.

Man. She wouldn't even look at him.

Gracie ran a manicured nail down the menu. "Does the beef stew have MSG in it?" She gazed up at Paige with a tight expression.

Well, that was just peachy. Seemed he was on his own. His mother wasn't about to score him any points with her.

"I don't know." Paige matched her severe tone, which was pretty impressive, seeing how Gracie tended to intimidate people.

"MSG makes her constipated," Julia said loud enough to inform the whole room.

"Julia!"

"Love you, Mom." She winked, and just like that the tension faded. Had to hand it to her. J was a master at making people smile.

"I'll have the porterhouse," Gracie said through a martyr's sigh. "No seasonings. Medium-well. And no garlic potatoes. Just fresh steamed veggies."

Paige's lips clamped in a fake smile as she jotted notes on her pad. Then, finally, she glanced at him with a raised brow.

He pretended to peruse the menu. Now that he finally had her attention, he planned to make the most of it. He gazed up at her, let his eyes wander all over her face. "What's your favorite burger?"

"I don't have one," she answered frostily.

J must have gotten it wrong. She didn't like him. Not at all. Of course that'd never stopped him before. "Why not? Too many to choose from?"

"No," she said, looking right through him. "I haven't tried them. I'm a vegetarian."

"Oh, good Lord." Gracie hid her face behind her hand.

"Sorry." J smiled at Paige. "She has a hard time trusting people who don't eat beef."

A vegetarian? Ben rubbed at the stubble on his chin. She was a vegetarian? How'd he miss that last year?

She flicked a gaze at him. "Are you ready to order, or should I come back?"

"I'll take the hot and spicy burger," he said before she could walk away. That was the only one that'd stuck in his mind. He liked a burger hot and spicy. Just like he liked a woman.

"I'll put that right in." Her voice was drier than the Texas prairie. She stalked away like her heels were on fire.

As soon as she was out of sight, J wrinkled her nose like she was impressed. "I like her. She's got moxie."

Gracie practically leapt over the table. "Do *not* encourage him."

"Oh, Mother." He reached over to pat her hand. "I already have all the encouragement I need." All he had to do was look at Paige. She did something to him. Something that the average woman couldn't. She made him wonder.

"What about Cecily Banks? She's a lovely girl." Though she tried to veil it, panic widened his mother's eyes. "Hubert and Beth Ann are such wonderful people. So benevolent and well-groomed."

Translation: she comes from a wealthy, well-respected

family. But maybe he wouldn't end up with someone like Cecily. Maybe he didn't want to.

"Cecily has to be, what? Twenty-three now? She was always such a beautiful girl."

"No." J shook her head. "She's as dumb as a box of rocks. He'd get bored after the first week."

"I'm with you on that." Last time he'd seen Cecily at one of his mother's charity events, she'd managed to yammer on and on about her party planning business like she was some benevolent humanitarian in the business of changing lives for nearly a half hour without taking one single breath. He couldn't sit and listen to that day in and day out without multiple stints in rehab.

"Okay." Determination bolstered Gracie's shoulders. She was like a steady old mare. "Mallory Emerson, then. She's still single, from what I hear. And you two always got on so well."

That was because he was pretty sure Mallory was gay. Lately, there'd been rumors she was dating her law professor's daughter. "Yeah. That's not gonna happen."

J erupted in laughter. "I'd love to see that. You and Mallory Emerson. That'd be something, Benny."

It'd be something all right. He took a swig of water. "Thanks for the ideas, ladies, but I don't need any assistance." There was no way in hell he'd let Gracie have any say in who he dated. Besides that . . . "I know what I want." Might've taken him forever to figure it out, but now that he knew, no one was gonna talk him out of it. Not even Paige.

"I'll tell you what I want." J's eyes glimmered. "The redhead in a Speedo."

Ben choked on a sip of water.

"Honestly, Julia." Their mother sighed. "You're ruining my appetite."

"Yeah." For once Ben agreed with his mother.

"Besides, darling," Gracie went on. "There are plenty of eligible bachelors who would line up at your door, *if* you'd give them the time of day."

It was true. Julia was considered a serious catch by all of their wealthy family friends. And hell, with her trust fund, a man wouldn't have to worry about providing for a family. Gracie'd been trying to find her a match for three years.

"The guys you keep throwing at me are so boring."

"Boring?" Gracie demanded. "You're calling Cal Worthington boring?"

J made a disgusted face. "Isn't Cal a butt doctor?"

"Proctologist," Gracie annunciated. "A *world-renowned* proctologist. And he is the most *interesting* man." His mother launched into an impassioned speech on good ol' Cal's research work in colon cancer while J pulled out her phone and started texting and Ben searched the restaurant for Paige.

Where'd she disappear to, anyway?

He got up to go to the restroom so he could make a sweep around the joint, but he didn't see her anywhere.

By the time he got back to the table, their food was out.

"Here we go." Red interrupted Gracie's monologue, balancing a tray of their food in his hands.

He plopped a plate in front of Gracie. "Porterhouse." He slid Ben's across the table next. "Hot and spicy." Taking his time, he presented Julia her burger like she was the queen of England. "Mushroom burger with extra cheese." Then he winked at her again, the son of a bitch.

"Can I get you anything else?" His gaze seemed locked on J's.

"No," Ben answered before J could say anything. "We're good."

"All right. Holler if you need anything." He grinned and disappeared again.

Ben reached for a knife and cut the burger in half. Juices oozed out onto the plate. *Damn.* That was some burger. Onions, green chilies, peppers, and a thick slice of pepper jack all smothered in hot sauce. Brought tears to his eyes. "I wonder why Paige didn't come out." He'd never stop wondering about that woman.

"Hopefully they fired her." Gracie focused on cutting her meat. "The young gentleman is much better at customer service."

What? Why wasn't Julia getting lectured about who she should and shouldn't be interested in? *Whatever.* Wasn't worth the effort that conversation would require. He picked up the burger and took an enormous bite. The heat rushed all the way down his throat. His favorite kind of burn. For once, the three of them ate in silence, which only proved one thing. The place might look like a dive, but the food was top-notch. Hell, it even shut up Gracie.

Just after he'd taken his fourth monstrous bite. Paige emerged from the kitchen. Ben swiped a napkin and wiped up the hot sauce that had to be dripping off his chin. Not that he could feel it. The burger packed so much heat, his mouth had started to go numb.

"Did everything come out okay?" She kept her distance from the table.

"Amazing," J said around a mouthful of food. "Best burger ever."

A genuine look of happiness flickered, but when she looked at him her expression went dark again.

Well wasn't that just dandy?

"And your steak, ma'am?"

Ben glanced down at Gracie's plate. The steak was perfectly

cooked, pink on the edges, red in the middle, juices oozing out everywhere. But his mother was on a mission to thwart any possibility of him reconnecting with Paige. He cringed.

"It's dry." She pushed it around with her fork.

"Can I take it back to the kitchen? Bring you another?" She didn't even pretend to smile this time.

"No need. I'll manage with it. I absolutely hate wasting food."

"Suit yourself," she muttered and walked away.

During the rest of the meal, Gracie and J chatted about a possible shopping trip later that afternoon. No sign of Paige. Of course they were really the only customers minus some old couple in a booth and a group of firefighters playing cards in the corner.

Finally, Ben had to push away his plate. He'd never met a burger he couldn't finish, but then again, he'd never had the hot and spicy burger at the High Altitude Café, either.

"I'm so full." Julia groaned. "But that was worth it."

Wouldn't argue with that. Ben popped a mint into his mouth, just in case Paige came back to talk. Yeah, right. He could dream.

"I need to freshen up in the restroom." Gracie stood gracefully and headed in the direction of the bathroom.

As if aware that their mother had left, Paige approached the table and started to stack their plates.

Ben handed her his. "Sorry about Gracie. She's not always such a pain."

She wouldn't look at him. "It's no problem."

"Just be glad you don't live with her," Julia said.

A smile changed Paige's face. Her eyes came alive when she smiled. He had to make her smile again.

She stood up straight, holding the stack of plates with both hands. "Can I get you anything else?"

"No. I've never tasted a better burger."

Well...no smile, but her at least her expression softened. "Glad you liked it."

She'd actually replied to him. That was progress in his book. "So I guess we'll be hittin' the river together?"

Was it just him or did her cheeks light with a blush?

"Um...yeah. I guess s—"

"That bathroom needs a good cleaning."

At the sound of his mother's voice, Ben closed his eyes. But he still heard Gracie take her seat and effectively trample any possibility of continuing his conversation with Paige.

"Excuse me?" Paige's tone teetered on a brittle edge.

He opened his eyes. Sure enough, she'd reclaimed the fiery expression that pursed her lips like she was trying to trap a few choice words. He could relate. He had some for Gracie, himself.

"A good scrub would get rid of all that grime in there." His mother went on. "You should see it. What a disgrace. The white tiles are practically black. It's disgusting."

He slid his gaze to Paige, who seemed to be doing some sort of meditative breathing exercise.

"I think we'll take the check now," J sang in a chipper soprano.

"Great idea." Paige slapped it down on the table, turned on her heel, and stalked away.

Gracie's jaw hung open. "Well, what on earth is her problem?"

Ben ripped his wallet out of his back pocket. "Tough to tell," he ground out, aiming an accusatory glare.

"I was just trying to be helpful, Benjamin," she said with a wounded look.

"Mother," he sighed. "Go sit in the car." Before he really

lost it with her and Paige got to witness his not-so-charming side.

"Come on." J herded their mother out the door. "Out you go, Gracie."

He pulled out enough cash to cover the meal plus an extra hundred for what they'd put her through. Not that it would get him anywhere. If those glares meant anything, she wanted nothing to do with him.

Grinning, he stood and tossed the cash on the table.

Good thing he had a whole week to change her mind.

CHAPTER SIX

Well, who the hell did Benjamin Hunter Noble III think he was, anyway? Paige stormed across the Walker Mountain Ranch's large front deck, her sandals clomping against the freshly stained wood.

Woofing happily in a greeting, Moose trotted next to her. But she didn't have time to stop and pet him today.

The crumpled hundred-dollar bill burned like a lump of hot coal in her pocket, scorching her with the burn of humiliation. She didn't need his money. When she's seen it lying on the table like an announcement to the world that he was filthy rich, she'd almost chased his rented Jeep Wrangler down the block so she could give it back to him and tell him exactly what she thought of that gesture. There would've been one problem with that plan, though.

She'd promised Bryce she'd be sweet. Her job *depended* on her being sweet this week. Sweet to Ben, sweet to his sister—which wouldn't be a problem seeing as how the woman was the only likable one in the Noble clan. And sweet to his mother, which meant she'd have to battle every natural instinct she had to tell that lady where she could stuff her high-and-mighty attitude. The thought curled her toes.

Yeah, she was in trouble. If she was going to get through this, she needed a serious intervention.

She approached the door, but Moose plopped down in front of it, blocking her access. "Sorry, boy." He wasn't allowed in the lodge anymore. Not since they'd become a commercial establishment. He'd been confined to the office and great outdoors. "I'll throw the ball for you later," she promised, nudging the dog aside.

Once inside, she jogged across the Walker Mountain Ranch sitting room and headed straight for the kitchen, dodging members of the waitstaff who milled around to set the rustic tables that were strewn throughout the room.

Sunlight streamed through the floor-to-ceiling windows that graced the far dining room wall and added to the overall cheerfulness the room always seemed to possess.

On a normal day, she'd stop to admire the view—the evergreens that lined the ornate stone patio and fireplace outside, the mountain peaks thundering above them, but Ben could be lurking anywhere and she wasn't ready to see him again. Not yet.

She needed a pep talk, some coaching. That's why she'd come to the pros.

As soon as she crashed through the swinging kitchen doors, relief opened her lungs. The Walker Mountain Ranch kitchen happened to be her favorite room on the property. She liked it even better than the sauna room next to the pool. It didn't have much to do with the tidy granite countertops or the happy yellow color of the walls or Elsie Walker's collection of cuckoo clocks hanging above the sink; it had more to do with the exact sight she saw when she stepped in.

Clad in a ruffled apron and a polka-dotted chef's hat, Elsie stood at the stove, humming to herself as she stirred a pot with rosemary-scented steam curling off the top. Bryce's mother was hands-down the kindest person Paige had ever met. She ran the kitchen at the ranch, but she also ran an unofficial counseling service, which Paige had used on more than one occasion.

On the other side of the kitchen, near the commercial-grade stainless refrigerator, Ruby James, Elsie's new kitchen assistant, was rolling out a pie crust.

The door closed behind Paige with a loud thud.

Elsie spun, her spoon flinging sauce through the air. "Paige!" She tossed the spoon aside and bustled over to gather her in one of those signature, cinnamon-scented hugs.

"Hi, Elsie." She squeezed her back and fought off a bittersweet pang. With her sculpted white hair and deep smile lines, Elsie reminded her so much of Gramma Lou, sometimes it hurt.

"I haven't seen you for ages." The woman let her go and looked her over like she suspected she might be dying from some rare disease.

Not all that surprising seeing as how she normally did spend a lot of time in the kitchen. What could she say? She'd always been a good eater. "I've been covering some shifts at the café."

"Well it's about time you came to visit us, isn't that right, Ruby?" Elsie glanced over her shoulder.

"It sure is," Ruby answered, leaning her back against the counter. "I expected to see you long before now. Especially since we made chocolate chip oatmeal cookies two days ago." Ruby had kind, emerald-colored eyes and a heart-

shaped face that instantly put you at ease. Paige had always
envied girls with those full cheeks and perfectly shaped lips.
Speaking of lips, her own were chapped.

She dug into her pocket and pulled out a tube of Burt's
Bees. *There.* She smacked them together. They'd never be
pouty-model lips, but at least the skin wasn't flaking off anymore.

"I could package you up some cookies, if you want,"
Ruby said with a tempting lift of her eyebrows. She'd only
been working at the ranch a couple of months, ever since
she'd been stranded when her car broke down as she drove
through Aspen. Paige had heard that Ruby had nowhere to
go, and no money, either. Somehow Elsie heard about her
and offered her a job. The woman never turned down a charity case.

Even though she didn't know anything about her, Paige
liked Ruby. They were about the same age and had connected right away. She was easygoing and quiet, but just
when you were ready to label her as shy, she'd come up with
some witty zinger.

"Thanks, Ruby. But I stole some cookies last night,"
Paige admitted, though she wasn't ashamed. She knew Ruby
would take it as a compliment. The woman could bake. Before stepping into Elsie's kitchen, she couldn't even bake
refrigerated cookie dough, but in two short months, Elsie
had turned her into a five-star pastry chef. "I took enough
cookies to keep me stocked for the week." Lord knew she'd
need some good cookies to get her through their little whitewater rafting excursion.

Her friend laughed. "You're always welcome to them.
You know that."

That was exactly why they got along so well. Because
Ruby was open and friendly and she needed more people

like that in her life. Maybe someday Ruby and Elsie would rub off on her. Probably not before the seven o'clock pre-trip meeting with the Nobles, though. Anxiety rushed in and prickled up her neck. "Thanks. But I'm actually not here for cookies."

"Oh?" Elsie's sparse eyebrows peaked. "What else can I get you then, dear?"

Paige plopped down on a stool at the kitchen island, which happened to be as big as an ocean liner. "I didn't come here to eat." *Shocking, I know.* "I need help."

Concern furrowed Elsie's lips. "I'll get you a slice of cake and coffee." Because Elsie firmly believed that no problem could ever be solved without some type of delicious home-made temptation. Paige loved that about her. And though she wasn't exactly hungry, she knew there was no point in politely declining. Elsie lived to feed people.

"So are you looking forward to your next trip?" Ruby crossed to the coffeepot and poured a mug, then set it down in front of Paige. "That senator guy is pretty cute, huh?"

Her face got as hot as the burner's on Elsie's stove. "Oh, I don't know about that," she lied. Cute wasn't exactly the best phrase to describe Ben. Sexy. Tempting. And totally arrogant, the hundred-dollar bill reminded her from inside her pocket. She'd dated a man who threw around his money before. She'd let him lie to her, let him make her all kinds of promises he never intended to keep. She'd given him everything, a huge slice of her heart and in the end she wasn't good enough for him, and she'd already decided that she would never let anyone make her feel so small again.

"Here we go, dear." Elsie slid a fat piece of chocolate cake in front of her.

The scent of expensive dark cocoa and powdered sugar woke her appetite. She picked up her fork and sawed off a huge bite, let the sweetness of it melt in her mouth. *Okay.* How did Elsie do that? Things seemed better already.

"Ben Noble looks like a young John Wayne, if you ask me." Elsie sighed in the way of swooning southern belle.

Despite the lack of humor threatening her very near future, Paige laughed. Any remotely good-looking guy resembled John Wayne in Elsie's world. She still had the tattered pinups of the man in her office.

Ruby leaned into the counter and propped her chin on a fist, staring off into a dreamy space. "Mmm hmmm. I bet he knows exactly what a woman needs, if you catch my meaning."

She caught it. But those were the kinds of thoughts she was trying to ignore.

"Tsk." Elsie's frown reprimanded them both. "You girls. Always thinking about jumping right into bed with someone. In *my* day we thought about commitment. Marriage."

Paige raised her brows. She couldn't help herself. "You never thought about jumping into bed with John Wayne?"

Elsie's cheeks flamed. She fanned her face, hiding a smile. "What is it you needed our help with, dear? Is your family giving you a hard time again?"

"No. Well. Yes." That would never change unless she agreed to "do her part" and work at the café. "But that's not why I'm here." She snuck in another bite of cake and finished chewing. Might be best to start at the beginning and that could take a while. She set down her fork. "Bryce said customers have been complaining about me."

"I find that hard to believe." Ruby straightened and poured some cream in her coffee, then fished a spoon out of the drawer. "I know I haven't been here long, but you're the best guide out there."

The compliment filled in some of the cracks that had

started to spread in the foundation of her confidence. "I'm glad *you* think so. But Bryce told me I need to be nicer."

"Psshaw." Elsie poured her own mug of coffee. "Bryce doesn't know what he's talking about, dear. You mark my words. You're perfect the way you are." She squeezed her forearm as if willing her to believe it.

"He's right, though. I'm not very nice sometimes." She decided to spare them the Hal Funkleman story.

"Being nice is overrated," Ruby said quietly, her finger-nail chipping at a blotch of food that had been encrusted to the counter. For the hundredth time, Paige wondered about the woman's past. She never mentioned it, but every so often, she'd notice a wounded look creeping into Ruby's eyes.

"Whatever do you mean, 'you're not very nice'?" Elsie clucked her tongue. "That's the silliest thing I've ever heard. You're a gem, Paige. And phooey to anyone who can't see it."

She winced. "I'm pretty sure Bryce doesn't see it." Apparently most of the customers didn't, either.

Elsie threw up her hands. "He's one to talk!"

That earned a laugh. "I guess it doesn't matter as much for him. He doesn't exactly hang out with the customers."

"There's a reason for that." Ruby's smirk hinted at her impression of Bryce.

Paige couldn't hold back a smile. Maybe Ruby wasn't all sweetness, either. Maybe no one was.

"Thanks for the support. But I have a meeting with Be—" She cleared her throat. "—Mr. Noble and his group in a few short hours and I need some pointers. I have to impress them." And somehow keep things professional so his mother would give her a good evaluation, which meant no shoving that hundred-dollar bill back in his face. She'd donate it instead. Surely the local humane society could use some extra cash.

"Just be yourself," Elsie insisted with a definitive nod of her head.

Yeah, that wasn't working so well for her. She looked back and forth between Elsie and Ruby. "Should I straighten my hair? Wear khakis and a cardigan? Maybe take out my nose piercing?" Though it was only a simple stud. That shouldn't get anyone riled up, should it?

"And look like a yuppie princess?" Ruby grinned. "No. That's not you, Paige."

It might not be her, but she had to spend the next few days with a crew of seasoned yuppies. "You don't understand. This is huge. The campaign guy'll be taking videos and pictures. The media'll be around. I mean, he's kind of famous."

"I wouldn't worry about that." Ruby pulled out the stool across from her and sat. "Who cares what he thinks about you? You're fun. You're tenacious. In fact, I wish I was more like you."

"No. Trust me. That would be bad." She polished off the rest of her cake and licked the fork while she thought about all of the customers she'd pushed. Ruby didn't know the half of it.

"You stand up for yourself. That's something I never learned to do," she murmured.

"Look at you two." Shaking her head in a disappointed cadence, Elsie scurried over to the coffeepot and poured them each a refill. "So different, but exactly who you were made to be. Don't wish that away, dears."

She was about to tell Elsie that she would definitely wish away her prickly nature if she could, when the door opened. Bryce sauntered in, followed by his cousin Sawyer. And Ben.

The sight of him in those jeans started that flutter in her heart again. She instantly ducked her head and stared at the counter. What was he doing in here? In her safe place?

"Ladies." Bryce approached them. "We were hoping to get some of those cookies I heard about."

With her head still down, Paige strained her eyes to catch a glimpse of Ben.

He swaggered closer, like he had been in this exact spot hundreds of times—stopping a roomful of women dead in their tracks.

Ruby fiddled with her hair.

Elsie beamed. You would've thought John Wayne had just walked into the kitchen.

Well he didn't impress her. No, sir. *We beg to differ,* certain regions of her body cried out, but she silenced them with a harrumph. He wasn't all that great. To prove it, she focused on Sawyer. Out of the three men, he was the only one she wanted to talk to at the moment. Though he resembled Bryce with that dark hair and square jaw, Sawyer was actually nice. She reached over to pat his arm. "Good to see you, Sawyer."

"You, too," he said, but his gaze focused on Ruby. He shoved his hands into his pockets. "You wouldn't mind sharing some of your famous cookies, would you?" he asked.

Without an answer, Ruby turned away and busied herself with a bowl of something on the counter.

Paige watched her friend carefully. She was definitely avoiding Sawyer. But why? What'd Sawyer ever do to Ruby?

"Of course we'll share the cookies, Sawyer dear," Elsie answered after an awkward silence.

"I'll get them," Paige offered, but before she could stand, Ben slipped right in front of her. "Hey, there Paige," he said in the sexy, husky voice that'd worked so well on her last year at the gala. Good gravy. What did he do? Practice in front of the mirror?

Determined to ignore him, she squeaked past. While she retrieved the cookies, Elsie nestled herself right up against Ben's shoulder like a puppy begging for an ear scratch. Paige resisted the urge to roll her eyes. That woman was such a sucker for charming men.

"Did you just get in, Ben?" she purred. "Why, you must be starving. Let me make you a nice big snack."

Oh, please. Paige handed the container of cookies to Sawyer, then sat back down.

Eyes still focused firmly on her, Ben smiled. "A snack sounds perfect." He pulled out the stool and plopped down across from her as easy and carefree as if they sat down across from each other every day. "I'll take a slice of whatever she's having." He looked her over again, in a way that made her keenly aware of her wild hair. He was used to sitting across from women who'd probably spent half their life at the spa, and she hadn't even found the time to brush her hair that morning.

Rising, Paige pushed away her plate. "Actually, I'm done. I have work to do before tonight." She hugged Elsie and shot Ruby a desperate look that hopefully communicated *follow me.* She had to get herself ready for that meeting, ready to face Gracie Hunter Noble again. And it'd take a damn village to transform her into a likable yuppie traditionalist. She'd only worn eyeliner once in her life. "Thanks for the cake. And the coffee." Avoiding Ben's curious stare, she planted a kiss on Elsie's cheek, then made a point to wave good-bye to Sawyer since he was the only man in the room who wasn't making her life more difficult.

"Are you sure you have to go right this second, dear?" Elsie frowned. "Ben just got here."

Exactly. He'd only just walked into the room and her heart had already sped into dizzying circles. Space. That was the only thing that would get her through the week. She had to wedge space between them whenever possible. "I have work to do before the meeting," she insisted as she twirled toward the door, but her foot caught the leg of the stool and knocked her off balance.

Ben hopped up and caught her arm as she stumbled forward.

The bolt of electricity from his skin against hers nearly laid her out flat.

"You okay?" His breath tickled her neck.

She fought the rising pulse that had taken over her body. "I'm fine," she squeaked.

In the corner of her vision, she saw Bryce swipe a hand down his face.

She forced out a laugh and yanked her arm out of Ben's very firm, very manly grip. "My foot's asleep, that's all. It'll be fine." With another coded glance at Ruby, she headed for the door. "I'll see you all later."

"Can't wait," Ben called behind her.

With Ruby by her side, she escaped into the dining room. But they weren't fast enough to outrun the sound of footsteps that echoed behind her. Heavy footsteps. Boots if she wasn't mistaken.

She spun. Sure enough, Bryce stood three feet behind her.

"Um...I'll wait over there..." Ruby indicated the other side of the dining room with a wave of her hand and meandered away.

"What happened at the café?" Bryce demanded.

"Nothing." Darn squeak. *Ahem.* "His mom isn't a very nice person, that's all." And that was putting it mildly.

He nodded like he knew exactly what she meant. "She won't be the easiest customer. Will it be a problem?"

"No."

"Because I'll get someone else to lead this trip."

"It's fine." She tried to smile, even with that hard knot of panic tightening under her ribs, cinching her breaths tighter. "No big deal. I'll be on my best behavior. I swear."

"We need this to be perfect," he reminded her for the hundredth time. "There'll be cameras everywhere."

"You have nothing to worry about. Okay? Please, Bryce. Trust me. I'll make sure everything runs smoothly."

"I trust you," he finally said.

"Thank you." Her chin lifted in confident defiance, even with the throb of Ben's touch still beating through her.

If only she trusted herself.

CHAPTER SEVEN

Ben knew three things about Elsie Walker. One, she didn't use recipes, but she could outcook Julia Child any day. Two, she'd lost Bryce's daddy young, and even though she'd never remarried, the woman was a hopeless romantic. She'd had a big hand in bringing Bryce and Avery together after they'd met last year. Three, and most importantly, she'd known Paige her whole life, which meant he'd just won the gossip lottery being left alone in a room with her.

Yes, sir, and he intended to mine for every detail he could.

"Here you are, dear," Miss Elsie sang as she slid a hunk of layered chocolate cake in front of him. A glob of fudgy frosting oozed down the sides and pooled on the flowered china he happened to know she only used for special company. He inhaled deeply, let the rich scent fill his senses. "Mmmm. Smells better than a rack of ribs on the smoker," he gushed, feeding the woman's pleased blush.

She clasped her hands in front of her. "Can I get you some coffee to go with it?"

"That'd be mighty nice, Miss Elsie." He straddled the stool and reclaimed his place at the island, hovering over that slice of cake. "Black as crude oil, if you don't mind."

"I don't mind one bit." She hustled over to the coffeepot near her desk and filled two mugs, then set one in front of him and pulled out a stool on the opposite side of the counter.

Ben savored a bite of the cake, letting it melt into ecstasy before chewing and swallowing. Then he turned up the wattage on his grin and aimed it right at her. When it came to figuring out how to get through to Paige, he wasn't above usin' what the good Lord had given him. He'd never met a woman who didn't appreciate some good old-fashioned flirting. If he played his cards right, Miss Elsie could become an ally in his quest, unlike Bryce.

He lifted the mug and sipped the dark brew. Wasn't quite cowboy coffee, but it'd do the trick.

"It's wonderful to see you, dear," Miss Elsie cooed. "It's been much too long since you've visited."

Yeah, well. He'd hadn't been back since the whole debacle at the gala. Paige had made it clear as that bright blue sky outside that she didn't want to see him. He eyed the older woman sitting across from him. Had Paige told her about that night? "Say, Miss Elsie. Everything all right with Paige?" He rested the fork on his plate and drooped his eyes into innocent concern. "She seems mighty uptight today."

Her eyes shied away from his in a telltale sign. The woman had a terrible poker face. She knew something had happened or she wouldn't suddenly be so fascinated by her coffee, now, would she?

"Don't you worry about Paige," she said briskly, stirring

the spoon round and round in her mug. "She'll be fine. I'm sure she's nervous, seeing as how this is such an important trip. She wants everything to be perfect."

"Perfect is overrated," he replied with a sly grin, clueing Miss Elsie in on the fact he was onto her. "Trust me. I should know." In his experience, perfect meant fake. Superficial. And he wanted to dive past the surface, sink into Paige's depths. "I happen to think Paige is perfect the way she is."

Taking his time, he let that sink in and sawed off another bite, enjoying the chocolate the way he'd enjoyed Paige's kiss last year, slow and thorough.

Miss Elsie smiled in her knowing way, but didn't offer him anything that could help him decipher Paige's feelings. She only sipped her coffee across from him. Good thing he was a patient man. When he'd finished chewing, he set down his fork in a silent threat to leave the cake unfinished. "Thing is, I'd sure like to know if I've done somethin' to upset her." In his mind, honesty was always the best policy. "I happen to like her a whole lot, but she seems bent on ignorin' me."

"Oh. Well." Elsie's nervous gaze drifted to the door and back to his face. She was a loyal woman, no doubt about that, but she was caving fast.

"Do you have any pointers?" he prompted. "I'd sure appreciate the help."

"When you put it that way..." Elsie kept an eye on the door. "Be careful with her, Ben dear." Her voice lowered. "She's more fragile than she looks."

"Fragile?" She didn't look fragile to him. Not one bit. The woman looked strong and capable and...almost untouchable.

"She's been hurt by people who were supposed to love her," Elsie said quietly. "If you like her, don't tell her. She won't believe you. Just treat her right. She'll come around, eventually."

And there it was, the wisdom that made Elsie famous for her good advice. She should start charging.

Treat her right.

That he could do. He grinned. "You know what I always say…treat a woman like a racehorse and she'll never be a nag." He'd picked up that bit of wisdom from Granddad, and it'd earned his grandfather sixty good years of marriage and counting. "Can't imagine anyone hurtin' Paige," he said as he reclaimed his fork and finished off the cake. A guy would have to be as dumb as a cow patty to run Paige off. Of course he'd done it once himself. But not on purpose.

"Yes, well…" Elsie checked the door again. "She was young and the boy was older. He led her on for years and then he didn't want her." An angry look stretched her mouth thin. "He knew what he was doing. Broke her heart in two, the poor dear."

Ben stood, walked his plate and mug to the sink, and rinsed them as Gracie had taught him. "Thanks, Miss Elsie," he said, pushing in his stool. "That helps." More than she knew. If Paige had let someone get close enough to hurt her once, that meant she had a vulnerable side. Though it seemed she'd buried it down deep.

Which meant he had some excavating to do.

* * *

Going home was all Paige needed to do to remind herself that she was way out of her league with Ben Noble. Not that her studio apartment wasn't charming. It happened to be right downtown, a couple of blocks from the slopes, on the third floor of a historic brick building that housed a T-shirt shop, a local art gallery, and a Japanese restaurant. She'd always been a big fan of diversity, though she didn't love the scent of fried dumplings that had been engrained in her burlap curtains. But she practically lived off their veggie udon noodle bowls, so she figured the trade-off was worth it. Speaking of...she unloaded the takeout boxes and set them out in front of Ruby. After stopping by Ruby's place to shower with some flowery-scented soaps and oils and whatnot, then dressing in one of her friend's girl-next-door outfits, she was famished.

"Check this out." Ruby set her iPad in the center of Paige's round bistro table, flipping through a series of horrific pictures.

"Oh my god." Paige quit eating. Ben Noble was a jerk. No. Worse than a jerk. She leaned over and gawked at the images, the brown cow's droopy, innocent eyes tugging at her heart. "I can't believe he beats his animals." But really, why should she be surprised? There had to be *something* wrong with him. The man couldn't be as perfect as he looked.

The memory of his face gave her a hot flash. Speaking of his looks, what a waste of hot cowboy genes.

"You really think he beats his animals?" Ruby squinted, her nose wrinkled, and pushed her face closer to the screen like she was trying to solve one of those mind-bending puzzles.

"Pictures don't lie." She flicked a finger across the screen. There had to be twenty of them posted on various news sites. Ben raising a shovel over the cow's head, a pond on his ranch oozing trash. "It's disgusting." To think that she even gave the man a second glance. And a third. Fourth. Okay. She'd looked him over as many times as she could, but that was before she'd known about those horrible pictures.

"Actually, pictures *can* lie," Ruby corrected as she shoved in a big bite of noodles. "Just look at all those skinny models in the magazines. Don't tell me they have no cellulite."

She opened her big, fat mouth to argue, but the woman had a point. Normally, she gave people the benefit of the doubt, but she was grasping at anything to make the next week easier, to keep that professional distance intact even while he smiled and drawled and swaggered in those close-fitting jeans.

Unfortunately, it was hard to convince herself that Ben could hurt his animals. He wasn't that kind of guy and she knew it.

"I mean, you read the articles. No one has any proof, yet. Maybe he pissed off his girlfriend and she wanted revenge." Ruby clicked the zoom until they both had a clear view of Ben's ex. "You want my opinion, she doesn't look like Little Miss Innocent."

No. That was true. Ben's ex-girlfriend looked like Little Miss Surgically Enhanced, if you asked her. And not just in the bust region. Either the girl had a lip-swelling allergy problem or she favored Botox. Of course, if that was the kind of woman Ben preferred, she had nothing to worry about. He wouldn't want her.

And that called for more noodles. "It doesn't matter, anyway," she said between heaping bites. "It's not like he's interested in a relationship." One night stand, yes. Commitment, no. That'd been pretty clear the one night she'd spent with him.

Moving on...

She glanced at herself in the thrift-store mirror that hung above Gramma Lou's antique mahogany buffet, taking in her attire, the borrowed powder-blue cardigan, the pressed khaki pants, the string of Ruby's pearls around her neck. "I hope this getup appeases his mother."

"Are you sure it's his mother you're trying to impress?" Ruby asked, eyebrows peaked into a probing glare that heated Paige's cheeks.

Whew. Time to open a window, get some fresh air flowing.

"Of course I'm sure," she insisted, popping out of her seat to crank open the small kitchen window above the sink. She stole an extra second there, closing her eyes as the breeze washed over her. "Ben is nothing special."

Her friend snorted in disagreement. "Is that why your neck gets all blotchy when you talk about him?"

"It does not." She reached up to soothe the burn that inched past the neckline of her shirt and trudged back to the table. "I get heat rash easily."

"Heat rash," Ruby laughed. "Yes. Well, he's definitely hot."

"Exactly," she conceded. "Which is why he dates girls like her." She stabbed the iPad screen with her pointer finger. "Valentina the catalog model with the ten-thousand-dollar boobs."

"Yours are way better than hers." Ruby lowered her eyes and grinned. "And they're a hundred percent natural."

"Thanks for that." It was no secret men were drawn to her chest, but who wanted the dilemma of wondering if they were really interested in her or just her cup size? In her previous experience, it'd turned out to be cup size. Take Luke Simms, for example.

"When Ben walked into the kitchen earlier, he hardly even looked at Elsie and me." In between bites of noodles, Ruby unloaded the ungodly amounts of makeup and hair products she'd brought to complete Paige's transformation. "His face lit up when he saw you. And you didn't exactly look indifferent."

"That's ridiculous." Air conditioner. She should invest in one of those window units. She shrugged off the mounting heat. "I'd never hook up with him again. Not after what happened at the gala." Even if he didn't abuse his animals, there were plenty of other reasons not to let herself fall for him again. He went through women like Kleenex and…"That man's mother is horrible. I couldn't even fantasize about a man who had a mother like her. He must have some serious baggage."

Ruby rolled her shoulders back in a seductive pose, but humor flashed in her eyes. "I'd help him carry that baggage, if he asked."

Yeah. Carrying it was one thing. She just didn't want to be the one sorting it all out. Speaking of baggage…she eyed her friend. "So I noticed you didn't say much to Sawyer." If Ruby was looking to carry a hot guy's baggage, she couldn't do much better than Sawyer Hawkins. "He's pretty good looking, too. Don't you think?"

The fork dropped from Ruby's hand and clattered onto the table. "Oh. Um. I don't know. Didn't really notice."

Yeah, right. Every woman noticed Sawyer. "He seemed to notice you," Paige observed casually. The man had his gaze locked on Ruby's backside, and she suspected he wasn't only staring at the stack of cookies next to her, either.

"He did?" Most women would've squealed at the suggestion that Sawyer had been checking them out, but Ruby's face paled. She pulled her hands into her lap and knotted them like she was worried.

"He's a nice guy." A real catch by most women's standards. Wasn't hard to understand why all of the local women in town called him Officer Hotness. He had dark wavy hair, almost as black as Bryce's, and piercing blue eyes. But it was his smile that got to most of them. He'd been stopped by many a woman in the grocery store who'd asked him about showing up to a friend's bachelorette party. Legend had it that he could've earned a lot of extra money, if he'd been that type of guy. Except he wasn't. While he may have looked like a fantasy, he was as wholesome as they came. Unlike Ben Noble.

Instead of agreeing with her, Ruby sat awkwardly still and quiet.

"I heard he's getting a divorce," Paige said between bites of noodles. "Which means he'll be single soon..."

"I don't date cops." The tremble in Ruby's voice held so many things—rage, fear, desperation. But before Paige could ask her what had happened to her, the woman pushed away her dinner and stood. "We should get started. We'll need every second we have to tame that hair of yours."

Paige forced herself to smile, even with a blinding rush of sympathy. Whatever had happened to Ruby, she sure as hell didn't want to talk about it.

"Why don't you dry your hair first," Ruby asked, seeming to assess what she had to work with.

Paige's dramatic sigh puffed her bangs. "Let's get this over with." She snatched Ruby's blow-dryer off the table and plugged it in over the kitchen counter. Who the hell knew it took two hours to actually groom yourself? What a waste of time. On a normal day, she hopped out of bed, showered—well...sometimes showered—ran a brush through her hair, and got dressed. That was it. She could be ready in ten minutes, start to finish, if she had to.

After plugging the thing in, she examined it. "How do you turn it on?"

With a disbelieving shake of her head, Ruby walked over, confiscated the blow-dryer, and flicked it on. "The *on* switch," she said.

"I knew that." Paige took the blow-dryer from her friend's hand. Hot air puffed out her hair.

"No, no, no," Ruby said like a mother correcting a toddler. You have to use a brush and straighten your hair. Like this." She picked up the brush and stole back the blow-dryer, then caught a lock of Paige's hair in the bristles and smoothed the blow-dryer over it.

"Sure. Okay. I can do that." Paige took over, awkwardly trying to catch of a lock of her hair the way Ruby had.

Her friend stepped back and watched, arms crossed, mouth alternating between a smile and a grimace.

Turning her back, she bent and flipped her hair. How the hell was she supposed to brush and dry at the same time? She turned her head to get a better angle, but the back of the blow-dryer sucked up a wad of her hair. "Ow!" A crackling sound rattled. The smell of burned hair polluted the air. She tried to pull the blow-dryer back, but it was stuck.

"Turn it off!" Ruby rushed over.

"I'm trying!" But where was the switch?

"It's smoking!" her friend screeched and somehow found the off switch.

The blow-dryer quit, but her hair was still stuck.

"Oh, boy." Ruby held the blow-dryer in one hand and tried to untangle Paige's hair with the other hand. "I might need to get the scissors."

Panic soared through her. "But I have to be at the meeting in an hour!"

"Okay. Don't freak out." Ruby carefully picked clumps of her hair out of the back of the blow-dryer. "There. I think I've got it." She finally pulled the thing away and laid it on the table.

Paige spun to look in the mirror. A frizzed ball of hair stuck out against the back of her head. "It looks like I have bed head!"

"Here." Ruby found a tube of something on the counter and squeezed clear goo into her hand. "This is frizz control.

It'll help smooth it down." She spread it evenly across the back of Paige's head, then ran a brush through it.

She glanced in the mirror again. Half of her hair was curled in waves and the section that she'd blown dry hung sleek and smooth. "Oh, screw it." She grabbed a hair tie and pulled her hair into a messy updo, securing it in place.

"Hmmm…" Ruby pulled out some strands and curled them around her fingers, then sprayed everything in place until Paige was gagging on the fumes.

"Sit." Her friend pulled out a chair and she obediently plopped down, still smelling the burned hair now intermixed with the chemical scent of hairspray.

"I smell like an old lady's hair salon," she complained, gagging.

"Relax." Ruby sat in the chair across from her and applied foundation, then powder. "Close your eyes." She came at Paige with the eyeliner pencil. "Stop blinking. Seriously. I feel like I'm putting makeup on a five-year-old."

"I don't like things touching my face," she whined. It was one of her things.

"Just stay still. Almost done," her friend grumbled. A few more swooshes of eye shadow, a heavy coating of mascara, and she leaned back. "There. What do you think?"

Paige stood, smoothing creases out of her pants, and glanced in the mirror. *Whoa.* She stared for a long time, then turned to Ruby. "I don't know what I think." She looked so different. "What do you think?"

"Um. Well." Ruby rolled those pretty green eyes up to the ceiling as if searching for the right words.

Great. "What's wrong?"

She sighed and leaned onto the table, propping her chin on her fist, her eyes giving Paige another once-over. "You just…don't look like *you.*"

She glanced in the mirror again. Couldn't argue with that. It definitely wasn't her usual ensemble of hiking shorts and a moisture-wicking T-shirt, but that was the idea, right? She fluffed her updo. "You haven't met this guy's mom. She's nuts. And she looks like Barbie's grandma." Perfect skin stretched over high cheekbones, soft and silky hair that she obviously colored. And who could forget the piercing gaze that made you feel like she could incinerate you. "She already hates me. I have some ground to make up."

Ruby handed her a tube of lip gloss. "You'll win her over."

"Right." She clomped to the mirror in Ruby's two-inch heels and smeared the strawberry-scented goo on her lips. The shine actually hid the dryness pretty well. Smelled good, too. Maybe makeup wasn't *all* bad.

"Just be yourself, Paige," Ruby offered.

"Myself doesn't seem to be cutting it." Not for Bryce, not for Gracie Hunter Noble, not even for her own family.

"Come on. You're funny and smart. You don't have to be the preppy girl next door. She'll see through it anyway."

Not if she could help it. "Anyone can change." Smacking her lips once more, she pocketed the gloss in case she needed it later. "I can turn over a new leaf. I'll be polite and soft-spoken and no matter what, I won't let that woman get to me again." And if all else failed, she'd keep putting on that lip gloss. Maybe the sweet scent would make everyone believe she was sweet, too.

"Oh, boy," Ruby muttered. "Good luck."

Luck. Ha. She'd never relied on luck for anything. Determination, that was her way. She'd muscle through this meeting, wrestling back every natural urge she had to argue. She'd become the shining example of a customer service star.

All while ignoring the way Ben Noble jarred her carefully constructed inner walls.

CHAPTER EIGHT

Ah. Now this was the life.

Ben reclined in the zero-gravity patio chair and let the evening sun warm his face. At the moment, he couldn't imagine a more stunning place to sit than the Walker Mountain Ranch's patio. Built in tiers, the stones resembled slate tiles, all rustic and varying shades of the earth—gray and brown and a dusty red. The first tier, where he and Bryce sat for their pre-dinner drink, had killer chairs and furniture strewn around for lounging. A step lower, there sat a gigantic gas fire pit with handmade log benches angled on every side. The lowest tier, down at ground level, held a sparkling blue in-ground pool and three hot tubs that would surely call his name once the warm sun slid behind the mountain peaks.

Tall, lanky evergreens and pines decorated the patio edges and stretched into an endless forest that cut off the rest of the world, and wrapped him in its seclusion and mystery.

Speaking of mystery…he flicked down his sunglasses and glanced at the man who'd once played his wingman in college.

Bryce was kicked back in the chair next to him. His faithful dog, Moose, sprawled out between them.

"So what's Paige's story, anyway?" Ben asked casually.

Bryce took a swig of sweet tea and set the glass on the table between them. "Whadda you mean?" His eyes narrowed the same way they used to when he'd lecture him about commitment during their sophomore year.

What could Ben say? He'd never lucked out in the dating department like Bryce had. The guy met his first wife, Yvonne, when they were like six, dated her forever, then married her. After he'd lost Yvonne in a Jeep accident, he'd met and married Avery in less than a year. And Ben had never seen two people so perfect for each other. Somehow the guy had found the real deal twice. Damned if he could find it just once.

He shrugged and gazed out at the peaks. "Elsie mentioned some asshole had done a number on her. Just wondering who it was." The more information he had on the situation, the better off he'd be. Then he could figure out how to undo the damage that guy had done.

"Okay. You wanna know about that guy?" Bryce leaned in, got in his face. "Actually he reminds me of you."

"Me?"

"Yeah. His family was filthy rich. He thought pretty highly of himself," Bryce said, easing his back against the chair again. "He was known for racking up the marks on his bedroom wall."

The comment hit its intended target. "Sophomore year was a decade ago, man." He'd be the first to admit it wasn't his best year. He'd gotten wrapped up in the parties, the booze, the women. Took him a while, but eventually he did get his head on straight. Bryce knew that.

"For some reason the guy decided he was interested in Paige," Bryce went on. "He was a senior, she was a sopho-more. They dated, got close. After he went to college, he'd come in and out of the picture. But she never slept with him because she wanted something real first. A *committed* re-lationship." The way Bryce emphasized the word made it sound like Ben didn't even know what it meant.

"When she was nineteen, he came back to visit. Told her he'd need something to remember her by. Something to bond them." Bryce didn't have to finish. He caught the meaning. He'd talked her into sleeping with him.

"Then the guy never called her again," Bryce growled.

Blood pumped through Ben's arms hot and fast. "What a prick."

"Yeah." Bryce gave him a pissed-off look. "Only reason I know about it is 'cause she showed up here the next day, shitfaced and heartbroken." Bryce pointed at him, face stern as a grumpy old man's. "Which is why you shouldn't get any ideas about her, Noble. I've seen how you are with women, remember? There's no way I'm letting you go after my little sister."

"I'm not saying I'm gonna go after her." He hadn't said it, but that didn't mean he wouldn't. "Just curious about her, that's all. What the story with her family?"

Leaning back, Bryce swiped his glass off the table and stared at the mountain peaks. "She's had it rough. They're a piece of work."

He grinned. "Whose family isn't?"

"Yeah, well at least your mom's the only crazy one in your bunch. She's got four siblings who give her all kinds of shit for not pulling her weight with their precious café."

Lord help him, he couldn't hide his amusement. "So a vegetarian is forced to serve a bunch of charred meat to a room full of carnivores."

Bryce laughed. "Sounds about right. She avoids it as much as possible, but sometimes they guilt her into it."

He thought back to the restaurant, to how Paige's face had been so flushed, so flustered. "It didn't seem like waitressing was her thing."

Bryce finished off his tea. "How bad was it?"

"Let's just say, J and I had to get Gracie out of there before things exploded. Not Paige's fault, by the way."

"That's what I was afraid of." Bryce kneaded his forehead as though fending off a headache. "Will your mom be okay with this? I mean, I know she's not planning to go on the trip with you, but will she have a problem with Paige?"

She already had a problem with Paige. That'd started the second she'd seen the interested look on his face. "Yes. She most definitely will have a problem with her. But she'll get over it."

"You sure? The last thing I need is Gracie Hunter Noble making trouble for me around here. We're still trying to get established."

His mother wouldn't make trouble. He wouldn't let her. "You guys have done a great job with the place, by the way," he said, glancing around the pool area again. "Can't believe the difference from when I was here last."

Bryce looked around, too. "It's taken a lot of work. And money. Can't afford any bad publicity right now, if you know what I mean."

"Gracie'll be fine. Don't worry about her. I'll take care of it." Just like he always did. He'd learned how to manage his mother.

Wind rustled the pine needles. Ben's gaze drifted back to

the pool, the shimmering water. He could see himself and Paige there. His arms wrapped around her slick, wet skin...

Bryce gave him a suspicious look. "Don't get any ideas about Paige. Got it?"

Too late. He'd already gotten ideas. One glance at the pool's glassy surface and he couldn't stop thinking about how great it'd be to meet her for a midnight rendezvous, swimsuits optional.

"Seriously. She's had enough assholes disappoint her."

Ben slipped off his glasses and leveled Bryce with a glare. "I know you're not calling me an asshole."

"I'm saying she doesn't need a fling."

"Who said anything about a fling?" He'd had plenty of those. It was time for something different in his life.

His friend didn't seem to agree. "You're here for a week, then you go back to your world. We both know there's no place for her in your world, Noble."

Why couldn't he decide who and what fit into his world? "I have to say, I'm a little hurt that you don't think more highly of me. You don't think I'm worthy of your little sister."

"I didn't say that." He sighed. "She doesn't have anyone else to look out for her, that's all. She never has."

Ben nodded. He got it. Bryce had been the only one who'd looked out for her.

Well, maybe it was time for him to lift that burden off his friend's shoulders.

* * *

Ben set out the saucers and cups the way he'd seen Gracie do hundreds of times. The kitchen of their three-bedroom guest cabin offered more than he ever would've thought, extra-tall hickory cabinets, stainless, gleaming stone countertops, professional-grade appliances, and Bryce had it stocked with all of their favorite things, including Gracie's jasmine and lavender tea.

The teakettle whistled, and not a moment too soon, because he heard the Escalade's wheels crunch in the drive. They'd been out shopping all afternoon, poor Julia, and now he was on a mission to tell Gracie about Paige and convince her that it wouldn't be a big deal.

Good luck with that. Gracie had a talent for making everything a big deal. Hearing the wheels of J's chair grind up the wooden ramp, Ben quickly set out the milk and honey and gave one last glance at the table. *Here we go.*

The door opened and Gracie pushed his sister into the room, bags and boxes from all those fancy stores piled high in her lap. Good thing J had the chair. Where else would Gracie stack all of her purchases?

"I told you, Mother. I don't like the silver shoes. I liked the red ones."

"The red ones were so noticeable, Julia, darling. They were overstated. There's something to be said for subtle elegance, you know."

J gave their mother the you're-an-idiot look reserved specifically for Gracie. "Oh, like people don't already notice me. Hello! I'm in a wheelchair, Mother! Pretty sure that puts me way past subtle."

Gracie uttered a long-suffering sigh and started to unload the packages from J's chair.

At least they'd had an afternoon of shopping. Shopping seemed to be one of the only things that could loosen Gracie up.

He sauntered over. "Hey there. Anything left in the stores for all of the other poor divas?"

J rolled her eyes. "There wouldn't be if she had anything to say about it. She wanted to buy me a fur coat, Ben. A. Fur. Coat."

"It was on sale," Gracie snapped.

"Yeah. For three thousand dollars."

"Ouch." He winked at her. "I'll just go out and shoot somethin' for ya. Make you your own fur coat."

"Don't be vulgar, Benjamin." Gracie walked toward the kitchen table. "What on earth?"

Ben swept out his arms and bowed. "I made tea."

But instead of smiling and saying thank you like any normal mother who was grateful that her son had turned out to be such a gentleman, she crossed her arms and tilted her head. "What do you want?"

"Nothing." He turned up the charm in his smile. "Can't I make my mother and sister some tea?"

J's eyes narrowed like she was calibrating her BS detector.

Keeping her distance from the tea spread, Gracie glared at him. "I was not born yesterday, young man. I am onto all of your shenanigans. You forget you raised you."

"I have some news, that's all." He pulled a chair away to make room for J at the table. Then he moved to the other side, pulled out a chair, and gestured for his mother to sit. "You'd best sit for this."

Keeping a wary eye on him, Gracie sat straight and tall in the chair. "Really, Benjamin. Just come out with it, already."

He waited for Julia to wheel herself to the table. Well, waited to give himself a minute. Every time he even thought about Paige, his pulse kicked up, his forehead got all hot, and he couldn't let his mother see how much that woman shook him.

"Well?" Julia reached for the teapot and poured herself a full mug. "This better be good, Benny. I'm expecting something earth-shattering."

Earth-shattering. That was one way to put it. Earth moving would be even better. At least the earth would move when he got his hands on Paige...

Heat pulsed through him. *Okay. Now's not the time*... He pulled out a chair and slouched next to J. "Guess who our rafting guide will be?"

Gracie folded her long arms on the table and tapped a nail against the wood. "I couldn't begin to guess."

"Denzel Washington!" J yelled with mock enthusiasm. "No, wait! Tony Romo!"

He gave her a look. "Okay, smart-ass. It's none of your pretend boyfriends." God knew she had hundreds of them. "It's Paige."

"Paige?" Gracie's lips curled with disdain. "That waitress girl?"

"That'd be the one," he answered in a cheery tone.

"No." Gracie's palm smacked the table. "Absolutely not. The girl can't even carry a stack of plates! How on earth can she guide a boat down a river?"

Ben rose and poured her tea. Even added the exact amount of milk and honey to bring some sweetness. "Bryce assured me she's the best."

"Tell him to find someone else." His mother's lips puckered with stubbornness.

"There is no one else." He scooted the tea closer to her. She'd never be able to resist the aroma.

Sure enough, Gracie picked up her mug and took a sip.

"Oh, this is gonna be gooooood." J scrubbed her hands together. "And you were talking about my pretend boyfriends. I do believe you're blushing, Ben Noble."

There was no denying it. His face felt like a thousand fire ants had bitten him.

"She's incompetent." Gracie set down the peace offering and pushed it away.

"So she's a lousy waitress. She only works there once in a while to help out her family."

J's eyes got all big. "So if her family owns the café, that means she's related to that hot redhead."

Don't get any ideas, missy. "I would assume he's her much *older* brother."

"Hmmm." J raised her cup to sip and bounced her eyebrows. "Maybe she'll give us a proper introduction."

"Not if I have anything to say about it." And he'd have plenty to say. Trust him. J was still too young and naïve to understand men. And since he was one, he knew exactly the way they thought.

Gracie pushed back from the table and paced. "If there are no other guides available, we'll have to cancel. There must be another company we can—"

He jumped out of his chair and squared off with her. "What are you so afraid of, Mother?"

Her gaze avoided his. "I already told you. She's incompetent."

Yeah, and he was Santa Claus. He didn't have to be a mind reader to figure out Gracie's problem with Paige. She knew him well enough to know he saw something in her. "You've never seen her on the river. If Bryce says she's the best, I believe him. She's the best. The trip has to be flawless and he guaranteed me she'd deliver." That was stretching the truth, but Gracie didn't have to know. "So you need to behave. Be polite to her. Don't make any scenes like you did at the restaurant. Do we have a deal?"

"Fine." His mother's lips slithered into that smile he

hated, the one that said she was about to pull one over on him. "I'll agree on one condition."

Shit. "What's that?"

"You keep your interactions with her strictly professional. If I so much as see you flirt with that girl, our deal is off."

"Good luck with that," J said around another slurp of tea.

He stared into his mother's scheming eyes and curled his lips to accept the challenge. "Deal."

Even as he said it, he knew there was no way it would stick. Gracie wouldn't be around all the time. Besides, he never let his mother have any say in who he did or did not flirt with.

Deal or no deal, he'd get to know Paige on his own terms.

CHAPTER NINE

Paige had gone through the pre-rafting-trip spiel hundreds of times with hundreds of customers, but as she walked into the Walker Mountain Ranch sitting room, she braced herself the way someone might for an impending car wreck, tightening her upper body into a rigid posture, pulling in a stabilizing breath. She eased the front doors open quietly and stealthily snuck across the foyer, edging her way along the wall until she could hide behind the rock fireplace and get a read on who would attend the meeting.

She peered across the sitting room and there she was, Gracie Hunter Noble, sitting on one of the leather couches, her back as straight and stiff as a two-by-four. Some dark-haired, pale guy Paige didn't recognize sat next to her.

Bryce perched in the chair across from them, and even with the distance, she could read the pained look on his face. At least he saw Gracie for what she was, a royal pain in the ass.

"Hey."

Ben. It was Ben. Coming from the direction of the patio doors behind her.

Stop fluttering. Just stop it, she commanded her heart, but that thing had always had a stubborn streak.

Her eyes shifted left and right, but before she could escape, a large warm handprint in the center of her lower back buckled her knees.

"Whatcha doin'?" He sidled up next to her, his hand still lingering against her, his spicy scent wrapping around her.

What was she doing? Convulsing. Practically gasping for air because his large, capable hand pressed against her and, even though she couldn't forget the humiliation he'd caused her at the gala, she also couldn't forget how it'd felt to kiss him, those sly, smiling lips claiming hers, coaxing out that surge of warm, tingling want from the vastly neglected regions of her body.

Seemingly oblivious to her inner chaos, Ben glanced down in that lazy way of his, soft brown eyes lit by the glow of the soft chandelier lighting overhead. "You look... different."

Usually she didn't care much how she looked, especially considering that she spent her days out in the sun and wind, out tending to horses that didn't care much how she looked, either. But standing next to him—so close she could feel the warmth of his body—made her acutely aware of every detail about herself, the small scar over the bridge of her nose from when she'd crashed her mountain bike, the freckles across her cheeks, the cracks in the dry skin on her hands...

"Sorry." One side of his mouth lifted. "I meant to say you look nice."

Except the word sounded confused, like he wasn't quite sure exactly what he was looking at.

"I like the new look," he tried again.

Her body went stiff and she stepped away so he couldn't touch her. He thought she was trying to impress *him*?

Blood rushed to her face. Hardly. So typical of a wealthy bachelor. She'd dressed up and put on makeup and he assumed it was all for him. The pulsing in her cheeks verged on a nuclear meltdown. "Your mother made it clear she likes things a certain way." *So there.* She hadn't spent two hours getting ready for him. She'd done it all for his mother.

Ben slipped in front of her. She only came up to his chin, but he lowered his head until they were nearly eyes-to-eyes, nose-to-nose, lips-to-lips. "The only person who values my mother's opinion is her."

He was too close. Too intense. She strained her lungs to slow her breathing so her breasts didn't heave out and collide with his chest.

"I make my own opinions, Paige. In case you can't tell, I like what I see when I look at you."

His gaze lowered to her lips and she had to pull back. She couldn't stand there teetering on the edge of that cliff. She couldn't let herself close her eyes and fall, not with Bryce and Mrs. Noble over there, not with her job on the line. And not with Ben being a cowboy Casanova who dated catalog models. That would not end well for her, just like it didn't at the gala. Just like it didn't after Jory convinced her to give him a piece of her heart, then threw it in the trash like a cheap dollar-store ring.

She stumbled back a step. "It doesn't matter if you like what you see," she snapped. "I'm not interested."

"Can I ask why?" he drawled.

"It would be unprofessional," she breathed, inching more space between them.

His lips quirked as he studied her, the expression calling

her bluff. He raised a hand up to the wall, trapping her against him. "If I'd have known I was gonna to meet you that night, I never would've even looked at another woman. You can't fault me for not bein' able to see into the future."

Resist the drawl. She had to resist the drawl. Inching more space between them, she raised her gaze to meet his and tensed her face to send him a message. "That has nothing to do with it," she insisted, then shrugged out from under him so her voice would quit trembling.

But his eyes wouldn't let her go. They seemed so settled on her, so comfortable staring into hers. "Get to know me. Then you can decide what kind of guy I am." He rested his hand on her upper arm in a gesture of sincerity, but she jerked away.

He shouldn't touch her. Shouldn't look at her that way. "I don't want to get to know you." Because what good would it do either of them?

His hand dropped to his side, but his eyes wouldn't let hers go. "I'll change your mind."

"I doubt that." Before he could make good on the threat, she sidestepped him and hurried into the sitting room. Suddenly, sitting next to his mother seemed a lot less dangerous than standing so close to him.

"Paige." Bryce's overly enthusiastic welcome revealed his distaste for the present company.

Wonderful. Should be a fun meeting.

Gracie sat taller and stared over Paige's head without so much as an acknowledgment. "Benjamin. There you are."

"Gracie." His head dipped in a polite nod that indicated both distance and respect. Typical Texas boy, always regarding his momma.

"Kev. Glad to see you made it." Ben sat next to the guy she didn't know.

As much as Gracie Noble seemed determined to ignore her, Paige couldn't afford to be ignored. She stepped closer to where Gracie sat and smiled. "Mrs. Noble. It's wonderful to see you again."

That seemed to stump the woman. Her hands fidgeted with the strap of her Coach purse. She cleared her throat. "Yes. Well. It is interesting, isn't it? It's hard to believe you're a waitress *and* a guide." Gracie gave her a cool look, to which she beamed her brightest smile.

"Sure is." Paige sat on the opposite side of the coffee table. As far away as she could get from Ben and his mother.

Ben scooted forward in his chair and gestured to the man sitting next to him. "Paige, I'd like you to meet my campaign director, Kevin Mackey."

"Very nice to meet you." She snuck a glance at Bryce. See? She knew how to be polite and refined and all of those other things he didn't think she could do.

"Nice to meet you as well." Kevin lifted a glass of red wine off the coffee table and sipped. "Thank you for accommodating us on such short notice."

Bryce waved him off. "Anything for Noble."

Anything except a date. Paige gracefully crossed her legs all ladylike and folded her hands in her lap. "Mr. Mackey, why don't you give us the rundown on plans for the publicity aspect of the trip and the ceremony?" she offered in a professional tone. "Then I can go over a couple of safety items and preparations we'll need to make."

"Sounds like a good plan to me," Bryce said with a hint of pride in his voice. He gave her a look of approval.

"We've got big plans." Kevin set his wine on the coffee table. "During the trip, we'll be live blogging and tweeting updates. A local station back home will run a series of videos we capture." He drummed his fingers against his knee. "Oh, and we'll need plenty of footage that shows Ben out in the woods, one with nature, et cetera, et cetera."

One with nature? She glanced at Ben, who hadn't stopped looking at her even for five seconds. *Great.* He was going to be a problem.

"The ceremony is planned for three o'clock Saturday afternoon. It's a big deal. Food, bands, the local government," Kevin continued in his monotone. "Everything'll be set up near the property line, where there's access from the road. We'll need to arrive via boat by two o'clock to get ready."

"Sounds wonderful," Paige lied. Sounded like a headache and potential disaster. Things were too unpredictable out there. But...the customer is always right, so she moved the meeting along. Quickly, she walked them through the waiver they had to sign before the trip and reminded them what they needed to wear: swimsuits, and the ranch would provide wetsuits and booties. "Don't forget to slather on the sunscreen," she reminded them, glancing at Gracie's perfect pale skin. "You'll also need sunglasses that are secured with a band around your neck." She sat back, relaxed by the shift into professional mode. She could do this. She could make it through the week. "I think that's it for now. I'll give you more information on safety procedures before we get on the river." Her face hurt from smiling so much. "Does anyone have questions?"

For the first time in a half hour, Gracie looked at her. "I'd like to go along," she said, lips curled in a smile.

"What?" Ben practically shouted. "You? *You* want to come on a whitewater rafting trip?"

"Yes." Gracie directed a smug look at Paige. "It sounds awfully exciting."

Exciting her ass. This woman was unbelievable. She

wanted to go to keep an eye on her. But why? What had she done to deserve her scrutiny?

"You do realize there's no shower, right? No mirrors? No gourmet meals?" Ben looked at his mother like she'd dyed her hair purple.

"Of course. I'm fine with no shower. Really, Benjamin. It will be wonderful quality time for us."

Quality time. Right. Because they clearly enjoyed each other's company. Paige shook her head but bit down hard on her lower lip. *Don't say anything.*

Ben jumped to his feet. "You're not going on this trip, Gracie."

Bryce made a show of checking his watch. "Wow. Would you look at the time? I'm gonna go make sure Ma is good with the meal plans." He stood and gave Paige a look that clearly translated, *give them a minute.*

"Yeah. Wow. I have to…" She mentally cataloged through a list of excuses. "…make a phone call real fast. I'll step outside."

Slipping past Ben, she shot him a good-luck look. He could argue until he ran out of breath, but something told her Gracie Hunter Noble always found a way to get what she wanted.

* * *

Paige escaped outside and closed the door behind her. The chill in the air offered a welcome change from the stuffiness that clouded the sitting room.

Outside the French doors, tiki torches flickered a glowing perimeter along the edges of the stone. Farther down, the fire pit sputtered and glinted a warm glow that never ceased to draw her in. She took the steps two at a time, craving the space, the solitude. How would she manage the trip if Ben's mother came along? How would she survive his ogling glances and Gracie's snide comments with her job intact? How could—?

She stopped.

The girl from the restaurant—Ben's sister?—sat in her wheelchair a few feet away from the fire pit. "Hi there," she said, setting down the paperback in her hand.

"Hi." Paige walked slowly to the bench. Seemed like his sister had the same idea she did. "Sorry to barge in. I didn't know anyone was out here."

"Oh, please. Don't worry about it," she said, patting the bench beside her. "The more the merrier." The girl grinned at her. She had an ease about her, a pretty but approachable face. "I hear you're guiding the rafting trip."

"Yep." She settled on the bench next to her. "Just so you know, I'm better at that than I am at waitressing."

She waved her off. "You were great." When the girl smiled, dimples snuck into her full cheeks. "We haven't been properly introduced. My name is Julia." She held out a hand, which Paige shook with a smile. Too bad Julia wasn't going on the trip with them. If her attitude at the restaurant was any indication, she seemed to know exactly how to defuse her mother.

"The meeting's over already?" Julia asked, turning her chair slightly so they were facing.

"Not exactly." Paige widened her eyes with a sharp intake of breath. Something told her the meeting between Ben and Gracie could last all night.

Ben's sister seemed to get the picture. "Let me guess." Her mouth pinched like she was deep in thought. "It ended in a fight between Mother and Ben."

"Something like that," she sighed. For being only nine o'clock, she was suddenly so damn tired.

"What happened?" Julia asked, leaning forward with a look of anticipation.

"Your mother wants to go on the trip with us."

She burst out laughing, the high-pitched giggle contagious. "You've *got* to be kidding me." Julia dabbed at her eyes with the corner of her sleeve.

"I wish I was." Oh, how she wished it was all a big joke.

"You know why, don't you?" Julia asked. "It's because Ben likes you."

"So he said." She groaned. So he'd been saying since he'd seen her again.

"You don't like him?" Julia drew the question out into an investigative tune.

That was a loaded question. She liked certain things about him. The way his backside looked in his jeans, for instance. The charm of his drawl. She'd always had a thing for cowboys. "I don't *know* him," she admitted. "And I'm kind of focused on my job right now." She didn't have room for someone like him, someone larger-than-life, someone who lived in the spotlight. She'd had that before and her heart still hurt to think about how it had ended.

"Actually, my brother's a pretty good guy." Julia's eyes sparkled in the fire's light. "He takes me all over the world with him. Makes sure I get to see everything he gets to see, even if I can't experience it." A hint of sadness, or maybe loss, weighted her words.

"He does seem like a good guy," she confessed, because she wasn't a liar. He really did. Especially bringing his sister along everywhere. A lot of guys wouldn't think twice about that. But…as nice as it was, it didn't seem fair that Julia always had to sit on the sidelines. She *shouldn't* sit on the sidelines just because she was in a wheelchair. She could do anything Ben could do…

Wait a minute. Her heart lifted into that joyous elation she felt whenever she thought about chasing her dream. "Have you ever ridden a horse?" Her eyes were probably too wide and her voice was probably too wound up, but she couldn't help it.

"I used to. Before my accident, I loved to ride." Julia's eyes narrowed. "Why?"

The fatigue that had blanketed her dissolved into a burst of energy. Her pulse thrummed and her hands clasped. "I can take you. I used to work at a therapeutic riding center. We've got a stable full of horses." And she'd worked to train them for this exact thing. "There's the most amazing view of the Bells from the ridge." That would be a short, easy ride for a newbie. "Do you want to see it? Tomorrow?"

Julia only blinked back at her, hands gripping the armrests. "I...can't." Her gaze fell. "I mean, I would love to, Paige, but I haven't been on a horse since—"

"I've taken paraplegics." And though she hadn't yet learned about Julia's injury, she'd seen the woman shift in her chair and move her legs, which meant she hadn't severed her spine.

Really?" Julia breathed like she was almost afraid to believe. Tears glistened in her eyes. "Are you serious?"

"Of course!" She scooted to the edge of the bench so their knees were almost touching. "We can go first thing after breakfast. Meet me at the stables. I'll have everything ready."

The tears made their way down Julia's cheeks. "Oh, wow. Thank you, Paige. Thank you so much."

In the radiance of Julia's open-mouthed grin, the impending week turned brighter, hopeful. She might never please Gracie Hunter Noble, or her own family for that matter, but this...*this* she could do.

CHAPTER TEN

Quality time? *Now* Gracie wanted quality time with him? She'd hired a nanny raise him, but now, when he was thirty years old—a grown man who shouldn't have to run everything by his mother—she wanted quality time.

Undeterred by the twenty solid minutes of arguing with her, Ben strode to the fireplace and back, jaw clenched so tight his temples ached. "Why don't you try being honest for once?"

His mother's eyes widened into a fabricated innocence. "Whatever do you mean?"

Oh, yeah. Right. Like she didn't know. "You don't trust me."

"Benjamin." She swept her hand down his arm and squeezed his hand in hers. "You're wrong. Of course I trust you." Gracie's other arm gestured to the French doors where Paige had disappeared. "It's her I don't trust. Look at what you've been through. You have to be very selective when you're in our position."

In other words, you were only allowed to interact with people on the preapproved list. Every item had to be checked off. Wealthy? Check. Well-respected family? Check. Designer clothes, hairstyles, shoes, handbags, etc.? Check.

Well, he was done checking items off the list. He was done with her list. It was time to make his own.

He shut down her mollifying smile with a pointed glare. "It has nothing to do with careful and everything to do with judgmental," he bit off. "You don't like her because she doesn't come from money. Very honorable."

"Gracie has a point, Ben." Kev spoke up from the side-lines. "Now wouldn't be a good time to start a relationship with anyone."

"Who said anything about a relationship?" He was well aware that his volume had exceeded a normal conversational level, but he didn't care. All he wanted to do was get to know Paige. Spend time with her. Figure her out. It wasn't like they were getting married or anything.

Kev and Gracie shared a look. "Even being seen with someone new could work against you right now."

"I'm not worried." If they wanted a pawn to cater to the attitudes and prejudices of everyone out there, they should've found someone else to run for senator and represent the family. When he was in Congress, people actually liked his honesty, his lack of superficiality. He pointed at his mother. "You can dislike Paige all you want. But I won't treat her like dirt just because you don't like her."

His mother stomped closer, heels click-clacking on the wood floor. "How I feel about that girl has nothing to do with it. You have a reputation to repair." Her mouth pinched into the same crease she wore when he used to come home drunk. "I'm going on the trip with you and that's that." Stifling any further argument, she stalked away from him. "Now if you'll excuse me, I need to rest. This day has completely exhausted me."

With a roll of his eyes, Kev followed her into the foyer. "I'll see she gets to her cabin."

The door slammed shut and Ben had the urge to run after her, to keep arguing until she changed her mind, but he knew better. Dad always called her a stubborn old goat, and the only way to get her to change her mind was to convince her he didn't even notice Paige. Which would be quite the challenge.

Ah, hell. What a mess. He needed a beer. Leaving the unresolved business behind, he hoofed it to the kitchen.

Bryce was already raiding the huge stainless refrigerator. Which meant he'd be having a Coke, seeing as Bryce was a recovering alcoholic.

"You two can still put on quite the show." His friend dug out two Cokes and handed one to Ben. "You really think she'll go on the river?"

"No." He gave his head a firm shake. She absolutely could not go. She'd complain about everything—the bugs, the dirt, the cold water, the fishy smell. He could take his mother in small doses, but all day on the river with her would be an overdose and someone wouldn't make it out alive. "I have two days to talk her out of it."

Bryce cracked open his soda. "Seems like she made up her mind."

He took a long drink. Then he'd have to find a way to change her mind. "I'll talk up the dangers. Risk of death, injury, bear attacks, her son going postal on her..."

Bryce laughed. "Whatever you think, man. From what I've seen, her and Paige on the river together would be a disaster."

"You're telling me." Gracie seemed to know exactly how

to push Paige's buttons. That was the only reason she wanted to go. She wanted to make sure to keep a wedge firmly between them. "Don't you have some kind of age limit on the waiver? Under fifty-five?"

"I wish," Bryce said, raising his Coke in a toast. "I could always write in a clause about yuppie senator wives."

He laughed again. "Nah. That'd only make her more determined." As much as it got to him, he knew because he was cut from the same stubborn cloth. Tell him he couldn't do something—or have someone—and he wanted it even more.

Bryce clapped him on the back. "You'll figure it out." He glanced at the door. "I should head home. Promised Avery a quiet dinner."

A quiet dinner. He pictured it. Sitting across from a wife who loved him, a baby in her belly. Jealousy stabbed him. "You've got it good."

"Don't I know it." Taking another long drink, he cruised to the back door.

Ben followed. There had to be a secret, something he was missing. As crazy as his mother was, his parents had actually been happily married for almost forty years. And he couldn't get a relationship to last more than three months. "How'd you know she was it?" he asked before Bryce could leave.

He got a funny smile on his face. "I knew when I met her. She got to me pretty good. Fought it hard like the dumb-ass I am." He held the door open for Ben and gave him a meaningful look. "I guess when it's right you just know."

Ben glanced to the doors where Paige had disappeared earlier. *She got to me.* He could relate to that. The only problem was, how could he get to her?

"Shoot. I'm late. See you in the morning." Bryce flicked him a wave and trotted across the dining room and out of sight, leaving him all by his lonesome.

Far as he could tell, he had two choices. One, go back to the cabin and apologize to Gracie so he could rekindle their argument. Or two, go outside and see if Paige was still around.

Without wasting any brainpower on that decision, he opened the French doors and slipped out into the darkness.

All around him, torches flickered and gave off the perfect mood lighting. The perimeter of the patio was so dark it reminded him of being on the ranch, underneath a wide-open sky with pinpricks of light. Except these stars and washes of galaxies looked so close it seemed as if he could reach up and feel their heat.

Yep. Looked like the perfect ambiance for a conversation with a certain guide. He strode across the patio, but stopped when he heard voices. Straining to see in the dim light he gazed down at the fire pit.

Well, damn. Paige and Julia sat side by side chatting away like they'd been friends for years. Not that it surprised him. J made friends wherever she went. Probably because she got so bored in that chair. She'd talk to anyone about anything. And that was what made him nervous right now.

He crept down the steps, clinging to the edge of the shadows and straining his ears.

"He's always had issues with women," J said in her know-it-all tone. Damn her. Of course she was telling Paige the abridged version of his love life. Of course. Leave it to his sister. He hurried the rest of the way down before the little informant could spout off more information that wouldn't help his cause.

"Evening, ladies."

Was it his imagination or did Paige's back go stiff?

"Ben!" Julia's face was pink with the chill in the air. Reminded him of the way her face would glow with excitement when she was little.

"Paige said she'd take me riding tomorrow!"

His chest locked. "I'm sorry. What?" Riding? As in on a horse? He eased down onto the bench beside J, wondering how to put his next sentence. "Not gonna happen, J. Understand? You can't ride a horse." He spit it out before he could tame the words into something pleasant.

"Actually—" Paige leaned forward and draped her elbow on her knee. It was a nice knee. His gaze drifted higher. Attached to a pretty sexy leg...

"It's safe. I have tons of experience helping riders with special needs."

Uh, huh. Still studying her toned thigh, he realized he was nodding. *No. Wait.* His head shook. He peeled his gaze off of her tan, sculpted body. "Sorry. What was that?"

A shy smile softened Paige's mouth. She raised her gaze to his. "I said I have tons of experience helping people like Julia ride."

"That's great." It was. In addition to being a knockout, she seemed compassionate, which was a trait most of his exes seriously lacked. "But J doesn't want to go riding."

His sister jerked her head to gape at him. "Yes, I do."

He ignored the flash of anger in her eyes. "It's too dangerous. What if you fell off? Or got thrown?" After everything she'd been through, why risk it? Why let a horse finish the job?

A reddish hue stained J's cheeks.

Oh, boy. Here we go.

"I'm *sorry*. You want me to sit around all day and do nothing like I've been doing for the last twelve years? That's not fair!"

Nothing was fair. Her accident wasn't fair. But he

couldn't let anything happen to her. He wouldn't. "I'm not gonna let you ride a horse, J, so you can forget about it."

She looked at him like she was trying to figure out the most painful way to kill him. "Forget what I said earlier." She glanced at Paige. "My brother can be a real ass." In a huff he recognized all too well, she wheeled herself past the fire pit and up to the ramp.

"Come on J," he called.

"Leave me alone. I'm going to bed."

He jumped up. "I'll get you back to—"

"I don't want your help. With anything." She cruised up the ramp and disappeared from sight.

He took two steps in J's direction before Paige tugged on his hand.

Her skin was chilled and he had an overwhelming instinct to wrap his hand all the way around hers to warm her.

"She's a lot more capable than you give her credit for."

He looked down. Realized he still held her hand in his. She'd only meant to stop him from chasing J, but he couldn't seem to let her go.

She tore her hand away. "Also, I'm pretty sure she's an adult and can make her own decisions." Her eyes flashed with the same intensity he'd noticed at the café. "She doesn't need your permission. If she wants to ride, I'll take her riding." The edge in her voice challenged, but there was something else there, too. Something almost fearful.

He said nothing. Only stared down at her, the softness of the wily waves that had escaped from the bun-thing on top of her head plunging down past her shoulders. He stared at the way her cheeks curved to her mouth, at the way her lips held firm, neither smiling nor frowning.

She's more fragile than she looks.

Elsie would know, but to him she didn't look fragile. She

looked like the most intriguing mystery he'd ever wanted to solve.

"So my opinion doesn't matter at all. You'll take her riding, even if I don't want you to." He sat next to her on the bench, fully aware that he was too close, violating her personal space.

Her shoulder tensed against his, but she didn't move away.

Good. He liked a woman who could stand her ground. Even if he'd never in a million years let her get her way.

"If I have to, yes." Her shoulder shrugged against his. "I'll ignore your opinion and take her anyway," she murmured in a formal tone, which he saw right through. She wouldn't. She was too worried about what Bryce would think.

He turned so that his knee brushed hers, so he could study her face, gauge the reaction in her eyes. "In twelve years, J's had seventeen surgeries on her legs." He'd been at the hospital for every one of them. He'd seen her coming out of the anesthesia, sick as a dog. He's seen her anguish during physical therapy. He'd seen her weep when the doctors told her, yet again, it'd all been for nothing. Her legs would never regain the strength they'd lost when they'd been crushed. She wouldn't walk.

His gut ached the same as it did every time he relived the direction her life had suddenly taken because of his adolescent stupidity. Felt exactly like his Arabian had kicked him in the stomach again.

He forced his gaze into Paige's. "After four of those surgeries, she contracted a raging infection." Four times as he'd held his sister's weak hand in his, he'd begged God, made all kinds of promises that he'd never be able to keep. Four times he was willing to give up his own soul for her. The memories lured him into the cold darkness that leaked through him whenever he let that truth sink in. He moved away so Paige wouldn't feel his weakness. "Four times I thought I would lose her."

He heard her slight intake of breath, although her neutral expression didn't change.

"She's experienced enough pain, Paige. I'm sure you can understand why I wanna protect her from more."

Paige stared down at her hands, eyes shifting as though she was caught in some internal argument with herself, and when she finally gazed up at him, something in the world had changed. Some wall between them had fallen down. She was no longer so guarded, so distant.

"You want to protect her. I get that." Sympathy widened her eyes. "But what does she want, Ben?"

This time he looked away. Studied the shadowy outline of the trees that bordered the patio. The fire's light flickered and danced over them, lighting their pointed tips, then retracting back into darkness. He couldn't think about what she wanted, only what was best for her.

"You should've seen her face when I told her about the horses." Paige bent her head so he had to look into her eyes. "She lit up. She said she'd give anything to be able to ride again."

It was stupid. He knew it. He should let her ride. But he still carried the trauma of being the first one on the scene of the accident. Seeing her covered in blood. Gasping for every breath. Unable to move. And he'd been useless to her. Helpless.

"She can do this. *I* can do this. I spent three summers working at an equine therapy center. We have special equipment designed for this very purpose." Paige laid her hand on his shoulder.

The touch wiped the lexicon clean out of his brain. He'd given speeches in front of a room full of media wolves, baring their ugly questions, and he hadn't once lost his ability to talk. He could yammer on and on until his cows came in from the pasture, but Paige laid one touch on him—one touch that left him with a stark, yawning yearning, and he was done. It was over.

"I know how to keep her safe." A new energy seemed to bubble over into her voice. "Trust me. Please," she begged, even though she didn't have to. He already knew he'd be no match for Paige.

Exhaling a sigh of surrender, he shook his head. "Fine. You win. I'll bring her to the stables in the morning."

"Thank you!" She squeezed his shoulder, and he glanced down at the shimmering swimming pool below them, clamoring for the sweet heat of her body against his.

Ah, hell. He was whipped. He'd pretty much agree to anything, if it would make her happy.

CHAPTER ELEVEN

Everything has to be perfect."

For what could have been the thousandth time, Paige tightened the modified saddle that hugged Sweetie Pie's wide back.

The massive Arabian stood obediently still, head and neck tall and straight, exactly as she'd been taught.

"Atta girl, Sweetie Pie." She gave the horse's glistening neck a good scrub with her fist, then wiggled the saddle to make sure there was no give.

"It'll be fine." Standing across from her, Shooter rolled his eyes. Stable Boy, she called him, though she had to admit, he had a way with horses. That was why Bryce had put him in charge. Most people thought of Shooter as an oaf, and once upon a time, she had, too. But he kind of grew on you after a while, with those tufts of reddish hair sticking up all over his head, and his large, teddy bear frame.

"Man, you're obsessed," he complained. "You've adjusted that thing for a half hour."

She'd adjust it another hour, if that's what it took. Running her fingers along the leather, she inspected the straps and buckles once more. "I promised Ben nothing would happen to his sister. And I intend to keep my promise." She had to prove to him that Julia could ride, that she could do so much more than he thought she could. Or should.

Though she had to admit, the whole protective older brother thing was pretty damn appealing. The thought of Ben made her heart squeeze in a painfully exhilarating clench that seemed to bunch up her throat. After he'd told her about Julia's surgeries, she'd had to fight hard not to throw her arms around him. Seeing that blank look of pain in his eyes, hearing the sorrow in his voice...it'd *done* something to her.

Pathetic as it was, she'd actually brushed her hair and applied makeup that morning, careful to mimic the natural look Ruby had taught her. Then she'd spent a half hour sorting through her closet, instead of the five minutes she usually took to get dressed. Finally, after consulting with Ruby, she'd selected her nicer jeans—the ones without any holes or snags—and a faded flowered button-up, leaving the top buttons undone for good measure. Yes, she had to keep things with Ben professional, but a little cleavage never hurt anyone, right?

And what could she say? It'd been a while since someone had looked at her the way Ben did. He didn't gawk at her boobs like other guys did. He took his time, swept a long gaze over her before settling on her face. He looked into her eyes when she talked, too, which was more than she could say about most men.

After she'd finally gotten dressed, she'd stood in front of the mirror for a good fifteen minutes and decided she looked decent. Good, even.

And yet she still felt like a peasant girl waiting to see the king.

Straightening, Paige gave the stables a critical glance. It definitely wasn't a palace, but it was everything a stable should be. Comfortable stalls for six horses, a small tack room, and a packed dirt floor covered with hay. Though she'd arrived at six that morning to muck it out and straighten things up, the grassy scent of manure still lingered, mingling with the sweet smell of the lilacs Avery had planted right outside.

After she'd cleaned, she took Sweetie Pie on a warm-up ride, telling her all about Julia and how she'd have to use all of the training she'd had to give this special girl a great ride. Sweetie Pie was a great listener.

"Come on." Shooter lumbered over in his ex–football player's unsteady gait. "Nothing'll happen to that girl. You spend all your spare time doing this stuff. It's your life." His strategic emphasis on the word *life* raised her hackles.

She zoned her gaze in on his smug face, ruddy cheeks, freckled skin. "What're you saying?"

"You know what I'm saying." He hobble-stepped to the opposite wall and pulled down a bridle. "You don't have a life."

"I'm focused." She stalked over to the other horses, Hooligan and Gypsy, and checked their saddles, too. Just in case. Couldn't have Ben falling off, either...although legend had it that a horse accident was how Bryce and Avery had fallen in love. They'd gone on a ride much like the one she was about to take Ben and Julia on. Then Buttercup threw Avery into a pile of rocks and the rest was history.

Behind her gate, Buttercup snorted and pawed the ground.

"Not this time, girl." The appaloosa was too unpredictable.

Going senile at a young age, too, the way she tended to wander off the trail.

Shooter popped up behind her and spit past the wad of chew in his mouth. "You're boring. You used to be fun. Go out and have a drink. Play some pool. Now all you do is hang out with the horses."

"That's because the horses smell better than you." Sidestepping the brownish splotch he'd spewed on the ground, she crossed back to her favorite horse in the whole wide world and smooched Sweetie Pie's nose, feeling the tickle of her whiskers. "They're nicer, too." Paige dug a carrot out of her pocket and balanced it on her flat palm. She held it under the horse's nose. "Wait, Sweetie, wait."

A slight quiver was the only sign that Sweetie Pie was dying to eat the carrot. She stood still, ears perked, but totally in control.

"Okay, girl," she gushed. "You can take the carrot."

Gently, Sweetie Pie gobbled it out of her hand, those huge horse teeth crunching in the cutest way. She laid her cheek against the horse's snout. Sweetie Pie was ready. She'd trained her and worked with her and bonded with her. She'd be the perfect one for Julia. "You're a good girl, aren't you, love? Such a sweetie pie."

Shooter gagged.

She shot him a look over her shoulder. "Make yourself useful and get that ramp set up. Will you?"

Muttering to himself, probably obscenities—he had more intriguing combinations than anyone she knew—he dragged over the aluminum ramp that would enable Julia to wheel herself up and get settled in the saddle.

Taking a knee, Shooter fiddled with a socket wrench and started to twist the parts into place. "What's so special about Ben Noble anyway?"

Her stomach lurched the same way it did when she sat on a plane and the wheels left the ground. *Stay grounded,* she commanded herself. She had to stay grounded. "He's a senator."

Shooter stood and stared right into her cleavage. As if her boobs could respond to him. "Not yet, he ain't."

"Well, he will be." If his charm got its way. "Not to mention, he's a good friend of Bryce's so we have to impress him." *Yeah. Keep telling yourself that.* It had nothing to do with the fact that she lay awake most of the night thinking about the way his manly-man hand had clasped around hers, about the way his eyes seemed to follow all the contours of her body, about how warm his powerful shoulder had felt against hers...

"'Morning y'all." At the deep drawl, she spun to the door in time to see Ben wheel his sister into the stables.

A burn raced up her neck and exploded in her cheeks. Um, yeah. It could be a challenge to keep things professional if he insisted on wearing those body-hugging jeans every time she saw him. *Just sayin'.* The tight white T-shirt and straw cowboy hat didn't help, either.

"Hi there," she managed to croak, then covered the weakness in her voice with a cough. It seemed to be a common problem when Ben was around. Most of her body went weak at the sight of him.

"We all set?" He scanned the stable the way a spy would, his eyes narrowed into slits of suspicion.

"Sure." Somehow, she found her footing and went to kneel in front of Julia. "Are you ready?"

"So ready!" She leaned over and dusted off adorable red cowboy boots. "Ben bought these for me in town this morning."

Of course he did. Her heart melted into a warm puddle deep in her chest.

"Everyone woman should own a pair of boots." He

sauntered closer, his eyes doing that lazy inspection of Paige's body, as if he had all the time in the world to simply take her in.

Patting her hair, she stood and rewarded his thoughtfulness with a smile. "They're perfect."

"Ahem." Somewhere on the other side of the stable, Shooter made a production out of clearing his throat.

Oh. Right. She waved him over. "Ben, you remember Shooter?"

His chin dipped in a single nod.

"And this is Julia." She stood protectively in front of Ben's sister. Didn't want Shooter to get any ideas.

"Nice to meet you, Julia." He craned his neck to peer around Paige.

"Shooter helped me get everything set up this morning." *Help* was a bit of a stretch, but she was feeling generous. Mostly he'd come to badger her about hitting the bar with him later that night. As if she hadn't learned *that* lesson.

"Thanks so much." Julia beamed at him.

But Ben's chin tilted up as he inspected Shooter, the easiness in his eyes replaced by something harder. "How's it goin', Shooter? What're you up to these days?"

"Whatever I'm told," he answered like a sulky child.

And they thought she had issues with customer service!

Instead of rolling her eyes and punching his shoulder like she wanted to, Paige gave his back an affectionate pat. "Shooter'll actually be going on the rafting trip with us."

Despite the unimpressed smirk that pulled down the corners of Ben's mouth, he offered Shooter a hearty handshake. "Great. Glad to have the extra help."

"We're all here to help," Shooter said in his affable way. "But my work here is done." He faced Paige. "I'll be fishing when you get back. Make sure you put everything away."

"Of course." She always put everything away.

"See you around." Shooter lifted his hand in a wave and left.

Ben watched him walk away, then tilted his head toward Paige. "He seems about as fun as he was the last time I met him."

She waved him off. "He's not so bad once you get to know him." And as long as you didn't get to know him too well.

"How *well* do you know him?" Ben's easy look had returned. His gaze lowered to the collar of her shirt and lingered there before making its way to her eyes again.

A flush crept up her neck. *Shoot.* Was the cleavage too much? Maybe it was too much. Maybe Ben thought she'd left those buttons undone for Shooter and not for him. "Um. Er. I've known him since junior high. Unfortunately."

"So it's one of those pesky brother relationships, then?"

"I know all about those," Julia piped up behind them. "I'll share all my coping mechanisms later."

Ben laughed and turned to ruffle his sister's hair. "Don't forget, I bought you boots today. Those suckers cost a small fortune, too."

"At least my brother is an expert at buying my affection," she said with a smirk.

"I'd take that," Paige laughed. The only thing Shooter'd ever bought her was a Coors Light after she'd schooled him in a game of pool.

"I bet you would," Julia quipped, her voice a singsongy tune that made Paige's cheeks prickle with heat. It was clearly all meant in fun, but it hit a little too close to the truth.

Before either one of them could see her face glow, she

pivoted to the horse. "This is Sweetie Pie." Burn subsiding, she glanced over her shoulder. "I've spent hundreds of hours training her, and she's the best horse in the entire world."

Julia wheeled herself close enough to reach up and pat Sweetie Pie's neck. "Hi there." The wispy mixture of awe and love in her voice swelled Paige's heart until it felt like it might float right out of her chest. This experience could change Julia's life. And she got to be part of it. She blinked past the burn in her eyes.

Sweetie Pie gazed down at Julia with those glassy, gentle eyes.

"Here." She dug another carrot out of her pocket and handed it to Julia. "Carrots are her favorite."

"Want a carrot, Sweetie Pie?" Julia held her hand flat and lifted the carrot to the horse's mouth. "God, I've missed horses." She shot an accusatory look at her brother. "Someone doesn't even let me *near* the stables."

"I'm letting you ride, aren't I?" Ben shot back. "Against my better judgment," he muttered.

"She'll do great." Paige's hand somehow landed on his arm.

He looked at her hand, then into her eyes. "I know."

Let go of his arm. Let go. She pried her hand off him and silently swore never to touch him again. It could seriously compromise her better judgment. Whirling away from him, she positioned herself behind Julia's chair. "Let's get you settled in the saddle. Ben," she said without looking at him, "...why don't you stand in front of Sweetie Pie? Just in case she needs a reminder to be still?" She wouldn't need a reminder, but he needed to get comfortable with the whole thing.

"Sure." He backed to the front of the horse, but kept a firm gaze on Julia.

"Up we go." Paige took the handles and wheeled her up the ramp. On the platform, she locked the wheels in place.

"Wow," Ben said. "The horse is like a statue. Her ears aren't even twitching."

She shot him an I-told-you-so smile. "She knows. Don't you?" She gave the horse's rump a love pat. "Okay, Julia. You ready?"

"Sure am." She scooted forward in her chair.

"I'll get your legs situated. Then you can take hold of the saddle and we'll slide you in." Carefully, Paige tugged Julia's leg and rested her ankle on the horse's back. Then she supported Julia around the middle. "Whenever you're ready."

"Here goes nothing," Julia said.

Paige glanced up and saw Ben watching, a slight twitch in his mouth. She gave him a reassuring smile as she slid Julia into place. It was a flawless transition, if she did say so herself. She hurried down the ramp and buckled the straps over Julia's legs. "This'll help your balance. Let me know if anything feels too tight or uncomfortable."

"Not at all." Julia marveled. "That was so easy."

"And that was the hardest part." She made her way down the ramp. "Now Sweetie Pie will do all the work. Won't you, girl?"

Julia looked like a queen up there, face glowing with joy. She could see it reflected on Ben's face, too.

They shared a smile before she led him to his horse. "Ben, meet Hooligan."

"Hooligan, huh?" Walking alongside, he scratched his way down the horse's flank and patted.

Hooligan responded with a bend of his neck, a silent plea for more.

"He's a beauty," Ben said with obvious appreciation. He knew a good horse when he saw one.

Paige backed away as he wedged his boot in the saddle and mounted the horse, giving her a nice view of his backside. She should look away. Turn away and hop on Gypsy . . .

Ben took the reins and straightened himself in the saddle, looking very much like the god of the cowboys.

All the pulse points in her body hummed. Geez. He *did* things to her. Things that could get her in trouble. Big trouble. Especially when he looked at her that way, with a secretive expression, like there was something private between them.

She turned away. There couldn't be anything private between them. That's all there was to it. Much as she enjoyed looking at the man, it would cost her too much.

As she walked around her horse, she quickly buttoned those top three buttons on her shirt. Then she propped her foot in the stirrup and hoisted herself onto the horse's back. Giving Ben no chance to pull her into his mesmerizing stare, she steered Gypsy toward the doors. "I'll lead. Ben, why don't you follow Julia?"

At a distance. In the back. That was the best place for him. When it came to Ben Noble, she needed all the space she could get.

CHAPTER TWELVE

Wasn't a bad view, really. He might not have the chance to stare at her face, but Paige happened to have a stellar backside, too, so he couldn't complain. Of course, by assigning him to the rear, she'd pretty much made it impossible for him to have a conversation with her. Was that her plan? Just like last night. The second he'd asked her a personal question she'd ducked out on their romantic fireside ambiance and said she had to get to bed early. He'd offered to go with her, but she turned him down. She laughed, though. And he loved her laugh. It was the most unexpected sound, high and breathy. Carefree. Normally she didn't seem too carefree. But when she laughed, she let go of something. Not that he knew what held her back...

Ah, Paige. Little did she know, putting him off wouldn't help. He loved a good mystery, but patience wasn't his virtue.

With a flick of the reins, he eased Hooligan up to his sister's side. Much as he hated to admit it, she didn't seem to need him watching over her. Though she hadn't been on a horse since the week before her accident twelve years ago, it all seemed to come back to her. She held the reins like a professional, and that horse Paige had trained, well...he'd never seen anything like it. It seemed to sense J's movements. Even with the steady incline they'd been treading for the last twenty minutes, J remained sturdy and still, the horse's easy gait slow and smooth.

He edged closer to his sister. "Whoa. Slow down there, Trigger. You're fixin' to leave me in your dust."

"That's the idea," she chirped.

"Red boots. Genuine Italian leather," he reminded her.

She slid her gaze sideways. "I might need a pair in blue, too. Maybe yellow."

"Damn, woman. I'll have to get another job to support your shoe habit."

She laughed.

He loved to hear her laugh, too. For so many years it had been a rare sound. Looking at her face now—radiating with joy—he realized he had to take part of the blame. He'd done his best to keep her safe, but that didn't exactly allow her to have much fun, either.

He thought about the time she'd begged him to take her paragliding. It was right after he'd earned his certification in Aspen. She'd watched him take off the side of the mountain over and over, then begged him to take her on a tandem run. He'd said no, of course. He'd said no when she begged him to take her skiing, too, even though he knew there was special equipment. His gut twisted. Paige was right. J was far more capable than he'd given her credit for.

Reaching over, he latched his hand over hers and slowed Sweetie Pie. "Seriously, J. Forgive me. Please. I never meant to hold you back from the things you loved."

She tugged the horse to a stop and turned her head. "I forgave you a long time ago." An unusually serious expression hardened her face. "I'm not the only one who hasn't been living, Ben. Maybe you need to forgive yourself."

Yeah. That was easier said than done.

"Everything okay back there?" Paige had stopped her horse a few yards ahead of them and turned around.

"Everything's amazing." J fluffed the reins and Sweetie Pie responded with a gentle swagger that didn't rattle her at all.

Ben nudged Hooligan with a clip of his heels. "I'm having a hard time keeping up with you ladies." Unless he missed his guess, that was Paige's plan. Keep him on the outside. Good luck with that. They were about to spend a whole day together in the great outdoors. It'd be impossible for her to avoid him then.

He fell in step behind Julia and Sweetie Pie as the evergreens and aspens thinned. Patches of sun lit the tall green grass and hundreds of white and purple wildflowers, making them glow. The terrain grew steeper. Hooligan snorted and chugged, but not Sweetie Pie. The horse didn't utter a single sound. She simply bent her head down and eased Julia up, up, up as they crested a small ridge.

At the top, Julia gasped. "Oh, wow. Oh, Ben...look at that." She pointed to the horizon, her hand reaching like she wanted to grab the view and take it home with her.

He looked in that direction, and that same appreciation washed over him. Off in the distance, mountain peaks soared to the blue sky, stretching down into a glistening green valley dotted with trees. Like back home, the sky was vast and overpowering, but the rest of the landscape held more color, more dimension than the Texas prairie. And with Julia situated in front of it, he wanted to remember it forever. Yanking

Hooligan to a stop, he dug his phone out of his pocket. "Smile. I'll take your picture."

She didn't just smile. She beamed like she'd seen the eighth wonder of the world.

"Cheese!" She stretched her arms out on either side of her, giving his gut a good blow.

"Careful," he called.

Her glare scolded him. And reminded him. No more hovering. No more helicoptering. No more holding her back. This whole letting-her-have-freedom thing would take some getting used to.

But she sure did look free without that chair confining her…

Paige trotted back to him and held out her hand. "Give me your phone. I'll take your picture together."

Taking his time to enjoy another view of her—the best view—he handed it over. It was a shame she'd buttoned up those top three buttons.

"Go over by your sister," she said, obviously flustered that he liked to look at her. What could he say? He'd never been one for subtlety.

With a pointed raise of his eyebrows, he trotted over to Julia's side and slung an arm around her. On any other horse, he would've kept his distance, but Sweetie Pie didn't seem to mind Hooligan encroaching on her space. "Say cheese, sis." He shot Paige his best grin.

"I'll take a couple," she called as she maneuvered her horse with one hand like a natural cowgirl.

When the photo shoot was done, she slapped his phone back in his hand without making eye contact and practically galloped away. "We should head back. I'm sure your mother's expecting you for lunch."

"Do we have to?" J whined. "I love it here. This view is the most beautiful thing I've ever seen."

He had to admit, it was pretty incredible, but he kept getting distracted by the scenery in front of him. Every time Paige's rear popped off that saddle, he nearly fell off his horse.

Digging his heels into Hooligan's wide girth, he urged the horse after Paige. When he'd finally caught up, he cut off her path. "We've got time. Let's let J enjoy the view for a few more minutes."

Paige's eyes narrowed, analyzing him like she wanted to decipher his motives.

But he wasn't one to keep secrets. Didn't like playing games, much, either. He surely hadn't kept his interest in her to himself. Just in case, he leaned close. "That'll give us a chance to talk. Lord knows, I've been waiting for that chance all morning."

She didn't look at him. "I really should keep an eye on Julia." Wrenching the reins, she maneuvered the horse past him.

"Good idea. We can both keep an eye on her." Not that she needed either of them, at the moment. She was steering Sweetie Pie back and forth across the meadow, videotaping the scenery on her phone.

Though Paige seemed intent on outmaneuvering him, he kept stride alongside her. "So how'd you get into equine therapy?" he asked in a purely innocent voice.

Those hazel eyes flashed at him. "Just so you know, it's against company policy to have a fling with a customer."

"Who said anything about a fling?" He backed Hooligan in front of her so she could see his eyes. Well…that and so she couldn't gallop away again. "I'm not looking for a fling, Paige. I've had enough of those." Too many. And every one left him emptier than the last. "I want something real. Someone real." He'd learned enough to recognize it when it stood right in front of him. "I'm not making a pass at you. I'm asking you a question. An innocent question." It was probably the most innocent conversation he'd ever had with a woman. "But it's because I want to know you. Not because I want to sleep with you."

She glanced past him, presumably at J, who was now adding commentary to the video.

"Ben's so pigheaded he almost didn't let me come on this amazing ride, but he finally came to his senses..."

So the whole world would know he was an ass, if that fact wasn't already obvious.

Paige looked at him again, this time with a smile playing at the corners of her full lips.

Thankfulness for J swelled in his chest. Somehow she showed his ignorance in the best light. She was the best sister in the world. "So." He tried again with Paige. "How did you get into equine therapy?"

Her gaze lowered to the horse. She smoothed her hand down its mane. "I spent a lot of time with my grandma when I was little. She practically raised me." Her eyes dared a look into his. "She loved being outdoors. Fishing, hiking, kayaking. But when I was ten, she got diagnosed with MS. It went fast. Within a few months, she couldn't get around anymore. It killed her not being able to spend time out here." Pain edged into her voice. "Eventually she lost the will to live."

A breeze blew, carrying her hair away from her face, which had flushed with emotion. Her eyes had grown hard, unyielding. He recognized that look. The look of steeling yourself against the deepening pain of a loss that still haunted your life. If she hadn't been sitting on a horse so far away, he would've touched her to bring her back, to remind her she'd made it past that time. The same way he had to remind himself sometimes. But he couldn't offer any words of consolation because he knew. You make it past, but you never really feel whole. You cope but you don't forget.

It always used to piss him off when people would gloss over J's new reality. After her accident, after his father died. *I'm so sorry. You're in our thoughts and prayers.* Were there more generic words in the entire English language? Something told him Paige hated those words, too. So he said what he'd always wished people would say to him. Something to acknowledge the person he'd lost, or the part of J they'd lost. "I bet you're a lot like your grandma."

Her face relaxed into an open-mouthed smile that tugged at the corners of her eyes. "I am, actually. More like her than anyone else in my family."

"She'd be proud of you." He watched J trot to the edge of the meadow, laughing and patting Sweetie Pie's neck. "You changed her life, you know. I can't remember the last time I saw her this happy." Which only proved that he was, indeed, a complete ass.

"Ben…" Paige eased her horse closer so that their knees touched. "What happened to her? How'd she get hurt?"

There was a painful jolt inside of him, the emotions stampeding their way out. His jaw locked. His hands tightened on the reins. But she'd answered his question. And now he owed her an answer.

"She was in a bad car accident with three of her friends. No one else survived." That was the easy part. The part his parents had made him rehearse over and over. Usually, that was when the platitudes came. *Oh my god, I'm so sorry. Your poor family.*

But Paige said nothing. She only waited. She wasn't so gullible. She knew that wasn't the end of the story.

Don't look away. But damn was it hard to look into her eyes and tell her the truth. "I was a senior and I let her come to a party with me. She was only fifteen." Too young to have to watch out for herself, but he'd been too busy beating all of his buddies at a drinking game. "She said she wanted to go home, but I was too wasted to drive her. Told her she'd have to wait."

Her eyes tapered like she felt his pain. "But she didn't wait."

"No. Her friend had just gotten her license. I didn't even know they'd left." He would've stopped her.

Beneath him, Hooligan stomped with impatience. He felt that same itch. Move. Run. Gallop. Let the wind carry it away.

Paige reached over and steadied a hand on the horse's snout. "Easy, Hoolie. We'll get moving soon." She peered up at him, waiting. Again.

For once she didn't seem to be in a hurry to get away from him. That was something, he guessed. With a deep inhale, he let the rest of the ugly story flow from the dam of memories. "They crashed just down the road. I heard the sirens." He blinked against the images. How he'd gotten that sick feeling, how he'd run through the house screaming for her, and, when he couldn't find her, how he tore out onto the road, all the way down to the scene. He remembered the sounds she made more than anything else. The gasps. The cries for help...

"Was it her spine?" Paige asked in a reverent quietness.

"Her legs were crushed. She almost lost them both." In some ways, she had lost them.

Paige turned her head and looked at his sister.

She'd leaned her head down like she was whispering something to Sweetie Pie, her new best friend.

"She's pretty incredible, you know," she said with a smile so genuine it made him ache.

"I know. She reminds me of that all the time." It felt good to lighten the mood and let that weight slide off. At some point over the last twelve years, he'd learned to drag it instead of carry it. Somehow that made it easier to bear.

"She's lucky, too." Paige urged her horse to his side and laid her hand on his arm. "To have someone in her family love her so much. That's something of lot of people don't have."

A lot of people, as in her? What about the guy at the restaurant? And what about her parents?

She must have seen the questions rising in his eyes because she cranked the reins and took off in Julia's direction. "Race you to the trail!" she yelled, already stealing the lead from him.

"Hey!" He clipped his heels into Hooligan's sides, hunkered down, and tore after her. Paige could run from him, but she couldn't hide.

Not anymore.

CHAPTER THIRTEEN

Ya! Go, Gypsy, go!" Paige crouched lower over the saddle horn and flipped the reins.

Ben was gaining on her, she could feel it. A glance over her shoulder to check on Julia, then she dug in her heels. "Come on, girl! Don't let Hoolie beat you."

She squinted. Fifty yards, then the race had to stop. The trail was too steep and rocky.

Hooves pounded the soft ground. Gypsy's head jutted, stretched.

A familiar ache crept up her lower back—her favorite kind of pain. Tension gripped her hands. She should slow down, but...she couldn't let him win.

Hooligan's shadow inched up on Gypsy, black mane flowing behind. His snorts and chugs got closer...closer, until they were neck-and-neck.

Shooting her that knee-wobbling grin, Ben bent lower. "Giddy up, Hooligan!" He clipped the horse with his heels.

Dammit! With an obnoxious whoop and holler Ben stole her lead and pounded toward the trail.

Defeat colored her cheeks. "Fine!" It came out harsher than she intended, but she hated to lose worse than she hated horse manure in her boots. "You won." Pulling back on the reins, she slowed Gypsy to a canter, then a trot. The edge of the meadow bounced about thirty yards ahead, disappearing into a thick forest. Beyond that, the trail dropped a good three hundred vertical feet. And, of course, Ben kept his pace at full throttle.

Her grip on the reins tightened. She could throttle *him*. "Hey! We're not racing down the trail!" It was too dangerous, rocky and steep. Even for someone as experienced as him, navigating at that speed would be a challenge. She cupped her hands around her mouth. "Stop!"

Either he didn't hear, or, more likely, he didn't want to hear. Without a glance back, he disappeared into the trees.

Grrrr. She was wrong about him. He wasn't the sweet big brother. He was a total show-off, an eighteen-year-old trapped in a man's body.

"He likes to live in the fast lane," Julia said as she trotted up behind her. "I gave up telling him to slow down a long time ago. He's pretty stubborn."

She could think of a few other words to describe him, but Julia didn't need to hear them. "He doesn't know the mountains." He could probably ride fifty miles back in Texas without seeing one small hill. "This isn't the kind of terrain he's used to."

"Ben never backs down from a challenge." A sly grin implicated Paige as an accomplice to his juvenile behavior. "I'd apologize for him, but it'll be way more fun watching him grovel at your feet."

"If he gets the chance." She flicked the reins to get Gypsy

moving again. "We'll probably find him lying on the side of the trail somewhere." Hopefully unconscious so he couldn't relay to Bryce the colorful string of curse words she'd spewed at him all the way back to the ranch.

Slow and careful, like skilled riders should be, she and Julia ambled side by side down the rocky slope, lower and lower toward the stables. Still no sign of Ben. Shaking her head, Paige looked over at Ben's sister. For coming from such a rich family—and such a stuck-up mother—she was so down to earth and easy to talk to. Maybe because of the suffering she'd endured or maybe simply because that's who she was. Either way, Julia felt like someone who could be a friend, and she didn't often feel that connection with people. Ducking to avoid a low-hanging branch, Paige glanced over. "I hope you had fun today."

Julia turned to her, her eyes full of tears. "You don't know how much this has meant to me."

And that was all it took to dissolve the tension that had tempted her neck to snap. Who cared about Ben? This so wasn't about him. It was about his sister, about helping her experience life again. The warm glow inside of her radiated into a grin. "It was nothing. Really. I'm happy we made it work."

"*You* made it work," Julia insisted. "You're the one who talked Ben into it."

"I don't know about that." Something told her Ben never did anything he didn't want to do. Whether he'd admit it or not, he felt bad about holding Julia back.

"Trust me." Julia reached down to pat Sweetie Pie's neck. "If he didn't have such a serious crush on you, this never would've happened."

A forced laugh choked her. A crush? Is that what she called it? Ha. "No. Trust me," she mumbled. "He doesn't have a crush on me." Ben didn't have feelings for her. Not real feelings anyway. He was the kind of guy who lived for the chase, and the more she resisted him the more persistent he got. "There's nothing there." Because she wouldn't let there be. She wasn't a stupid girl. Not anymore.

Julia shook her head. "You're about as stubborn as he is," she said through a billowing sigh.

"Your brother isn't stubborn. He's reckless." Tearing down the trail like that. Didn't he get it? He was her responsibility. If something happened to him, it would be on her. She could lose her job...

"You should give him a chance, Paige," Julia murmured. "For even as pigheaded as he can be, he really is a great guy. And he needs a great girl."

Without meaning to, she eased her heels into Gypsy's ribs. The horse clomped faster. "We really should get back." Because her fantasy world didn't need any encouragement when it came to Ben.

"You don't like him?" his sister asked, her large, dark eyes doing a cross-examination.

The sun beamed down hot and intense on her face. "It's more complicated than that," she muttered.

"For what it's worth..." Julia's smile reached up to squint her eyes. "...I think you'd be great for him. He doesn't belong with these hoity-toity bimbos my mother keeps throwing at him."

She was pretty sure their mother had already decided her son didn't belong with Paige, either. Ben Noble lived in a different world than her. She craved freedom, anonymity. And his escapades with women made it into the entertainment sections of all the Texas newspapers. In an evasive maneuver, she turned her head. "Oh, look. We're back already." *Thank god.*

Or not, she thought when she spotted Ben.

He leaned against the corral fence looking like a young Marlboro man, one knee bent, boot kicked up on the rail and a piece of tall grass hanging from his mouth.

It was a sight she would've enjoyed if she hadn't been so irritated with him. Sure, the guy could easily win a Brother of the Year Award, but he wasn't that different from most guys she'd known. Arrogant. Wild. Impulsive.

Besides that, his whole good-old-cowboy look could stop traffic at a beauty pageant parade and he knew it. As much as it all tempted her, she'd never been one to cater to anyone's ego.

Steering Gypsy right past the fence, she made sure her eyes glossed over him. "Glad you found your way back," she said coldly.

"Hooligan found his way back." Ben straightened and strode over to her. "Seems like once that horse knows he's headed for home, he's hard to stop."

Ignoring the way his eyes searched hers, she dismounted and went to grab Sweetie Pie's bridle. "All right, Julia. I'll get Sweetie Pie lined up with the ramp. Then we'll get you back into your chair."

"Thank you so so much." The girl's eyes were shining. "That was amazing, Paige. The best day ever."

Despite Ben's hard stare directed at her face, her heart swelled. If she could start that therapy program, she'd get to see a smile like Julia's every day. That would make every day of the last five years of her life worth it. She focused her gaze intently on the horse. She could not let Ben Noble derail her. This is what she was about and she had no room in her life for anything else. She smiled back at Julia. "I'll take you out anytime. It's great practice for Sweetie Pie."

"You were right. She's the best horse ever." She leaned in

against Sweetie Pie's mane, hugging the back of the horse's neck.

Still avoiding Ben, Paige led the horse to the ramp and lined her up. "Here we are, Sweetie Pie." She looked into the horse's wise eyes. "Stay now, you hear?"

Sweetie Pie didn't have to answer. She always heard.

"Want me to hold her?" Ben asked somewhere behind her.

Unfortunately, ignoring him hadn't made him disappear. But that didn't mean he wouldn't. Eventually. "Sure. Whatever." Without turning to acknowledge him, Paige climbed up the ramp and positioned Julia's chair. Then she leaned over and slid her arms around Julia. "On three, we'll slide you over. Ready? One. Two. Three."

Another easy transition shifted Julia back to her chair. The woman didn't look exactly thrilled about it, either.

She gazed up at Sweetie Pie with a wistful longing. "I'd love to go out again before we head back to Texas." She carefully wheeled herself down the ramp.

"I'm sure we can make that happen." Paige followed behind her. "Maybe after the rafting trip."

"That'd be great!" Julia's strong hands pushed on the wheels of her chair. She spun herself toward the stable entrance. "Thanks again, Paige. I should go clean up before lunch."

Ben stepped to the edge of the ramp to cut off her path, but Paige simply dodged around him, still evading the question in his eyes, pretending she couldn't read them, even though they were clear.

What's wrong?

Why are you avoiding me?

"Thanks for the great company." She waved at Julia. "See you soon."

"I guess I should go, too." Ben started after Julia, but his sister shooed him away.

"No. I don't need you following me around." A sly grin made her look ten years younger. "You should stay. Help Paige put things away."

What? Her head snapped up. *Um, no. Bad idea.* Alone time with Ben would make it impossible to ignore him. "That's okay. I've got it. I do this myself all the time."

"Well, he's not coming with me." Julia gave her brother a stern look. "Besides, it's the least he can do after that stupid stunt he pulled."

For a few seconds, Ben's eyes shifted back and forth between her and Julia like he was torn. Then he shrugged. "Okay. I'll help out."

Paige ducked toward Sweetie Pie to hide the glow on her face. Julia was almost as persistent as Ben...

"See you both later!" She chirped, then she was gone, the little sneak.

"So...what can I do for you?" Ben spread his arms like he was her personal genie.

"Nothing. Seriously. I don't need your help," she replied, her tone airy and light. Impassive. She refused to give him the satisfaction of knowing he got to her.

But he must've seen right through her because his hands went straight to his hips. "What're you so pissed off about?"

"I'm not pissed off." She unlatched the saddle and ripped it from Sweetie Pie's back, hauling it over to the stand. "I'm busy, that's all." Too busy to stop and look at him. To let him apologize. She needed a reason not to like him, to keep her distance. She'd been through this before. It was shocking how similar he was to Jory, how he kept pursuing her, how he complimented her and looked at her like he wanted to see her. Well she knew how that turned out. Once he had her, he'd toss her aside. Same dance, different song. Jory had been classic rock. Ben was country.

"You're obviously pissed off," Ben said with amusement playing on his lips. He strode over in his cowboy gait. "Tell me what I did and I'll apologize."

She slipped past him. "This is me, Ben. See? I'm not as sweet as you thought." *So leave me alone. Move on to some other girl who fits better with your life.*

"Sweet is overrated." She heard the grin in his words.

What could she say to that? Nothing. So she went about her work silently, removing Sweetie Pie's blanket, brushing her down.

"If you don't put me to work, I'll find somethin' to do on my own." Ben leaned next to her so she had to look at him. "I'd hate to ruin your system."

His closeness sizzled on the bare skin of her arms. *Dammit.* Why did he have to shake her up like that? "Fine." She pushed off her knees and stood, desperate to get away from him. It was too hard to think clearly, to hold him off when he got close to her. So she pointed him away. "Get Hooligan settled. The saddles and blankets go over there." She gestured to the stand across the stables. "Brush him down. Make sure he gets a drink. Think you can handle all that?"

He didn't move, still stood inches away, close enough that she felt the hum of his energy, close enough that the storm clouds of want gathered in her chest.

"Sure. I can handle it," he assured her with a look that told her he could handle a hell of a lot more than that. "*If* you let me take you out tonight."

Impossible. This guy was impossible. "Sorry," she said with an exaggerated shrug. "There's a company policy against flings with customers." Okay, so there was no policy, but there really should be. In fact, as soon as she was done in the stables, she'd go straight home and write up a whole employee handbook for Bryce and Avery. Rule number one: No flings with customers.

"I'm not a customer," Ben reminded her. "I'm a friend."

"You're not my friend," she said through a laugh. How stupid did he think she was?

His crooked grin turned on the charm. "I'm not looking for a fling, Paige. I just want to get to know you."

"We can't get to know each other." The ache under her rib cage reminded her to breathe.

"Give me one good reason why."

There were about a thousand reasons why, but the best one... "Bryce would kill me. This week is important to the ranch, and I refuse to mess it up."

Ben stepped closer, those eyes bringing her somewhere else, into a realm of possibilities where she had no business being.

"You're not gonna mess anything up. Trust me. He's a good friend of mine," Ben murmured, his gaze drifting down her body in that slow, lazy way of his, threatening to put her under a spell. "I'll talk to him."

No. Huh-uh. She could not get sucked into his magic. She backed up a couple of steps, refocusing on the horse. So much safer. "Fine," she said in a formal tone. "You might be able to convince Bryce...," though she doubted it. "But there're plenty of other reasons I won't go out with you." She went back to scrubbing down Sweetie Pie. "Your mother, for example. She hates me."

"Not true," he argued. "She doesn't *hate* you."

"She doesn't want you going on a rafting trip alone with me." She mocked him with a glare. "Which, by the way, is hilarious, considering you're a grown man."

It was the first time she'd ever seen his face flush.

"My mother doesn't matter," he said, still blushing.

Satisfaction warmed her stomach. Ha. She could get to him, too. Straightening, she tossed the brush to the nearby bucket. "Don't take this the wrong way, but she makes herself matter in a way that's not exactly appealing to your potential girl*friends*."

His hand latched on to her arm. "One date. That's all I'm asking for."

No, no, no. Don't touch me. Don't make me want something I can't have.

"Ben." She sighed. *Leave me alone* didn't sound nice. And he thought she was nice. As much as he was mistaken, she hated to burst that particular bubble. It was a rare occasion that someone thought she was nice.

He stepped closer. Too close. "One date. Three hours. What are you afraid of, Paige?"

"That's a complicated question," she whispered because that was all she could manage. Her lungs squeezed. She couldn't tell him the truth. She was afraid once he saw past everything, he wouldn't like what he found. Just like everyone else.

But he didn't back off. He didn't move away. He stared at her until the world fell silent, until his gaze fell to her lips. She knew he would kiss her before his lips pressed into hers. She knew, but she didn't back away, either. Her heart pounded so hard it ached and when his lips were finally on hers, she kissed him back, letting her knees go weak, letting her herself sink into him, letting go.

And he knew where to take her. Holy shittles, he knew. His strong hands caressed up her back and gentled into her hair. His soft, warm lips pried hers open, shooting bursts of warmth down her arms and legs. Something in her chest unlocked and she opened her mouth to him, let his tongue stroke hers. And it was a good thing he was so solid and sure because she wouldn't be able to stand if she wasn't leaning against him.

His lips moved over hers, slow and sensual, with a reverence no one had ever offered her. And it was so different, the places he was taking her, so open and giving, demanding nothing for himself. Her body responded to his with a shuddering gasp that made her want to give him more, everything. Chest heaving with a stifled breath, she glided her tongue along his lower lip, then bit down on it lightly.

His low groan lured her hands to his chest. They slid down, feeling the solid muscle under his shirt. Warm satisfaction filled her body to the point of brimming over as a sensual desperation flickered in his movements, making them faster, harder. His tongue mingled with hers, loosening her control, only proving the theory that one kiss could lead to so much more. He could give her more. So much more, judging from the way he seemed to know exactly what she wanted...

A foreign sound froze her. Her hands gripped Ben's shirt as she strained her ears.

Moose. Barking. Somewhere close by. Which meant Bryce wouldn't be far behind.

"Paige?" her boss called.

Bryce!

She jerked back and shoved her hands into Ben's chest so hard, he stumbled backward into the feed buckets. Everything clattered as he fell, landing right in a pile of horse oats.

"Paige?" Bryce yelled again. "What the hell?"

Moose bounded into the stables and launched himself at Ben, smothering him with happy kisses.

Eyes wide and bewildered, she looked down at him, still crumpled on the ground, trying to wrestle the dog away as he laughed his ass off.

Oh, no. She squeezed a hand over her mouth, face pulsing

with a scorching heat. Her shaking hand reached up to smooth her hair, sure that somehow the evidence of that kiss was all over her.

"What's going on?" Bryce demanded as he jetted through the stable doors.

"Ben fell," she blurted out. "He was helping me put stuff away and he..."

"Tripped over my own feet." Eyes watering from the laughter, he pushed Moose away and stood, brushing himself off.

The dog tore away and disappeared from the stables like he'd caught some juicy scent. "Some things don't change. I'm still a klutz. Remember when I fell down the steps at the old frat house? Broke my arm?"

Bryce eyed him with suspicion. "As I recall, that was because you'd consumed about half the keg."

He grinned at Paige. "Beer was definitely not my problem today."

She fought a rising blush that would surely engulf her whole body if she let it.

Back to work. She had to get back to work. Shakily she stumbled over to start disrobing Hooligan and catch her breath.

"Glad you're here," Ben said to Bryce casually behind her.

How could he be so casual? Like nothing had happened? Like the world hadn't spun so fast she'd lost her head...

"I was wondering if you could spare Paige for a few hours tomorrow morning."

She peered around Hooligan's wide rump and glared hard at Ben. What was he doing?

He pretended not to notice.

Bryce frowned. "Why?"

"J's birthday's coming up and I have no idea what to get

her. She and Paige are about the same age. I was hoping she could help me find the perfect gift."

The man was such a liar! He knew exactly what Julia loved. Case in point, those amazing red boots he'd given her that very morning. "Actually," she spoke up, still hiding safely behind Hoolie, "I'm not much of a shopper."

The fabricated innocence rounding Ben's eyes mocked her. "J thinks the world of you. I was hoping you could help me pick something that'd remind her of our ride this morning. A keepsake, if you will." He turned back to Bryce. "Okay with you, boss?"

"Sure. Yeah." Bryce craned his neck and sought her out. "Everything'll be ready for the trip, right?"

"No." She smirked at Ben. "I still have a ton to do." *So there.* "I haven't even started packing." Which wasn't exactly true, but she was desperate.

Bryce waved her off. "Shooter can pack. He's gotta start pulling his weight around here, anyway. Wouldn't kill him to take on more responsibility."

"Awesome." With a victory grin directed at her, Ben clapped Bryce's back. "Thanks, man. You always come through for me."

"Yeah," she muttered as she bent back to Hooligan. "Thanks a lot." She rubbed her lips together, trying to rid them of the tingle that still lingered from Ben's warmth.

Oh god. She was in trouble. Kissing that man was like dipping a spoon into mocha almond fudge ice cream. One spoonful, you swear to yourself, that's all. But it's so delicious, so creamy, so fulfilling...

And before you know it, the whole carton is gone. That was Ben Noble. Mocha almond fudge. Sinfully delicious. And all wrong for her.

He was an indulgence she couldn't afford.

CHAPTER FOURTEEN

Ah, the beauty of family dinners.

Ben licked the back of his fork—finishing off the miraculous strawberry balsamic glaze Elsie had slathered on the almond-crusted rainbow trout that tasted as fresh as if someone had yanked it out of the mountain stream right outside. He pushed his plate away and leaned back in his chair, crossing his legs at the ankles. Might as well settle in. From the looks of Gracie's stern pout, he could be in for a long night.

Next to him, J prattled on and on about their horseback adventure, about the incredible mountains, about how much she loved Paige. The mention of her name alone made Gracie's lips pull so tight they looked like a rubber band about to snap. Their mother didn't look at Julia. Instead, she glared at him like he was about to ruin her life. Which only made his lips fumble back and forth between a smirk and a smile. *That's right, Mother. I live to embarrass you.* If she wasn't so damn uptight, it wouldn't be so easy.

Kev sat next to his mother, worry folded deep into his forehead. He nodded politely at Julia, but his eyes shifted like he had a thousand concerns scrolling through his mind.

"Paige was the best," Julia cooed. "I mean, you should've seen her horse. Sweetie Pie's so well trained. And Paige knew exactly how to do everything. It was so easy!"

He shot his sister a grateful look. He appreciated the effort, no matter how futile it was. Julia was always the hero, but talking up Paige wouldn't change Gracie's mind about her. There was no way in hell Gracie would back off. Not that it deterred him. No, sir. His mother's approval had never been all that important to him. Julia's? Yes. His father's? For sure. But something told him his father would've liked Paige. Ben Senior had quite the independent spirit himself, much to Gracie's disappointment. He could almost hear his father's approval. *She's a keeper, son. I've always appreciated a woman who doesn't fear your mother.* Because Paige didn't fear Gracie. That wasn't her hesitation about getting to know him. She simply didn't like his mother. And he didn't blame her at all.

"Did you help Paige get everything put away?" Julia glanced at him, her stare probing for more information.

"Yep. Sure did." His tone maintained an air of casualness, but his face must've colored because Gracie folded her arms across her chest.

"Benjamin, I thought we talked about this."

Julia wrinkled her nose. "Uh-oh," she muttered under her breath.

He clasped his hands on the table in his typical patient son stance. "About what, Mother?" he asked as innocently as a four-year-old.

"About you steering clear of this girl."

"Paige," he enunciated. "Her name is Paige." His eyes met hers. "And I never agreed to steer clear of her."

"I see." She sat straight, regal as always, but he'd learned to read the panic that rose in her eyes. "Well." She turned and gave Kev some silent command. "I didn't want to have to do this."

Kev handed her a manila folder and frowned apologetically at Ben.

"Wow. This is so CIA." J went to snatch the folder, but Gracie swiped it back. "A secret folder. I wonder what it could be." She smiled sweetly at their mother. "Is it your colonoscopy report? Do tell. Please. We can't wait to hear."

Ben sniffed out a laugh. If only. Something told him the contents of that folder had nothing to do with Gracie and everything to do with Paige.

His mother slid the folder across the table, mouth bent into that know-it-all look she'd worn during every single argument they'd had since he'd turned thirteen and decided he could think for himself.

He didn't pick it up. Didn't have to. "This is so typical. I find a girl I like and you find the nearest private detective."

Gracie nudged the folder closer to him. "She has a past, Benjamin. I knew it the moment I saw her. And I was right." Her palm slapped the folder. "She was arrested, for heaven's sake!"

Hmm. Paige had gotten herself arrested? Now that sounded interesting. He opened the folder and flipped through the papers, scanning the report. Arrested for underage drinking, disorderly conduct, disturbing the peace. "So what?" Who didn't have a misdemeanor or two in their past? He'd had plenty of them, but he'd been too smart to get caught.

"So you know what the media will do with this." She pointed a manicured nail in his direction. "It'll destroy you. Everything you've worked for. We can't afford another scandal right now."

"Scandal?" He laughed. He couldn't help it. "I'd hardly call drinking and making some noise a scandal." He tossed the papers onto the table, scattering them like the trash they were. "I couldn't care less if she was arrested."

"You want to win this election, you have to care," Kev shot back. "After what your last girlfriend did, your image is shit, Noble. There're hundreds of people working their asses off for you. It's time to start caring."

He blinked back at the man who rarely raised his voice, who only offered his opinion when he was asked. Is that what he really thought? That Ben would waste the opportunity he'd been given? That he was so spoiled he didn't realize the sacrifices everyone had made for him?

He cleared the anger out of his throat. "I know exactly how many people work for me. I know every volunteer's name. Hell, I know their families' names." He sucked in a breath. *Simmer down.* Before he made a scene. "Talking to a girl is not gonna kill this election for me. I've worked my ass off, too, Kev."

"I know. I know." His hands raised in surrender. "All I'm saying is now's not the right time. Give it a year. After you're elected, come back. Date her all you want. Hell, you can marry her, for all I care."

"Oh, dear Lord, Kevin," Gracie said through a gasp. "Let's not get ahead of ourselves."

"Awww! Yes! You have to marry Paige!" Julia hugged herself. "You two would make the perfect couple. And she'd be the best sister-in-law ever!"

Ben jerked his head and scanned the room. Last thing he needed was for someone to inform Paige they were getting married. Luckily, all of the waitstaff seemed to be hanging out in the kitchen.

"No one's getting married." He ignored J's pout. "And I couldn't give a shit what the public thinks about my love life. If people don't like me, they don't like me. I'm not gonna pretend to be someone I'm not. I like Paige. I don't know if it'll go anywhere, but—"

Across the room, the kitchen door slammed. Everyone's head turned. A panicked squeal erupted from Julia.

He jerked himself upright and peered over his shoulder. Paige was headed straight for their table.

Everyone got eerily quiet. Even Gracie seemed to dread the impending conversation.

"Shit." His hands fumbled to gather the papers, but she was too fast. Before he could hide anything, she stood at the head of their table, an overly polite look about her. "I'm glad I caught you all before you finished dinner." Her detached glare made the rounds before landing on the papers that dangled from his hand.

Those powerful hazel eyes narrowed. "What's that?"

"Nothing." He shoved it all back into the folder and closed it firmly. "It's nothing."

"Hi, Paige!" Julia waved. "Thanks again for that awesome ride this morning!"

It was a stellar effort, but Paige didn't seem to hear. Her mouth gaped, and those eyes fixed on the folder like she could see right through the cover, like she could see right through all of them.

"I don't believe this." She stalked over and ripped it out of his hand.

He fired a *happy-now?* glare at his mother while Paige flipped through the wonderful memory of her arrest. Gracie studied her nails and smoothed a cuticle like it was just another family dinner.

"If you'll excuse me." Kev pushed back his chair. "I need to use the restroom." He hightailed it out of there like he was being chased by a bull.

Damn it. Ben squeezed his eyes shut but when he opened them, Paige still stood there, eyes suspended in disbelief, cheeks growing harder by the second.

Finally she slammed the folder shut and waved it in his face. "You did a background check on me?"

"Actually, I did a background check," Gracie said coldly. "It seemed like the prudent thing to do. And I'm glad I did, by the way."

Silent breaths raised her shoulders, but Paige didn't look at his mother. She looked at him, her tanned skin donning the reddish hue of humiliation. He hated seeing her like that, hurt, embarrassed, but he stared back anyway.

"I came to tell you all that I e-mailed you a checklist for packing." A carefully controlled anger gave the words a brittle edge. "Don't. Forget. Anything."

"Why, that is so thoughtful." His mother batted her eyelashes. "We'll make sure we pack absolutely everything."

Ben swiped the sweat off his face. His mother sure knew how to lay it on thick.

"I can't tell you how much we're looking forward to the trip," she continued. "Thank you so much."

"No problem," Paige spat at him. "Enjoy the rest of your evening." With a flip of her long flowing hair, she spun and bolted for the door.

"Way to go, Mother." Julia whacked him. "What are you waiting for, Ben? Go after her!"

She was right. He had to go. Even if Paige looked at him like she wanted to castrate him...

"Come on!" J gave his chair a good shove and he scrambled to his feet, hoofed it out the French doors and onto the patio right as Paige's shadowy form disappeared around the corner.

"Wait!" He called and sprinted after her.

She didn't stop. Of course she didn't. This was Paige. She'd stomp all the way home, probably hoping he'd choke on her dust.

When he finally caught up to her under the dim light of a rod-iron lamp, he hooked her shoulder and turned her to face him.

Fury lit her eyes. He tried not to like it, but good god, her fire got him going. He tugged her closer, smelling honey and mint, the same scent he couldn't rid himself of after he'd kissed her...

She jerked away. "Don't touch me."

Right. No touching. Definitely no kissing. No matter how good she smelled. No matter how giving her lips had been earlier.

She posted a hand on her hip, a clear indication that her patience was waning faster than a crescent moon.

An explanation. He had to give her an explanation. But first... "I'm sorry about all that." Hopefully she could read the sincerity in his eyes. "My mother's crazy. She does stuff like this all the time."

"She humiliates people?" Her raised brows revealed that wasn't exactly a sales pitch for getting to know him better.

He almost took her hand. Almost. "You shouldn't be embarrassed. I could've been arrested for underage drinking more times than I can count."

Her shoulders let down and she dismissed his ignorance with a roll of her eyes. "I don't care that she found out I was arrested."

Wait. His head dipped to the side. She was so...bewildering. "Then why are you so upset?"

"That time in my life really sucked." She looked past him. "It wasn't long after my grandmother died. I was mad at the world."

He waited. He wanted to hear more. Everything. But she turned away. "Don't worry about it, Ben. Okay? She's looking out for you. I get it." Without a glance back, she started to walk away.

"Hold on." He lunged in front of her like some desperate chum. Man, she made him do crazy things. "Are we still on for tomorrow?"

"No," she sighed. "Don't make me go. Please. I hate shopping. And you obviously have no problem picking out gifts for your sister."

"Yeah...about that." He shot her a smile. "I have a confession to make."

There was that look again, the one that wavered between trusting him and walking away. Before she could make good on the silent threat, he continued. "I wasn't gonna take you shopping."

"Why am I not surprised?" She folded her arms, which only accentuated her amazing curves.

Eyes up, cowboy.

"So," she said all haughty and fired up again. "Where were you planning to take me?"

This oughta be fun. "Paragliding."

She laughed. "Paragliding. Seriously. You're crazy. You. Are. Crazy." Her arms flew up. "You can't just go paragliding. That requires a certification."

"I have it. Got certified here last summer."

She rolled her eyes. "Of course you did."

He tested out his footing by moving a step closer. "Come on, Paige. You like adventure."

"Yeah. Adventure with a safety plan."

"You're afraid," he taunted with a grin.

Her back went as straight as the lamppost next to them. "I'm not afraid."

"Then come paragliding with me," he challenged. "Tomorrow morning. You come with me, I won't bother you again. We'll go on the rafting trip, be all professional like you want. I won't ask you out anymore."

Now that seemed to get her attention. Her eyebrows perked up. "You promise?"

"Swear on my daddy's grave." He forced his eyes to stay in hers, even though they were tempted to drift down to the point of her V-neck shirt. Man, the woman knew how to wear a shirt.

"Fine. I'll go." She stabbed a pointer finger into his chest. "But only if you swear to stop making passes at me."

"I swear." Did it still count if his toes were crossed?

"And you've gotta stop looking at me like that, too."

"I have to look at you. And you can't blame me for liking what I see."

She shook her head and sighed like a diva, but a smile played with her lips. "Fine. I'll see you in the morning."

"See you then." He watched her walk away, admiring the tight curve her backside. With any luck, this shared experience would open her up.

It was a gamble, but then again, he'd never lost a bet.

CHAPTER FIFTEEN

She was going to hurl. Seriously. Everything that had gone down so easy last night—Elsie's oatmeal chocolate chip cookies, the chips and guacamole, and the margaritas she'd consumed for dinner (in that order)—might come back up all over Ben. It would serve him right.

Wrapping a weak arm around her stomach, Paige gave the man a sideways glance. He bent over the steering wheel, focused on navigating the Jeep along the rugged road that switchbacked up Aspen Mountain. Once they reached the top, they would run and jump off a cliff with a flimsy nylon parachute attached to their backs. And to think...he got his graduate education at Stanford University. She'd always thought smart people didn't do stupid things like jump off a cliff, but then again Ben didn't seem to hold up to any clichés. Cowboy, yes, but he was more refined than the typical ranch hand. Politician, sure. He could talk his way out of a paper bag, but he also had an underlying genuineness that most people didn't. Casanova, definitely. She had to remember that today. He was also an adrenaline junkie, apparently. But he wasn't antsy like most of those types she'd dated.

He was hard to peg, that was for sure. And she didn't like when she couldn't peg someone. So the prospect of jumping off a cliff was scary enough, but doing it attached to Benjamin Noble seemed to carry an exponential risk. Because she was a woman, after all, and he was warm and solid and he looked so good in those worn Carhartt work pants.

"You seem nervous." He peered over at her and she had half a mind to smash her hand in the side of his face and direct his gaze back to the road. Hello! Watch for rocks! The cliffs! Tree limbs!

"I'm not nervous at all." Terror earthquaked through her and cracked her voice.

He eyed her with suspicion. "You good with heights?"

"Sure." She was perfectly fine dangling a hundred feet above the ground off the side of a rock face, firmly secured in a harness and belay. Soaring thousands of feet above the ground, though...that wasn't heights. That was extreme madness. But it would be worth it, right? He'd leave her alone and she wouldn't have the distraction, the tension with his mother. She could do her job and prove to Bryce she was a professional in even the toughest situations.

"You're gonna love this, Paige."

"I love walking. Flying has never been on my list of fun experiences." Best for him not to get his hopes up.

"Oh, this isn't flying. It's more like floating." He rubbed at the stubble on his chin—the sexy few days of growth that had lightly scraped against her neck when he'd kissed her...

Goosebumps pricked at her arms, but she rubbed them away with her hands. Focus. She had to focus.

Ben's eyes turned upward toward the royal-blue sky. "It's

like you're weightless. Completely free. You won't believe how peaceful it is up there."

Huh. Not *it's a rush* but *it's peaceful*. Interesting philosophy about falling out of the sky. Her heart jackhammered until the pulse of it jarred her vision. She crossed her arms tighter and tried to wrangle it into a normal rhythm. "You know what I think is peaceful?" she asked, because she couldn't resist.

He raised his eyebrows in a silent question.

"Waterfalls. Wind whispering through the evergreens. Babbling brooks."

"Ha." He gunned the engine and they shot up a steep incline.

Paige gripped the *Oh shit* handle with a force from somewhere deep inside. She could've ripped that sucker right off the ceiling. "Seriously. Where did you learn how to drive?"

"On the ranch." He jerked the wheel this way and that, bouncing her head. "We didn't have roads. Not really, anyway."

Steadying a hand against the glass, she stared at her hiking boots. Much safer than staring out the windshield or at Ben's face, gorgeous face that it was. "Well, we do have roads. Can you slow it down? I'm sure you don't want to have to explain to the rental guys why there's vomit all over the dashboard."

"No worries. We're there." He gunned it up one last hill and hit the brakes.

She remained still, trying to regain her equilibrium, while he jumped out of the Jeep and unpacked a huge bundle of stuff from the back. She watched him lay out the gear, harnesses, ropes, helmets—because, great, if something goes wrong and you find yourself barreling out of control toward the earth at least you'll have head protection.

What the hell was she thinking?

"You okay?" Ben came back to the Jeep and unloaded another bundle—the parachute presumably—and rolled it out on the ground.

"Great." The words scraped her throat, which seemed to have swollen shut. She got out of the car and wandered to the mountain's edge. About two feet from her boots, the earth dropped off into a ravine that no one in their right mind would want to float over. It was rocky and steep, unforgiving even for a simple fall. She inched her toes to the edge and peered down. Whoa. The earth seemed to shift under her as the beginnings of a panic attack made her heart palpitate. *Breathe. Breathe.* She lifted her gaze. *Don't focus on the rocks. Focus on the beauty.*

Normally, she loved the view from up here. The town of Aspen looked like rows of dollhouses from so far up, a miniature city with a quaint mixture of brick buildings, manicured streets, and old Victorian homes nestled safely in the lushness of an emerald-green valley that rolled and stretched between granite-studded mountain peaks. She drew in another calming breath, closed her eyes, let the high-mountain breeze stabilize her inner chaos. The wilderness was where she always found her true self. It was vast and unforgiving but also serene and beautiful…

"You ready?"

Her eyes popped open. She spun. At some point Ben had crept up behind her, though she had no idea how long he'd been standing there.

"Sure." She stumbled to him, and oh-Mona-Lisa, she couldn't feel her legs. Energy buzzed through her and made everything shimmer like waves of heat rising from the ground. Or maybe from Ben. He stood with his back to the sun, a surreal glow hazing around him, solid build filling out the fleece pullover he wore, polarized Maverick sunglasses glinting, and that all-American smile flashing.

Yes, there was heat. It flowed to uncharted regions inside of her. Parts of her that had been locked up, blocked off, barricaded by constant disappointment.

Ben plunked a helmet on her head and strapped it under her chin. "In order for this to go well, you've got to trust me. Okay?"

"Sure," she muttered in a robotic tone. She forced her stiff arms to her sides because she was torn between shaking some sense into him and yanking him against her so she could feel his hard body once more before she plunged to her death. One last sensuous kiss before death… maybe more than a kiss? Maybe that was how she could distract him…

But before she could seduce him, he galloped away and put on his gear. "I'll be steering, braking, reading the wind currents. All you have to do is hold on."

"I'll try." It would be a lot easier if she could actually open her fists, but they seemed to be stuck.

"You'll also be harnessed to me, so there's nothing to worry about."

Nothing to worry about? Was the altitude getting to him? Not only did she have to worry about equipment malfunction, a rogue wind current, a freak bird accident, she'd also have to worry about him brushing against her ass. That would comprise her judgment, make her think things, maybe do things…

"Here. Let's get you into the harness." He knelt in front of her and held out the leg holes of the contraption. She stepped into them like a little kid. Then he got busy tightening the straps against her upper thighs. And, oh yes, his hands brushed against places they had no business touching.

"There we go." He slid his fingers in between the straps and her thighs and tugged gently, which was the most action she'd gotten in some time.

"Seems about right. How does it feel?"

How could she possibly answer that question? Everything in her traitorous lower hemisphere was clenched in anticipation. "Great," she squeaked.

He clipped something that looked like a small pad to the back of her harness. "You're gonna sit back into this little chair and relax."

She stretched her neck to look over her shoulder where his hands worked. There was definite touching. Quick electric pulses worked through her. Yeah, there would be no relaxing out there, not with him spooning her from behind.

"The conditions are perfect," he said. "Got the wind report on my phone. It's now or never."

Never. Please? Was that an option? She remained silent as he strapped himself into some crazy harness with too many ties and pulley things to count. Then he came up behind her, stood so close his breath warmed her neck, and strapped her to his chest and waist so that they were one entity, so she couldn't escape.

Ben reached down and clipped some carabiners into place, attaching them to the parachute that would carry them across the clear blue sky.

Her fists pulled tighter. She had no control, nothing to hold on to except for him. And maybe that was his plan all along. To take away everything else so it was only him and her.

"Ready?" The depth of his voice vibrated against her skin.

Her chest felt full and warm and she didn't know if it was because he was there, so close, or because they were about to step into oblivion.

When his arms encircled her, she couldn't help it; she leaned back into him, breath suspended, heart aching.

He leaned his chin on her shoulder, slipped off his glasses, and gazed into her eyes, steady and clear, like he saw everything. "What's wrong?"

"Nothing," she murmured.

His big, manly hands came to rest on her shoulders. "You're shaking."

"Rrrrrreally?" Her teeth chattered.

His arms slid around her, not to secure a clip this time, but to hold her. "I know this isn't easy. Letting go of control."

"What are you saying?" She tried to joke.

"Are you sure you want to do this?" His voice quieted into a somber challenge. "It's not too late to back out."

Yes it was. It was too late to go back. Ben was too good at prying her open, too good at probing those places no one else had ever bothered to touch. "We had a deal," she said, stronger than she felt. "If this'll really make you leave me alone, I'm in."

"Okay, then." He gave her that wicked hot grin. "When I say go, we're both gonna run straight for the side of the cliff."

"That's not crazy at all," she managed to wheeze between heart palpitations. Because they were really doing this. They were really running straight off the side of a cliff…

"Go!"

Ben's legs, his strength, pumped behind her, propelling them forward. She tried, she really tried, but her own feet stumbled and scraped the ground in a drunken jog. In her peripheral, she watched the chute mushroom over them. Then there was a serious drag, yanking back on her—on them. Ben's legs fought through it, but hers failed. The drag pulled harder, stronger, until the solid earth vanished and she dangled from Ben.

Her stomach lurched into her chest as they soared, wind whipping her ponytail, the chute dragging them higher, higher. The land beneath swirled into greens and browns and grays, then everything glowed blue and surreal, the white-hot sun above them, or maybe next to them...

Ben whooped, his forearms bulging as he pulled down on the handles gripped tightly in his capable hands.

A pain shot through Paige's chest and she realized she wasn't breathing. The air came out of her in a long groan. She sucked in new air as they lifted higher.

Ben leaned forward, his stubble scraping that tender place right beneath her ear. "What'd ya think? Pretty incredible, huh?"

"Incredible," she repeated in an aching whisper. And it was. Beautiful. More beautiful than anything she'd seen in her life. She was so small, a mere mark on the earth compared to the vastness, the wildness of what stretched out underneath her. It was a painting, a wash of colors and textures all flowing together in a divine harmony. She soared above it all, above every heartache, above every ugliness that confined her, that tried to define her. Oh, god, oh, god, oh god. Ben was right. She felt completely weightless. Free. "I love it." Her face turned to his. "I love it."

He laughed against her cheek. "Do I still have to leave you alone?"

"No," she whispered. Because up there, suspended above reality, Ben seemed possible. Anything seemed possible.

"Good," he murmured, then pressed his lips to her neck. "Because I don't know if I can."

That touch, the smoothness of his lips on her skin trembled all the way through her. She closed her eyes and waited but he didn't kiss her again. He'd gone back to his steering, his watching, his command over the skies. So she went back to making sense of everything below. There were the mansions on the east side of town, their pointed eaves poking through the canopy of trees. Then there was the river, small as a grayish blue ribbon, bending and meandering through the green valley. They were lower now, but it was still all so far away, so small and insignificant compared to the views that filled her eyes and made them burn with tears. Though the wind pressed against her and pinched her cheeks with life, Ben's chest against her back kept her warm. His sturdiness kept her grounded.

The white chute that plumed above them dipped and pulled in a gentle rhythm that could have lulled her to sleep. She closed her eyes. Peaceful. Yes. She understood. So much—

A jerk twisted her upper body. What the—

With a start she opened her eyes and looked back at Ben.

He yanked hard on the strap again and again, lips twisted with the effort.

Then a series of jolts made her heart race. Something was wrong. Oh, god. They were still so high. Five hundred feet?

"Paige?" Ben sounded like an impostor, his tone no longer deep and soothing, no longer in control. "Paige, hold on. Okay? Hold on."

"Wh...why?"

"The wind shifted. It's picked up. We've gotta land. Now."

"Now?" She looked down. *Oh, god.* Don't look down. Never look down. The ground came up at them so fast. So damn fast. Her eyes fixated on the valley floor, coming into focus with each passing second. Trees dotted the river. Rocks littered the meadows.

Above them, the chute flapped madly in the wind like a balloon losing air. It shook her hard. Or maybe she shook. Her hands were too sweaty to catch a grip of the bar in front of her.

They were gonna die. They were both gonna die. "Ben." Her stomach swelled and her mouth went dry. "Please. No." Exactly what she'd feared stared her in the face, ugly and consuming, looming in front of her. What about her family? Would they care? Would anyone care? Maybe Elsie. Probably Elsie. She took loss hard...

"We'll be okay," Ben shouted at her. "But brace yourself. It's gonna be rough."

Oh, god. Their momentum sped up. It felt like that time she'd flown to Costa Rica and the plane had gotten caught in massive turbulence. They were falling but somehow Ben was slowing the force of it.

Pressure built inside her head.

On the ground, she could make out the individual trees, cars. The homes didn't look small anymore. Nothing did.

"Brace yourself!" Ben yelled. "Tuck your head!"

But she couldn't move. She could only watch the ground zoom up, up, up. Raw fear squeezed her lungs and expelled all the air. What should her last thoughts be? Her last words? Nothing came. Nothing! Her brain filled with the clouds that were now so far above them.

"Ben," she whispered, gripping her hands over his forearms. "I'm so scared."

He didn't seem to hear. His arms jerked and pulled on the straps. Their momentum slowed.

Then there was a hard jolt and everything stopped.

CHAPTER SIXTEEN

Perfect. Landing. Son of a pistol—if that would've been a bull riding competition, he would've scored a ten. He'd be walkin' home with the damn trophy. Ben looked up at the lanky oak tree branch that had snagged their chute. Not ideal to be swinging a good thirty feet off the ground, but it sure beat the hell out of broken legs, so he'd take it.

"Hallelujah!" He swung his arms around Paige and pulled her close, the blitz of adrenaline still fresh in his blood. "That was somethin', huh?"

But Paige didn't seem to share his enthusiasm. Her body went stiff. "Get. Away. From. Me."

He laughed. "Sorry, sweetness. That's impossible right now." Besides, that's not what she'd said at three thousand feet. He seemed to recall that she'd leaned back into him, dropping her head to the side, and maybe even moaning when he'd kissed the sweet-tasting skin of her neck...

In fact he'd like to pick up right where they'd left off.

Could be difficult hanging from a tree, but not impossible. He leaned in to nuzzle her neck again.

"Stop it!" Her legs swung. "You almost killed me!"

The tree branch swayed with her frantic movements.

"Hey." He captured her in a bear hug from behind. "Settle down. You wanna fall?"

She went still again and peered down at the ground.

Yeah. He didn't think so. "We weren't gonna die, Paige. Didn't you hear me? I said, '*rough*. It's gonna get *rough*.' Not, 'brace yourself for death.'" He could've gotten them down on the ground. It would have been bumpy, but not catastrophic.

"You had no control up there!" He didn't have to look at her to know her jaw had clenched and made those hot, pouty lips pull tight.

"We could've been killed," she shrieked. "Something could've gone wrong. Something did go wrong. Now we're stuck in a tree!"

He cleared his throat to cover another laugh. "I could think of worse places to be stuck." He didn't mind it at all, no sir. Thanks to the seat harness, she was practically sitting in his lap. Now, if he could get her to face him, somehow...

"Hey." He brought his lips close to her cheek. Sure enough, a gasp escaped, a small sound torn between acceptance and frustration. Ha! She wanted him as badly as he wanted her.

"Oh no you don't." She flailed again. "You stay away from me!"

He backed off, eyed the branches above. Last thing they needed right now was a bad fall. "Easy, trigger. You're gonna break us loose. Then we'll be talkin' major injuries."

Her shoulders rose and fell against his chest in heated

breaths. "Don't tell me to take it easy." She jerked her head and glared. "And don't touch me. You said if I did this, you'd leave me alone."

"Oh, no, sweetheart. That deal's off."

"Excuse me?"

"You severed it midair. Remember?" He sure as hell did. He remembered the exact words. "I asked if I still had to leave you alone and you said, 'no.'" He moved in close to her neck again, let his breath flow out in a long sigh. "Then I kissed you."

She stared straight ahead and crossed her arms like she felt nothing, but her shallow, quick breaths betrayed her. "I changed my mind. You still have to leave me alone."

"Too late." That wouldn't be possible now. Not when he'd gotten a taste of her. Not when she'd let her guard down and he saw what really lived inside of her, fear, but also hope and a desire to let go. He could help her with that. They could help each other.

"How the hell are we supposed to get down from here?" Paige was still playing like he didn't affect her, as if she didn't want him the way he wanted her. But every time he brushed a touch against her skin, she trembled.

As much as he'd like to explore what that meant right here, right now, he couldn't seduce her up in a tree. So he slowly, carefully, dug out his phone from the zipper pouch attached to his coat. "I'll call Avery. She's probably close by. I asked her to pick us up."

"Avery?" Those tendons in Paige's neck pulled tight. "As in Bryce's wife?"

"She seemed like the best option, considerin' you didn't want Bryce to know."

Paige strained to look back at him and made a big show of rolling her eyes. "Like she's not gonna tell him."

"She won't. She's all about secret romances." He bounced his eyebrows for effect and waited for the fiery reaction in her eyes.

Sure enough, they flashed.

Man, that'd never get old. "I reckon it's more than likely he'll find out now. Everyone's gonna find out."

Her tanned face suddenly looked pale. "Whadda you mean?"

Didn't she know? Once this hit police scanners, they'd have no place to hide. Avoiding the answer he knew she wouldn't want to hear, he dialed Avery's number.

"Ben." Her tone didn't mess around. "Whadda you mean everyone's gonna find out?"

He held the phone up to his ear. "There's no way we're gettin' ourselves outta this tree. Avery'll have to call the fire department."

"No." Paige's head shook like they were watching a horror movie and the serial killer was about to murder his last victim. "No. Please. No."

"It'll be fine." Definitely not the ideal situation, especially considering Gracie would find out, too, but there was nothing they could do about it, now. He'd explain it all to Bryce. After Gracie's heart attack, she'd get over it.

The phone rang into his ear. Finally Avery picked up. "Hey, Ben! Where are you?"

"Well…" He gazed at their surroundings. "You see that big grove of oaks by the river?"

Movement scratched across the line. "Oh. Yeah. I see it."

"We're about thirty feet up in the tallest tree."

"Oh no!" she gasped. "Are you kidding? Are you okay?"

"We're great," he said, aiming a smile at Paige. She deflected it with her signature, I'm-going-to-kill-you-in-the-most-painful-manner-possible glare. Which he saw right through, by the way. She wouldn't get so fired up if she felt nothing, now, would she?

"Drive on over," he said to Avery. "I'm thinkin' we'll need to call in the big guns to get us out of here."

"I'm on my way!" she yelled, then the line went dead.

"See?" He clicked off the phone and stuffed it back into the pouch. "Nothin' to worry about. She'll be right over."

"Nothing to worry about? I can't believe this," Paige growled. "I can't believe you did this to me. I could lose my job, Ben. Don't you get that?"

"You're not gonna lose your job. Bryce'll know this was all my idea. Trust me. He's known me long enough." He'd pulled enough stunts like this in college. Bryce wouldn't be surprised that he'd convinced Paige to jump off a cliff with him. Just another ordinary day in Benville. Unfortunately, at the moment Paige didn't seem exactly thrilled to be visiting his world, but he could change that.

Gliding his hands up her back, he kneaded her muscles in a gentle massage.

Her shoulders let down in a sigh. "Ben..."

He ignored the warning in her tone and kept going, working his hands in circular movements between her shoulder blades. Her head bent forward, giving him access to her neck.

His fingers grazed the skin at the base of her neck.

He heard her breath catch in her throat...

Below them, Bryce and Avery's black F-450 barreled toward the tree at about a hundred miles per hour. Right before a head-on collision with the tree trunk, it screeched to a stop and kicked up a cloud of dust.

Damn. He hated to take his hands off of her.

Avery leapt out of the truck and stared up them. "Oh my god! Paige! Are you okay?"

"We're great!" Ben yelled and waved cheerfully.

"No we're not!" Paige snapped.

"Don't worry!" Avery waved her cell above her head. "I'm calling nine-one-one right now. We'll get you help!"

"Great," Paige spat at him. "We'll probably be front page news tomorrow morning."

Yeah. No way to avoid the media on this one. Kev would probably have a coronary. But there was no such thing as bad publicity, right? Besides, voters always loved a romantic story. What could be more romantic than this? At the moment, there was no one he'd rather be stuck in a tree with, and he planned to make the most of it. He eased his hands onto her shoulders again, inching his fingers over the tops of them, as low down her front as he dared without getting slapped. "It's not so bad. Think about all this extra time we'll have to get to know each other."

She didn't answer. If fact, she seemed hell-bent on staring straight ahead so she didn't have to look at him.

"Don't worry guys," Avery called up. "They're on their way. Ten minutes, tops."

"See there?" Hands still on Paige's shoulder, he leaned in close, so his lips were against her cheek. "Help is on the way."

"Great," she muttered, but she did glance back at him. Their eyes met and the force of it was like a punch to the gut.

Wind rustled the leaves around them and spread her hair across her face. Sunlight beamed in through the shadows and lit the hazel depths of her eyes. Good god, she was gorgeous.

Before he could tell her so, she cleared her throat and looked away.

He relaxed against the harness. Patience. Timing was everything. He gazed up at the infinite blue of the sky, thought about how her breath had caught when they took off into the wind, about how she'd gasped and whispered. He gathered her hair in his hand and smoothed it down. "You didn't like it up there?" he asked, teasing her, because he already knew the answer. "Not at all?"

Under the influence of his touch, Paige seemed to have relaxed, too. Well...at least her shoulders weren't cranked so tight.

She lifted one shoulder in a small shrug. "It was... different."

"Good different, right?" he prompted.

She peered back at him again. "You're impossible."

That was an improvement. At least she wasn't flailing to get away from him anymore. "I like to think of myself as an optimist. Someone who doesn't give up easily."

"That's putting it mildly," she said with a hint of a smile.

"Hey, guys!" Avery interrupted. "Do you want me to call Bryce?"

"Yes!" he yelled at the same time Paige shouted, "No!" She looked back at him, her face tight with exasperation.

"Might be better for him to hear it from Avery," he offered. "Rather than find out later."

Her eyes closed. "Yeah. I know."

"I'll take care of it. Don't worry. You won't lose your job." He and Bryce had covered for each other for years. He'd understand. He might not love it, but he'd understand.

She opened her eyes, her gaze drifting away from his into an almost a shy retreat. Silence ticked away, but he didn't mind it. Finally she darted a glance at him. "It was amazing up there. I've never experienced anything like that."

He grinned. He knew she'd feel that way, once the initial shock wore off. That's what he'd been hoping for, anyway. Paragliding was a lot like sex. The rush of it, the thrill of it, the danger of it, tended to bond two people together in a shared intimate experience that could either end in a perfect connection or a catastrophic fall. They'd had that connection. He'd felt it. And then he'd gone and ruined it with a stupid stunt like landing them in a tree.

He slid his hands back over her shoulders. "Sorry I scared you. I should've warned you about the landing." That was always the hardest part, rough and unpredictable. But worth it, anyway, to feel that free. As scared as she'd been at the top, she probably wouldn't have gone with him if he'd told her how hard it was coming back to earth.

"It's okay," she whispered, and for once, the woman didn't look away. She looked right at him, into him, brave and sure. Terrified but strong. Her lips parted and he heard a labored swallow. "Ben...this is such a bad idea."

He pulled her closer, threading his arms around her. He couldn't help himself. "I know." But he pressed his lips against hers, anyway, and when her perfect chest expanded with a gaping breath he pressed in harder, tasting the sheer extravagance of her lips, her mouth, her tongue...

Then he kissed her again, with all the reverence she deserved, until the sound of sirens serenaded them.

CHAPTER SEVENTEEN

"S top," Paige whispered, her lungs bulging with empty gasps. "Stop, Ben. Please." Because she couldn't. She couldn't pull away from the tender warmth of his mouth, the draw of his capable hands. With every touch, she lost more of herself, lost that stinging awareness that this could not happen. Every hypersensitive nerve in her body submitted to his touch, until she felt completely powerless.

Below them, chaos erupted, engines and slams and shouts and the distinct scent of a diesel truck. Sure enough, the fire department's tower truck grumbled to a stop right below the tree. Four of Aspen's finest hopped out, and damned if Luke Simms wasn't one of them. Of course he'd be on duty today. Of course.

"It'll take them a while to get up here." Ben went to kiss her again, but she held him off. Half the town was down there beneath them, scurrying around, shouting, pointing. She'd already spotted Bryce's 4Runner, Elsie's robin's-egg blue convertible, and Sawyer's police cruiser drive in. How could he even think of kissing her at a time like this?

He peered over her shoulder at her face, a slight pout on his lips, and even though she tried to fight the smile, it rose anyway. One look at his gorgeous, comedic face was all it took to distract her from the shit storm that waited below. Bryce had asked one thing of her. Make sure everything goes smoothly. Make sure you don't mess this up. Ben was in Aspen for publicity, and she was pretty sure this was not the kind of publicity he needed.

Leaning forward, she peered down past her toes.

Luke held up the megaphone. Static crackled. "Everyone okay?"

"We're perfect!" Ben shouted down.

Why'd he have to be so cheerful all the time? Like this was simply another adventure to record in his log. If she didn't know better, she'd have thought he landed them in a tree on purpose.

"We're sending up the bucket," Luke called.

That finally made Ben pull back, but his large hands still rested on her shoulders. She braced herself. If he started caressing her again, she'd be in big trouble.

"Promise we can pick this up later?" he asked, his voice tingling down her neck.

Promise. She couldn't promise him anything. Just like he couldn't promise her anything. They didn't know each other, not really. And if her previous relationships were any indication, he'd find something about her not to like. Case in point, Luke Simms, who was currently being raised toward them in the tower truck's bucket, their knight in shining fire gear.

"Paige?" Ben drew out her name into a question. One she couldn't answer. There were too many things in the way— her scarred heart, her job, Grace Hunter Noble, the fact that

Ben was running for senator. None of that seemed to matter when he his hands were on her, when his lips commanded hers, but now each of those things glared at her, hands on their hips, shaking their heads. No. No, no, no. Don't you dare go there. "You told me you'd leave me alone. I jumped. Now you have to keep your word." She turned her back on his lengthy sigh.

The bucket inched closer and closer, propelled by the soft hum of a motor. Finally Luke came into view.

His lips quirked. "Well, well, well. Who do we have here?" He jammed his finger into a button and the bucket stopped. "Paige Harper. Stuck and needing my help."

He'd always known exactly what to say to light her inner fire. "Shut up, Luke." It was common knowledge that she hated needing anything from anyone. Especially help. People who knew her well made jokes about it at the hole-in-the-wall bar she used to frequent. *Paige would cut off her own arm before she used the cell phone in her back pocket to call for help.*

Which is why Luke seemed to find her predicament so hilarious.

"Aw, Paige. Come on. I've missed you. Been meaning to call you."

Behind her, branches rustled. Ben's movements jerked her upper body. *Yeah.* Like he could defend her honor up here. In a tree. She had this overwhelming urge to unshackle herself from him, if only to make a point. She didn't need him to get all offended for her. She could handle Luke.

"What's the matter? You in between hookers right now?" she asked as innocent as Laura Ingalls Wilder.

Luke busted out a laugh. "Damn, Paige. We were good together." He looked past her and nodded at Ben. "But I see you've moved on. Name's Luke Simms. And you are...?"

"Ben." It was quick and sharp, obviously meant to sever any further discussion.

"Nice to meet you, Ben. Gotta say, I'm impressed. Aren't many guys out there who could sweep Paige off her feet like this." He clamped his huge hand onto her shoulder.

"How about you do your job and get us down?" Ben growled. "Taxpayer money and all that. Save the commentary for another time?"

"Happy to." He smiled and cranked open a small door. "Go ahead and scoot forward 'til you can climb in. Then we'll unclip the chute and you'll be home free."

Paige eased forward, feeling Ben right at her back. The tree shook. Leaves fluttered down around them.

"Easy." Ben's arms encircled her, guided her slowly onto the bucket floor. Then he went to work unclipping all the strappy things like he didn't want to give Luke the opportunity to touch her.

When they were all set, Luke pulled a small lever. The bucket lifted. "We've gotta get up there and untangle the chute." He shot Ben a mocking glance. "Nice landing, man. Takes real talent to find the one grove of trees in the entire meadow."

Ben's face turned the shade of the fire truck beneath them.

Great. Just what she needed. A macho showdown thirty feet above the ground. She shifted her weight and blocked Ben and Luke's view of each other, then chatted with Luke as he moved the bucket up, cut a couple of branches, and tugged the chute loose from the tree.

Ben balled it up, his hands working like he was furious. But at least it kept him busy. There was barely enough room in the bucket for the three of them to stand. Definitely not enough room for a brawl.

The tower motor pulled them lower. Luke helped her climb down the steps to the ground.

"Thanks," she muttered. "Appreciate the rescue."

"Anytime. Seriously, Paige." He eyed Ben. "I meant what I said. We had fun together, right? Can I call you sometime?"

She was pretty sure that last question was only for Ben's benefit. She shook her head. Men. What was it with the macho-caveman-this-woman-belongs-to-me-thing? She and Luke might have had some fun, but it was nothing worth repeating and he knew it. "Probably shouldn't call me," she said as sweetly as possible. Because she hadn't changed her mind about putting out.

"Okay then," he said with a teasing smile. "You know where to find me if you change your mind." Luke walked back to the truck.

Ben glared at her. She glared back.

"Mr. Noble?" Fire Chief McCormick interrupted their stare down. "I'll need your help with the incident report."

Ben's face colored again. "Of course," he said briskly, then followed the chief toward the truck.

"Paige!" Avery ran over and smashed her into a hug. "Oh, I'm so glad you're okay." She pulled back and looked her over. "You are, right? Nothing hurts?"

"I'm fine," she assured her, which was mostly true. Her legs had even stopped shaking. But then she looked past Avery and saw Bryce standing a few feet away, arms crossed, dark expression, talking to one of the firemen.

Avery glanced over her shoulder, then leaned close. "He's ready to kill Ben," she whispered.

"Well it wasn't *all* his fault," she admitted. She never should've agreed to go with him anyway. It was dangerous in more ways than one. "I only hope this won't mess things up with the trip." Not now. Not when she was trying to prove herself.

"I'm sure it'll be fine," Avery said with a reassuring smile. "I'll go talk to him."

As soon as she walked away, Ben sauntered over. "Have you dated all the firemen or just that guy?"

Paige eyed him. "You sound jealous."

"Maybe because you seem happy to go out with an ass like him and you won't even give me a chance."

How could she explain it to him? She'd dated Luke because she knew nothing would ever come of it. She'd never fall for someone like Luke. It was easy. Fun. Then when they parted ways, there were no hard feelings. Her heart didn't hurt.

Ben's touch carried more weight. It had more depth. With Ben, there'd be expectations. It wouldn't be enough for him to know Paige the cool guide who joked around like one of the guys. He'd want to know all of her, even those parts of her she hardly knew herself.

"Benjamin!"

The sound of his mother's shrill voice tensed her body.

Gracie Hunter Noble sprinted past her, her pricey designer coat flapping in the breeze, and threw herself at her son like he'd returned from the horrors of war. "Good heavens! You can't do this to me, Benjamin! You know my heart can't take it!" His mother pulled back and inspected him. "Why, you could've been killed! How many times do I have to tell you—" She looked up. Her eyes met Paige's.

Well damn it all, the woman hadn't even noticed her. She should've made a break for it while she could've.

"You." She pointed one of those red shellacked nails in her direction, then turned back to Ben. "You agreed you wouldn't get involved with her."

Ben shook his head, but before he could say anything, Paige marched up to Gracie. *Thank you for making this so easy.* "You have nothing to worry about, Mrs. Noble. We are definitely not involved." She refused to let herself wither under the power of that woman's gaze. "In fact, I was just telling Ben that I'm seeing someone." She gestured over to the cluster of firemen, and, yes, it was a desperate move, but he hadn't exactly given her a choice now, had he? "Luke Simms. He's right over there in the uniform," she gushed. "So you obviously have nothing to worry about. Ben knows I'm not available."

"Oh." Gracie gazed over at Luke. "Well. How wonderful. He looks like a nice boy," she said, no longer glaring.

Ben didn't seem to think the news was wonderful. He came at her. "Paige—"

"Luke!" she yelled to cut him off. Because she didn't need Gracie Hunter Noble breathing down her neck. And she sure as hell didn't need Ben.

Luke trotted over to their awkward circle. "Yeah?"

"You busy tonight?"

A slow smile spread across his face. "Nope."

"How about dinner?"

"You got it," he said, looking her up and down. "I'll pick you up at eight. Take you someplace nice. Elevation 8,000?"

"Sounds perfect." She tried to gaze at him like a woman in love. "See you then."

"Yep. See ya then." Luke sauntered back to his truck.

Ben stepped up to her. "This is shit."

She looked past him. "I really should get back to the lodge." With a fake smile at Gracie, she wiggled her fingers in the kind of wave the woman would appreciate. "I'm looking forward to our trip. Bye now."

Before Ben could stop her, she stomped over to the tree

where Bryce stood. From the dark look on his face, he'd witnessed the whole scene.

"I need a ride home," she said, fashioning her eyes into a repentant plea.

He simply straightened, rested a hand on her shoulder, and guided her to his 4Runner. She climbed in and slammed the door, keeping up the facade until Ben had walked away. Releasing a long breath, she clicked in her seat belt and hid her face in her hands.

The engine started.

She dropped her hands to her lap and looked over at Bryce. His gaze bounced between her and the road.

"What?" she finally demanded.

"I'm only gonna say this once," he said, shifting gears before he punched the gas. "I'm not your big brother. I'm not your parent. But I know Ben." He slowed the car and looked at her carefully. "I've seen it enough. Some woman screwed him over and now he's on the rebound."

"I know that." She waved him away like the whole thing didn't get to her. Like her heart didn't pound when she was around Ben. "You heard what I told his mother."

"I also know you're not dating Luke. And I see the way you look at Ben." He stopped the car and draped his arms over the wheel, stared out the windshield. "Worse, I see the way he looks at you." He frowned in that stoic, don't-want-to-say-it-but-have-to way. "Last thing I want is for you to get hurt. This isn't the first stupid stunt he's pulled. He's reckless. Half the time he doesn't think."

"Are you sure?" Because that didn't seem right. The Ben she'd seen was deliberate. Smart. Funny. And yes, so damn hot. He had a lot going for him...

"I lived with him for three years in college," Bryce reminded her. He slipped the Jeep back into gear and headed for the road. "Look. If you want to have some fling with him, it's none of my business. But at least wait until this trip is over. I can't afford to have Gracie come after me right now."

"Relax." She'd taken care of it. Ben had looked like he was about to explode when she said she was seeing Luke. "Anyway, the only reason I went with him today was because he promised he'd leave me alone. One paragliding trip and he'd quit asking me out. That was the deal." Though she had a feeling the whole thing was a setup. He knew what that free fall would do to her. He knew she'd let down her guard.

Bryce still didn't look convinced. He had that worried furrow he got whenever something didn't seem right. She'd seen it so many times. He didn't say much, but she could tell when he was worried about something. "Remember, Paige. He's gone after this. Back to Texas, then headed for DC, most likely."

Reason five hundred and seventy-eight why they didn't belong together. "I know he's leaving. And I'm starting the therapy program like we've been talking about." She wasn't about to let him forget that. "This is too important to me, Bryce. I won't do anything to mess this up, to threaten the ranch."

Not even Benjamin Hunter Noble was worth that.

CHAPTER EIGHTEEN

He should know better. Give Gracie Hunter Noble one stinkin' centimeter and she'd take fifty damn miles. Just like she'd done when she took over the high school prom his senior year, just like she'd done in his campaign, and just like she'd done now in this whole thing with Paige. He never should've let her believe she actually had any say in his love life, never should've made that deal with her.

Well, no more deals. Mother or not, it was high time he put Gracie in her place.

Ben threw her rented Escalade into gear and gunned the engine.

"Good gracious, Benjamin!" Gracie braced both hands against the dash. "Will you slow down? I never should've let you drive! You're fixin' to kill me!"

"If I wanted to kill you, I would've done it a long time ago. Trust me." He jerked the wheel and they left the chaotic scene in the meadow behind, firemen still milling around, probably tweeting about what a dumb-ass he was. He turned onto the dirt road that led back up Aspen Mountain.

"What are you doing?" Gracie looked over her shoulder. "The highway is back there."

"We're not taking the highway. I have to pick up the Jeep." Which still sat at about ten thousand feet on the mountainside. The half-hour drive would give them plenty of time to talk.

Steering over the rugged terrain with a not-so-careful hand, he buzzed down the window. The air was still cool, even though the sun blazed its high-altitude warmth. Man, he could get used to that mountain smell—crisp and fresh, a tinge of evergreen.

"Really, son. Must we have all the wind?" Gracie grimaced and smoothed her white hair. "I have a luncheon and I'd rather not look windblown."

"I'm hot." Mostly from the way Paige had set his blood to a boil when she'd asked out that loser right in front of him. So she refused to give him a chance, but was obviously willing to hang out with some man who had clearly blown his chance with her a long time ago.

Not that he blamed Paige. It was Gracie's fault, with all of her old-biddy comments and glares. When it came to Paige, she'd been as cold as a mortician's mistress, and he intended to put a stop to it.

"Better hold on." He swung the wheel and sped up the first switchback.

"This doesn't look very safe." His mother ducked her head and looked upward at the cliffs towering above them. "I'm not sure I'll be able to drive back down."

"You'll be fine." It would be something to watch, that was for sure, seeing as how she usually had a driver cart her around like a queen. Back in the day, before she'd risen to near-dignitary status, she'd grown up on a ranch. He knew for a fact she'd been driving on the Texas back roads since she was twelve. He'd seen pictures of her, barefoot and clad in overalls, a handkerchief tied over her head, capricious grin on her freckled face. What happened to that girl? There was a time Gracie hadn't cared about whose last name was what or how much someone had stockpiled in their bank account. He had to wonder if that girl still lived inside of his mother somewhere.

Keeping an eye on the ruts in the road, he turned down the twangy country music she loved. "Why'd you marry Dad?"

Pain gripped her features like it always did when anyone mentioned his father, but she covered it up with a scowl. It'd start with a sad twinge of her mouth, but she'd steel it so fast you'd miss it if you didn't know what to look for.

"That's a silly question." A wave of her hand dismissed him. Her eyes focused hard on the windshield, like she was reading a script for her next lines instead of gazing at the scenery.

He wasn't about to let her off that easy. "Was it because he had money? Because his daddy was a senator?" He already knew the answers to those questions, but he wanted her to remember. He wanted to hear her say it.

"Of course not." A tremor ran through her voice before it thickened with anger. "Don't be ridiculous, Benjamin. I loved your father. I loved him very much."

Another turn faced them east, where the midmorning sun still sat low. He pulled down the sunshade to save his eyes. "Why?"

"What on earth do you mean, 'why'?" Her posture changed, shoulders stiff and straight, chin tipped too high. It spoke for her. *Please stop. I don't want to talk about him.* Because it was too painful. She'd told Ben once, after the funeral when she'd drunk herself honest, that she never should've let herself love someone so much because it hurt too bad. She'd lost part of herself and she was afraid she'd never find it again.

In his book, that was the only kind of love worth having. If it didn't change you, what the hell was the point?

He slowed the SUV, navigated a rocky section of the road slowly. Wouldn't do to nick the oil pan and distract her with a breakdown. "I want to know. Why'd you love him? Why'd you stay with him for so long?"

"I...it was because..." Chin still jutted, she shook her head. "Why are you asking me this?" An accusation hid in the words. Like he was being cruel. Nothing spawned guilt trips like fear, and Gracie was more skilled at guilt trips than a Catholic headmistress. A long time ago, it had worked on him, but it didn't get to him so much anymore.

"You must have loved something about him. Or maybe it was the money. The fame."

"He made me feel free," she said, her regal, soothing tone almost desperate. "It had nothing to do with money, Benjamin. Your father..." She bit her lip and exhaled through her nose. "...he wanted me. The way I was. Even as a silly eighteen-year-old girl."

That was putting it lightly. Even he could tell from the pictures of their early days together that his father was smitten. He'd had it bad. He remembered one image clearly. His mother sitting on a horse. She wore a long, flowing skirt and her hair was parted into loose braids that fell down around her shoulders. She was laughing. And Dad...he was staring up at her with a look of awe, like he couldn't believe what he saw. Ben had come across the picture when he was about eight. It'd been tucked into a box with everything else that existed pre-fame. Like Gracie wanted it all to be forgotten. To his young eyes, his parents looked like movie stars from those old Westerns Granddad sometimes watched. Sometimes, when Gracie was gone on her long trips to Paris and Rome and the South of France, he'd dig out that picture and wish that was still his mom. She looked happy. Gracie the Senator's Wife smiled all the time, but it never changed her eyes, never made them sparkle the way they did in that picture.

"We were so young," she murmured. "Hadn't the faintest idea what we were getting ourselves into. But I never got over it. How he chose me."

Ben glanced at her. Tears glowed in her eyes, but in true Gracie form, she blinked hard. "He chose me every day for all those years. Even the day he died. He chose me."

Ben let silence settle between them. Listened to the gravel and stones ping the undercarriage, let the breeze erase the anger. Dad might've chosen her every day, but she didn't choose him. She was cold. Controlling. No wonder she didn't want to talk about him. She knew she didn't deserve him.

It took a while, but the irritated curl of his fingers subsided. His words would still cut her, but he couldn't let them go. "He chose you even though you didn't come from money. Even though your daddy was a drunk."

"How could you—?"

"I'm gonna pursue Paige." That's what this was about. Much as Gracie hated to acknowledge it, everything didn't revolve around her. "And you can't do a damn thing about it. So I'd like you to stop tryin'."

She twisted to face him, her eyes widened into a warning. "You can't pursue her. She's seeing someone else."

"She said that to get you off her back. You've been awful to her and I won't have it. Not anymore."

"I don't know what you're talking about."

He glared at her. "Innocence is one thing you can never claim." He turned the car up another switchback and caught a view of Aspen, growing smaller and more distant the higher they climbed.

"Benjamin, please—"

"I see something in her," he interrupted. "Something worthy of choosing."

"But your campaign..."

"I'll still run my campaign. I'll still win that Senate seat. And I'll do it on my terms. Dating who I want to date. Living the life I want to live."

Her cheeks tightened into that stubborn old mare look. "It will never work out. Not with her."

"What makes you so sure?"

"A girl like that doesn't commit, Benjamin. She's too free-spirited, too naïve."

He hit the brakes so hard, Gracie jolted forward. He waited until she looked at him, then pointed straight at her, in case she really didn't see the irony. "You were that girl."

"Exactly," she snipped. "So I know what I'm talking about. Trust me. Please. She's not right for you."

He eased a foot back onto the gas because this was pointless. If they didn't get to the top soon, one of them won't survive the trip. "I don't understand. You stayed with Dad for almost forty years. You were free-spirited, too. Once."

She folded her arms. "I did things I'm not proud of."

Heat flared in his gut and spread through him. "What things? What the hell are you talking about?"

"We had a hard time in the beginning," she said to her hands. "His schooling, all his political aspirations. I felt neglected."

Something in her tone—regret?—crushed the air from his lungs. Good god. "You cheated on him." He wanted to gag on the words, they made him so sick. She made him sick. "When? With who? Did he know?"

"He knew." She blinked like she saw nothing in front of her. Like all she could see was a disgusting truth she'd swept under the rug for years.

It was nauseating. Here she pretended to be this prim and proper moral goddess and the whole time she's no better than the rest of them. He blasted the outside air to cool down before he completely lost it.

"It was a mistake," she said firmly. "A horrible, horrible mistake. We had a long road after that. I'm trying to save you from all that pain." Her hand curled around his wrist. "Paige doesn't want the life you want. It took years for me to adjust."

He ripped away from her slimy touch. "Don't do that. Don't you compare yourself to her." Paige was nothing like Gracie. She said whatever the hell she wanted, but at least she was honest.

"We have to protect your father's legacy, Benjamin," Gracie said quietly. "Everyone loved your father. He was a good man."

"His legacy has nothing to do with me." And neither did her secrets. All those secrets did was confirm that fact that he needed space from her, from the family. He had to become his own person. Do things his way.

"How can you say that? If you go into politics, no one will remember what he did. They'll be watching you. And I won't let you tarnish his reputation with another scandal."

"Paige is not you," he ground out, jaw locked with disgust. And thank god for that.

"No. She's not." The words were patronizingly soft. "But is that really what you want for her? To never feel like she fits in, like she will never measure up to everyone's expectations?"

Despite the shock of it all, he almost smiled. Something told him Paige couldn't give a shit about everyone else's expectations.

"You lived that life, too. You know what that world is like. Do you really believe it's right for her?"

He hit the brakes again so he could face her, so he could look in her eyes and let her see the truth. "I don't know. I don't have to know right now." For the time being, he had all the information he needed. Paige was different, real and unafraid and tough as nails but fragile, too. He leaned closer to Gracie, so her eyes couldn't escape his. "But I'm gonna find out. I'm gonna spend time with her. Don't stand in my way. Don't do anything that you'll regret later."

Because if she tried to get between them, he'd sure as hell make sure she regretted it.

* * *

Good god, what had she done?

Tricking Luke into asking her out seemed like a good idea at the time, and she was definitely in a pinch, but something about the way Avery gaped at her made her stomach hurt.

"Are you crazy?" Avery paced across the kitchen with her hands resting on her pregnant belly. "I mean...Luke? Really? Luke Simms? You want to go *there* again?"

"Luke *is* pretty hot." Ruby fished a gallon of fudge gelato out of the deep freeze and set it on the island between her and Paige. She pulled out three spoons. "Something about a fireman. Especially in uniform." With wide, devious eyes, she cranked off the lid and dipped in her spoon.

"This from the one who's sworn off men for some mysterious reason." Never one to resist a good temptation, Paige picked up her spoon, too. Ruby insisted she didn't need a man to be happy. She steered clear when anyone tried to flirt with her at the lodge. And yet she was one of those gorgeous, voluptuous women who made men forget their own names. "Maybe we should discuss your love life instead of mine." Maybe she should try to bring up Sawyer again...

Ruby's radiant eyes darkened. "No thank you. Nothing to discuss. Yours is way more interesting." She shoveled in a huge bite of gelato.

If it was anyone else, Paige would push more, but there was something too delicate about Ruby. Anytime they asked her questions about her past, this horrible look took over that pretty face, a look that blended pain and fear, and Paige almost didn't want to know what had happened to her. Whatever it was, it left a serious mark.

Avery paused at the edge of the island and snatched the third spoon. "Really, Paige. Forget Luke. I think you should give Ben a chance."

"That's not what your husband thinks," she reminded her. "Or Ben's mother." Or her, for that matter. "It's not practical, you know."

"Love shouldn't be practical!" Avery's arm waved and the blob of gelato shot across the room, splatted against the refrigerator door. "Oops." She licked the spoon.

Smiling, Paige hopped off her stool and tore off a paper towel. Elsie kept her kitchen spotless. She'd die if she found a splotch of gelato.

"I'm with Ruby," she said as she wiped it up. "I don't

need a man to complicate my life right now." She had things to do. Big things, if she could make this trip a success for Bryce.

Avery scooped out another spoonful of gelato. "You only date men who have no potential," she accused, shoving the whole thing in her mouth.

"Excuse me?"

"That's what Bryce said. He said ever since you dated that one prick, you haven't gone out with anyone who had potential for a serious relationship."

"Like Bryce knows anything about relationships."

"Is that why you won't go out with Ben?" Avery demanded.

Her face flamed. "Of course not."

Avery leaned into the counter, watching her carefully. "So you're not attracted to him?" she asked, skepticism etched into her smirk.

Her stomach pulled into a tight knot and threatened to implode. "Of course I'm attracted to him." She was a woman, after all.

Avery smiled victoriously. "Then what's the problem?"

She shook her head and made disgruntled face. "You're as bad as Ben." Except he wasn't bad. He was good. So good. God, the way he'd kissed her...lips so firm and generous. The memory sent her stomach rolling.

Ruby whapped her shoulder. "Wow, girl. You've got it bad. You can't even say his name without blushing."

"I knew it!" Avery pumped a fist in the air. "You so want him. As bad as he wants you."

Paige focused on the gelato so she didn't have to look at them. Wanting him didn't mean she should have him. She smirked. "I want Gerard Butler, too. Preferably in a Scottish kilt, but that doesn't mean I'm gonna get him."

Avery rolled her eyes. "Ben is so much sexier than Gerard."

Her jaw dropped. So did Ruby's.

"What?" Avery demanded. "Believe it or not, a happily married woman can still recognize sexy." She waved a finger in Paige's face. "And believe me. Ben is sexy."

She didn't have to tell her. She'd been trying to ignore that fact since she'd met him.

"Seriously." Avery leaned into the counter and propped her chin on her fist. "Look at Bryce and me. That wasn't exactly practical, now was it? And look how happy we are."

She laughed. "You should've heard his pep talk on the drive back. He all but forbade me to date Ben."

"Bryce will come around." She licked her spoon suggestively. "I do have influence in that area, you know."

Paige made a face. "Gross. He's like my brother. I'd rather not hear about how you influence him."

Ruby laughed. "I love working here. You're so lucky to have each other." Her eyes looked sad again, but they were determined, too.

"We're glad you're here, too." Paige squeezed her shoulder on her way back to her seat. "Now instead of talking about the man I can never have, let's start talking about the trip. Is the food packed?"

Before Ruby could answer her, the door cranked open and Petey peeked in.

She did a double take. Her brother never came to the lodge. And what was he doing poking his head into the kitchen?

His eyes met hers and he pushed the door open all the way. "Paige. Bryce told me I'd find you in here."

"You found me," she said, the uncertainty weighing down her voice. Something had to be wrong...

"Um...I need to get back to the office." Avery waddled to the kitchen door. With a soft smile at Paige, she scooted past Petey. "Nice to see you again."

He nodded at her, then strode to the island looking nothing like the most carefree of all the Harpers.

"Yeah, I should go, too." Ruby stood, eyes wide with concern. "I gotta check on the dining room. Make sure they're all set for dinner." She disappeared before Paige could stop her. Before she could tell her she might need reinforcements. Because Petey's mouth had a sad twist and his eyes kept looking down. He didn't tease her at all. That was how they communicated. He teased. She griped at him. And it worked. But now his face was too serious.

He waited until the door closed behind Ruby, then rested his palms on the island across from her. "There's something you should know."

"Okay." She wished her heart would stop hammering, that her hands would stop shaking. Whatever he had to say, it obviously wasn't good news.

"Mom has MS," he said, his voice tighter and an octave too high.

"What?" Too much air escaped. She gulped some back in to fill her lungs. *Please. No.* Images of Gramma Lou's gnarled body flashed in her mind. She pulled out the stool and sank before she collapsed. "MS? Are they sure? How do they know? How—?"

"They found out yesterday." Petey spoke slowly, like he was afraid she wouldn't understand what he was saying. And she didn't. She didn't understand at all.

"Doc says it's pretty advanced. She's had symptoms for a while, but you know her."

"No." She shook her head. "No, Petey. I don't know her." Tears stung her eyes, but she fought them back. "You know why I don't know her? Because she was never around. Gramma Lou raised me." Even with all of the blinking, tears slipped out.

He walked around the island and steadied a hand on her shoulder. "I know things haven't been easy with Mom and Dad. But they did their best. That's all they could do."

They did their best. Did they? Maybe they did. Maybe that was all they had to offer by the time she came around. Maybe they'd used up their patience and love raising her siblings and they had nothing left for her...

"Thing is, Paige, we're gonna need some help to keep things running. They can't afford to hire someone right now." Pete stuffed his hands in his pockets. "I know it's not your gig, but it'd be pretty great if you could help out. For a while."

She blinked at him but couldn't speak because her heart was breaking apart in her chest, dislodging the things that had been stuffed so deep down...disappointment, hurt, but also guilt because she hadn't tried hard enough. It was easier to distance herself when she felt like she didn't fit in, but she could've worked harder. She could've tried.

Petey let go of a sigh and for the first time ever, he looked smaller and weary. "Once the ski season starts, things'll pick up again. We'll hire more help. But until then..." he paused and looked at her with sadness drooping his eyes. "She shouldn't deal with all the stress. She shouldn't be on her feet so much. You know?"

Tears built again. It didn't make sense. None of it made sense. She pressed a hand to her mouth to stop a sob. "Why didn't they call me? Why didn't they tell me they were doing tests?" Why did they pretend she wasn't even part of their family?

"You know them. Dad's as stubborn as an ox. He'd die before he'd ask for help. But I thought you should know."

Her eyes closed on another round of hot tears. "Thank you," she whispered, then opened her eyes and let the tears fall.

"I know you love your job." He glanced around the kitchen. "Maybe Bryce will give you a leave of absence or something. It should only be a couple of months."

"I'm sure I can work something out," she said, more confident than she felt. Summer was a busy time at the ranch. They needed a full-time guide. If she went to work at the café, Bryce would have to hire someone else. He'd have to give away her position.

She gathered in a deep breath and let it raise her head, her shoulders. It would be worth it. For her to spend time with her mom. To try to get to know her the way she'd always wanted to. Before it was too late.

Too late. God, how could the world change so much in one minute? How could there be a time limit on reconciling with Mom? Sorrow nearly gagged her. "Did they say how long...?"

"No." Petey's eyes reddened. "But you remember how it was with Gramma Lou. Mom's pretty depressed about it."

So was he. She could tell. The light was gone from his eyes. He hadn't given her a noogie or tousled her hair once. She stood. "I'll try to get by and see them today."

"I'm sure that'd mean a lot." He turned toward the door, then paused and glanced down at her. "They love you, Paige. You've gotta know that. Even if things haven't always been easy."

"Thanks," she whispered.

He offered her a sad smile, then left.

They love you...

She'd never felt loved by her parents. Tolerated, but never loved. They didn't love her the way Gramma Lou had, gig-gling with her, pretending with her, getting down on the floor and playing with her. But maybe that was simply who they were. Maybe she had to learn to accept them for who they were, for what they could offer her.

Before they were gone forever.

CHAPTER NINETEEN

Funny how one conversation can change the way you see everything. Paige stood outside the café, but instead of focusing on the cracked bricks, the tacky signage, and the dingy windows, she studied the curtains her mother had sewn herself—from red-and-white checkered material she'd found on sale in a store a few towns away. She remembered Mom sitting at the dining room table sewing those curtains night after night, long after everyone else had gone to bed. Mom had done little things like that all the time. Things Paige didn't bother to notice. Like those curtains. Had she ever even looked at them in all the years they'd hung there?

A heaviness settled inside of her—the weight of sadness and regret bearing down.

Paige pushed open the door, knowing that, even though they were closed on Wednesdays, her mother would be there. She'd be taking inventory and doing her weekly cleaning, scouring the stoves and ovens and refrigerators, working her fingers raw like she could somehow scrub away the new reality she found herself living. Gramma Lou had tried it, too, that desperate denial. She'd planned a three-day backpacking trip for her and Paige the day after she'd been diagnosed. They'd packed and prepared, both pretending nothing had changed, both denying the changes they'd already seen taking place for the last year, the weakness in her right leg, the tremors, the tingling numbness she'd complained about. On day two of the trip, when they were cresting a small ridge, Gramma Lou had lost her balance and taken a fall. She'd only broken her wrist, but that day marked the start of a rapid deterioration. It had been her last trip in the wilderness.

Blinking against tears, Paige made her way to the kitchen. The café sat dark and empty. Instead of chatter and laughter, a profound silence hung heavy and solemn. It was the same silence that had weighted her thoughts for the last three hours.

A clang from the kitchen lured her to the back. She inhaled deeply, then held the breath tight in her chest until the ache receded. Quietly, she crept to the kitchen doorway and peered inside.

Mom was up on her toes, yanking pots and pans off the shelf above the stove and stacking them on the stainless counter next to the sink. She looked the same, but that was the funny thing about a disease like multiple sclerosis. Things were only changing on the inside, nerve damage, muscle weakness. It might not be what killed her, but it would bring pain and frustration. It would make her life harder. In the end, those were the things that stole Gramma Lou's life. That made her believe life was not worth living.

And she wouldn't let Mom come to that same conclusion.

She would do whatever she could to make things easier for her, to do what she hadn't been able to do for Gramma Lou. Straightening, blinking out tears, she marched into the kitchen. "Need some help?"

Her mother froze, still holding a saucepan. She stood that way for what seemed to be an eternity, that saucepan dangling like it was about to fall from her hand. Finally she set it on the counter. "Pete told you," she said without looking at her.

She didn't deny it. "Why didn't you? I was just here. You could've told me about the appointment." *You should've told me.* Because mothers were supposed to tell their daughters those kinds of things so they didn't have to go through them alone.

Mom wiped her hands down the plaid apron she wore. When she turned to face her, Paige sucked in a breath.

She *had* changed. Dark circles gouged underneath her mother's eyes. Her face had thinned, sharpening her cheekbones.

Sadness flooded through her, overflowing into guilt. She braced a hand against the counter for support.

"I kept thinking the test would come back negative," Mom said with a ghost of a smile. "That the aches and pains and numbness were all part of getting old."

Paige closed her eyes because it was so hard to look. So hard to see reality instead of what she wanted to see. "How bad is the pain?"

She shrugged. "Not terrible. It comes and goes. The doctor says it will get worse."

It would. She remembered Gramma Lou lying in her bed moaning. Begging for medication. She remembered feeling so helpless that it hurt her, too. There was nothing she could do for her except sit there, show her pictures of their adventures, open the windows and let the breeze spawn memories.

Looking at Mom, knowing what she knew, caused something to shift inside of her. Whenever she'd looked at her parents, she'd always felt like she stood on the other side of a canyon, wondering how to get there, how to build a bridge that would bring them together. Now she realized it was up to her. They'd both put the distance there, but she could be the one to leap over it. Once she'd been too afraid that she'd fall, that it'd all be for nothing. Funny how a diagnosis could give you the courage to do what you should've done a long time ago.

Paige waited for Mom to look at her, waited for their eyes to connect, then she approached her. "I'm so sorry." For so many things. For not being the daughter they wanted. For not trying harder.

Silent tears puddled in her mother's brown eyes, spilling over one by one. "Paige." She reached out her arms and pulled her in, enfolding her in a softness she'd never known. "Don't be sorry. Not for anything."

"But I haven't been here." She pulled away. "I will be now. I promise." The therapy program could wait. Mom couldn't. "I'll help out as much as I can."

With a frustrated groan, Mom broke away and snatched a towel off the counter. "I won't let you do that." She mopped her eyes, then tidied her mascara with her fingers. "I want you to be happy. And you're not happy here."

The words speared her because they were true. She didn't want them to be true but they were. Happiness wasn't the most important thing in the world, though. Not to her, anyway. "You're my family. I want to be here." It would be their only chance to repair the damage they'd each done. Even if it wasn't her dream job, it'd be worth it.

Mom smiled at her, but another round of tears slipped down her cheeks. She leaned back into the counter, marveling at Paige, shaking her head like she couldn't believe what she saw. "I've always envied you."

Her? Mom envied *her*? Out of everyone in the family... Penny who was beautiful and graceful and refined. And then there was Pearl, shy and sweet with a singing voice that could soothe a colicky baby...

"You're stubborn enough to follow your heart, Paige," Mom said, mopping her eyes again. "You chase your dreams. I've never done that. Did you know your father and I haven't traveled farther than Denver since any of you kids were born?"

"No. I guess I didn't realize that." God, how sad.

"I regret it now, knowing it'll get harder for me to travel. Your father..." She looked around the kitchen, shaking her head like she didn't know how she'd gotten there. "He loves this place so much."

What about her? She'd put as much into it as he had. She'd made it her life. "You should sell it," she blurted out, suddenly desperate for Mom to live, *really* live, before it was too late. "If you really want to travel. If you want to have a life... it's not too late."

"It'd kill him." Mom gave her head a firm shake, pressing her lips together. "I'd love to travel, but I love your father more." She turned back to her pots and pans, stacking them carefully.

"What about you?" Paige whispered. "You still have so much time. You can do so many things."

Mom didn't turn around. "You're the bravest one out of all of us. You know that, Paige?" *Clang, clang, clang.* She moved the pots systematically. "The way you walked with Gramma Lou those last months. We were all too afraid, but you stayed with her. You took care of her. She was lucky to have you."

"You have me, too." Her eyes heated again. This was the right thing to do. She couldn't deny it, not with the way her heart pounded. "I'm gonna work here."

Abandoning the pans, Mom spun. "I won't hire you." Her eyes glinted with a stubbornness Paige had never seen. "I won't let your father hire you, either. You're doing good things. You'll get your therapy program going. I won't let you give up on that for me. We'll find a way to manage. We always have."

"But—"

"No." Mom took Paige's shoulders in her hands, gazing down at her with this loving, soft expression that penetrated her defenses.

"Let me do this for you," she sniffled. "I know it might not seem like it, but we love you. You're our baby girl. We let this place get in the way of a lot, but I hope you can forgive me for that.

"I forgive you." She threw her arms around her mother. "And I love you, too, Mom." Just like that, the bitterness that calcified her heart was gone.

* * *

"Things are not looking good, Ben." Kev's worry furrows deepened into jagged lines that cut across his forehead. "We're tanking. Crashing and burning. According to the latest polls, twenty percent say they'll vote for you. Twenty freaking percent."

Not the best news he'd heard all day. Not the worst, either, though. Not by a long shot. Paige had a date that night. With someone else. That was bad news.

He glanced around the cabin's kitchen-turned-war-room. Kev had set up a whiteboard, which was littered with unreadable chicken scratch. Something about the statistics on how many senatorial candidates had ever overcome such a shitty deficit in the polls. Didn't have to be a genius to figure out the odds weren't exactly in his favor.

"Did you hear him?" Gracie angled her head to interrupt his blank stare.

Seeing his mother's head bob around in front of him flipped the switch on his temper the way only she could do. "Of course I heard him."

"What are you going to do about it, Benjamin?" she demanded.

"The naked show is always an option," J interjected from the sofa where she had been parked for at least an hour reading the latest *People*. "Chicks dig that kind of thing. Naked men."

"How would you know?" he shot back.

"Yes, Julia. That is a wonderful question." Gracie assumed that daunting motherly stance, backs of her hands laid against her hips, head sticking out like a rooster's. "How, exactly, would you know?"

"It's my favorite show. A girl's gotta get action somehow." She flipped to the next page in her magazine like they were discussing the weather while Gracie squeezed her eyes shut and raised her hands to the heavens as if imploring God to save her wayward daughter.

Kev collapsed in a kitchen chair, shoulders hunched in defeat, wide forehead shining with sweat. Ben couldn't help but feel bad. The man was killing himself for his benefit. The least he could do was come up with a plan to turn things around. When he'd run for Congress, he'd had the stats on his side from the beginning. For the most part, he'd been well liked. Amazing what one deceptive woman could do to a man's reputation.

Since those fabricated pictures had come out, he'd kept quiet, thought it would blow over. But now it was time to fight back. "How about a press conference?" he asked. "I've never directly addressed the rumors. So maybe it's time." He heaved himself out of the armchair and stood in front of Kev. "We could make it a big deal. Introduce the land trust, invite everyone to follow a live blog while we're on the river..." If nothing else, it'd generate publicity for what he was about to do.

Gracie clasped her hands. For some reason she always looked like she was posing for a camera. "It's a wonderful idea. Exactly what we need right now."

Kev's frown perked up only slightly, but it was something. "I'll set it up for tomorrow morning," he said as he dug out his phone.

"Great. I'll be ready." Addressing the media wasn't exactly his favorite pastime, but it'd be worth it. It'd get Gracie off his back and it'd show Kev how grateful he was for all the work on his behalf. If it weren't for Kev, he wouldn't even have that twenty percent of the population. He never would've been a congressman.

"We should write out a script," Gracie insisted as she floated to the table and retrieved her laptop.

Ben checked his watch. "Actually, I'll do it later. I was thinking I'd take J out tonight. Go have some fun out on the town." At a certain restaurant. Where he happened to know Paige would be with Smokey the Bear.

His sister eyed him with suspicion. "Why would you do that?"

"It's been a while since we've been out, that's all." He avoided eye contact so she wouldn't see through his lie. The last thing he needed was for his mother to find out he was going after Paige. "I thought you'd enjoy seeing Aspen's nightlife." Elevation 8,000, specifically. He'd looked it up on his phone right after he'd ditched Gracie at the top of Aspen Mountain. Looked like a swanky place. "Better put on a dress and some heels. You never know where we'll end up," he said with a mysterious undertone, even though he knew good and well where they'd end up. He'd already made reservations.

With a shrug, J tossed her magazine on the coffee table. "I guess it beats sitting around here." Releasing the brake on her chair, she wheeled herself over. "Give me twenty minutes."

"You got it." Then, because his mood was getting lighter by the second, he went back to the table and sat across from his mother, who was typing furiously on her laptop. Never mind that he said he'd do it later. Not like she ever let him write his own speeches, anyway. He leaned over to take a peek. "Don't forget to focus on the positives." Knowing her, she would write a novel insulting Valentina. "Make sure it's all about the land trust. The good things we're doin'. Only give a mention to the accusations."

"Of course," his mother intoned, still giving him the cold shoulder after their little chat earlier.

Kev sat down next to him. "Are you really up for a live blog?"

"Sure." He didn't see any problem with it. They had a satellite phone so there should be coverage the whole way. "We can upload videos and pictures."

"What about Paige?" Kev asked a little too innocently.

"What about her?"

"Will she be fine with that?"

Gracie stopped typing and looked up at him, another lecture brewing in her eyes.

He pushed back and jolted to his feet. Nope. Not going there again. He and Paige were none of their damn business. "Sure. She'll be fine." He pulled out his keys and headed for the door. "I'll go warm up the car. Tell Julia I'm outside." He didn't want to be late, after all. Not since he'd come up with a new game plan for how to win her over.

No more hitting on her. No more checking her out. No more asking her out. Instead, he planned to take Elsie's advice. Treat her right.

That's why he had to get to the restaurant. Because something told him that was the one thing Smoky the Bear didn't know how to do.

CHAPTER TWENTY

Elevation 8,000 was not Paige's typical scene. Case in point, the twenty pairs of stilettos she'd seen click-clack by her in the fifteen minutes she'd been waiting on the bench right inside the door. She didn't wear stilettos. Didn't even own a pair. Paige glanced down at her black ballet flats. What was she thinking setting up a date with Luke? After the day she'd had, she should be soaking in the hot tub at the Walker Mountain Ranch, sipping one of Avery's famous strawberry basil margaritas. Instead, she was at some snobby restaurant waiting for a fireman who'd already proved he was an ass once, and who was now...she glanced at her watch...nearly eighteen minutes late.

He had two minutes to show or she'd have gotten all dressed up for nothing. Well. If you could call it dressed up. After the whole blow-dryer incident, she'd decided she wouldn't go too far in the "dressing up" department. Wasn't worth it, the time, the effort. The potential fire hazard. So after she'd visited Mom, she'd gone home, showered, let her hair air dry into the typical waves that most of her friends told her they envied. She'd applied a hint of powder to even out her skin, then a touch of mascara. The only thing she kept from Ruby's stash was that yummy lip gloss.

And she hadn't agonized on what to wear, either. She'd picked a short, flowy black skirt that fell above her knees and a ruched shirt the same color as the Caribbean Sea, with a nice high neckline, seeing as how Luke's eyes tended to wander. When she looked in the mirror, she'd been surprised. She looked pretty good. Well, better than okay, anyway. At least she'd thought so until she showed up at the restaurant designed for the rich and flawless.

It was the trendiest place in town, minimalist-chic, they called it. Quiet and dim, with round booths and hanging lights and exposed brick. One steak cost as much as the shoes she wore, and they were genuine leather. She'd only eaten there one other time. Jory brought her when he was home from college for a visit. She'd eaten the most decadent stuffed portabellas, then he'd ordered chocolate crème brûlée. After that, they'd driven out to the old ghost town on Castle Peak Road and he'd convinced her he needed something to remember her by. The thought made her sick. She'd wanted her first time to be with someone who actually loved her. She wanted it to be memorable and special. That night Jory proved she wasn't worth memorable and special. And Avery was right. She bailed out of every relationship before the man could do what Jory did to her. That's why she was here. With Luke. It wasn't for Gracie's benefit. It was so she could run from Ben...

"Hey, gorgeous." Luke strode over to where she sat. He looked nice, dressed in a green button-up shirt and khakis but his eyes were bloodshot and he wore a sloppy smile on his face.

She stood and assessed him. "You're late."

"Sorry," he said with a sheepish grin, and sure enough, the smell of alcohol hazed around her.

You've got to be kidding. "Did you stop and drink a keg on the way here?" she asked in a harsh whisper. Not that she was one to judge, but really?

"The guys and I went for happy hour," Luke whispered back. "Damn, Paige. Lighten up. You used to be fun," he complained.

She shoved the strap of her purse higher on her shoulder. "Yeah. Well, this was a bad idea."

But before she could walk away, Luke linked his arm through hers. "I rescued you from a tree today," he reminded her, nudging her ribs. "Come on. Have dinner with me. It'll be great to catch up."

"I don't know—"

"Mr. Simms," the hostess interrupted her. "We have your table all ready." She batted her eyelashes exactly like most women did in Luke's presence.

With a hand on her back, he prodded her to follow the hostess. "It'll be a blast. I'll even pay," he promised.

"Fine." She ground her teeth, but let him nudge her across the restaurant, following the hostess's swaying hips. She did love the crème brûlée...

"I reserved a quiet table in the corner," Luke murmured, resting his hand on her ass.

"Great." She swatted his hand away and walked faster. What had she gotten herself into?

* * *

"What's going o—"

He shushed J with his hand and tried to hear, but they were too far away. He'd give his left arm to hear what she was saying.

He stood. "I'll be right back. I'm gonna try to get closer..." Maybe take a quick trip to the bathroom, since he'd have to walk right past their table...

"Take notes for me!" J called happily. He stared straight ahead, but glanced toward Paige every other step.

She was still on her feet, but now Luke was talking...

He ambled closer, stumbled over some lady's purse. "Oh. Sorry," he mumbled.

The gray-haired woman scowled, but then smiled when their eyes met. "I recognize you!" She had a distinct Texas twang. "You're Benjamin Noble." She scurried out of her chair and captured his hand in hers, shaking it like he was the president of the United States. "I loved your daddy. What great man! Handsome devil, too, wasn't he?"

He tried to smile back. "Yep. He was amazing."

"Well, honey." She whapped his arm in a friendly, slightly flirty gesture. "I'm from Dallas, and I want to assure you, you've got my vote come November."

"Thanks." He looked up right as Luke grabbed Paige's arm and yanked her back to the table.

Oh, no. Hell no. He did *not* touch her like that. "Excuse me." He shoved past the woman, vision narrowed on that guy's pretty-boy face. He made it to their table just as Paige wriggled free.

"Come on, Paige. Don't get all pissed off," Luke whined.

"What's going on?" Ben demanded, blood pumping through his arms, up to his face.

Paige spun. "Ben? What the hell are you doing here?"

"I'm here with J." He swept an arm toward their table.

Julia seemed to suddenly realize they were all staring at her. She waved, then picked up a menu and hid her face.

Luke scrambled out of his chair and threw a wad of bills on the table. "We were just leaving. Weren't we, Paige?"

Her face was molten. "Are you kidding? I'm not going anywhere with you, Luke. You're completely wasted."

"Paige." The man swiped his meaty paw through the air again, but Ben stepped in front of her. "Why don't you sit down and finish your dinner?" He kept his tone even and discreet. No sense in making a scene.

Luke's massive arms crossed over his chest. He looked down at Ben like he was a mere snack. "And if I don't? What're you gonna do about it, cowboy?"

Good question. Ben glanced around. Heads had definitely turned and some of the waitstaff moved toward them at a brisk but calm pace. It'd been a while since he'd been in a brawl, but it had to be like riding a bike, right? He rolled up his shirtsleeves. "Whatever I have to. Seems to me you should have a little more respect for a lady."

Luke laughed, his bloodshot eyes wide and disgusting. "That what she is? A lady?"

"Sit down and I'll make sure Paige gets home." Ben applied a firm hand to the asshole's shoulder and directed him back to his seat.

"You can't tell me what to do." Luke flailed, then charged, arms outstretched like he was going to strangle him.

"Luke! No!" Paige cried, but his fist flew through the air.

Ben ducked the first punch. *Yep.* Like riding a bike. But he couldn't get away from the second blow. Luke's fist collided with his face. Pain shot through the bridge of his nose. Warm blood flooded his lips. *Ow.* He opened his eyes. Saw the ceiling. Three ceilings...

Luke bent over him. "How'd that feel, Cowboy Pete?" He asked with a slur.

"You asshole!" Paige shoved Luke away. "You're such a jerk! I can't believe you did this..."

Waitstaff buzzed around, but Ben still only saw stars. He scrambled off the floor. A man dressed in a black suit with an earpiece directed both him and Luke toward the doors. "It's time to go, gentlemen. Or we'll have the police sort this out."

Ben looked over his shoulder and tried to focus on Paige. "Go help Julia," he said, swiping at the blood with his sleeve.

Nodding, she turned away from him.

The security's guard's grip on his arm tightened. He forced Ben around tables, past the bar, through the elaborate entry. "I suggest you two don't come back. We won't be so friendly next time."

Before Ben could turn and make sure Paige had Julia, the security guard shoved him out the door.

CHAPTER TWENTY-ONE

Julia. Find Julia. Hands shaking, Paige shouldered her purse and started a clumsy search across the restaurant. People stared at her, shaking their heads. She overheard one woman on the phone.

"Yes, of course I'm sure it was Benjamin Noble. He started a brawl right here in the restaurant!"

Uh-oh. That was bad. Very bad.

"Paige! Over here!" Julia waved at her from a small booth. "Oh my god. Is he okay? That looked horrible."

She winced at the thought of Luke's hand colliding with Ben's nose. Her stomach turned. "It didn't sound good, either." When the security guard had shoved him out of the restaurant his face had been a bloody mess.

Julia snatched her purse off the table and dug around.

"Here." Paige maneuvered her chair next to the bench. "I'll help you slide over. Ready?"

After tossing some money down on the table, Julia nodded, then pushed herself off the bench. Paige threaded her arms around her and shifted her into the chair.

"I can't believe Ben did that," she said as she wheeled Julia to the door. "Why'd he do that? I had things under control." She was about to walk out the door. But no, Ben had to show up and make a huge scene.

"You really have to ask why?" Julia smiled up at her. "He's crazy about you. Seeing Luke touch you like that pissed him off. He's got a temper for that kind of thing. Trust me." She patted her hand. "He defends my honor at least three times a week."

"I don't need anyone defending my honor." Though it was so...thoughtful. No one had ever gone to that much trouble to make sure she was being treated with respect.

The hostess opened the door for them. "Thank you for visiting Elevation 8,000," she purred, apparently oblivious to what had happened in there. "We hope you come again."

"You bet," Julia answered. "Thanks for the show."

Paige eased the chair out the door and scanned the sidewalk. Ben sat on a bench with a white cloth over his face, and Luke was laid out on the sidewalk next to his feet. *Great.* "What'd you do to him?" she demanded, rushing over.

He pulled the cloth away from his face and she almost wished he'd put it back. Dried blood crusted his skin around a hideous purplish bruise that spread from the bridge of his nose underneath his eyes.

She reached out her hand, but stopped before touching his face. "Is it broken?"

"Nah." He wrinkled his nose a few times. "It's nothin'. I've been kicked in the face by an Arabian. I can handle a punch."

"Two shiners. Very distinguished," Julia laughed.

"You wanna talk distinguished." He peered down at Luke.

"How about passing out mid-threat." He stood, still wincing like he was in pain. "The idiot was in the middle of telling me he'd break my legs, too, when all of a sudden he keeled over."

Paige skirted the chair and stared down at Luke. Pathetic. This whole thing was pathetic. "I'm so sorry, Ben." Next time she wanted to make a point, she'd do it without a man's help. "I guess I should drive him home."

"We'll help you get him home." Ben stooped and heaved Luke up to a standing position. "Come on, buddy. Let's get you to the car." Luke groaned and leaned heavily against Ben's shoulder.

Feeling that warm glow that only Ben could light in her, she grabbed the handles on Julia's chair and followed him to the Jeep. "Think I should tell him that woman was talking about him on the phone?" she whispered to Julia.

"Nah. He'll find out tomorrow." She waved the whole thing off. "Don't feel so bad. It's not your fault he's madly in love with you."

How could she not feel bad? She could've ruined his political career. Could a senator get elected after getting into a fight at a high-end restaurant? Was that even possible?

Ben loaded Luke's limp body into the backseat, then helped his sister into the car. He was so careful with her. So sweet.

And insisting on helping her get Luke home after what she'd pulled earlier...

God, he really was a nice person. She surrendered the wheelchair to Ben and climbed into the backseat. What little backseat was left with Luke laid out like that, anyway. The smell of alcohol nearly choked her.

"So where does this yahoo live?" Ben asked, dabbing at his nose again.

Paige clipped in her seatbelt. "Take a left up there. Then we'll go straight for about four miles. Then right on Second Street." She scooted as far away from Luke as she could get, hugging the window.

Ben drove in silence, and she didn't know what to say. Thank you? It didn't seem like enough. Or should she yell at him for trying to be a hero and getting himself hurt?

"So that was fun," Julia said cheerfully.

"Yeah. Fun," Ben muttered.

"What will I do for entertainment while you're on the river?" His sister sighed. "Guess I'll have to buy some new magazines."

Wait a minute. Paige shoved a snoring Luke away and leaned forward, peering between the seats. Why should Julia have to sit around while they were out having fun?

Ben glanced over at her. She met his eyes, an idea brewing a smile on her face. "You should come with us, Julia," she said, still smiling at Ben.

"Really?" his sister squeaked.

"No. No way." His eyebrows lowered in a stern expression. "Definitely not safe."

"I'm the queen of safe," she reminded him. "I've taken paraplegics down the river and nothing's ever happened."

Quick breaths shot in and out of Julia's open mouth. Her eyes fixated on Paige. "Yes. I want to go. *Please.*"

"You're not going," Ben growled, looking borderline mean with those shiners under his eyes.

Paige laid a hand on his shoulder to soften him up. "I'll take good care of her, Ben. Don't you trust me?"

He eyed her. "Sure. I trust you. It's nature I don't trust."

"The water level is perfect for it." Last time she'd checked it'd been low enough for a safe, easy ride. "The boat won't be moving too fast. I'll put her right in the middle."

"Middle doesn't matter if the boat flips."

Julia's eyes pleaded with Paige.

"I've never had any incidents at this water level," she continued in a soft, sweet tone, trying to remind him this would be good for Julia. "We take every precaution on the water..."

Staring straight ahead, he tapped his fingers against the steering wheel.

"Please? Please let me come." Julia folded her hands and shook them in his face. "I'll never ask you for anything else as long as I live. I swear."

He stopped the Jeep at a stop sign and looked back at Paige.

"She'll be fine. I promise." She pressed her gaze into his, letting their eyes stay connected long enough that a burst of warmth ignited deep in her belly and floated up to her chest.

Ben's cheeks went soft. "Okay. I trust you."

"Yes!" Julia raised her hand for a high five. "I can't wait!"

"I've got a ton of river clothes you can borrow," Paige told her. "I'll get them ready tonight."

Julia squeezed her hand. "Thank you so much."

Ben simply smiled. He turned right on Second and she pointed out Luke's apartment house.

He pulled up in front and together they got Luke inside, depositing him on the couch with a heavy thud. "Sleep it off," Ben muttered. Then he opened the door for her and they went back to the car.

"You want me to take you back to your car?" he asked, looking at her in the rearview mirror.

"No. I'll go back to the lodge with you." She gave him a small smile. "I know where Elsie keeps a first-aid kit. We can at least get your face cleaned up."

He grinned back. It was the first real smile she'd seen on his face all night. "That sounds perfect."

* * *

Though it was only ten thirty, the kitchen was deserted and quiet, exactly like she'd hoped. They didn't need to explain to anyone how Ben had gotten his face messed up. Hopefully, she could repair some of the damage so it didn't look quite so bad in the morning.

She led the way to the island and pulled out a stool. "Have a seat."

He obeyed with a smile. "Yes, ma'am."

They hadn't said much since they'd gotten Julia back to their cabin. Luckily, Gracie had gone to bed, though Ben's campaign manager had given Paige the third degree about what had happened. She'd answered every question, but when it came to talking to Ben, she almost didn't know what to say. *I'm afraid of you* didn't sound good, even though it was the truth.

He'd kept his distance from her. Because he was like that. A gentleman. He seemed to sense her hesitation, her internal battle against the way he made her feel. The pull between them was so crazy intense. She knew if she touched him, if she let him touch her, it would all be over. Just like stepping off that cliff earlier that morning. They wouldn't be able to go back. She wouldn't be able to stop anything.

Taking her time, she made her way to the cupboard near the sink. Sure enough, Elsie's huge red bag with a white cross stood out. She removed it and walked slowly back to Ben.

His eyes followed every move and he had this soft, content look on his face. She pulled another stool over and focused intently on unzipping the first-aid bag. "This might sting." She unwrapped an antiseptic pad and dabbed at the cut across the bridge of his nose.

He winced.

She pulled back her hand. "Sorry."

"Didn't hurt." He grinned. "You would've made a good nurse."

Her skin flamed. She dabbed again. "I hate the sight of blood." Always had. "Getting through my wilderness EMT certification was a nightmare."

"But you did it." His eyes tracked with hers. So intense...

She set down the trash in her hand and moved away to break the spell. "Yeah. You do what you have to do."

She unwrapped a bandage and evaluated the damage to his nose. Nice nose. And those lips...Focus on the nose. Only the nose. So much safer. "Doesn't look as bad as I thought." She carefully pressed the bandage against his skin. "Hopefully the bruise'll fade in a day or two. But you were right. I don't think there're any broken bones."

His eyes sought out hers, but he said nothing.

"I'm sorry about all of this," she murmured, because she couldn't stand the silence. And...what was he thinking? That it'd been a mistake sticking up for her? That she wasn't worth a facial wound? "It was stupid. I never should've gone out with him. Then you never would've gotten hurt..." And she'd be at home. Alone. Instead of aching over this man in Elsie's kitchen.

His lips turned up into that irresistible grin. "You're worth it." He didn't say more, simply gazed at her in a way that made tingles spread down her neck, across her chest. It was a feeling long forgotten. A feeling that had been submerged with disappointment and plans and dreams and goals. But she recognized it. It came rushing back, as strong as the river on a class-five section. Desire. Need.

Ben remained still but his eyes lured her closer. She felt the warm glow of his breath against her mouth.

His hand reached up, those rugged fingers, trailing a gentle line down her cheeks, but he still didn't move closer. He only stared at her. Like he had all the time in the world to watch her.

Such a sweet heaviness settled on her chest that she felt like it might cave in. Was she breathing? Could she breathe?

Her heart seemed to swell, sending signals, waking up her body. Her eyes closed and her lips collided with his, drowning her in a delectable warmth. His mouth was firm and demanding against hers, and the sensuality of his skilled touch weakened her legs.

His hands slid low around the back of her waist and he pulled her into his lap, her legs straddling him, tightening around his waist with the wonder of what his tongue was doing to hers, stroking and caressing and erasing every doubt.

He kissed her slow but hard, sure of himself, sure of them. And she was sure, too. So sure. Never more sure of anything because it had never been like this with anyone else. Powerful and real. So real it made her ache in a way no kiss ever had.

"Ben," she whispered against his lips.

He didn't answer, just stood, hands cupping her ass, and moved her to the island, settling her on the counter in front of him, looking her over. Every part of her, it seemed. Her neck, down to her chest, down to her waist. His hands clasped on her ankles and he worked his way up her shins, massaging, caressing, higher, higher, up her thighs, over her waist.

Her body trembled and her lungs burned. This was different. Not fast and sloppy in the backseat of a car. Slow and sensual. Like she was worth the extra time . . .

Ben's lips drifted to her neck, right below her ear. "I love the way you smell."

The whisper hit the right spot, bringing out a shiver followed by goose bumps prickling every inch of her skin.

"The way you taste." His tongue slid down her neck, forcing her to grab a fistful of his shirt. Suddenly her skin felt this heightened sense of awareness. The slightest brush of his lips against the tender spots on her neck tightened her grip until her knuckles hurt. He went back to her lips and they fit together so perfectly. "I want you, Paige," he panted in a hoarse whisper. "I want you like I've never wanted anyone."

Okay. Didn't have to tell her twice. But she couldn't say so. She couldn't utter one syllable...

He pulled away, looked around. "This is Elsie's kitchen," he said, his eyes shifting like he was afraid she'd planted hidden cameras.

Paige laughed. He had a point. "Um. Yeah." She licked her lips. Couldn't seem to form a cohesive thought.

He leaned his forehead against hers. "We can't do this here."

Her mouth opened to protest. They could. Technically, they could do it right then and there. No one was around...

Except he was right. Elsie would kill her. She'd drag her to confession or something...

Ben looked at her forever without speaking. Then he lowered his head to her eye level. "Do you want me to take you home?"

She knew exactly what he was asking. Did she want to end this now? Before it was too late? Before they couldn't go back?

"I'm not lookin' for a one-night stand," he warned her, his eyes solemn. "I'll drive you home right now and leave. If that's what you want."

No. She didn't want to go home. Not alone, anyway. She

wanted to know how it felt to be loved. No one had ever been able to show her that.

No one.

"Let's go." Ben pulled back, seeming to have misread her silence.

"No." She planted her palms on the counter behind her to hold herself up. Every part of her felt weak. "I don't want to go home." Because she'd hidden for too long.

His expression went from solemn disappointment to surprised, open-mouthed grin. He lifted her off the counter and set her feet on the floor. "Then come on." He linked her arm through his. "There's somethin' I want to show you."

Half floating, half walking, she let him lead her out the door.

CHAPTER TWENTY-TWO

Body still shuddering with what that woman had done to him, Ben whisked Paige out the kitchen door and down the patio steps. No one sat around the fire pit, and even though the warm glow beckoned, he urged her past it, down the last of the steps, past the pool—though that would've been fun, but a little too cold.

He dug his phone out of his pocket and lit up the flashlight app, shining it over the ground until he found the little path he'd discovered on a hike the day before.

There.

"Right this way." He nudged her into the darkness of the thick pine trees, and threaded his arms around her from behind, bringing their bodies closer, their steps in-line. They eased down the trail carefully, slowly, moving like one being. The perfect fit of her body against his reignited the flame of want, so he eased more space between them, but didn't let her go.

"Where are we going?" she whispered, as breathless as she'd been in the kitchen.

"You'll see," he murmured into her ear because he knew exactly what that did to her.

They hiked down a small slope, curved around a rock, and they were there, the oasis he'd discovered yesterday—a hammock right next to the soothing creek.

The waxing moon provided enough light for him to see a smile alter her face. "I always knew Bryce had a secret spot." She tugged on the hammock as if testing the reliability. "Seems pretty sturdy."

Ben slid behind her and sank his weight into it, pulling her down with him. It bent at the sides, cocooning them together.

Paige shimmied until they lay face-to-face, chest-to-chest, thigh-to-thigh.

They swung slightly. The trees creaked. Above them, stars burned and it felt like they'd done this a thousand times, wrapped in each other's arms, staring up at the unfathomable sky...

"I told Gracie to back off," he said because he didn't want her to think he was sneaking around. Looking for a fling. "She won't bother you anymore."

Paige gazed up at him. "She does make some good points." A concerned look gathered her eyes at the corners. "I mean, I want nothing to do with politics, Ben. Or the spotlight. That's not my scene."

Maybe that's why he loved her so much. Because she didn't care about fitting a certain mold. She never wanted to be someone she wasn't. "It's not exactly mine, either," he admitted. Or at least it wouldn't be if his life had gone differently. If Julia's life had gone differently.

"What *is* your scene?" she asked, weaving his fingers

with hers. He loved her hands, petite but strong and skilled.

"What if you don't get elected? What would you do then?"

The question stumped him. What would he do if he didn't get elected? He hadn't even considered it. He hadn't let himself. Julia had spent hours researching health care, insurance, alternative therapies for people with disabilities. She'd spent so much time writing that bill...

"I'd work at the ranch." Saying it made him feel like an ass, but Paige would understand better than anyone. Being outside. Having your hands busy. Feeling free...

"Then why are you doing it?" she demanded, that fire flashing in her eyes. "Why are you killing yourself to run for senator if it's not what you really want?"

"It's where I can do the most good. For Julia. *That's* what I want." He'd let her down once. He couldn't do it again. "She's writing a bill. To help other accident victims get more coverage for alternative therapies. Once I'm elected, I'll get it passed." Then all of J's suffering would matter. It would make a difference for others.

Sighing, Paige rested her head against his shoulder. "She's lucky to have you, Ben."

He smoothed her hair. It was so soft. Silky. "So have you ever considered moving to Washington, DC?" he asked, even though he already knew the answer.

Her smile strained. "I belong here. In Aspen. With my family."

His head tilted over hers. Her family? He searched her eyes. "I didn't think you were that close."

With a heavy sigh, she rested her head down against the fabric. "My mom has MS. I found out today..." Even in the dark, he saw the whites of her eyes grow brighter.

"Oh, god. Paige..." He wished he could wipe the pain out

of her eyes. "That's awful." Especially after what she'd told him about her grandmother...

"So I can't leave," she whispered. "I don't want to leave."

He rested his head against the hammock's pillow so he could stare into her eyes. "You don't have to leave."

Her eyes searched the sky. "So one night, then? That's all?"

He slid his fingers under her chin and turned her face back to his. "I don't think one night'll be enough."

"I don't either," she admitted with a small smile that made him want to ease that shirt up and over her head.

"We'll figure it out." He wrapped a leg over her and brought her body against his, feeling the fullness of her breasts against him, that perfect fit of her body and his. But he fisted his hands so they didn't wander. Not yet.

"So you saw your mom today?" he asked, breathing her in.

She snuggled against him. "Yeah."

"How's she doing?"

"She seems okay. Still in shock, maybe." Paige looked into his eyes fully, no longer afraid. "I guess I don't really know how she's doing. We've never been close."

He stroked her arm. "Why not?"

"She was forty-five when I was born. My next-oldest sibling was ten. It was like she had no idea what to do with me."

"Things'll change now." At least, it seemed something had changed for her.

"I hope so." She pressed her hand against his, fingers stroking his skin. That small touch, that intimate contact made him groan. Damn, he wanted her. The way his body was responding at the moment, you'd think he was an eighteen-year-old kid.

"My brother asked me to come back and work at the restaurant," she said quietly.

"What?" He half sat up. "You're not gonna do it, are you? What about the therapy program?"

"I don't know." She shifted to her back and stared up at the sky again. "I feel like I should. Bryce has been dragging his feet for a year. Who knows if we'll ever get it started."

"You can't give up on it." He lay back down next to her. "God, Paige. You saw Julia out there. That changed her life."

She shook her head. "It'd take years for me to find the funds. Not every family has a reserve like yours."

"I'll talk to Bryce." Shit, all he'd have to do was show him the pictures of Julia strutting around the meadow like she'd found the Holy Grail.

"Bryce warned me about you, ya know." Paige stabbed a pointer finger into his chest.

He gave her a questioning look.

"About how you are with women." Her expression was playful, but there was a hesitancy there, too. "About how you're a player. Love 'em and leave 'em."

Well, that was great. His buddy was really doing everything he could to help him out. "That was true. Once." He was man enough to own up to his past. "College was tough for me."

She lifted her head. "Because of Julia's accident?"

"Yeah." Crazy how Paige already knew more about him than most people. "I wanted to escape. From everything." And he had for a while. "Then my dad got sick. Cancer. He fought it for years. But we lost him last summer."

"That's terrible." Paige's free hand rested on his chest. "I bet you miss him."

"Yeah. The man was a saint." He narrowed his eyes. "He had to be to put up with Gracie all those years."

"Amazing, isn't it?" she asked. "How some couples make it work no matter what? I thought my parents were the only ones who've stuck it out."

"She didn't make it easy on him, that was for damn sure. But Dad fought for her. I guess she fought for him in some ways, too." She'd royally screwed up in those early days, apparently, but she was fiercely loyal to the end. Trying to atone for it the rest of their marriage, he supposed. "I guess you take it one day at a time." He touched a kiss to Paige's neck. One arm niggled its way under her waist and the other wrapped around to meet it at her belly button.

"One night at a time." She kissed his mouth with that feisty smile.

"I like the sound of that," he murmured as he wrapped her in tighter and held on.

* * *

Ow. Oh, ow. Whoa. Damn it. Paige tried to free her foot from the twist in the hammock. The thing swung madly, swaying the trees above them.

Laughing, she pulled away from Ben and untangled herself. "I've never made out in a hammock before." Chest still heaving, she gasped in a breath. Never made out with a man like him before, either. *Good night,* the man made kissing an art form.

"Always a first time for everything." Raising his eyebrows, Ben shimmied Paige's shirt up, up, caressing the exposed skin on her stomach. "Making love in a hammock might be tough, but I'm up for the challenge."

His lips lowered to hers again, but a breath caught in her throat and nearly choked her. Making love...

Her body went stiff. She looked away from him, tried to

inhale, to calm her nerves. How could something from five years ago still haunt her?

"Paige?" Ben rolled her shirt back down, his eyes questioning her. "What's up?"

She opened her mouth to tell him it was nothing, to tell him to keep going, that she would be okay, but she couldn't trust her voice.

He rolled off of her and rested on his side, head propped up on his hand, looking at her, waiting...

Busted. She forced herself to look back at him, even though humiliation pricked her cheeks. "Um...well..." Her fingers fidgeted with the hem of his shirt. *Okay.* This was hard. Much harder than she thought it would be. Her eyes raised back to his. "I've only been with one other person."

He seemed to consider that, then raised one shoulder in a shrug. "So?" He brought his face close, a soft, caring expression tugging at her heart. "That's a good thing, Paige. Trust me. It should be about commitment, love. When it's not, things get complicated. You're better off without the baggage."

"But it wasn't a good thing." Tears nipped at the corners of her eyes. "It was...humiliating." Her shoulders shuddered and she couldn't tell if it was from the cool breeze or from the buried emotions that had started to surface. "I mean, I didn't want to have sex with him. But he made me feel like I had to. And it was horrible." Three minutes of sharp pain. He hadn't said anything afterward. He'd hardly even looked at her, like she was some big disappointment. They'd silently gotten their clothes on and then he'd driven her home, dropping her off on the curb without even a kiss goodnight.

"That's why I never..." She gulped a painful swallow.

"...let anyone else get close enough. So I didn't have to do that again."

Ben stared at her unblinking, his cheeks rigid, his mouth pulled with anger. "Paige..." he whispered, his fingers reaching up to brush her cheek. "That never should've happened. It should never be like that." He drew his lips close to hers, but didn't kiss her. "I'll be right back," he said, then eased off the hammock. "Wait there."

She propped herself up on her elbows, the hammock swinging beneath her. "Where are you going?" To kick Jory's ass? She hadn't told him his name, had she?

Ben leaned over her and kissed her forehead. "I'll be back. Ten minutes, tops," he said, backing away. "Don't move." He turned and disappeared into the darkness.

She didn't mind being alone in the wilderness. In fact, usually she preferred it. But without Ben's warmth next to her, something about the echoing quietness felt lonely. She sat up and turned her body so her feet dangled over the side of the hammock, and made it more like a swing. Pushing off the ground, she swung herself gently, listening to the sound of the rushing creek, the breeze rustling the pine needles, trying not to count the minutes as they passed.

When she was sure it had been three hours, footsteps thudded nearby. *Please let that be Ben.* Because she was cold and she wanted to be in his arms again.

Sure enough, he appeared out of the trees, now wearing a headlamp and carrying a huge cardboard box.

"What's that?" she asked, trying to get a glimpse of what was inside.

"Never you mind." Ben turned his back to her and kneeled, setting the box on the grass. He pulled out a bottle of wine and two glasses, then used a corkscrew to pop the cork. He filled both glasses and handed one to her. "This is a 2006 Jasper Hill Emily's Paddock shiraz. We drank it the night you danced with me at the gala," he said, swirling his glass, then taking a sip.

How could he remember that? She sipped, too, inhaling the minty tea-like scent, remembering the smooth velvety taste. But she never would've remembered what it was called.

"You were wearing a long red dress with a fitted bodice," he continued as he unpacked a blanket and spread it over the ground, smoothing a second fuzzy, thick blanket on top of it as though building a cozy nest under the stars.

Her heart picked up, but he wasn't done.

"You wore a string of pearls around your neck. Dangling pearl earrings." Ben removed a couple of the kerosene lanterns that she recognized from the ranch's guest rooms, and set them around the blanket. "You wore those sexy strappy shoes on your feet." Using a lighter he ignited the lamps in a soft glow.

"Ben..." She sighed, but she couldn't say more because there were no words powerful enough to tell him what she felt, how much she needed him...

"You had a cut on the back of your hand," he said, reaching into his magic box again, and removing an iPod docking station. "When I asked you what happened, you said it was from rock climbing." He fiddled with the iPod thing until it turned on, until the soft notes of Norah Jones's "Come Away with Me" drew out her breath in a way that made her feel light and free.

Still on his knees, Ben scooted over to her, sipping his wine. His gaze rested in hers, so strong and powerful it stopped her heart. "The woman who confronted me that night...the one from the bar..." He shook his head. "I didn't even remember her name, Paige." He set down his wine and covered her hand with his, stroking her skin in a way that opened her heart enough to let him in.

"But I never forgot every detail about you." Eyes lowering to her lips, he smiled. "One look at you and I memorized everything." His lips drew close enough to brush hers. "I knew I'd never meet anyone else like you."

Tears heated her eyes with a happy burn because he'd turned a cold lonely night into a safe place. And now she knew how it felt to be cherished.

"You deserve to feel beautiful. And sexy." Ben tugged on her hand until she eased off the hammock, until they were both on their knees gazing into each other's eyes in the flickering light.

"I do feel beautiful." When she was with him. He made her feel what no one else ever had.

Taking away her wine, he set it off to the side, and his smile lured out hers because it promised so much, that he knew how to make her forget, how to build her a new reality when it came to intimacy. His smile promised he would make this night special and lovely.

And fun. Ben was nothing if not fun.

The music continued the soft rhythm. Ben swept her hair over her right shoulder, and kissed her neck, weakening her legs until she started to sink into him.

"This is what it should be like," he breathed against her ear. His lips closed on hers again, and his hands followed the curve of her hips, up to her waist, underneath her shirt. The sensation of his skin against hers shuddered through her, sending her heart dipping and soaring until she was almost dizzy with the physical elation. His light touch crawled higher, climbing up her ribs, shrinking her lungs, sending a radiating burn down her body.

A helpless sigh escaped.

Ben smiled against her lips. He pulled away and looked at her, *into* her, lifting her shirt slowly over her head and dropping it next to her. The brisk air felt good against her skin, but it didn't soothe the burn that radiated inside of her, glowing brighter and brighter in her core, softening her, swelling through her...

His eyes focused on her breasts, and for the first time ever, those D cups were coming in handy.

"Damn, Paige." His fingers traced the outline of her bra, and he glanced up at her face through heavy-lidded eyes. "You have no idea what you're doing to me. How long I've thought about this..."

"Enough thinking, Ben Noble," she said, feeling the power her body had over him. And she reached back, unclipped her bra, slowly sliding it down her shoulders until she was bare before him. His hands slid up her ribs, this time moving over her breasts, fingers drawing circles over her nipples. No one had touched her that way, carefully and deliberately, knowing exactly how to awaken a neglected longing. He kissed her harder, a groan in his throat, then lowered his lips to her neck, building a splintering anticipation as he worked his way down, gliding his tongue over her skin, leaving a pulse of heat with each kiss.

He pulled back and smoothed her hair away from her forehead, eyes connecting with hers like he wanted to make sure she was okay.

Hmmm. Yes. She was definitely okay. "You're still wearing too many clothes," she murmured, then peeled off his shirt and worked her hands down his hard muscled chest and abs to his jeans. Smiling innocently, she unbuttoned them and shimmied his boxers and pants off his hips.

"Now I'm feeling shy," Ben lied, then captured her in a bear hug and took her down to the blanket, slowly inching her skirt down her legs like he enjoyed the anticipation. Hovering over her, he examined her underwear—good thing she'd chosen the lacy ones—then took them down with his teeth.

"Wow. You've got some moves," she laughed.

"Just wait, Paige. You just wait," he drawled. Pulling back the blanket, he tucked her inside the bed he'd made and lay next to her, trailing his fingers down her breasts, over her belly button, then lower. Gently, he spread her legs, teasing her inner thighs before caressing her, his whole hand rubbing places she didn't even know existed. Small explosions of pleasure rocked her. "Wow. Oh wow," she whispered over and over... so many times she couldn't count. Half numb with pleasure, she groped her hand over his body until she found what she was looking for.

Ben stilled while she closed her hand over him, his eyes shutting, that strong tension in his jaw releasing, making him look helpless under the influence of her touch.

His eyes opened and found hers, like he'd suddenly remembered what he was doing. "Paige," he groaned. "Oh, god, Paige." His fingers worked her over again, and she kept her hand on him, massaging him, spurred on by his persuasive moans.

He leaned over to kiss her, slowly, as though savoring the taste of her.

"This is so different," she whispered. Like nothing she'd ever experienced. "I didn't know..." The impact it could carry, the significance. Yes, the physical sensations stunned her, but they were also handing themselves over to one another, surrendering to each other, open and unguarded.

"Make love to me, Ben," she whispered. She wanted to experience the fullness of that connection, the extravagance of giving themselves fully.

"Thought you'd never ask," he said, his smile teasing her. Easing his body over hers, he stroked her hair, kissed her mouth, and carefully worked his way into her.

The movements were slow and tender, like he could anticipate what her body needed. "Tell me what you like," he whispered, as breathless as she was.

"All of it." Her fingers dug into his back. "I like all of it." The feeling of his weight over her, the force of him inside of her.

He thrust deeper and deeper, groaning with pleasure. The friction made her body heavy with desire.

Wrapping his arms around her, he gathered her against him, then rolled on his back so she was straddling him, and sweet mercy, the angle touched all the right places at once.

"Is that good?" he asked, his own expression twisted with restraint.

Yes. Yes. Oh, holy wow, yes. But all she could manage in response were short, ragged breaths.

"How good?" he asked with that spoiled-boy grin.

"Ben," she rasped. "Please..." She didn't even know what she wanted, what to do...

His hands guided her hips into a rhythm that sent stars circling in her vision. Every thrust reverberated through her, swelling a thrilling burst into her lower abdomen. Ben seemed to sense she was close. Oh, wow. So, so, so close.

He moved her faster over him, their ragged breaths breaking the night's silence. "Paige...you're perfect," he gasped.

All she could manage was a moan before one last thrust crashed a wave of sheer pleasure over her, making her weightless, making her fly and fall at the same time...

Ben held her tight, shuddering beneath her, breathing her name.

Collapsing under the weight of a satiated exhaustion, she fell over him.

"Wow," she whispered, still unable to inhale a solid breath. "Just... wow."

Laughing, Ben shifted her, so they were both lying on their sides, facing each other in the dim light. He took her cheeks in his hands. "This is what you deserve, Paige. Nothing less."

Pressing a kiss against her forehead, he nestled her in the shelter of his arms and held on.

CHAPTER TWENTY-THREE

W arm. So warm. Love like an old quilt wrapped around her heart, her mind, her body. Warm and soft. Comfort. She opened her eyes.

Patches of sunlight illuminated the blanket that entwined her and Ben. The canopy of pine needles above her glistened with the magic of morning dew. Somewhere a barn finch sang. The brisk morning air chilled her cheeks, but the rest of her felt bundled and cozy. She didn't dare move. Didn't want to wake Ben, to disturb the perfection. He breathed softly, as though he felt it, too. The peace that gave her limbs a lazy heaviness. His body faced hers, spooning her, and at some point during the night he'd wrapped a leg over her. She peered over at his face and smiled. Ben her human blanket. Slowly, she eased herself up until she had a better view of his face, the curve his lips, the hard angle of his jaw.

What kind of man was Benjamin Hunter Noble III? Not the kind she'd ever met. Not the kind she'd ever been with.

She traced her finger along his cheek, pressed it over those very capable lips, feeling her limbs go limp again, like they did last night about a hundred times.

A slow smile worked its way into Ben's cheeks. "Morning, beautiful."

God, she loved that twang.

His eyes opened halfway and found hers. Lazy smile still intact, he smoothed her hair and guided her to his mouth.

Even though they had to have spent half the night kissing—in between the necessary formalities of life stories and all that—his kiss still hit like a quake, reverberating through her with tingling aftershocks. "Careful," she whispered. "You don't want to start something you can't finish."

Laughing, he stretched his arms over his head and groaned. "Oh, I can finish. Pretty sure I proved myself last night." Light from the sun illuminated his eyes, made them almost the same color as honey. His strong arms pulled her onto his hard, wonderful body.

She rested her cheek on his shoulder where it fit so perfectly.

One of his hands drew concentric circles on her back. "I'm thinkin' that was the best night's sleep I've had in a decade."

"Me too." Under normal circumstances, she had to admit, she wasn't much of a cuddler, but there was something restful about the warmth, the comfort of being nestled against someone. Not someone. Ben.

"What time is it?" he asked through a sleepy yawn. "Seven?"

Her lips pouted. "I guess I can check. If you really must know."

An apologetic crease crinkled in his forehead. "Sorry. I'd

stay here all day if I could. Trust me. But there's a press conference at nine."

Heaving a dramatic sigh, she unearthed her arm from the blanket. Blinked at her watch. No. That couldn't be right. Shading her eyes, she glanced up at the sky. The dimness from the trees had made it seem so much earlier...

Ben propped himself on an elbow, eyebrows peaked. "Seven-thirty?"

"Eight-forty," she said through a grimace.

"What?" His body jolted into motion, scrambling, but he tripped and landed on top of her. Smirked. Kissed her again. As far as she was concerned, he could kiss her as many times as he wanted. He was so damn good at it. He should compete for an award or something.

"Whoops. Sorry, Paige." Only he didn't look sorry. Not at all. He pushed himself up to his feet and reached for her hand. She gladly offered it to him.

He whisked her off the ground and into his arms like she was some dainty little thing. The feeling was kind of a nice change...

"Thank you for the best night of sleep I've had in months." He pulled her against him, tight enough she could feel the impressive outline of those award-winning pectorals. "I don't want to go..." His lips trailed kisses down her neck.

"You have to go. Your mom will kill me." She pushed him back, but her arms were about as useful as twigs.

"My mother will love you. Someday. Trust me. She won't have a choice." He stooped to get dressed, and, Lord have mercy, she couldn't seem to tear her eyes off of him.

But he pulled on his boxers and pants, dressing quickly, and she had no choice but to do the same.

"Speaking of your mother, she'll have a heart attack when

we show up at the press conference with my hair all knotted and my clothes wrinkled." Paige tried to smooth down her wild hair, then her shirt and skirt, but it was useless. Her current look screamed, "Yes, I camped out in the woods and made love to the hottest cowboy in the world!" But she didn't regret it. His mother could string her up by her toenails and she still wouldn't regret it.

He rested his hands on her shoulders and gazed down at her. "You don't have to come with me. If you're worried."

His concern was sweet, but they'd crossed over to another dimension last night and Gracie had to know. Paige had to send her own message. "I'm good. I can take whatever your mother dishes out." She'd taken crap from her own parents for years. And she learned it was best to face it head-on. Besides, she could at least attempt to smooth things over with Gracie. For Ben's sake. "Come on." She tugged him toward the path that led back to the lodge. "We'd better hurry. You're on in ten."

Hand in hand, they raced up the hill, past the pool, up the steps all the way to the lodge's back doors.

With Ben right behind her, she plowed through into the sitting room. Stopped cold. Everyone was there. And she did mean everyone. Gracie and Kevin sat on the leather couches. Julia was positioned at the other side of the coffee table. Sawyer leaned up against the wall looking very cop-like in that crisp blue uniform. Avery sat in a chair staring at the floor. Bryce stood near the phone, arms crossed, scowl in place. He didn't look happy. "Where the hell have you been?"

"Yes, Benjamin." Gracie rose. "Where have you been all night?"

Ben still wore his calm expression. "We were out." He draped an arm around her and stood all cool and casual, even while the blood swooshed through her ears. She tried to avoid the murderous look on his mother's face.

"Technically we're adults and we don't have to answer to any of you," Ben said, smiling down at her.

She tried to smile back but her lips were temporarily out of order.

It was easy for Ben to stand there like this was no big deal but she watched her boss swipe a hand down his face. Something he only did when he was trying to rein in his temper. Sure enough, his jaw bulged like he wanted to refute Ben's claim then and there, and tell them that they sure as hell did have to answer to him, but Avery scurried over to him and clasped Bryce's hand in hers. She gave him a look that told him to mind his own business, then led him toward the kitchen. "Come on, love. We still haven't finished our coffee."

Bryce didn't move.

Paige held her breath, but after one more stormy glare at them, he followed his wife without another word.

Phew. She'd have to remember to send Avery a thank-you note later.

"All right, people." Ben scrubbed his hands together. "Let's get this thing going. Is everything set up outside?"

Tension still clogged the room, but his campaign director jumped into action, sidestepping her and taking Ben by the elbow to lead him away.

"Here're your talking points," Kevin said briskly. "Now let's get you changed." He escorted him across the room. She couldn't hear anything the director said, but Ben didn't look too happy, if the frantic wave of his arms was any indication. They disappeared around a corner.

"I should go help with crowd control," Sawyer said, heading for the door.

Crowd control? Paige edged to the window and peered through the curtains. The parking lot was full.

"So..." Gracie marched over to her, back as straight as a two-by-four, eyes icy, and mouth curled into a counterfeit smile. "Won't you join us for the press conference?"

"Mother." Julia wheeled herself over. "I'm sure she has more important things to do than hang out and give Ben an audience."

"Don't be ridiculous, Julia. I'm sure Paige is interested in Ben's political career." Even though the woman couldn't have been more than five-foot-four, somehow she always managed to look down on everyone. "Right, Ms. Harper?"

Something told her there was more behind the request, that Gracie was setting a trap, but what choice did she have? "Of course. I'd love to stay and support him."

"Wonderful." Gracie curled her fingers around Paige's shoulder. It wasn't a warm touch, not by any stretch. It was a touch that said, *I will tell you where to go, where to stand, how to blow your nose...*

"Kevin," Gracie called.

The man jogged back into the room. "Yeah?"

"Why don't you find Julia a seat where the press can get her picture with Ben?" she suggested.

"Sure." He lumbered back to them and took the handles of Julia's chair, pushing her in the direction Ben had gone.

Which left Paige and Gracie. Alone. *Well, this is awkward...*

"We should find a place to watch, as well." Gracie guided her out the front doors.

When they stepped outside, Paige stopped. There were people everywhere. Members of the press stationed all along the front deck, their cameras ready. Oh, god. She backed up a step, looked down at her clothes. They were wrinkled and dirty. And her hair...holy moly. What would all of these people think of her?

"Here." Gracie pulled her to a stop about fifteen feet from where the podium sat on the porch. "This will be perfect. We can hear everything that's going on, but we won't steal the spotlight."

"Mmmm hmmm," she answered, but she wasn't paying attention to Gracie because Ben was taking long strides up to the podium. He'd changed into a suit, and his hair had been neatly gelled into place. Chaos erupted then, flashes and a cacophony of questions.

"Mr. Noble, can you tell us what happened at the restaurant last night?"

"Who beat you up?"

"Who's the mystery girl you were seen with?"

Oh, no. This was bad. So bad. She stole a sideways glance at Gracie, but shockingly, the woman simply stood tall and proud, the perfect picture of a proud mother. She didn't seem the least bit upset about last night's brawl.

Weird...

"Thanks for coming out here, everyone." Ben leaned into the mic and pasted on some smile she didn't recognize. Reporters shouted more questions, but he raised his hand to quiet them.

"First, I'd like to make a brief statement about last night." Paige waited for him to seek her out, to glance her way and smile, but he didn't. He looked like a statue, standing tall and straight, perfectly posed.

"Last night, I was enjoying dinner with my sister when I noticed an altercation at another table."

Wait. Altercation? She'd hardly call Luke's paw on her an altercation. It probably would've become an altercation if he hadn't interfered, but still...that felt exaggerated, somehow.

"I grew concerned for the woman at the table..."

Woman. No mention of her name. No mention that he actually knew her. That he'd actually followed her to the restaurant, that she was actually standing twenty feet away from him...

Was he ashamed of her?

"...so I went over to make sure she was okay. When I arrived at the table..."

Arrived at the table? That didn't even sound like him!

"...I discovered the man had consumed too much alcohol. When I offered to drive his date home, he gave me a pretty strong right hook to the face."

No. Paige shook her head. That's not what happened at all!

"What happened then, Mr. Noble?" One of the reporters shouted.

Ben held off in a dramatic pause—he was obviously very skilled at this. Very skilled at a lot more than she'd realized.

"Well..." He delivered one hell of a humble-guy shrug. "Honestly, I felt bad for him."

"What?" She gasped. He did not!

"He passed out, so I made sure he got home. It seemed like the right thing to do." He half shrugged like this was totally his gig, like noble deeds were just another day in the ordinary life of Benjamin Hunter Noble III. Paige crossed her arms and tried to breathe normally. Well, wasn't he a regular superhero?

Murmurs buzzed through the crowd, and weren't they all impressed? Who wouldn't be? Some jerk had messed up his face and what does good the senatorial candidate do? He gives the man a ride home, keeps the street safe from another drunk driver like some kind of cowboy savior.

Fake. It was all so fake. Color seeped into her cheeks. She was an idiot. Such. An. Idiot.

Gracie leaned close. "This is absolutely the best thing that could have happened for him right now."

The best thing? Instead of warmth and tingles, her body felt sticky hot. Gross. "What do you mean?"

"If it hadn't been for that scene at the restaurant, the media wouldn't love him so much right now." She looked at her son with blatant admiration. "Thank you, Paige. You have no idea what this will do for us at the polls."

Paige blinked because the anger was breaking apart, crumbling into a deepening sadness that stung her eyes. She couldn't give a damn about the polls. This was her life. Not some stupid publicity stunt. She gazed at Ben standing there so at ease with the crowd. How could she have been so stupid? His life was one big publicity stunt. And it always would be.

"This was a mistake," she whispered. Another huge mistake.

Gracie didn't seem to hear. For once her plastic face looked genuinely happy. "Benjamin is a wonderful politician. Don't you think?"

The sting in her eyes blurred everything—the crowd, the lodge. "I have to go." She stumbled away from Gracie, ballet flats pounding the porch as heavy as if she were wearing boots. She couldn't cry in front of his mother. She couldn't look at her, knowing how foolish everyone must think she was. She didn't belong with someone like him. She couldn't live the way he lived. Always pretending, always spinning everything to her advantage. She wouldn't survive the questions, the cameras, the constant scrutiny.

"We'll see you in a little while," Gracie called from behind her. "I'm looking forward to our river trip."

She pretended not to hear, escaping back into the lodge without turning around. Once inside, she headed straight for the kitchen.

* * *

Pausing outside the kitchen door, Paige swiped the tears off her cheeks and inhaled deeply. Five minutes. She had to pretend to be fine for five minutes until she found someone to drive her to her car, which still sat at the restaurant. Then she could go home and cry in the shower. Easing in long breaths, she tried to soothe the pain in her chest as she pushed open the door.

Bryce, Avery, Ruby, and Elsie all sat at the island chatting, sipping their coffee. The room silenced when she walked in.

"Paige!" Elsie bounced up from her stool and ran to greet her.

"Want some coffee?" Ruby asked, already retrieving a mug.

"Nope," she belted out cheerfully. She could tell by Bryce's hard stare at the opposite wall that he had a pretty good idea what had happened between her and Ben last night. But she couldn't let him think that. So she marched over to him, holding her head high. "I'm sorry we were so late this morning," she said, forcing herself to maintain eye contact.

"Don't worry about it, Paige." Avery's smile said she wanted details later. But she'd never tell. No one could ever know. She grinned at Bryce. "Just so you know, nothing happened between Ben and me." The lie pierced her.

Last night she'd thought something wonderful had happened. She'd thought she finally understood how it felt to be loved. But Ben was a good actor. Did he even mean anything he'd said? How would she ever be able to know what was real with him? Tears threatened again but she kept her smile intact. "After the scene at the restaurant, he asked if I could help him with talking points for his little speech today," she said, praying her face didn't flush and expose the truth. "So we went over to the café."

"Really?" Avery tilted her head like that wasn't exactly what she'd expected to hear.

"Yep," she chirped. "We figured he could spin this whole thing into something that would help him in the polls." Because that's what his job demanded. Spinning everything that happened in his life to put himself in the best possible light. That's what his job would always demand. And she wanted nothing to do with it.

"Huh." Bryce's lips dipped into a thoughtful frown. "Didn't realize that. Sorry if I seemed a little pissed off."

Casually, she sipped the coffee Ruby had set in front of her, making an extra effort to look from one face to the next, still smiling. "By the time we'd finished, it was so late, I let him crash in the apartment above the kitchen."

"Wait. There's nothing going on between you two?" Avery demanded, her blue eyes narrowed with suspicion and maybe a hint of disappointment.

Paige laughed, and, wow, it sounded so real. "God, no. A Republican senator?" She rolled her eyes. "He's so not my type." That was the truest statement she'd ever spoken. How could she have let things go that far with him?

"What a shame," Elsie murmured with a sad shake of her head.

Paige looked at Ruby, and, judging from her friend's sad, soft smile, she saw right through the whole act. She let her eyes confirm what Ruby already seemed to know. "Can you give me a ride back to my car?" she asked her friend, barely holding her voice together.

"Definitely." Ruby slipped the apron over her head and left it on the counter.

"I'll be back in an hour to get the trailers loaded," Paige told Bryce, then raised her hand in a happy wave. "See you soon. Can't wait for the trip," she gushed.

Then, before the threatening tears gathered, she followed Ruby out the door.

CHAPTER TWENTY-FOUR

Leaving the podium behind, Ben didn't even bother to turn and give that one last charismatic wave to the crowd the way he'd been trained. Kev had a point that introducing Paige to the media would only make her life harder, but the whole speech had felt all wrong, especially knowing Paige stood there watching. Withholding certain details from the media had never bothered him before, but somehow she put everything in a different light.

He'd wanted to show her off. Hell, he'd wanted to tell everyone he was falling in love with this brave, beautiful girl. He'd wanted to tell them all that she was tenacious and smart, that she wanted to change people's lives.

And she would. No doubt about that. When Paige wanted something, nothing stopped her. That much was obvious. That was one of the things he loved most about her. That and her enticing body . . .

Searching her out, he walked the length of the front deck before turning to head inside.

Compared to Paige, what good was he doing, really? Standing up there and giving speeches. What good did that do Julia? Nothing even close to what Paige had done for her in one morning of horseback riding. Somehow she'd taken the pain in her past and used it to do something important. He thought he could, too, being a senator. But standing up in front of the media sure didn't make him feel the way he'd felt when he saw Julia riding, when he saw her smile and laugh and savor every moment.

Paige had done that. She'd made Julia come alive again. And he loved her for it.

He might not be able to tell the media that, but he had to at least tell her. Pausing at the edge of the deck, he glanced around. Where'd she run off to, anyway?

"Benjamin." Gracie approached him wearing a wide, fake smile that showcased her dental implants.

"Where'd Paige go?" he demanded. Even the sound of her name gave him that kicked-in-the-gut feeling. Nerves and pure excitement. Nothing better. Couldn't remember a woman giving him that feeling before. A Grand Champion steer, maybe, but not a woman.

"Why, I'm not sure where she is," his mother drawled, looking around like she'd misplaced her sweet tea. But Gracie's eyes always gave her away. They widened into the same look Julia had worn when she'd crashed the tractor into the barn when she was seven.

"Mother," he ground out. "Where is she?"

"She said she had to get going," his mother lied. Because whenever she lied, her lips twitched in the corners, but he always called her bluff.

"What'd you say to her?"

"You were wonderful up there, Benjamin." She leaned to the side to see past his shoulder. "Wasn't he, Kevin? Brilliant. The press ate it up!"

Kev now stood behind him. It was like an ambush. "She's right. That was quite the save, Ben." Kev whacked him on the back. "The local Dallas affiliates all carried it. Not sure about Houston, but it doesn't matter. Can't wait to see the new numbers."

"Great." Who cared about the damn press conference? "Where'd Paige go? Why'd she leave?" He glanced at his sister, who had wheeled herself up behind Kev.

"I'll give you one guess," she said, glaring at their mother.

Gracie looked away as though enjoying the scenery, so Ben turned to Kev. "What's going on?"

"Wow. It's getting late." Kev turned and hoofed it across the porch. "I'd better get packed. We're meeting at ten-thirty for the trip, right?" Without waiting for an answer, he jogged down the steps. "See everyone soon."

Coward. Ben narrowed his eyes at Gracie and posted his hands on his hips so she'd know he meant business. "Where is she?"

"I don't know," his mother responded, and this time she wasn't lying. "That's the honest truth, Benjamin. She simply left."

She must've left for a reason, but he was wasting time trying to drag the truth out of Gracie. He'd have to ask Paige what happened.

Without another word, he booked it down the porch steps and followed the dirt road to the boat sheds where they stored all of the rafts. Maybe she was getting things ready for the trip...

He peeked inside. Deserted. Huh. If he didn't know better, he'd think she was avoiding him.

Not knowing where else to look, he stopped into the office and pounded on Bryce's door.

"Yeah?" came from inside.

He pushed it open. "You seen Paige anywhere?"

"Sure." Bryce was sitting behind his desk, Moose by his side. He looked up from his computer screen. "I saw her about twenty minutes ago. In the kitchen. She asked Ruby to give her a ride to her car."

Okay. So maybe she wanted to go home and change, but wouldn't she have at least waited to say good-bye? Wasn't she still thinking about last night as much as he was?

Ben stepped inside Bryce's office and closed the door. "Did she seem okay?"

His friend shrugged. "Sure. Why?"

"I thought she'd stick around. After the press conference." Not that he'd tell Bryce why without her permission. "Did she say anything?"

"Guess she felt like she had to explain herself for last night," Bryce said. "But I get it. She was helping you out."

Huh. That was an interesting way to summarize their night together. He sank into the chair in front of Bryce's desk. "What'd you mean she was 'helpin' me out?' "

"You know." He looked at him like he was stupid. "Helping you write the script for your press conference."

"*What?*" Where'd he get that idea? "What the hell are you talking about?"

Frustration colored Bryce's face. "Did you two hang out at the café last night to work on your talking points or not?"

His mouth opened, but he didn't know what to say. Is that what Paige had told him? Was she worried about getting fired or something?

"Paige said you were at the café all night," Bryce repeated, looking the slightest bit pissed off.

Best not to answer any questions without talking to her first. "Look, I just need to talk to her," he said, standing. If she didn't want anyone to know, he wouldn't be the one to share, even though it was hard keeping it to himself.

"She said she'd be back in an hour," Bryce said, refocusing on his computer screen. "We've got a lot to do before the trip."

"Sure. Okay." He'd have to catch her before everyone else met. Hopefully, he'd be able to track her down. "Thanks, Walker. Guess I'll see ya soon." He started to leave.

"Hey, Noble," Bryce called.

He stepped back into the office.

Bryce leveled him with an intense glare. "I've got a favor to ask you. Don't want things to be awkward, but seeing as how Paige said you're not her type, I don't suppose it will be."

The words knocked the wind out of him. "She said that?"

"Yeah. In the kitchen."

Not her type? He wasn't her type? That wasn't what she'd told him last night...

"I need you to report back on the trip," Bryce said, leaning over his desk.

"Report back?"

"Yeah. Tell me how things went. How she did. We've gotten some complaints about Paige."

Some weird defensive heat pounded his forehead. Was Bryce implying she was incompetent? "From what I've seen, she's a professional."

"I didn't say she wasn't." Bryce shot him a simmer-down look. "She's been talking about this therapy program—"

"And she'd be damn good at it," he shot back. He couldn't stop himself. Why'd it feel like Bryce had Paige under the microscope?

His friend looked away. "We're running some numbers, looking into insurance and all that. But I'm not convinced she's ready to take it on."

"She's ready." He sat across from Bryce. "Trust me. I couldn't believe it when we took J out. She was a total professional."

"I need to know if anything happens on the trip," Bryce said, dismissing his arguments. "If you see any red flags or anything."

"Sure. I'll let you know." He didn't have to worry. Nothing would happen. Paige had already proven to him she could handle anything.

"I need unbiased feedback." Bryce's frown revealed that he knew something was up between him and Paige. "I would've asked Gracie, but I had a feeling that'd go south quick."

"Yeah. She doesn't need help picking on Paige." Hopefully his warning had remedied that situation. But something about Gracie's odd behavior earlier told him he hadn't made a dent in her determination.

He popped out of the chair. Man, he had to find Paige before they went on this trip. "If you see her, tell her I'm looking for her."

Bryce went back to his computer screen. "Will do."

* * *

Ruby pulled over the car and parked behind Paige's Subaru, which still sat a few blocks down from Elevation 8,000. "So he lied to the media?" she asked, slipping the car into park.

"Not exactly." Technically, he hadn't lied; he'd only omitted critical facts from the story.

"Maybe he was trying to protect you." Ruby rolled down

their windows as if she knew they'd be there for a while. "Seriously, Paige. He's so into you. It's obvious. Maybe he was worried you didn't want him to tell the world about you. Talk about being in the spotlight."

"Exactly." She turned to look at her friend. "Can you imagine dealing with that all the time?" Last night, Ben had made it sound so simple, but nothing about a relationship with him would be simple. What? Did he expect that she'd up and move to Washington, DC, when he won the election? The thought of living in a crowded, polluted city made her shudder. If only she'd been more rational last night...

"You sure you're not scared of a relationship?" Ruby asked, tilting her head in a way that invited Paige to spill her guts. "From the sound of it, you two had quite the amazing night."

Right on cue, her cheeks blazed. Amazing didn't begin to describe it...

"Trust me, Paige. I get the whole fear thing." Her friend's head bobbed in a sympathetic nod. "I understand it better than you realize." The weight in the words hinted at empathy, at the secrets that she kept. "But if he's as perfect as he sounds, then all of that might be worth it." A dreamy smile made her green eyes glisten. "I mean, he remembered what *wine* you drank the night you met."

"Yeah. That blew me away," she admitted. "But I can't do it, Ruby. I couldn't love both sides of him." The Ben she'd spent the night with, yes. She could fall in love with him. But not the Ben who'd stood in front of the cameras. "It's easier to cut it off now. Before things go further." Before she gave him her heart and he broke it. She couldn't do that again. There'd be nothing left.

"You slept with him," her friend reminded her. "How much further—?"

A siren whined behind them and cut her off. Red and blue lights flashed across the car's interior.

Ruby's hands froze on the steering wheel as she looked in her rearview mirror. "Oh, no. Paige. There's a cop," she whispered, like they sitting there smoking crack instead of having a normal conversation.

"Relax." Paige looked around and spotted the NO PARK-ING sign they tended to post in tricky spots all over Aspen. The city had to pay the bills somehow. "We weren't supposed to park here, that's all. No biggie."

But Ruby's face had paled. "This is not good. This is really not good."

Good god, hadn't the girl ever gotten a speeding ticket? A warning? She hadn't pegged Ruby for the goody-goody type. "It'll be fine." She waved her off. A parking ticket was nothing to panic about, and this definitely wasn't *her* first rodeo with the law. "The cops here get bored." She grinned to put Ruby at ease. "But you're gorgeous, so we'll probably get off with a warning."

Ruby didn't look amused. "No, you don't understand," she whimpered. "I can't get a ticket."

"Why—?"

"Mornin'." Sawyer ducked his head toward Ruby's window.

Paige let out a breath. She had no idea why Ruby was so panicked, but at least it was only Sawyer. He was harmless.

"How's it goin', ladies?" he asked, like he'd fully expected Paige and Ruby to be sitting there.

Ruby sat statuesque, hands still positioned firmly at ten o'clock and two o'clock.

"Hi, Sawyer," Paige said quickly, to compensate for her friend's obvious fear. "What's up?"

"Ben was looking for you at the ranch," he said, even

though his eyes kept drifting back to Ruby, but the woman stared straight ahead as though watching a horror movie.

Paige's heart did a flip at the thought of Ben looking for her. *That* would have to stop. "Is that why you pulled us over?" she asked hoping to move this along for Ruby's sake.

"This isn't a legal parking spot." Sawyer pointed to the No Parking sign a few feet in front of the car.

"Yeah. Sorry about that. Ruby was giving me a ride back to my car." After a serious walk of shame...

Ignoring her, Sawyer leaned down, resting his bulging forearms on the edge of the window. "Hey, Ruby. I've been meaning to tell you...you make the best chocolate chip cookies I've ever tasted. Don't tell Aunt Elsie I said that."

Paige fought a smile. Sawyer obviously had a thing for Ruby. He knew exactly who he was pulling over.

Except the feeling didn't seem to be mutual. Ruby's face went from white to pink. Her head turned slowly to face Sawyer, like it was on a crank. "Mmmm hmmm," she murmured, staring at him like he was a big, ugly black widow.

"So, Sawyer," Paige said, stealing the spotlight before he figured out something was up. "You're not going to give us a ticket or anything, are you?"

"Of course not." He studied Ruby's face carefully. "But is everything okay? Anything I can help with?"

Her friend looked like she was two seconds away from bursting into tears. Or throwing up? The poor woman. Paige suddenly had an overwhelming urge to rescue her. "Everything's great. Ruby was giving me some relationship advice." She clamped a hand on her friend's shoulder until the woman smiled and nodded.

"Does it have anything to do with Noble?" Sawyer asked innocently.

"I don't think that's any of your business," she said as nicely as possible.

Sawyer only grinned. "I'll let you two ladies get back to it, then." He straightened. "Oh, wait." Leaning in, he looked Ruby over again, his gaze trailing down her body and back up. "Noticed you have North Carolina plates."

Paige actually heard her friend swallow.

"How long have you been in town?" he asked in that official police officer tenor.

"A couple of months," she choked out.

His smile brought out the left dimple that had women all over town fanning themselves. "You'll get that taken care of soon, right?"

"Mmmm hmmm." She cranked her head away from him, staring out the windshield again.

"I'll help her," Paige promised.

"All right, then. See you ladies around." Gravel crunched under his boots as he walked away.

As soon as he was gone, Ruby closed her eyes, shoulders rising and falling with frantic breaths.

"What the hell was that about?" Paige asked, then reined in her tone so she didn't sound so brash. "I mean, what are you so afraid of?"

Ruby peered into the rearview mirror and smoothed her red hair back into place. "I'm not scared," she insisted, her voice full of steel. "I'm focused right now, Paige. On rebuilding my life. I don't want any distractions." Her head tipped back against the headrest. "And someone like Sawyer could be a serious distraction."

"That makes sense." She got it. Some things weren't worth giving up for a man.

Ruby's gaze drifted back to the rearview mirror like she was looking behind her, watching for a disaster. "Anyway.

You should get home so you can get ready for the trip. Bryce'll kill you if you're late."

"I guess so." She glanced at her watch. Only had a half hour until she had to load the boats. "But let's go out Friday," she said to Ruby. Because the woman obviously needed friends as much as she did. "I'll invite Avery and we can make it a girls' night." She might never know what had happened to Ruby, she might not be able to help her, but she could be a friend.

"I'd love that." Her smile erased the fear that hid in her eyes.

After saying good-bye and getting out of the car, Paige turned to watch Ruby drive away. She was rebuilding her life. And in some ways, Paige was building hers for the first time. Everything she had—every ounce of energy and hope and strength and time she possessed had gone toward building the therapy program. Ruby was right. Building something took focus. She didn't need any distractions, either. Especially a distraction she couldn't have a future with.

Paige walked to her car and slid into the driver's seat, then rolled down the windows. She inhaled deeply, feeling the sun on her face, the chill of the high-altitude air. Since he'd arrived in Aspen, Ben had been one big interruption.

But she couldn't let one mistake with him steer her away from her goal.

CHAPTER TWENTY-FIVE

After searching the whole damn property, Ben sprinted to the boat sheds, but, unfortunately, everyone else had already made it there. Bryce, Gracie, Julia, Kev, and yes, the one who mattered most.

Paige bent over the trailer, hands working on some kind of complicated knot that cinched the rafts down.

Whoa. Bryce was right. She'd gone home to change. The red swimsuit top that looked like a sports bra and black board shorts stopped him dead in his tracks. Son of a pistol, look at those abs. Dented and carved. Not skinny. Curvy. And hot damn, those weren't her only curves; he knew that for a fact.

Steering clear of the others, he approached her and whistled. "Just when I think you couldn't possibly get any hotter..."

Her head stayed low, hands working furiously to tighten the knot.

"Uh…" He leaned closer. "Is everything okay?"

She straightened and looked at him with cool eyes, like he was a complete stranger. "Fine. Excuse me." She slipped past him and hurried to the open van door.

He followed. "Can I help with anything?"

"Nope." Her eyes continued to avoid him.

"Did I do something to piss you off?" Only she didn't seem mad. She seemed…indifferent?

"Nope," she said like a damn parrot.

"What the hell happened?" he demanded. "What about last night? I thought…" they had some kind of connection. "Is this about the press conference?" Was she mad about what he'd said?

She finally stopped working. A sigh huffed out. "I can't talk about this right now. Okay? I have a lot of work to do."

"But—"

"I can't have any distractions. We'll talk later. Did you bring your bags down?" Seemingly intent on avoiding any meaningful conversation, Paige bounded away and loaded a duffel into the back of the van.

"Not yet." What did that have to do with anything? He assessed her with a long stare, taking in her rigid movements, her tight lips. Lips that had clung to his earlier that morning, thank you very much.

"I need your bags," she intoned. "I have to finish packing."

Like a chump, he hiked back up to the cabin, snatched his dry sack off his dresser, and hiked back. By the time he got to the van, Paige had everyone gathered around her.

"Benjamin!" Gracie stretched out her arms to greet him. He looked her over. "I see someone went shopping," he said, taking in her attire—blue dry pants and long-sleeved swim shirt, with the latest in high-end river shoes on her feet.

"I had to prepare for the trip." Gracie smoothed down her

shirt. "I was hoping for something in purple. Blue simply isn't my color."

"First-world problems," he muttered, Paige's apathy still gnawing at him. Like they couldn't afford to have a five-minute conversation.

"If everyone will give me your attention," Paige called. "We have to get through the safety talk before we can leave." Her face had turned to stone.

This ought to be fun.

In a professional monotone, she launched into the safety speech. What to do if the boat flips or wraps. The proper river swimming position. Paddle commands. All stuff he'd heard before. Nothing he'd ever had to use on any rafting trip he'd ever been on. Might as well take some time to investigate how he'd managed to screw things up with her. Only one person could help him with that.

He shuffled until he stood close to Julia, then lowered next to her. "Hey. Any idea what's up with Paige?" he whispered.

"No," she whispered back like they were in class and she was afraid they'd get caught talking. "But Gracie dragged her off to watch your performance this morning. I tried to run interference, but she had Kevin keep me away."

Of course it had something to do with Gracie. Of course.

"Pretty sure our fabulous mother took her down the stairs so I couldn't follow. I have no idea what she said to her."

He was almost afraid to ask . . . "How long did they talk?"

"Only a few minutes," J whispered with a sympathetic look. "Then Paige left. She looked upset, Ben. Really upset."

Oh, boy. That didn't bode well for him at all. He stood upright and shook his head. All that work to get her to give him a chance. Five minutes with Gracie and now he'd have to start all over.

"Okay!" Paige clapped her hands. "Looks like we're all loaded up. You can go ahead and climb into the van." She smiled at Gracie, then Kev, then Julia, but when he scooted past her to help J get into the van, she crossed her arms and looked away.

That was just dandy.

Kev and his mother climbed into the back row. Ben lifted J and settled her into the middle seat. Then he grabbed her chair, purposely brushing Paige's shoulder.

She jolted away like he'd shocked her.

Well, it wouldn't be the first time. And if he had anything to say about it, it wouldn't be the last, either. Though next time he'd prefer it to be in a more intimate setting.

When he got back into the van, he could've sat by J. Easily. But where was the fun in that? Instead, he squished into the first row next to Paige.

She rolled her eyes and turned her head, chin tipped up.

Bryce started the van. Country music twanged. Gracie started some boring conversation with Kev about the latest polls.

Perfect opportunity for him to get some answers. He pressed his lips close to Paige's ear. "What did I do?"

She stared straight ahead. "It's not what you did, Ben. It's who you are," she whispered back.

"What's that supposed to—"

"Once we get on the river…" Instead of giving him a chance to finish, she shifted to face the others, her ponytail flipping across his face. "…Shooter and I will unload the boats," she called in that formal voice. "You all should take time to put on your sunscreen."

"Really?" he growled. "You're not even gonna give me a chance to talk?"

"Hush, Benjamin." Gracie shushed him. "Paige is giving

us important information. Go on." She practically scooted to the edge of her seat like the suspense was killing her.

Yeah, right. She just didn't want him to find out what she'd said to set Paige off. Again.

"You'll also want to make sure your river shoes are strapped on tight." Paige talked over his head. "And that sunglasses are secured or put away."

Fine. Ben folded his hands. He'd have to be patient, wait for a lull so he could take another shot at dragging it out of her. She had to shut up, eventually.

Except she didn't. She went on and on. And on. And on. All about the history of the Roaring Fork River. The history of rafting the river. Blah. Blah. Blah. She talked until Bryce pulled into a small dirt parking lot right on the riverbank.

The van stopped and before he could even blink, Paige threw open the door and took off like a shot, leaving him in a confused wake. What the hell had happened? What did she mean, it's who he was?

And, more importantly, what could he do to fix it?

* * *

This. This is where she belonged. Setting up the boats on the riverbank, the rocky sand exfoliating the rough skin of her heels, the sun beating down on her shoulders and her cheeks, heating her to the point of perspiration.

Stein Park was the put-in for all of their Upper Roaring Fork trips, and it never failed to deliver that sense of anticipation that simmered now, a low rumbling in Paige's belly. The park itself wasn't much to look at, only one-and-a-half acres of open space managed by the city. A small dirt parking lot, an emerald green meadow that stretched and rolled down to the riverbank. Pretty standard for Aspen. But to

Paige, what set the place apart was the way the Roaring Fork River flowed beneath the bridge and wound around the bend, the opening to the mystery of what lay ahead. To her, the river was a lullaby. Soft, white noise flowing into her eardrums, a satisfying swoosh that welcomed her into this world. The *real* world.

But she knew from experience it wasn't a safe world.

She'd rafted this stretch of river maybe five hundred times, and no two trips ended up exactly the same. As beautiful as it was, the river was also a fickle schizophrenic. Depending on the rain and the snowpack and the general aligning of the planets, the boulders that made up the rapids could shift and alter the currents so that, half the time, you didn't know what the hell you were up against. Sometimes there'd be a new strainer, a jumble of logs, clogging one route so you'd have to find another. Sometimes a new sleeper—rock under the surface— would snag the floor of the boat. Seriously. There were days the river was a minefield.

Of course, every run down the river also depended heavily on the paddle crew. Paige sized up hers for about the hundredth time. Gracie Noble stood by the van, crouched in front of a side-view mirror, teasing her hair with a pick. Seriously? It already reached the clouds so it wasn't like she could get it much higher. The woman looked like some kind of geriatric actress preparing to shoot a Viagra commercial.

Then there was the campaign director, Kevin, who, judging from his pale skin, hadn't seen the sun since...well, ever. Upper-body strength didn't exactly seem to be his virtue. He, of course, stood with Ben, tweeting yet another ridiculous selfie for their phony campaign.

And Julia, who had perched her chair at the very edge of the river and was staring at it like it held the key to all of her dreams.

She had half a mind to only take Ben's sister and leave the rest of them behind. They'd have a great time, she and Julia, and she wouldn't have to listen to Gracie's blathering or Kevin's tweeting or Ben's phony speeches.

But she wouldn't let any of them ruin this trip.

Lucky for her, today happened to be a river day, and the river, with its soft swoosh and flowing grace, always revived her. Mustering a smile, she jogged down to where Ben had parked his sister's chair, right at the edge of the river so the water could lap over her bare toes.

"Hey, Julia. You ready for this?"

"Paige! Thanks so much for letting me come!" She leaned over and reached out to the water with her fingertips. "I can't believe I get to go whitewater rafting. I can't believe it!" Her dark eyes sparkled even more than normal, walnut-shaped globes of pure anticipation.

Paige leaned close to her. "You're actually the only one I want to bring," she whispered. "Don't tell anyone that."

Julia laughed, a twinkling sound that ratcheted up Paige's smile.

This was what the trip was about. That was what she was about. She had to keep reminding herself that, especially when Ben shot her those tempting glances only he could pull off, a mixture of predatory and wounded and completely irresistible, of course. She'd done her best to steer clear of him, but the truth was, she couldn't avoid him forever.

Now that they were about to push off, she needed his help to get Julia situated.

"The river's so beautiful." Julia gripped the wheels of her chair, pushing and pulling until she faced her.

Wow. The woman had some impressive upper-body strength. In fact, she could probably easily outpaddle Kevin. But she couldn't let Julia paddle. That was part of the deal, part of Ben's stipulation. His sister had to sit smack dab in the middle of the boat, the safest seat in the house.

"Did something happen?" Julia peered up at her. "Earlier? At the press conference? I know it's none of my business, but you looked kinda pissed off."

The bruise on her heart throbbed, but she smiled. "Nothing I can't handle." Julia didn't need to worry about it. She dealt with enough in her own life every single day. This day had to be about freedom for her.

"'Cause Ben's worried, Paige." She shaded her eyes from the blazing sun. "He thinks Gracie said something to upset you." The melodious pitch of her voice rose into a fishing expedition.

Paige ignored the implied question and focused on cinching a dry sack into the boat. "Trust me. That's not the problem." She didn't care so much what Gracie had said. It was the truth of her statement that had gotten to her. Ben's chosen profession demanded that he become a professional liar. A politician. Whoever ended up with him would live life in front of the cameras. They'd need to lie about things, too. And she couldn't. She needed freedom. She couldn't play a part like Gracie had done all those years. For so long, she'd tried to be who people needed her to be, and it had only turned her into a self-protective failure. Trying to be everything to everyone meant she would become nothing.

Julia tugged on her sleeve. "Hey, Paige—"

Gravel crunched behind them and his sister snapped her mouth shut like she was afraid she'd get caught butting in.

"Can I help you ladies with anything?" Ben asked, his voice dripping with that tempting-as-midnight-dark-chocolate drawl.

"Actually, yes." Paige refused to get lost in those eyes. They'd only make her think funny things. And she had to focus. "Can you get Julia in the boat?" She pointed at the foldable camp chair she and Shooter had secured onto the center tube of the raft.

"Wow," Julia murmured. "That's quite the seat."

"Yep." She hoped her smile didn't look as plastic as it felt. Feeling Ben's gaze burn holes through her, she tugged on the straps that held the chair in place. "It's pretty sturdy. Just remember our safety discussion."

She focused on Julia. *Don't look up.* Because Ben had moved over her. Too close. Scooting more space between them, she bent over and lifted the strap she'd rigged up in front of the chair. "It'll be a bumpy ride. You have to hold on the whole time."

"Deal," Julia said solemnly.

"All right, sis." Ben swept his sister into his arms, and even though she tried not to watch, tried not to notice the careful way he carried her with one arm secured under her arms and one secured under her knees, the scene dinged her heart. Did he have to be so kind?

Ben settled Julia into her special chair and the woman beamed the same way she had when she'd sat tall and straight like a queen on Sweetie Pie's back.

He seemed to watch his sister for a minute, which gave Paige the chance to watch him without getting caught.

Though his lips were supple and relaxed—and completely enticing—his jaw tensed and his eyes shifted back and forth from the river to Julia as if assessing the danger.

He was worried. He didn't have to say anything, she could tell. And she needed him calm and alert for this trip. "Ben," she called. "Can you help me load the cooler?"

He seemed to wake from the awful nightmare he was probably forced to relive every time he looked at his sister. "Sure. Yeah."

Paige headed for the van. His long stride caught her in a matter of steps.

"She'll be fine." She heaved open the van door. "You need to stop worrying."

"I'm not worried about Julia." He plowed his open palm against the metal, slammed the door shut, and wedged himself between her and the van, the space so tight she felt his muscles tense against her. But he didn't touch her. He only looked at her.

Her traitorous body responded with an overpowering rush, pheromones coursing through her the way they had when his hands slid up her stomach last night.

"What the hell happened, Paige?" His voice was low and rough and completely sexy.

She mentally backhanded herself. Not the time for that...

"We made love, for god's sake. Now you won't even talk to me?" His face inched closer. "I didn't peg you for the overdramatic manipulative type."

His eyes. Stop looking at those delicious lips and focus on his eyes, damn it. Why was that so hard? She nudged him out of the way with her shoulder and opened the door again, dragged the cooler out so there'd be a barrier between them. Thank goodness it was filled with ice. She might need that to cool herself down later.

"I realized something." She matched his anger in her own expression. "You're different in front of the cameras, Ben. You lied. You acted like you didn't even know me before. Like I was a stranger to you. Like you hadn't been *stalking* me at the restaurant."

"I wasn't stalking you," he shot back, face all red and passionate. "If I told them the real story, they'd be all over you. I went along with it to protect you."

"That's just it." Her heart got that sinking feeling, like it was stuck in quicksand. As much as her head knew it was best, her damn heart hated to think that he'd never touch her again, never kiss her the way he'd kissed her last night. But no. *No.* She always deferred to her brain when it came to things like this. Her heart was too fragile. She couldn't risk it. "I don't want that, Ben. I don't want to live my life dodging cameras, worrying about what everyone thinks of me." She'd worried about it far too long, though she never would've let anyone know. And now she only had regrets.

"Paige..."

God, the way he said her name, like he *knew* her, like he'd do anything—wrangle a rabid bull or whatever it was cowboys spent their days doing—for her, if he thought it would make any difference.

"I know it sucks, but that's not how it is all the time." He threaded his fingers through hers, the simple touch feeding her hesitation. "We can figure it out. How to have both..."

"Ben!" Kev yelled from the shoreline. "Come on, man! Time's a tickin'! Let's get a few shots of you and Julia for the blog."

And there it was, the only evidence she needed to refute his claim. There'd always be another shot. Another tweet. Another blog entry.

Ben squeezed his eyes shut.

Before he opened them, before he could sway her with another argument, she withdrew her hand from his, grasped the cooler's handle, and dragged it away. Good old Kevin had made her point for her.

There was nothing more to say.

CHAPTER TWENTY-SIX

Ben ran a hand over the god-awful orange life preserver that squeezed his upper body and stared at the swirling river a few feet away.

An intermittent pain pulsed inside his chest like a warning flare. Call it intuition, a premonition, a gut feeling. Whatever the hell it was, he didn't like it.

Of course, it could have something to do with the fact that nothing had gone right that morning. Not with him and Paige, anyway.

Paige. He fought back the squeeze in his throat with a long inhale.

She stood on a rock in front of the group, her goddess body backlit by the sun. She'd started the infamous whitewater rafting safety talk, but he was having a hard time focusing. Between her tight swim top and the weird churning in his gut, he'd hardly heard a word she said. *Focus.* Sure, he'd rafted all over in Canada and the North-west, but he'd never had his disabled sister on a trip with him. As many times as he'd heard the "talk" he should have it memorized, but nothing had ever gone wrong. He'd never been worried about himself swimming a rapid, but Julia...

"If the boat hits a rock sideways, it might wrap or flip." Paige demonstrated with the inflated miniature raft she held above her head. "If that happens, we'll all end up in the water."

Ben glanced at Julia. His mouth went dry. She couldn't swim through whitewater. Even with the life vest, the current could pull her under...

"If you fall out of the boat, point your feet downstream and steer with your arms so you don't hit rocks," Paige continued in that polite, no-nonsense voice.

The heads around him all bobbed in expectant nods, but visions of Julia bouncing off boulders in a violent current edged him closer to a panic attack. This was a bad idea. His sister didn't belong in a class-three rapid.

"By the way, it's critical that you never stand up in the river." Paige paused to look at each one of them. Well, each one except him. Apparently politicians didn't deserve a sturdy glance.

"If your foot gets stuck between the rocks, the current's strong enough to push your head under. We call that scenario a foot entrapment. It's a nasty one."

Perfect. Sweat itched on his forehead. How the hell many more scenarios were there? And why didn't he remember all of this from his other trips?

The expression on Paige's face relaxed from grim seriousness into slight concern. "If I think we're about to wrap or flip, I'll yell, 'high side.'" She tipped the toy boat on its side. "Everyone who is able should immediately move to the side that's tipping up. Hopefully, the weight will bring us back down and steady the boat."

"Hopefully?" The flesh in his throat felt like sandpaper. "Sorry, but hopefully's not gonna cut it."

Paige's lips bunched in a silent challenge. Her eyes narrowed into a cool indifference.

But hey, at least she looked at him.

"When done properly, the high side always works." She sounded like a monotone recording.

He crossed his arms. "So you've never flipped a boat?"

Julia whapped his leg. "Shut up, Ben. I want to get on the river."

He ignored his sister and stared back at Paige, matching her irritation glare for glare.

"Of course I've flipped a boat."

You idiot. She didn't have to say it. He heard it loud and clear.

"But I've never lost anyone." Her eyes locked on his and the force behind them could've stopped his heart.

"This is a team thing. We work together, do things right, we'll be fine." Her mouth went soft and turned his legs all rubbery again, damn it.

Gracie, who had been unnervingly quiet, he just realized, shuffled into the water.

"Good Lord in Heaven above! This water's colder than a well-digger's belt buckle!"

"Yeah," Paige said, as she jumped off her rock. "If it's this cold on your feet, imagine falling in."

Bryce walked through the group. "No one's gonna fall in. Right?" He eyed Paige.

"Right," Kev muttered, casting a wary glance at the water like it had the ability to reach out, grab his ankle, and pull him in.

Right. They had to work together. Which meant Paige had to communicate with him, talk to him, look at him. Maybe it wasn't too late to convince her he deserved a shot.

"Of course no one's going to fall in." Paige waded in up to her sculpted thighs and held the boat in place. "We should push off. We're already late."

He should move. He should really move. It would help if he could take his eyes off her legs...

"Ya know," Gracie drawled from behind him, "I'm thinkin' I may as well go on back to the lodge with Bryce. Meet up with y'all at the party a bit later. Would you mind, Benjamin?"

Back. Lodge. Gracie had said something to him...*Eyes off Paige's legs, chief.* He turned to his mother. "You're leaving?"

"I didn't realize the water'd be so cold. You know how my arthritis flares up in the cold..."

He had a tough time stifling a smile. Maybe things were looking up. Maybe it wouldn't be such a bad day, after all. "Fine? Are you kidding? That'd be excellent. Wonderful. The best thing that's happened since about eight-forty this morning." When he'd been lip-locked with the beauty in the sports bra swimsuit.

Did he imagine it, or did Paige's cheeks flame with a blush? Hopefully it was a blush. That meant he might still have a fighting chance with her. Lord knew things would be easier with Paige if Gracie wasn't around to muck it up again.

"Are y'all sure?" Gracie asked, but she was already out of the water.

"Yeah, it's no problem," Bryce said, but he shot Ben a dark look.

What can you do? He answered with a smirk and a shrug. Better to have her driving Bryce crazy than Paige.

"Bye, then! Y'all have fun, now, you hear?" She did her beauty-queen wave and followed Bryce back to the van.

"Okay." Paige assessed their boat. "That'll change things up. Ben, you'll be front left." She pointed to his spot, a slight glow still smoldering on her cheeks, if he wasn't mistaken.

"And we'll put Kevin front right." She waited for Kev to climb in. "Shooter and I'll take the back. Julia, you stay put and hold on. Okay?"

"Roger that," J sang happily.

Feeling the weight on his shoulders lighten, Ben climbed over the tube and took his assigned seat. He leaned over to grab his paddle off the floor and caught another great view of Paige's legs. So distracting…

The boat rocked while Paige and Shooter climbed into the back.

Ben faced forward so he could focus on something besides her tanned skin. Last thing he needed was to fall out of the boat. So it was probably a good time to check out some of the other scenery.

There was plenty of it, that was for sure. On both sides of their boat, rock-strewn slopes folded down right into the river. Rounded boulders of all shapes dotted the shoreline, separated by miniature pine and springs of aspen that dared to grow on such tenuous ground. The river sat too low to let him see much of Aspen itself, but mammoth mountains rose up on his left, catching him in a shadow that reminded him how small he really was.

Beneath him, the boat moved swiftly in the current and thudded against white-capped waves. Water splashed his face and arms. Cold glacial water that ran off the mountains and collected in the river. Good thing the sun was out.

"Let's practice some paddle commands," Paige called

over the roar of the river. "Our first rapid'll come up quick. We need to be ready."

"Right. Paddle commands," Kev said, voice an octave higher than normal. "What were those again?"

"Forward. Back. Right turn. Left turn," Ben answered just as Paige made a sound. He looked back at her and grinned. "I listen."

"Right." Her smile bordered on playful. "When I call forward, you all dig in and paddle hard." She demonstrated with her guide paddle. "Backward, lean back, plunge the blade into the water, and push."

Ben's gaze drifted down her body, lingered on the way her muscles tensed when she went through the motion.

It'd be a miracle if he didn't fall out of the boat today.

"Right turn means the left side paddles forward and those of you on the right paddle backward. Anyone want to guess what a left turn is?" Her eyes offered him an invitation.

He always did love being the teacher's pet. Especially when the teacher was such a babe. "Left turn means the right side paddles forward..." He did a few practice strokes, hopefully displaying everything his body could offer her in the process. "And the left side paddles backward."

"Right." She smiled, the real Paige smile, the one that showed her slightly crooked front teeth, the one that tugged on the corners of her eyes.

Wow. Gracie's absence definitely seemed to have improved her mood.

"Make sure you only paddle when I tell you to," she went on. "Especially in the rapids." Reaching over the side of the boat with those long, graceful arms of hers, she plunged her guide paddle into the water and pulled, turning the bow of the boat left in one effortless motion.

Her eyes shifted to him and suddenly he realized his

mouth hung open. Ah, well. Couldn't be helped. She had that effect on him. Didn't hurt to remind her that she had the power to make his jaw drop.

Her small smile and a shake of her head told him she got it, but then she was all business again. "First rapid is Entrance Exam. Class four." Droplets of water glistened against the browned skin on her shoulders and, god help him, he didn't hear what else she said.

Before he could ask her to repeat it, she and Julia started chatting. Something about J's new sandals and where she got her toes done. Which meant he could check out of the conversation for a while. He shifted and scanned the scene in front of them. The river churned and boiled, the water murky and brown. Calm for now . . .

"Say cheese." Kev snapped yet another photo of him.

"Really? Haven't you taken that same picture five times already?"

"Wanted to get that mountain behind you. Stellar shot." Kev slipped his phone back into the waterproof pouch he'd belted around his waist. It looked like a fanny pack. Very hip.

"Besides," Kev said, "the female constituency will fall all over themselves when they see you shirtless."

Paige made a gagging noise.

"Hey." Kev raised his hands. "We gotta do what we can. Thank god you work out, Ben. Every little bit helps."

Yeah. Not exactly what Paige needed to hear at the moment. Time to change the subject. "So . . ." He gave her "the eye." Never failed him before. "How bad is this first rapid?"

She shrugged. "Not too bad. Usually. Pretty straightforward run."

"Will we get wet?" Julia squealed. She was obviously enjoying herself. "I hope we get wet. The sun is so hot."

Paige laughed. God, he loved that sound.

"Wait 'til we're through the rapid. I guarantee you won't be hot after that," she said.

He'd beg to differ. As long as she sat mere feet away wearing those short shorts and tank-top bra thing, he'd be hot.

The boat floated around the bend, and almost immediately, the river started to move faster, louder. Whitecaps crested and crashed. A distant rumble thumped his eardrums. Splashing. Thrashing. Reverberating like wheels of a freight train.

"Is that the rapid?" Kev asked. "Holy shit. I think I'm gonna throw up."

Paige stacked her shoulders and stood on her toes, peering over the heads. "Yep. That'd be Entrance Exam." She plopped back down. "Relax, Kevin. You'll do great. It'll be fine because we're all gonna work together." Her eyes narrowed at Ben in a silent, *right?*

Right. Yeah. Work together. He'd do his best. He checked on Julia. Handed her the strap she was supposed to be holding on to. "Stop letting go of this," he said. It came out rougher than he intended.

"Ben's right, Julia," Paige agreed. "You need to hold on. The bumps can be pretty jarring."

Their eyes met. Hers were bright, intense. Like she'd come alive again.

J made a big show of rolling her eyes. "Yeah, yeah, yeah. I'll hold on." With a crusty look at him, she wrapped the strap around her wrist.

"Get ready." Paige shoved her feet under the rim of the boat like she wanted traction. "Paddle hard."

Ben faced forward, tightened his grip on his paddle.

"Don't forget to wait for my commands," she said over the thrashing water.

He waited. And waited. She said nothing. What the hell

was she doing? They were about to drop into the rapid and she wasn't calling any commands. He looked over his shoulder.

Her eyes were trained on the water in front of them. She had her guide stick in the river, but she was barely pushing or pulling or anything.

"Shouldn't we paddle?" he yelled.

"Wait," she replied.

He turned back around. They were about to hit a damn wall of water and they had no momentum. This was crazy. She was crazy.

The wall got closer, closer. Damn it! "Paddle! Forward!" he yelled at Kev. "Come on!"

Kev obeyed, paddling in a frenzied synchronization. Ben reached forward, pulled, leaned back. Adrenaline singed his arms. "Forward!"

"Stop!" Paige yelled. "Both of you, stop!"

But he couldn't stop. They'd never make it through without the momentum. He ignored her, kept paddling. Breaths shot out of his mouth. His muscles strained.

The boat rocked with the momentum, but they plowed through the first cresting wave with no problem.

"Woo hoo!" Julia yelled.

"Hold on, Julia!" Paige yelled. "Right turn!" She screamed. This time, he listened. The bow tracked to the right and the current caught them.

A sharp drop lurched him forward. He braced himself against the rim.

"Now forward! Hard! Hard!" Paige's yell scraped.

He paddled until his arms ached. The boat jolted and bounced, pinballing off rocks.

Julia laughed and squealed.

"Forward! Keep going!" Paige called behind him. They

bounced through the series of waves at the end, then the water calmed.

"Woo hoo!" Ben raised his hand to Kev for a high five, but the man only stared at him, wide-eyed and pale.

Fine, then. He moved to slap a high five to Paige, but she set her jaw and looked at him like he'd called her fat.

"Everything okay?" he asked, already having a pretty good feel for the answer.

She reached over the side of the boat and stabbed her paddle into the water. The bow of the boat turned to the shoreline. "Start paddling to the beach," she said. "We're gonna take a quick break."

"But our schedule..." Kev started.

Paige's heated glare shut him up. Shut all of them up, actually. Even though Ben was dying to ask...

What the hell had he done now?

CHAPTER TWENTY-SEVEN

Once they reached the shallows, Paige jumped out of the raft. "Ben, I need a word." She steadied the boat and pulled it up on the beach. "The rest of you can stay put. We'll be right back."

Without waiting for him, she trucked up a small embankment and out of earshot from the rest of the group. They didn't need to hear this.

Ben bounded up behind her. "That was amaz—"

"What the hell do you think you're doing?"

He gaped at her. "What?"

"You screwed up the whole run!" He'd put them all in danger. "You muscled right through and we totally missed the smooth run on the right."

"I don't understand..." he spat, his jaw flexed and hard. "We made it through fine."

"We hit every rock in the whole damn rapid. I practically

broke my arm trying to steer us against the current. You're lucky your sister didn't fly out of the boat!"

He got in her face. "You weren't paddling. Excuse me if I got worried."

"Damn it, Ben." She swiped the perspiration from her forehead. "I need you to trust me. I know what I'm doing."

"I do trust you." He took a step closer, looking down at her like he wanted take her in his arms and make love to her right there.

"Like hell you do." She kept her distance because one touch and it would be all over, judging from the way her body ached to be with him again. "It's time to give up this little savior quest and stop trying so hard to protect Julia. In case you haven't noticed, she's an adult. A very competent adult, from what I've seen. She doesn't need you controlling every aspect of her life."

"Me?" He laughed. "I'm the one with a control problem?"

"What's that supposed to mean?" she shot back, chest bursting at the seams with angry breaths.

"You find every excuse you can to push people away. You can't control them so you write 'em off." He smiled. He actually smiled like he thought he had her all figured out.

"You don't even know me," she seethed.

"Pretty sure I got to know you last night." He looked her body over in a blatant insinuation. "You act so damn tough but you're scared."

"I am *not* scared." But her shoulders exposed her lie, trembling in the charge of electricity that hemmed them in.

"Prove it. Give me a chance. We'll both be brave. I'll lighten up with Julia. You stop analyzing the future and go with your gut." He captured her in his arms, skin so warm against hers. "What does your gut tell you, Paige?"

To run. Her whole body wanted to run as far away from him as she could get so she didn't have to want him this bad.

"Uh, Ben!" Kev called from somewhere down below. "We really should push off. Can't be late to the party."

The distraction gave her enough space to squeak out of his hold.

She jogged down the slope but he caught her, pushed his lips close to her ear. "This isn't over."

And she knew he was right.

* * *

Paige approached the raft and ignored Julia's obvious smirk. Hopefully they blamed her red face on the sun. Ben sauntered behind her, much closer than an acquaintance would.

"You two done?" Shooter, asked obviously annoyed.

"We needed to get some things straight." At least that's what she'd intended to do, but as usual, Ben derailed her.

She waited for him to climb into the boat, then she pushed them off and claimed her seat, unable to look at him, at any of them, especially Shooter, who seemed to be taking notes on how this trip was going. Probably to report back to Bryce.

As they floated on the flat water before the next rapid, everyone chatted. Well, everyone except her. Ben glanced back in her direction periodically, but she managed to avoid eye contact.

She was actually thankful when they coasted into rougher water again. It gave her something to focus on besides him. "Next rapid is coming," she told them as she jabbed her paddle into the water to make a slight right turn and keep them in the current. "It's called Double-O-Seven. Another class four."

Ben swiped his palms down his shorts and picked up his paddle. He smiled at her, seemed to silently promise that he'd listen this time.

That smile. *Sigh.* It made her shiver even though she was boiling up in the sunlight. "Okay." She couldn't look at him. Had to focus. "This is a pretty straightforward route. Nothing fancy." As long as they all paddled together, she could even use the current to make the turns.

The boat moved faster. White water sloshed over the sides. "Let's paddle forward," she said, raising her voice above the water.

While Ben, Kevin, and Shooter dug in, she used the blade of her guide paddle to turn the bow whichever way the current pulled.

Slight right around the boulder at the top. Quick left to snake through the two boulders in the center. The boat dipped down a small drop. "Keep going! That's it! Forward!"

Water splashed in and sprayed her face, but the boat steadily moved with the current, smooth instead of jarring.

Then the whitecaps evened out, the water calmed, and they were once again on a Sunday stroll.

"I love this!" Julia laughed as she wrung out her shirt. "I'm freezing my ass off but I love this!"

Shooter dug in his dry sack and handed her a fleece. "Here, put this on over your jacket. It'll give you extra insulation."

"Thanks." She smiled at Shooter and he grinned back.

Ben moved between them to help his sister slip it over her head, but then saw Paige watching and jolted back to his seat. "Yeah. You can probably handle that yourself, huh, J?"

Her eyes widened with a surprise, but she shot him a sassy smirk. "Yep. Pretty sure I got it."

Paige couldn't fight a smile. Well, look at that. A grown

man really can change. His eyes caught hers and held them. It felt like the water was filling up her chest, scary and dangerous, but she forced her eyes to stay there. Brave. Maybe Ben was right. Maybe she needed to be brave.

"You two really need to get a room," Julia mumbled, but her eyes glimmered.

Ben seemed to ignore his sister. At least he wasn't blushing the way she was.

"Well done, back there, boss." He raised his hand to high-five her.

Ah, what the hell. She slapped his hand. His fingers clasped around hers and made her heart pump harder. With a small smile, like he knew exactly how that affected her, he let go.

"So what's next?" Kev's face drifted into view.

She tore her eyes off Ben. "Uh..." Where were they again? She glanced around, got her bearings. Right. Okay. "We've got Slaughterhouse coming up. Class four. This is one of the biggest we'll see." Not to mention, the most tricky. Hit the hole at the top wrong and you'd be up shit creek.

"Sweet," Ben said, and for some reason it made her tingle.

"This is a loud one, too," she said over the water's rising drone. "So make sure you're listening. Sometimes things in Slaughterhouse change fast. I might call a forward then a back then a turn." It all depended on how the river felt today.

They approached the bend, the current tugging on the raft faster, harder...

Here we go. Adrenaline leaked through her in that slow fervor the way it always did at the top of Slaughterhouse...

She jammed her feet between the outer tube and the floor to get some traction, but something was wrong. The floor was too soft. She stomped on it again. *Shit. Oh, shit.* This was not good. It had deflated. Instead of the water flowing out through the holes in the sides like it was supposed to, it pooled in the bottom of the boat.

Her hands shook. They had too much drag. The boat was too heavy. "Shooter," she hissed. "Get the bucket. Get this water out of here."

He scrambled to reach the bucket in the middle of the boat. "What the hell happened?" he demanded. "The floor wasn't pumped?"

"Of course I pumped the floor." She had, hadn't she? Yes. Yes. She always remembered...and it was fine when she'd gotten back in the boat after they'd stopped...

The boat stuttered and stalled, stuttered and stalled, like a car with a bad transmission.

"Damn it!" She stabbed her paddle into the water but couldn't even turn.

"What's wrong?" Ben asked.

"We're taking on water." The words burned her throat. God, this could not be happening. Not with Julia in the boat. She peered ahead. There was no time to get to the shore. They were about to drop into the rapid...

Shooter hit his knees and bailed water over the side of the boat. "It's coming in too fast," he yelled. "There's no way we'll get through this!"

"What? What the hell does that mean?" Ben growled.

"Get ready to paddle." She cranked her guide paddle against the current. "We have to get through the upper falls, then we can pull over and bail." Her voice croaked. She shot Ben a stern look. "Don't stop paddling. No matter what happens."

"Got it." He turned and crouched, ready.

"You, too, Kevin. You've gotta paddle hard."

His head bobbed in a silent nod, but he got that deer-in-the-headlights look.

"Julia," Paige wheezed. "Don't let go. You hold on to that strap."

"I've got it." She wrapped it around her wrist a few more times.

"Forward paddle!" Paige yelled.

They dropped. "Right turn! Right turn!" But instead of straightening them out, the current tossed them sideways. No! Not sideways. She fought to see through the water splashing her face.

They were headed right for the rock, the hole...

"Right turn! Right turn!" Her throat went hoarse.

Ben and Kevin fought to paddle, to pull, but the boat dragged. The floor. The damn floor!

The boat careened into the rock with a heavy thud. The left rim rose.

"High side! High side!" Paige screamed. She threw her upper body over the rim, but it was too late. They were going over.

"Come on!" Ben yelled as he climbed his way up the high side of the boat.

Kevin huddled on the floor.

"High side!" she yelled at him. Everyone. They needed everyone's weight.

Shooter pushed past her and got his hands on the rim, but then the boat spun.

Another jerk. Her body stretched and snapped like a rubber band. She went sprawling. Her kneecaps thudded into the rim in front of her. Freezing water oozed over her, splashing her cheeks, scraping her legs.

"High side!" She screamed again as she clawed the rim, but her icy hand slipped.

Powerless. She was powerless.

High-pitched screams rose over the thundering water.

Julia...

She looked up in time to see Ben's sister tumble over the side.

No! Flailing, she fought the momentum and tried to follow her.

Another tidal wave surged over the boat. She opened her mouth, closed her eyes. Water slammed into her face, knocked her head back.

Falling...

She was falling.

Bam!

The back of her head collided with a rock. Everything blurred into a surreal silence.

Julia...

Her eyes got heavy.

Light drained away.

A cold darkness swallowed her whole.

CHAPTER TWENTY-EIGHT

Light. Dark. Light. Dark. The current somersaulted Ben underneath the boat's hard neoprene.

Julia. He had to get to Julia.

He thrust his palms up, tried to push the boat off. It wouldn't budge. Damn it!

Air burned for release in his lungs. He dove down, swam hard, kicked. God, it was cold. So cold his bones ached. Light glowed above him. Light meant air. He needed air...

Harder. He had to swim harder. With long strokes, he pulled against the current, up, up...

Finally his head broke the surface. He gasped and coughed, gagging on the water he'd inhaled.

Thrashing water sputtered all around him. The current dragged him hard, but he fought it, fought to keep his head up, to see above it all. He scanned the river, the shoreline...

There!

Julia sat on a rock, thank god. Thank. God. Shooter was

with her. He must've pulled her out. Kev was there, too, drenched to the gills, hunched over, but fine.

He pulled his arms in a freestyle stroke. *Breathe, breathe.* Sweet air. The hard drag of the current tapped out his strength, but finally he pulled himself up on the sandy shoreline.

His legs felt like tree trunks as he stumbled out of the water. His eardrums still roared, but Julia screamed something at him...

"Paige! Where's Paige?"

He stilled. Swept a gaze down the shoreline and back up. But it was only the four of them.

"She's not here! I can't see her anywhere!" Julia sobbed. "Ben, where is she?"

He whirled back to the river, but the blood pounding in his head made it hard to see straight.

Damn it! He should've made sure everyone was accounted for before he'd gotten himself out.

Wading back in, his eyes scoured the water. White. Chaotic. A glimpse of red pulled his focus, but then it was gone. Behind a boulder.

Red. Paige's life vest was red.

He tore back into the water and threw himself into the current. The cold shock of the river sucked out all his air. Chugging out shallow breaths, he kicked and stroked. Forget the whitewater position. He had to get to Paige.

But the current. The damn current. It locked him in a vice grip and held him in its power, shooting him through the center, down the falls.

"Paige?" he yelled, but it ended in a gagging choke. Wave after wave smacked his face, blurred his eyes.

His frantic arms kept pulling. With a fierce kick of his legs, he rose above the surface.

Red. Just in front of him. The current had her, too. It started to drag him down again, but he kicked and struggled. Strained to see through the waves.

Paige's head flopped forward and submerged her face. In the water. She couldn't breathe…

"Paige!" he yelled as loud as he could. She wasn't fighting. Why wasn't she fighting?

His legs ached with fatigue, but he battled back. The water was slowing…if he could swim hard for another two minutes, he'd be able to grab her, get her out.

Another onslaught of adrenaline warmed his body. He freestyled close enough that he could snag her jacket and he pulled her against him.

Her eyes were closed.

"Paige?" he panted. "Hey."

No response.

Securing her with one arm, he pulled and kicked his way to the shore and dragged her out, her body as limp as a rag doll.

Tremors tortured him as he rolled her onto her back and tipped up her chin.

"Come on, Paige." He couldn't swallow, couldn't stop shaking. "Come on." Pinching her nose, he covered her mouth with his and breathed into her, again and again until he saw her chest rise.

Her body seized, arms and legs taut. Then a horrible strangled sound came from her throat. Her eyes popped open wide. Hands clutched at her chest. Water sputtered out of her. So much water.

The remnants of fear still clawing at his insides, Ben rolled her on her side. In between gasps of air, chokes racked her body until she threw up.

He rocked back on his knees, breathing. Just breathing.

Trembling with an empty coldness that wouldn't go away. She'd almost died. God, if she would've died...

"What happened?" she wheezed.

He couldn't answer because he couldn't talk. Couldn't utter one damn word. Couldn't touch her. Couldn't blink. Couldn't feel anything.

She shifted to her back, blank eyes staring up at the sky. Then they found his. She snapped up to a sitting position.

"Julia! Julia! Where's Julia?" Clumsily, she braced her hands against the ground and tried to stand.

Ben held her down. "She's fine," he managed, even with the uprising of raw fear inside of him. He'd never been so scared. Never. Not in his whole life. All he could see were her eyes sealed shut. Body so still...

"She got out?"

"Why didn't you?" he demanded, the fire from his throat leaking into his voice.

She flinched. "I...I'm not sure. I hit my head. I guess I got knocked out."

The adrenaline had drained, but in its place rage boiled. "How could you let this happen?"

Paige froze and looked at him, her mouth gaping. "What?"

"You promised nothing would happen. Julia could've been killed. *You* could've been killed." He pushed off the ground and paced out the energy on unstable legs.

"I don't...I don't know," Paige repeated. "The floor. It was deflated."

"You should've noticed," he said through his teeth, because, holy shit, she'd almost died. "You should've checked."

"Everyone take it easy," Shooter said as he walked over, carrying Julia in his arms. He set her carefully on a flat rock.

"Paige," she cried. "I'm so glad you're okay. I was so scared."

Paige scrambled over to her, took his sister's shoulders in her hands. "I'm sorry, Julia. Are you okay? Are you sure you're okay?"

"I'm fine," she said, wiping her cheeks with the backs of her hands. "I was barely in the water before Shooter pulled me out. I thought it was all pretty cool. Until I realized you were missing."

Missing. Nausea thundered in Ben's stomach again. He turned away. He couldn't sit there. Couldn't look at her anymore. Not until the burn in his chest subsided. He was so torn. Between kissing the life out of her and shaking her. He started to walk away. "I've gotta call Bryce."

Before he could whip out his phone, Paige stood behind him. "Everything's fine. I'll just pump the floor. We don't have to call Bryce."

"He asked me to. If anything happened."

She grabbed his shoulder and turned him around. "He what?" Shock flashed in her eyes. Something else, too. Extreme distrust.

Ben backed away from her. "He asked me to report back on how the trip went. He had some concerns."

"He told you to spy on me?" Her voice weakened into disbelief, like she couldn't believe he'd betray her, and it hit like a punch to his gut.

"Not to spy." But that's exactly what Bryce had asked of him. "To take some mental notes. So he could make a decision about your program." He braced himself for yelling, for that ferocious indignation that made her so hot, but she only whispered, "I can't believe this."

Don't say it. The words that fought for airtime were nasty, meant to punish her for what she'd put him through. He knew it. But he opened his mouth anyway. "After what I've seen today, I'm not sure the program's a good idea."

"God, Ben," Julia snapped at him. "Stop being such an ass."

He was. He was being a complete asshole, but he couldn't seem to rein it in. Because it wasn't worth it. Losing a life. And he couldn't see past Paige's closed eyes. He'd spent three days with her and he already couldn't imagine his life without her. It was too much. Too intense. If he pissed her off, maybe he could walk away without feeling anything for her.

"*I* will call Bryce," Paige spat at him.

Shooter stepped to the middle of their circle. "Everyone chill out." He gave Paige a pointed look. "I already called Bryce. When I saw Ben giving you mouth-to-mouth."

"Great, Shooter," Paige wheezed. "That's great. Now we'll have another scene with the damn fire department."

"I told him it looked like you were conscious. Didn't sound like he was gonna call in the big guns."

"He probably should." The words earned Ben a death glare from Paige. He threw up his hands. "What? You were practically dead. Might be a good idea for the paramedics to check you out."

"I wasn't practically dead. I choked on some water, that's all. I'm *fine*." She stalked away from him with an extra sway in her hips and damn his libido, this wasn't the time to get turned on.

"Come on, Shooter." She snagged his sleeve. "We have to take care of the boat."

"Or you could sit down," Ben called, knowing it was in vain. "And maybe . . . I don't know . . . *rest*, seeing as how you almost died."

She flipped him the bird, then busied herself with righting the overturned raft.

He plunked himself on the rock next to Julia. He'd never felt so tired. His muscles ached like he'd run a marathon, but at least he wasn't shaking anymore.

Speaking of shaking...Julia's head started swiveling the second he sat down. "What?" he asked her.

"That was smooth, Ben. Real smooth." She whapped the back of his head like an exasperated Italian mother. "You saved her life, for crying out loud! She would've been all yours. All you had to do was be the hero. Hug her, give her some love. Instead you were a complete jerkwad. That's about five steps lower than an asshole, in case you didn't know."

"Only five?" He hunched over and rested his elbows on his knees, stared at the swirling river. "I don't know what happened. I lost my head." It was true what people said about shock. You never knew how you'd react. Some people cried, some threw up, some went mute. Apparently, he got madder than hell. "It freaked me out, J. I can't imagine if she'd...I mean what if she hadn't made it? What would I do?"

"So it wasn't that she almost died. It was that *you* almost lost her." His sister smiled softly. "Don't you think that means something, Ben?"

"It would if she wanted to be with me." It would mean a whole hell of a lot. No woman had ever gotten such a reaction out of him. No woman had gotten this far under his skin. "But she's made it pretty clear she doesn't think it'll work."

"Are you kidding me?" J pursed her lips and gazed at the sky, a silent *why do men have to be so stupid?* "If she didn't care about you, you wouldn't have crushed her heart five minutes ago. And you did." She brandished a finger in front of his face. "You crushed that woman's heart. If she didn't want you, she wouldn't care what you thought about her."

She had a point. But even if that was true, even if Paige cared, he'd screwed up so royally that she'd never forgive him.

The program was the one thing she wanted in life. And he'd told her she shouldn't have it. He glanced up the shoreline and found Paige. She crawled on the boat's floor, hands running over the neoprene, searching. Her supple cheeks had hardened into the mask she'd worn the first few times he'd met her. "It doesn't matter. It's too late. She'll never give me another chance."

"Oh, please. That's a total cop-out," J grumbled.

"What's that supposed to mean?"

"Benjamin Hunter Noble the third," J purred like Scarlett O'Hara. "I do believe you're afraid. Maybe even more afraid than Paige."

He only looked at her. No use denying the obvious. He'd ridden bulls and had broken a wild stallion. But he was still afraid of a girl.

"Well, don't worry, dear brother. Lucky for you and Paige, I'm not afraid. Give me some time. I'll help you come up with a plan to win her back." His sister's eyes glistened with the prospect of a happy ending.

He wished he had her faith.

* * *

Boats don't just deflate. Paige ran her fingers along the slippery creased floor, feeling for any abnormality, a hole, a tear, a snag. Nothing. She found nothing. Shoulders shuddering, she rocked back and sat on her heels. Her lungs felt like they'd been filled with gravel, scratchy and heavy. Breaths squeaked in and out, but they didn't fill her, didn't calm her.

Ben was right. This was her fault. She should've noticed the floor had gone soft. She should've noticed they were taking on water. If she would've done her job, she could've pulled them over to the shoreline and pumped the floor before they'd hit the rapid. But she'd been too distracted, and Julia could've been killed. If Shooter hadn't been right there…

Bile splashed up the back of her throat. She fought the rising tide of nausea and reached for her water bottle to submerge the doubts that crept up.

After what I've seen today, I'm not sure the program's a good idea.

Tears burned her eyes and brightened the sunlight. The program wasn't an idea. It was her dream. The only thing she'd poured her whole heart into for the last five years. It was what had given her hope that her life could be worth more than her parents made her believe it was.

"Hey." Shooter tapped her shoulder.

Blinking hard, she peered up at him.

"You sure you're okay, Paige?" His eyes wouldn't meet hers. And how could she blame him? He'd pulled out Julia while she had to be rescued herself. He'd done her job. Bryce was going to kill her.

"Looks like Bryce is here." He nodded in the direction of the road.

Sure enough, the Walker Mountain Ranch truck sat on a dirt pull-off and her boss jogged toward them.

"Great." She shifted to her butt and scooted to the edge of the raft. "Guess it's time to face the music."

Ben appeared, carrying Julia. He settled his sister next to Paige and knelt down in front of her.

"Are you sure you're okay?"

She stared hard at the sand, at the colorful pebbles strewn around her sandals. "I'm fine." She was. Physically, anyway. Her head ached, her lungs hurt, but it was nothing compared to the arrow in her heart. She'd told him everything. Things she'd never told anyone else. After everything he'd said to her, after everything they'd shared, he had no faith in her.

He rested his hands on her knees and looked in her eyes. "I'm sorry."

"It was my fault," she whispered, her throat burning. "I shouldn't have talked you into Julia coming on the trip." She'd been so caught up in wanting to prove to everyone that she could turn the wilderness into a safe place for anyone. But this only proved she had no control out here.

"It was an accident," Ben insisted firmly. "Don't put this on yourself. I shouldn't have said that. I was scared—"

"What the hell happened?" Bryce huffed, as he skidded down the embankment.

She shook off Ben and stood to prove that she was fine. "We flipped. The floor deflated. I didn't realize it until we were headed in."

"It deflated?" He walked to the boat and ran a hand over the floor. "It's a brand-new boat."

"Yeah." She already knew he wouldn't find anything. She'd looked. She'd felt the whole thing over.

"How'd you miss that, Paige?" A reddish hue made him looked sunburned, but she'd seen it enough times to know he was pissed.

"I should've caught it." She couldn't tell him that she was too distracted with Ben. She didn't want Ben to know, either, because he'd made it pretty obvious back there that his feelings didn't go quite as deep as hers.

"It wasn't her fault," Julia snapped at Bryce. "She was amazing."

Bryce looked at Shooter and raised his brows like he wanted confirmation.

"I didn't notice the floor, either," Shooter said with a sympathetic glance at Paige.

"Yeah, well, you weren't the trip leader." He posted his hands on his hips and focused on her again.

"Julia's right." Ben stepped up to Bryce. "It wasn't her fault."

Oh. Sure. Now he wanted to defend her. A little late for that.

"She told me it was her fault," he shot back.

Ben spread his arms in a surrendering gesture. "Everyone's fine. That's all that matters."

Bryce didn't seem to agree. "Shooter said you were unconscious. Ben pulled you out?"

"I hit my head." Humiliation worked its way up her neck and seeped into her face. It was so ridiculous. A guide having to be rescued.

"Avery's on her way," Bryce said. "She's got the van. She'll give everyone a ride to the party." He snagged her shoulder. "We're going straight to the hospital."

She jerked away. "You can't make me go to the hospital."

"You were unconscious, Paige." Ben steered her back to Bryce. "You weren't breathing. Maybe it's best…"

She whirled to face him, too many emotions clashing— fear and desperation and this strange sense of longing. Damn him. "Now you're going to act like you care? After what you said earlier?"

His shoulders slumped. "I wasn't thinkin'."

Bryce placed a hand on Paige's back and nudged her in the direction of the truck. "We're going to the hospital. Avery'll be here in five minutes."

"It's not necessary," she insisted again. She didn't have time for the hospital. "I can fix this, Bryce. Give me another chance. Have Avery bring out another raft. We can still finish the trip."

"No." He opened the door for her. "I'm not risking anything else. Julia could've been seriously injured, Paige."

Tears gathered in her eyes. "I know."

"*You* could've been seriously injured."

"But I wasn't. No one was." She looked up at him, still hoping. Couldn't he give her another chance?

"Get in the damn truck," he growled. "We're going to the hospital."

And that was when she knew. He'd made up his mind. It'd only taken one accident to wreck her dream.

With a hard knot forming in her throat, she slid into the truck.

Moose whined in the back, scratching on the window like he wanted to climb into her lap. She wished he could. The dog always seemed to know how to make her feel better.

Bryce got in and slammed the door hard. He shoved the keys in the ignition and gunned the engine.

"You're not going to let me start the program. Are you?" she asked, staring at her hands.

"Sorry," Bryce sighed. "I ran the numbers. There's no way it'll work."

"You're not going to make it work," she corrected, but she wasn't angry. She had no right to be. It had never been his vision, only hers.

"It's not what we're about," he said, watching the road as he pulled out. "It's not our brand. It's not what we're trying to do. And insurance costs for a program like that are astronomical."

She stared out the window at the passing landscape, the colors of the mountains blurring together. So that was it, then. No more discussion. A strange sense of calm came over her. Someday. She *would* make it happen. She had to make it happen. It didn't matter if it took her twenty years, she'd find a way. It was something she could contribute to the world. A chance to make her life matter. Bryce wouldn't take that from her. Ben wouldn't take that from her. But right now, her family needed her. She could go back and remedy her regrets. Rebuild something with her parents. Or maybe build it for the first time.

Drawing in a breath for courage, she looked over at Bryce. "Consider this my two weeks' notice."

He eased the truck to the side of the road. "Don't do that. Don't quit."

"I'm so thankful for everything you've done for me, Bryce." She bit into her lip so she wouldn't cry. "Your family gave me a place when I didn't have one. And I'll always be grateful for that. But I need to move on. Mom has MS and they need me at the café. It's time for me to let go of the past." Forget about the disappointments, the unmet expectations. Those things had done nothing but hold her back. "I'll work there until I can figure out how to fund the program myself."

Bryce stared out the windshield as though holding back an argument. Finally he turned his head, his eyes sad. "You'll always have a job. If you change your mind. You know you can always come back."

"I know." She forced a smile to lighten the mood. "Don't take this the wrong way, but I hope I won't have to come back."

"You won't." He reached over and mussed her hair, still her true big brother. "I know you, Paige. You'll find a way to make it happen."

She held on to those words, stored them away. "I hope I can still come for Elsie's dinners."

"Always," he said with a grin. "She'll blame me, you know. For you leaving."

"It's not your fault." She understood. Not that she loved his answer, but she understood. "You're right. You and

Avery have built something amazing together. But it's not a therapy program."

"What about Ben?" Bryce pulled the truck out onto the road again.

She played dumb. "What about him?"

"I'm not as stupid as I look. I've known you both forever," he reminded her. "I knew you didn't spend the night at the café."

That night. Wow, that night. It would always be special to her. But she wasn't stupid, either. "Ben's great." So great. With those wild eyes and that all-American grin and those jeans. He was funny and good. Strong and compassionate. A swell of emotion scraped her throat. "But we wouldn't be great together." Not with him living in the political spotlight and her always trying to hide from it.

"You sure about that?" Bryce asked, taking his eyes off the road to study her face.

"I'm sure." Even as she said it, doubt rooted itself deep. It would go away in time, though. Especially if she kept busy. She'd work at the restaurant, work to restore her relationship with her parents. He'd go on to be senator. The currents of their lives would carry them in different directions and their weeklong whirlwind romance would be one of those distantly wistful happy memories that she'd tell her grandchildren someday.

Someday. That's what she counted on. Someday she'd be the director of a wilderness therapy program. Someday she wouldn't have to wish things were different.

Someday she wouldn't long for what she couldn't have.

CHAPTER TWENTY-NINE

All this for him. Ben shook his head as Avery skidded the van into the dirt parking lot on his land. The party was already in full swing. Kev had outdone himself with the preparations. Peaked white tents stood in the center of the flower-spotted meadow. One held a buffet that could've rivaled the one on the cruise he'd gone on with Gracie and Julia last year. Another tent sheltered a band, jazz from the sounds drifting in through the open windows. Yet another massive tent covered what looked like fifty round tables where people milled around, sampling the fine wines and food. Despite the outdoor venue, everyone seemed dressed up, women in silk sundresses and wide-brimmed hats. The men mostly wore khakis and button-ups, although a few braved suits.

Ben opened the van door and they all piled out.

"Wow, Kev. How'd you manage to pull this off way out here?" He went around back to get out Julia's chair.

Kev followed, smoothing his hair and his wrinkled river clothes. "We've got connections. Had to pay some of 'em to come, but you know your mother. She said price was no object."

Ben hoisted J's chair out and set it on the ground. Then he went back for his sister. "You had to pay people. To come to my event."

"Don't take it personally. We wanted a big crowd. Besides, technically we're not paying them. We gave out gift bags."

Yeah, he'd seen Gracie's extravagant gift bags. "You had to bribe them."

"It's part of the gig, Ben. You know that."

He lifted Julia out of her seat and shifted her into the chair. "You ready to party, sis?"

She smiled, but it looked forced. "I guess. I wish Paige was here, though. I hope she's okay."

Yeah. Tell him about it. He glanced at the keys still hanging from the ignition. He had half a mind to steal the van and take a joyride to the hospital. She didn't seem to be in bad shape, but you never knew with a bump on the head. Besides that, he had a lot to say to her. The drive over had given him some time to sort it all out. Nothing fancy. But he at least wanted the chance to tell her how he felt.

"I knew it! I just knew it!"

Oh, boy. He looked up, braced himself. Gracie was practically sprinting toward them.

"I knew something would go wrong," she moaned. No one could play the part of worried mother better than Gracie. "Oh, I'll never forgive myself for backing out. She clutched J's hands in hers. "I should have been there for you, Julia. I should've been there to protect you."

"Good god, Mother." J slid her gaze to the left, then right.

"You don't have to do this. No one's even watching so you can ditch the act."

"How could you say that? It's not an act." She gave Ben a wounded look. "After all I've done for her…"

J started to wheel herself away. "Paige is the only one who got hurt. Maybe you should go to the hospital and gush over her." She eased the chair down the gravel slope without looking back.

"Paige?" Gracie's face looked pale. "She's in the hospital?"

"Yeah." Ben glanced at the keys again. He should be there. He really should go…

"What happened? How bad was it?"

"Don't know, yet," Ben said, eyeing his mother. Suddenly the mask had fallen off and she looked genuinely worried. "What's wrong?" He watched her carefully. Something wasn't right…

Her eyes got too wide. "Nothing. I'm just… very concerned for her, that's all. I mean, I don't understand. How could the guide get hurt?"

"She hit her head. Got knocked out." The memory stirred up the nausea that had only started to settle.

Gracie gasped. "Will she be okay?"

"I don't know." He looked around. "Avery told me she'd let me know when Bryce called."

Gracie turned her back on him a little too fast for his liking. "I should go check on things. You'd best mingle, don't you think?"

"I guess." Though the crowd spread out in front of him held little appeal. They weren't there for him, anyway. Not really. It was another stunt. Another façade created by his mother and his campaign director. Hardly any of them knew what he stood for, why he'd even wanted to run.

Kev emerged from a beast of an RV. He'd changed into

his signature uniform—a neatly trimmed black suit, even though it had to be a good eighty degrees in the sun. "Let's get you dressed, Ben." He waved him up the steps. "Your mother went with a simple white button-up and those tan pants that seem to be so popular around here. They're right inside."

"Great," he muttered feeling more like a puppet than he ever had.

Kev gave him a good pat on the back. "See you in ten. Make sure you wash up, too. You smell like the river."

"Will do. Thanks for the advice."

It actually felt good to clean up, to scrub the river off of him, along with the memories of pulling Paige out, of thinking she wouldn't come back to him, of feeling helpless, like he wasn't enough. He wasn't. Not for someone like her. Someone larger than life. Brave and strong. God, look at the world he lived in. No wonder she didn't want any part of it.

Showered, changed, and dressed in the clothes his mommy had picked out for him, he stepped back into the fresh air. Avery passed him by.

He caught her arm. "Any word?"

"She's fine." She smiled. "No serious injuries. She's so lucky you were there, Ben."

Relief unlocked his lungs. For the first time since he'd watched Bryce lead her away, he felt like he could breathe.

Avery looked around, then leaned close. "There's something you should know, though."

"What?" he asked, not liking her sad expression.

"She quit. She won't be working at the ranch anymore."

The news settled the heavy weight of guilt right back on his shoulders. "Why?"

"Bryce told her we couldn't launch the program." She shrugged. "I guess she wants to move on."

Because of this trip. She'd been counting on Bryce to give her a shot at her dream, and Ben had ruined it for her.

"Ben," Kev called from the food tent. "Get over here! There're some people you need to meet."

"Sorry things didn't work out with you two," Avery said before walking away.

She wasn't nearly as sorry as he was.

For the next hour, he wore his politician smile, shook hands, held babies, posed for pictures, and made small talk about what a fabulous event it was, and how much the community of Aspen appreciated his generosity.

Every time he met someone new, he wondered if they were there because they wanted to be or because of the expensive cufflinks in their gift bag. He was almost afraid to ask.

Finally Kev trotted away from his side to go hit the buffet, which had started to run low. But he wasn't hungry. Instead of eating, Ben took the opportunity to wander away from the people and the noise and the smell of bourbon. He walked down to the river and found Julia parked next to the water's edge.

"Hey. You okay?" he asked, stepping close enough that he could get a good look at her face. She looked as down as he felt.

She didn't look away from the river. "After we get home, I'm packing up my stuff and moving away from the ranch."

"Pardon?"

"I'm moving. To Dallas," she announced, turning the wheels of her chair until she faced him. "Meghan's been begging me to be her roommate."

Meghan? Her flighty friend who worked at a hair salon? The idea was so ridiculous that he laughed. He couldn't help it. "Meghan can't take care of you."

"I don't need someone to take care of me," she said, her hands fisted, face red. "And I won't stay at the ranch and watch you ruin your life for me."

Ruin his life? "What the hell are you talking about?" She wasn't ruining his life. He was doing a pretty damn good job of that himself.

His sister shook her head like she couldn't believe what an idiot he was. "You never would've gone after Paige like that if it wasn't for me."

She had a point. That wasn't the first time he'd gone for a swim on a rafting trip. Usually that was part of the fun, part of the thrill. But with Julia in the boat...everything felt more out of his control.

"And do you even want this, Ben?" She looked at the crowd that milled around the tents. "Do you *want* to be a senator?"

He'd never lied to his sister, but there was a first time for everything. "Of course I want it." Faking conviction was harder than it sounded. "I mean...I wanted to do it for you, J." For her and *with* her. He could give her a voice...

"And what about Paige?" she asked quietly.

He looked down at his hands. "She wants nothing to do with it." And he didn't blame her. Look at all of those people up there. Look at the show he had to put on for them. Much as he hated to admit it, Gracie was right. "She'd never be happy in that world."

"Neither will you." J crossed her arms in the same pout she'd relied on since she was three. "I thought you wanted this for *you*, Ben."

That was because he'd led her to believe he wanted it, that he held all of these political convictions. Like a good Catholic, he'd been careful to never let his doubts show.

"I can't watch you go after things you don't really want

just so you can prove yourself to me." The tears in his sister's eyes jabbed at his heart. "You're a good man. The best brother in the whole world. You didn't get in that car with Kacy that night. I did."

His jaw locked. He didn't want to talk about this with her. Didn't want to hear her blame herself. "You were a kid. You didn't know."

She shook her head like it didn't matter. "I've made peace with it." Tears streamed down her cheeks. "I love my life. And I love you too much to sit there and watch you ruin yours."

His mouth opened but he couldn't say one damn word. Her sweet sincerity tangled his throat. "But what about all the work you've done? What about the bill?" She'd spent so many hours on it . . .

"We can lobby," she said, shaking her head like she couldn't believe his ignorance. "We have plenty of connections between you and Gracie. We'll find another senator to introduce the bill. You deserve to be happy." She used her shirt to dry her tears. "You should be with someone like Paige. You shouldn't be holed up in a DC office and sitting through endless sessions that don't do the country much good, anyway." She peered up at him, no longer the girl whom he'd sworn to protect. She'd grown up. She was wise and gracious. And right. Always right.

Every day Julia chose to be brave. Now it was his turn. Drawing courage from his little sister, he stood. She was right. It was time to let go of everyone else's expectations of him, to let go of that driving desire to prove himself to the world. To her. She was offering him his freedom. And he knew exactly what he wanted to do with it. "I have to withdraw from the race."

"Really?"

"Really." And that wasn't all. He looked around them at the rolling acres of land they owned. A land trust was great, but they could use it for something even better. Something that would change lives instead of laws. They could push all kinds of legislation, but that wouldn't stop tragic accidents, it wouldn't stop terrible diseases like the one that had killed Paige's grandmother, like the one that was eating away at her mom. "We can donate all of this to Paige. Let her run her program here." Let her give the gift of hope and beauty to people who needed it most.

"Are you serious?" J squealed, her happy self again. "Ben, that's perfect! I could help! I could work there and—"

"Whoa...easy." He crouched to put the brake on her chair so she didn't go rolling right into the river. "It's only an idea. A lot would have to happen first."

"It's the best idea in the world." For being confined to a chair, the girl sure could bounce. "Can we really do that? Give her the land?"

"I'm definitely gonna look into it," he promised. There'd be a million details to work out. And one more hurdle...

"But first I have to tell Gracie."

CHAPTER THIRTY

Someday...

Someday she'd be able to walk through the door of the High Altitude Café without dry heaving. That day was not today, unfortunately.

The smell of charred meat and sizzling grease descended on her like a cloud, holding her in its heavy haze. It wasn't only the smell that made her sick to her stomach, though. It was the nerves.

The place was packed with the dinner rush, which meant all hands on deck. Every member of her family would be there. Right inside the door, Paige scooted off to the left and slipped behind the coatrack to watch, to get her bearings. Pete moved from table to table, chatting with the customers, charming the pants off the women, judging from their ruddy cheeks and flattered smiles. Obviously, he played the part of the manager today. Out of all the Harper siblings, he had the most charisma, not to mention the most star power with the older women. Something about those dimples.

On the other side of the restaurant, her other brother Paul manned the bar like Tom Cruise in *Cocktail*. He'd actually studied the old classic, a favorite of his from the eighties, and learned how to flip and toss the bottles of liquor just like Tom had, although he didn't have Tom's lady-killing smile or slender body. He was big and beefy, like Dad.

Her sisters Penny and Pearl both floated about, taking orders, running food, and bussing the tables, in between catching up on the local gossip, judging from the way Pearl kept gasping and waving her hand in a No-way.-Are-you-serious? sort of gesture.

Back in the kitchen, behind the scenes, Dad no doubt stood at the grill, while Mom walked the line, sampling the food, judging the presentation—how many ways were there to make meat look nice?—while their part-time kitchen staff slaved away in the steam and heat.

An echoing hollowness yawned inside of her, taking up the space in her lungs.

She'd quit her job. And she felt like a stranger here.

Her siblings all had their places. They fit in. Not only that, they loved working there, loved the food, loved the chance to gab with the patrons. This was home to them, but it never had been to her.

She exhaled a breath. But that was her fault. Maybe instead of expecting her parents, her brothers and sisters to make a place for her, she should've made a place for herself.

On the outskirts of the camaraderie, she watched carefully and listened and finally felt it—the something bigger that kept her parents coming in every single day for the last thirty years. It was the laughter and the hugs. The hearty handshakes and whacks on the back. It was the way people shouted hello all the way across the restaurant. The low hum of country music playing the in the background.

The High Altitude Café was a gathering place. It might not be a wilderness therapy program that would change the lives of people with disabilities, but it had a purpose. It brought people together. All those years, it'd been her choice to stay on the outskirts of her family. She could've asked her parents for more. She could've given more, herself.

She'd been too afraid. Ben was right about her. She feared so many things. Him. That penetrating connection they had. She feared that deep connection with her own family. It required so much, too much risk. She'd made sure her family couldn't reject her. She'd shut them out.

And it was time to open herself back up.

Working here would never be her dream, but it would make her part of the family. And that was something she'd always craved, too.

Stepping out from the shadows, Paige headed straight for Pete. He'd be the easiest one to start with. He'd never really given up on her the way the others had.

She caught up with him right outside the kitchen doors. "Hey."

He whirled, somehow keeping the large tray balanced on his palm perfectly steady. "Hey yourself." A smile brightened his eyes. "To what do we owe this honor?"

"I'm here to work." She shrugged her shoulders. "I quit my job. Need to make some money."

The tray wobbled and dipped to one side, but he righted it before the empty glasses cascaded to the floor. Concern rounded his eyes. "Paige . . . you didn't have to quit."

She rested her hand on his arm to calm the worry in his eyes. "Yes. I did. It's time for me to move on." If she stayed at the ranch, she wouldn't be moving forward. At least if she eventually found a better-paying job, she could work toward her dream. "I can't stay here long-term." Because they wouldn't pay any better than the ranch. "Just through the end of the off season, then I'll help you hire someone else." And maybe she'd look into using her kinesiology degree...

"Aw, Paige. This'll mean so much to Dad and Mom."

"I'm doing it for me as much as them. I want to be here." She glanced around to make sure the coast was clear, then leaned closer. "Speaking of, I've been thinking...I have some money saved. If we all went in together, maybe we could send Dad and Mom on a cruise." While she'd been waiting on her release from the hospital, she'd read a travel magazine. Seemed like a cruise would be the perfect vacation for her parents.

"Mom would love it," Pete said. "Not so sure about Dad."

"But he'll go. He'll do it for Mom." This was something she could do for Mom, for both of them. Give them good memories together before things got tough.

Pete slid the tray onto a nearby table and pulled her in for a hug. "Let's do it, then. I'll spread the word to the others." He pulled away and did a double take, like he'd seen her for the first time. "What the hell happened to you?"

She glanced down at her attire. She'd come straight from the hospital as soon as they'd released her. She still wore her river clothes and her hair had dried into a matted mess. But she waved it all off, along with the memories of Ben's stinging commentary on the accident. "Long story. And not all that interesting."

"I doubt that," he said, but he didn't ask her to elaborate, thank god. She'd rather not think about it, about Ben, specifically. How could she already miss him? It'd only been a couple of hours.

"Come on." He led her into the kitchen, and sure enough,

Mom walked the length of the stainless counters, peering over the cooks' shoulders, keeping everything moving. Dad stood stationary, of course, while he flipped burgers at the grill with a practiced precision.

"Hey, Ma, Pops, look who's here." Pete presented her in an awed fashion, arms raised in a *ta-da*.

Mom finished redirecting one of the line cooks, then turned to Pete. Her body jolted to a stop. "Paige." It was a mere gasp, a happy puff of air. "You're here." Her cheeks did that crumple thing, then she started to cry.

"Of course she's here!" Dad's beefy chest seemed to swell. "She's back where she belongs." He slid his spatula onto the counter and lumbered over to grab her an apron. He tossed it at her all brisk and businesslike but his eyes smiled. "Well, what are you waiting for? The customers aren't gonna serve themselves." He went back to burger flipping, but she saw it, the hint of pride or maybe relief. He wanted her there. It had to be hard for him to deal with Mom's diagnosis. Maybe he knew they'd only get through it together.

While going over the specials with her, Pete tied her apron. She smiled down at the cheesy illustration. "I'm a terrible waitress," she whispered. "You know that, right?"

He patted an extra dose of confidence into her back. "You're right, sis. You are a terrible waitress." He swooped in front of her with that grin that made all the grandmothers swoon. "But you're a damn good person." He directed her toward the dining room. "Now get out there and break some plates."

A smile radiated from her heart as she headed for the dining room. She might not be a good daughter. Or the best guide. Or a good candidate for a serious relationship, though it would take some serious time and copious amounts of gelato to forget Benjamin Hunter Noble III. But Petey thought she was a good person.

And that meant more than all the titles in the world.

* * *

If he didn't know better, he'd suspect Gracie was hiding from him. Sometimes it seemed the woman had an uncanny ability to know when bad news was headed her way so she could get the heck outta Dodge.

Ben slinked around the back of the catering tent so as not to be seen by the crowd. He'd had enough shaking hands, smiling at people he'd never met, making small talk about the caviar. He had one mission and he wasn't about to get distracted. Edging to the tent's opening, he peered inside just as a large woman came around the corner.

"Goodness!" She jolted to a stop and did a double take. "Benjamin Noble! My Lord, you're even better-looking up close."

She tried to block his view, but thankfully he stood a head taller, perfect height to survey the scene right above her Texas bouffant.

"I saw you at the restaurant," she said. "It was downright heroic, what you did. Teachin' that awful man a lesson and rescuin' that poor girl."

"Actually, that poor girl rescued me," he said, and damn, it felt good to tell the truth. Because Paige had rescued him. If it weren't for her, he'd be fighting for a job he didn't even want.

The woman said something else, but he scanned the crowd. His eyes homed in on Gracie, standing near a melting ice sculpture. He tried to step around the woman, but she reached out and shoved her chubby hand in his.

"I'm Virginia Mayflower. From Dallas. I want you to know, Mr. Noble, you'll have my vote come November."

He withdrew his hand and slipped past her. "That won't be necessary," he mumbled as he charged straight for his mother.

"Benjamin!" Her exaggerated smile practically blinded him.

Uh-oh. He slowed. What the hell was she up to?

Gracie came at him, a blond woman trailing behind. "We've been looking everywhere for you."

"Why?" He checked out the woman who stood behind Gracie. Her platinum blond hair hung straight and sleek down her shoulders and her blue eyes sparkled with an awed shyness. She wore a flowered sundress that stood out against her evenly tanned skin and, despite his best attempt not to notice, that also accentuated her disproportional bust.

"You remember Cecily Banks, don't you, darling?" His mother purred. "The party planner?"

"No, I can't say that I do."

A red hue shadowed his mother's face. "Of course you do. Hubert and Beth's daughter. You met her at a party a few years back?" Her brows danced in a plea for him to be polite.

Ah, Cecily. Of course. How could he forget? Her hour-long monologue about the joys of party planning had gotten him good and drunk. *Nice try, Gracie.* He could see where this was going, so he shrugged. "Sorry. Guess I don't remember."

Cecily giggled as if that was the cutest thing she'd ever heard. "That's okay, Mr. Noble. I remember you."

Good god. He had to get Gracie alone.

"Cecily has been a godsend," Gracie gushed. "She put this lovely event together. I don't know what I would've done without her."

He offered the poor girl a token smile. "It's great. Thanks for the help." He looked at Gracie. "Can I talk to you for a minute? Alone?"

She backed away. "Don't be silly, Benjamin. I have so much to do, so many people to chat with. I'm sure you would love to get reacquainted with Cecily while I make the rounds."

His stern glare sent her a message. "We need to talk. Now."

"Of course," Cecily bubbled. "I have a million things to do, anyway." She looked up at him through her fake eyelashes. "I hope we can catch up soon, though."

"Probably not," he said, then dragged his mother to a deserted corner. No use making a promise he didn't intend to keep. Not anymore.

"Benjamin! Let go of me this instant." Gracie ripped her arm out of his grasp and straightened her blouse. "What are you thinking? Have you lost your mind? You were so rude."

"I'm pulling out of the race," he blurted out above the music.

"Don't be ridiculous." She glanced around and laughed softly. Her cocktail party laugh, he called it. "You can't quit. Not now. After all these months of work. And the money..."

"I don't want to be a senator." That was the bottom line. He'd caught a glimpse of what life could be like with Paige, and that's what he wanted. Maybe he didn't know her all that well, but he knew he'd never meet another woman like her. That was all he needed to know. "I'm makin' the announcement today. Here. And I'm holdin' on to the land."

Rigid breaths raised Gracie's shoulders. "Absolutely not. What do you think your father would say? He would be humiliated. After everything he did for you..."

"No." He wouldn't let her use that against him, to manipulate him. Not anymore. "Dad would want me to be happy. I have to believe that."

Her gaze fell to the ground, eyes shifting like she didn't know where to look. Then she staggered back.

"Mom?" She didn't look good, pale and unsteady, like she'd suddenly gotten dizzy. "Are you okay?" If she even tried to fake a heart attack right now...

"You're right," she murmured.

"Pardon?" Had she ever muttered those two words together in her life?

"You're right. He would want you to be happy." She looked around, drew in a lengthy breath, then closed her eyes. When she opened them they were full of tears.

Whoa. She hadn't even cried at Dad's funeral...

"I can't do this," she whispered.

"Can't do what?" he demanded, getting a few looks from the people around him.

"Hush, Benjamin," his mother hissed, tugging him to the side of the tent where no one could see them.

You've got to be kiddin'. Didn't she ever get tired of the dramatics? "I don't have time for this." He turned to walk away from her. From all of it.

"Ben, the accident wasn't Paige's fault."

He stopped. Wasn't Paige's fault. His knees buckled. He turned slowly, dizzy from his hammering pulse. Because she made it sound like it was *someone's* fault. Not an accident...

The fearful look on her face confirmed it.

Anger rushed in, making him lightheaded. "What. Did. You. Do?"

Gracie suddenly looked small, almost frail. "Kevin," she whimpered, squeezing a hand over her mouth. "I knew he was up to something. When we got to the river, he told me to go back to the ranch with Bryce. But I didn't know—"

"You didn't know what?" he asked, body boiling so hot he had half a mind to run down and jump in the river.

"While you were changing, I asked him what happened." She looked around like she wanted to make sure no one could hear. "He said he used his pocketknife to slit a small tear in the floor so no one would notice."

Blood rushed to his head. Everything went dim. "How? When?" But then it hit him. When they'd pulled over on the side of the river. When Paige had taken him up the hill and yelled at him. Shooter was in the back of the boat. He must not've seen...

"He didn't mean to cause an accident," his mother said, her voice still wavering with an uncharacteristic weakness. "He only wanted to make Paige look bad. So you'd stop pursuing her."

Ben scanned the crowd looking for the son of a bitch. "Paige was hurt. She could've been killed." Heat coursed through him and tightened his gut.

Gracie clamped onto his arm. "I didn't know. You have to believe me. He didn't tell me what he was up to. I would've stopped him. I never would've let him put anyone in danger, especially Julia."

"I believe you." As crazy as she was, she'd never do anything to hurt either one of them.

"What are you going to do, Benjamin?" she whispered like she was afraid to ask.

"I'm gonna let the authorities handle Kevin." Bryce's cousin, Sawyer, was a cop. He'd seen him earlier at the buffet table chatting with Ruby. He was probably still around somewhere. No matter how much Kev had done for him, he couldn't let him get away with this.

As for Gracie...well, she wasn't totally innocent either, especially with the way she'd treated Paige from the beginning.

"Don't worry, Mother." He linked her arm through his and strolled back to the party. "You and I are gonna fix this."

He already had a pretty good idea of how they could make it up to Paige.

CHAPTER THIRTY-ONE

In one week Paige had broken fourteen dishes. Yes, fourteen. Two bowls, six plates, and now, counting the two that lay in shards at her feet, six glasses. She tiptoed through the glass strewn across the floor, the Larsens' iced tea sloshing in her sandals. "I'm so sorry," she said to the older couple for about the hundredth time.

Mrs. Larsen swatted the air. "Not another word about it, sweetie girl. You'll get the hang of this gig. All in good time. You'll see."

"I hope so." They couldn't afford to keep replacing the dishware. At least Dad and Mom were out of town, thanks to the bargain she'd found on that last-minute cruise. He tried to hide it, but every time she broke something, Dad got that stressed look on his face. "At least no one got hurt," he'd mumble, but she could tell he wondered how long it would take before she did hurt someone, drop a plate on someone's foot, maybe. Lose a tray on someone's head.

Damn it. She tried, but she'd been so distracted. It didn't help that she'd first seen Ben again at the restaurant. He and Julia and his mother had sat at that table right over there. He'd sat in that chair. She still remembered the way he'd smiled at her, like they shared some secret she didn't know, yet. Now, every time she looked at that chair, she saw him, felt him all over her like he was the night in the hammock, and that torturous yearning would radiate in a warm pulse as she remembered how his hands had slid down her back…

"Are you all right, Paige?" Mrs. Larsen was peering at her over her bifocals. "You're as flushed as Ed gets in a lingerie shop."

"I'm fine," she squeaked out past the throbbing in her throat. Then she knelt to start cleaning up the mess. As soon as she figured out how to stop fantasizing about Ben, she'd be fine. Right? For a few days at first, she really thought he'd come by. Or at least call. Okay, she hadn't thought. She'd hoped. Hoped that he couldn't forget about her the way she couldn't forget about him. Hoped he'd forgiven her for risking Julia's life…

"I'll help you out." Luke Simms strode over to where she crouched, standing above her, peering down like he was looking right down her shirt. Just her luck that the elite members of the Aspen Fire Department had nothing better to do this morning than sit and drink coffee and harass her.

"Don't need help," she grumbled.

Luke crouched across from her with a grin. "Come on, Paige. Don't be mad anymore. Let me take you out again, make it up to you. This time, no drinking. I swear."

Right on cue, Pete strolled out from the kitchen with the small hand broom she used to clean up all of her messes. That'd become their system. He'd hear the crash of breaking glass and emerge from the kitchen like a dutiful little elf, saving her from having to have this conversation with Luke yet again.

"Here you go, sis." He handed off the broom and dustpan and returned to Dad's post—the grill, in preparation for the noon rush.

Heaving a sigh, she started to sweep up the glass, but Luke took the broom away. "See? I can be a good guy. What was so great about that senator, anyway?"

What was so great about Ben...his protective nature, his tenacity, his love for life, his carefree outlook. The way he loved his sister. The way he'd held Paige all night. God, his smile...

"A hobby. That's what you need, Paige," Mrs. Larsen insisted. "Then you'll be so busy, you'll forget all about that man."

For the last three days, Mrs. Larsen had offered her infinite wisdom on the subject of Paige's most recent romantic debacle while Mr. Larsen nodded and smiled at his wife. So far, in each of their brief counseling sessions while she'd taken their orders, Mrs. Larsen had concluded that Ben must, and she quoted, "be the dumbest son-of-yank she'd ever known because how could someone smart walk away from you, Paige?"

"I'll be your hobby." Luke elbowed her lightly.

While she appreciated the efforts to rebuild her self-esteem, neither Mrs. Larsen nor Luke had been able to help her find a way to kill that sweet vulnerability Ben had tilled up in her heart. Maybe she should turn to shock therapy...

"Belly dancing!"

Still on her hands and knees in the pile of glass, Paige looked up. *Uh...*

Mrs. Larsen clapped as if applauding herself for such a fabulous idea. "Oh, Paige, you would make a wonderful belly dancer. You've certainly got the abs for it. My daughter, Myra, said they've started a new class at the rec center. Why, we could go together! I could sew us some matching outfits, you know those little crop top numbers and flowy skirts with all the sequins? Oh! And we could drape beads all over ourselves."

"I'd love to see that." Luke raised his eyebrows and slid a sleazy glance down her body.

"Um…" She made eye contact with Mr. Larsen, and swear to god, his eyes bulged like he was choking on his own laughter. "Wow, Mrs. Larsen…that'd be so…fun. Unfortunately, I have no rhythm." No lie there. "But you're right. I need to start thinking about something else."

Something else.

Hmmm…something else.

Dogs! Maybe she should get a dog. She'd always loved Moose. She could go to the Humane Society after work. Then her apartment wouldn't feel so lonely. It hadn't been lonely before she'd met Ben. It had been fine. Her whole life had been fine because she hadn't known what she was missing. But now…

Mrs. Larsen gasped.

Her head snapped up. "What? What's wrong?"

The old woman's mouth hung open.

Was she having a heart attack? A stroke? Paige's hands splayed in front of her, training ready to take over. "Are you okay?"

Raising her hand, Mrs. Larsen silently pointed past Paige's shoulder.

She cranked her head.

Ben.

Her eyes blinked. But when she opened them, he still stood right behind her.

"Looks like my work here is done," Luke muttered, dropping the broom and dustpan and retreating back to his table in a sulk.

"Can I help?" Ben lowered to his knees right across from her.

"You're here," she whispered and her whole body sighed in relief because he wasn't gone.

He wasn't gone. He knelt two feet away from her in those jeans that made her knees wobble and certain parts of her body hum.

"My, my," Mrs. Larsen muttered. "He sure is a looker."

A looker. Yes. That was one way to describe him.

"Paige." He reached for her, like he feared she'd run away, but didn't he know? She couldn't run. She'd tried that already and somehow she'd left a piece of herself with him.

"Here." Ben's warm skin brushed hers as he picked up the broom and dustpan and swept up the glass.

His touch melted her. She stayed on her knees and watched him work. Stayed on her knees when he rose and dumped the glass in the trash. Distantly, she realized that Julia was parked near the door, and Gracie stood beside her, watching with those vigilant eyes. But they disappeared again when Ben came back to her and silently held out his hand.

"You're here," she said again, still dumbfounded, still trying to find her footing. But she didn't need to because Ben seized her hand and pulled her up in one strong motion.

"Now, that's a man." Out of the corner of her eye, Paige saw Mrs. Larsen fan herself with a napkin.

"Tell me about it." Her eyes locked on his.

"What the hell is going on here?" At some point, Pete had come out from the kitchen. He crossed his arms and sized up Ben with a long glare. "Whadda you want?"

"It's okay." Paige now regretted telling him all the things Ben had said to her that day. Because she knew he hadn't meant any of it. He'd only been worried about Julia. And about her, like he'd said. Her brother offered to track him down and "kick his ass," which they both knew was a fantasy, what with his wiry frame, and all. But at the time, it had made her feel better, nonetheless. She gave her brother a look that told him to back off and inched closer to Ben. "You'll have to excuse my brother."

A hint of that dizzying grin quirked his mouth. "Y'all have every right to hate me." He didn't let go of her hand. And it was a damn good thing because she might've toppled over and how would that have looked?

"You scared the sense out of me, Paige. When I pulled you out and realized you weren't breathing—"

She fisted his shirt and pulled him against her, silencing him with her lips because she didn't care what had happened three days ago. It didn't matter. She knew his heart. He'd offered it to her, repeatedly, and she'd been too stubborn to accept it gracefully. Too afraid. She didn't intend to make that mistake again. So she kissed him as deeply as she'd fantasized about kissing him for all of those long, lonely days, smiling against his lips because he was here and now she didn't have to learn how to belly dance and she didn't have to find some distraction to make her forget about the best night of her entire life.

Ben pulled back, shook his head. "Wait," he sputtered, out of breath. "There's something you should know."

Something? *No. No.* She knew all she had to know. That this man was right. He was worth risking her whole heart. There couldn't be anything more important than that, but she humored him and tilted her head. "You have about thirty seconds before I kiss you again," she warned.

He didn't grin back at her. Instead, his face tensed...
"Kevin slit the boat with his knife. He sabotaged the trip."

The revelation knocked the wind out of her. Okay. So.
Yes. That was a slight shock...

"We turned him in," Ben continued. "And the authorities
are dealing with it—"

"She could've been killed," Pete snarled. He strutted forward a few steps, but Paige held up her hand to stop him.
"Why would...why...how...?" She had trouble getting out
the words past the bulge in her throat. How could someone
she didn't even know hate her so much?

Ben turned to his mother. She slunk forward, hands
clasped tightly in front of her tiny waist, chin dipped in re-
pentance. "He was trying to ruin things for you. I can only
imagine he was following my lead." For the first time ever,
Gracie Hunter Noble looked her in the eyes. "I'm terribly
sorry for the trouble I've caused you. I was only worried
about Benjamin. About how a relationship would affect his
campaign. But now that he has withdrawn—"

"Withdrawn?" She gaped at him and once again his mother
faded to the background, an image with no significance.

"Someone reminded me that I never wanted to be a senator. I realized I could do more good with the ranch than I
could sitting in an office." He glanced over at J and grinned.

She waved in her happy, bubbly way.

Paige tried to wave back but her hand shook too much.
"But what about all the work you've done?" What about the
bill Julia had helped him write?

"If Ben wasn't so full of himself, he would've realized
there are ninety-nine other senators," Julia said, shaking her
head in that annoyed, sisterly way. "We'll find someone else
to introduce the bill. Someone who actually knows what
they're doing."

Paige laughed. And cried. Oh god, when was the last time a whole room full of people had seen her *cry*?

"Besides, your program is exactly the kind of thing we're hoping to see more of." Ben handed her an envelope. "We want to help *you* do more good. Change people's lives. Like you did for Julia. After a talk with my granddad, we decided this was the best way to use the land."

Paige carefully opened the envelope. Inside there was a deed. To the Nobles' acreage. In her name...

"We all want you to have it," he said while his mother nodded. "Even my granddad. He wants you to give others the same chance you gave Julia."

"And our family foundation will fund the therapy program," Gracie added. And now Paige could see past the coldness of her exterior to a genuine sort of kindness in her eyes. "Anything you need, all you have to do is outline your expenses."

Paige stared at the envelope, her heart burning. Tears flooded her eyes, and for once she didn't care who saw them. Because this man standing in front of her had freed her to feel again, and now she didn't want to escape the emotions that pounded so hard in her chest. She didn't want to protect herself anymore. Ben had just handed her everything she thought she'd ever wanted, but she realized it meant nothing if she couldn't share it with him.

She handed the envelope back. "I don't want it," she whispered.

He stared at her like he was afraid to touch her, but she wasn't afraid. She wanted to touch him, wanted to feel his solid warmth. So she smoothed her hands up his sides, over his chest, her knees so weak and inadequate because he felt like home.

"I don't want any of that nearly as much as I want you,

Ben Noble," she murmured, invading his personal space. "You're enough. You could've shown up here with nothing and it would've been enough."

He crushed her against him and lifted her off her feet. "God, I want you, Paige. You have no idea..."

"I think I do..." she whispered against his neck as she wrapped her legs around his waist.

A low groan droned in his throat.

"Get a room," Pete muttered.

She ignored him, ignored them all, and gazed into Ben's eyes so he'd know he had her heart, too. She wouldn't protect herself from him. Not anymore. "I want to build the program *with* you. You keep your land. We'll do this together."

"That's the best idea I've ever heard." He set her feet on the floor, holding her tightly against him, kissing her forehead, her nose, her cheeks, and finally—*finally*—her lips. She lifted her hands to his cheeks, holding him there. Right. There. Losing herself in the feel of those clever lips...never wanting the moment to end. It was perfect.

"Is this a good time to order a mushroom Swiss burger?" Julia called sweetly.

Pulling away from Ben, Paige shot her a look.

"Coming right up," Pete said. But instead of going to the kitchen, he approached Julia, positioning himself behind her wheelchair. "First I'll get you lovely ladies to a table."

Awww...was Julia blushing?

Before she could get a better look, Ben held her at arm's length, and gazed into her eyes. "You're sure? This is what you want? To run the program at the *Noble* ranch?"

"I don't know." Being coy had never been one of her strengths, but what the hell? She crawled a finger up the center of his chest. "I guess that would make you my boss?"

His eyes fixated on her finger as it lingered over his impressive pectorals. "I guess so."

"Staff meetings should be fun."

"Corporate retreats," he corrected with that sly grin that she would spend the rest of her life dreaming about every night. "Weeklong corporate retreats with team building exercises." Judging from the playful arch in his eyebrows, he had some ideas for what those exercises might be.

Mrs. Larsen giggled.

Now she was the one blushing.

"I'm offering you the chance of a lifetime, Miss Harper." He held out an arm like Fred Astaire. "What d'ya say?"

She untied her apron and slipped it over her head, then slung it on the back of a nearby chair. "I accept. But you should know, I've already committed to working at the café for a while."

"You stay as long as they need you." He shot Pete an accommodating look. "We've got a lot of work ahead of us, anyway. It'll take a while to get things goin'."

Pete acknowledged Ben with a nod of acceptance.

"So..." He linked her arm through his, and she couldn't help but notice how neatly she fit against his side. "Maybe we should go somewhere more private and discuss the details." Before the words were all the way out, he'd already whisked her to the door.

Insides glowing like rekindled embers, she peeked over her shoulder and smiled at the crowd behind them. "Don't wait up."

Even though it was only eleven o'clock in the morning, they had a lot to do.

EPILOGUE

Do you trust me?"

There was a time not so long ago, she would've said no. She didn't trust anyone. But over the last year, Benjamin Hunter Noble III had earned her trust about a thousand times, and she owed this to him.

"On the count of three, we're gonna run and jump right off the side of that cliff," he whispered in her ear, then took his time working his lips down her neck. This time, the trembling had nothing to do with a feeling of impending doom and everything to do with his hot breath against her skin.

"That's not crazy at all," she teased. Because, even though she wasn't as afraid as she had been the first time, they were still about to jump off a cliff with a flimsy piece of nylon attached to their backs.

He wrapped his arms around her and gave her a good squeeze. "I love you, Paige. You know that, right?"

It wasn't the first time he'd said it, but it was the first time she'd heard such somberness in the words.

She rested her head on his shoulder and peered up at him. "Please tell me you're not saying that because you have a bad feeling about this."

His gaze held hers and she saw the truth in his eyes. "I'm saying it because it's true."

In that case... She smiled up at him, soft and happy. "I love you, too." In one year she'd learned that Ben was charming and funny, slightly cocky, but real, too. And thoughtful. Optimistic. Protective of those he loved. Loyal to a fault. She'd also learned that she could love deeper and harder and fiercer than she dreamed possible. She'd discovered that an unfathomable connection between two souls really did exist.

And here they were, about to jump off a cliff because Ben made her believe anything was possible. Even flying.

"Wind report looks good." He shoved his phone back into his satchel. "Ready for this?"

"Of course," she replied snarkily with a lilt in her shoulder. Because experience had taught her that, when she was with Ben, she had to be ready for anything.

She waited for his countdown, then ran with him, chasing the wild blue sky. Behind her, his legs pumped hard and she let him propel her forward strong and hard into oblivion. As the wind carried them higher and higher, her heart lurched into her throat, starting that adrenaline-fueled fire in her belly. And then they were suspended, dipping and soaring over the peaks below like a majestic bald eagle bathing in the pinkish haze of a dwindling sun.

Paragliding at sunset. It had never been on her bucket list, but Ben had begged her, and, well, she was such a sucker for those puppy-dog eyes of his. Besides that, she'd never been so immersed in beauty that she'd actually felt it this way, the sheer perfection of the world, wild and overpowering with the wind whipping. And yet she still felt so safe and protected with the feel of Ben, warm and steady against her back, soaring over the place they'd built—Ben's modest log house, the extensive stables stocked with every piece of equipment she'd need to run the therapeutic riding program, the cattle runs that would bring in the cash. None of it seemed real...

"Are you warm?" Ben asked, so thoughtful, as always.

"Practically sweating," she laughed. But the heat pumping through her wasn't fear. It was reckless freedom.

Steering them lower, Ben nudged her. "Our pasture's right down there," he said over the wind, nodding to the left.

When she looked down, a flash of color caught her eye. Red lines and curves...words. Ben dipped them lower and her eyes strained.

Will you marry me? was spelled out in...roses? It had to be thousands of beautiful red roses.

The burn of happy tears flooded her eyes. "Ben..."

He leaned close, his lips next to her ear. "Paige Harper, you are sassy and sexy and compassionate and brilliant. And sexy. Did I mention sexy?"

Somehow her laugh prompted the tears to fall.

"This isn't my place. It's ours," he murmured into her ear.

She shook so hard she felt it in her bones, and it wasn't because they were so far above the ground. It was because she'd never known such happiness, such unrelenting joy.

"I want to be with you. Every day. I'm tired of you goin' home at night. I'm tired of yours and mine. I wanna move on, sweetness. Let's make everything ours," he drawled, the wind whistling between them. "I don't deserve you. But I'll do my best to try every single day," he continued.

And then, as if afraid her hesitation was because she wasn't sure instead of the fact that she wanted to savor this moment, he leaned his head over her shoulder. "The ring is in the truck. Didn't want to drop it," he said apologetically. "But I promise, it's a rock."

"Stop," she laughed…and cried, her emotions alternating between giggles and tears. "You don't have to prove yourself to me, Ben." Didn't he know he already had? "I couldn't give a damn about the ring. Of course I'll marry you."

His lips brushed her neck. Just when she thought she couldn't soar any higher…

"Too bad I can't kiss you on the lips. Or take you to bed." Ben murmured against her skin.

God, she loved how he made her laugh.

"Guess I didn't think this through."

"It's perfect." No one had ever gone to so much trouble for her. "How long did it take you to spell it out?" It had to be days…weeks…

"Doesn't matter. It was worth every second." He steered them lower, then nuzzled her again. "There *is* a pretty private spot down there in that meadow," he hinted. "To the left of the roses. I packed a blanket and some champagne in the truck…"

Paige stretched her neck to get a better view of the meadow. "Isn't that Bryce and Avery's truck? And your mother's Caddy? And Pete's Jeep?"

"Dammit," he muttered. "Word gets around, I guess. Should've waited to spill the beans until we'd consummated the pact." She didn't have to look at him to see the vibrant grin. She heard it in his voice. An overwhelming sense of gratitude started the tears again. She'd never get tired of that grin.

"Guess we should head down and get this party started," Ben said, steering them toward the meadow. "You ready?"

"Yes." More ready than she'd ever been for anything. Together, she and Ben sank lower and lower through the pink sky.

And this time, she didn't fear the landing.

Desperate for a new start, Ruby James heads for the mountain air of Aspen, Colorado. She'll be fine as long as she keeps her identity a secret. But that will be more difficult than she imagined when she falls for the gorgeous town deputy...

Please see the next page
for a preview of the next book in Sara Richardson's
stunning Heart of the Rockies series,

MORE THAN A FEELING

CHAPTER ONE

Morning is hands-down the most beautiful time of day in the mountains.

Ruby James stepped out of her Honda Civic and raised her face to the sky, closing her eyes, breathing in the fresh, sweet scent of the new, dew-kissed grass. At five o'clock the sky was still dark and studded with stars, but the frayed edges of the mountainous horizon glowed with the promise of light.

A new day. Fresh, clean air, a blank slate of possibilities. Each morning for the last year, she was the first one to greet it at the Walker Mountain Ranch. And for the first time in her life, she had started to understand freedom. It manifested itself in the expanse of mountainous space, in the stillness of a world still asleep, in the opportunity she'd been given to take care of herself, to pursue a life she wanted, instead of one that had been thrust on her by a broken system.

The air's chill infused energy into her blood as Ruby

tromped from her parking spot behind the Walker Mountain Ranch, lugging along a cloth market bag that held her very own personal set of stainless-steel measuring cups and a marble rolling pin. Elsie Walker, her boss and the head chef at the ranch, kept a set at in the kitchen, but she preferred to use her own for baking. Then she'd take them home each night to polish them and bring them back the next morning. It was something akin to having a briefcase— she imagined—except instead of a laptop and a cell phone and whatever other devices were popular at the moment, her briefcase was filled with kitchen utensils. They were the best ones she could find at that gourmet kitchen store in town, solid and unbendable, the highest-quality materials for baking. And this morning she had to do her best baking because their best clients would be coming off the trail later this afternoon, and everything had to be perfect.

Each year in the spring, before things got busy, the Walker Mountain Ranch welcomed a group of foster kids from other towns in the area. They came to stay for free. They went on a backpacking trip. They went whitewater rafting. They did the ropes course and zip line and had the chance to just be kids without a care, for once in their lives.

She would've given anything for that chance back when she was being carted to foster home after foster home. So when Elsie had told her about the group—when they'd started planning—Ruby had decided she would do everything she could to make this week at the ranch the best of these kids' lives, cooking for them, volunteering to help out while they were at the ranch—anything to make them feel wanted and accepted and free.

She approached the lodge's back door, the familiar scent of wood stain greeting her. The massive logs stacked one on top of each other always reminded her of the Lincoln Logs she and her brother Grady used to play with before Mama went to prison. They'd build structures almost exactly like the one that stood in front of her, grand mountain palaces where magical things happened—where families gathered around fireplaces and drank hot chocolate. Where there were no drugs and no cops and no fears. They'd set up the fences and add in small plastic farm animals they'd shoplifted from the drugstore, pigs and cows and chickens, and even a crotchety rooster they'd called Slim.

Back then, she'd believed things could turn around for them. She'd believed Mama would go to rehab like she always said, and then things would be normal. Once, she'd even shoplifted an apron for Mama—a frilly thing that looked handmade. As if when Mama put it on, she'd be magically transformed into the woman Ruby had always dreamed she would become. The mom who made chocolate chip cookies and drove the car pool and cut her peanut butter and jelly sandwiches in funny shapes that'd make her giggle at school.

But Ruby didn't believe in magic anymore.

Shaking her head at herself, she paused to study the Walker Mountain Ranch's lovely façade. Maybe that's why she'd ended up here. When she'd gotten in the car, she didn't know where to go. She'd never had a place, and god knew Aspen, Colorado, was worlds away from Cherryville, North Carolina. But it was either stay there with Derek and live with the bruises that always splotched her skin, or go. Disappear. Build a new life, a new name, a new future for herself.

So she'd chased freedom. As she'd worked her way west, the mountains had called her name. She'd seen mountains before, of course, but nothing like the Rocky Mountains. Instead of mounded green hills, they were massive and sharp, lovely but impenetrable. Exactly the refuge she was seeking. While there was a certain fragility to her new life—her new identity—this was the first time she'd felt rooted since before Mama'd been put away.

As always, that thought burrowed deep in the tomb where she normally kept all of those memories vaulted. That was where they belonged. Stashed away. 'Course with Mama's birthday being today, those crushed hopes and dreams were getting restless, feeling almost uncontainable. Was she still in jail? Had Derek contacted her mother after Ruby had run away? Cold dread washed over her, and she plowed through the ranch's kitchen door before the tide of fear dragged her back into the currents of the past.

The kitchen was dim with only the under-cabinet lighting turned on, but it was warm, too, scented with cinnamon and yeast. Inhaling the familiarity soothed the tremble out of her hands. No one here knew a lick of anything about her past, and she had to keep it that way. She couldn't risk Derek tracking her down, not after the threats he'd made the last time he'd beat her up.

Holding her breath, she willed her heart to stop pounding so hard. She had to calm herself down. Derek couldn't find her here, she'd made sure of that. She'd been sad to hear of her old neighbor's passing, but Ruby James's death had given her the perfect opportunity to escape.

The woman hadn't had any children of her own, and she'd always had a soft spot for Ruby. Still she'd been surprised to hear that Miss James had left her everything. Her house and her car. She'd never told Derek. She'd simply sold off everything, except the Civic, and used the proceeds to fund her trip out west, paying cash for absolutely everything.

As a cop, Derek would have the means to look for her, to watch for a ping on her credit card, to scan reports from all over the country. That's why she'd been so careful. That's why she'd used Ruby James's name. That's why she'd cut up all of her credit cards.

No. He wouldn't find her, she told herself again as she marched to the other side of the room and set down her bag. It was time to stop thinking about him. About Mama. A new day. A new life. And she had cinnamon rolls to bake.

Bryce and Avery Walker didn't open the ranch until nine during the slow season, but Ruby and Elsie made all the baked good from scratch, which meant Ruby had to get an early start every morning. She preferred it, anyway. Being alone. It was easier because she didn't have to pretend. She didn't have to watch herself so closely, to guard every word and every thought so she wouldn't risk confusing her new identity with her old life. When she was alone, she could let down her guard, turn on some tunes, and put her hands to work, rolling out scones and cinnamon roll dough and whatever else was on the menu for the morning.

Just the thought of that therapeutic process of kneading and rolling and mixing was enough to set her emotions right. Even though she'd left it behind, her old life was always there in the dreams, in the memories. Sometimes they leaked out, spilling over into the present, but she could usually outrun 'em as long as she stayed busy.

And speaking of busy...she shimmied out of her fleece coat and hung it on the hook behind the pantry...she had a whole mess of baked goods planned for those kids—gooey chocolate chip cookies as big as their heads, fat, fluffy cinnamon rolls that would melt in their mouths. Smiling at the thought, she started to unpack her supplies. First, the heavy marble rolling pin that had cost her a small fortune. Admiring the swirled gray and white stone, she pulled it out of the bag and—

Crash!

The jarring sound stilled her. A breath lodged in her throat. She strained her ears, listening.

A series of thuds and rumbles sounded again from the pantry.

Oh, god. A swallow tangled her windpipe. Something was *in* there. Her grip tightened on the rolling pin's handle. Was it a bear fresh out of hibernation? Scenes from that damn grizzly bear documentary she'd watched two days ago flashed like a horror flick, the bear towering over her on its hind legs, teeth gnashing, claws slashing through the air. Aspen had a major bear problem. They broke into restaurants and homes, raiding the kitchens, rummaging through the trash...

God. Oh, dear god. Her heart catapulted into an arrhythmia. Perspiration beaded on her skin. She stared longingly at the kitchen door, all the way on the other side of the room. It might as well have been Antarctica! There was no way she'd get over there without the *thing* hearing her! The pantry's half-open door stood between her and a clean escape...

More clatters cinched tension into her neck.

"Damn it!"

Ruby inhaled a gasp. Not a bear! Definitely not a bear! A muffled string of curses edged her back against the wall. A man. There was a man in the pantry! Except there were no other cars outside. Bryce and Shooter, the ranch's other guide, had gone on a backpacking trip with the kids...

Wait a minute. She jerked her head and squinted in a futile effort to examine the kitchen door she'd walked through not five minutes ago. It hadn't been locked. Holy Moses, it was *always* locked! If she hadn't been so preoccupied with the past, she would've noticed. Someone had broken in!

An icy sensation spread over her shoulders and locked them tight, the remnants of past trauma seeping into her.

Derek?

No, no. He couldn't have found her.

Another crash seemed to shake the floor.

Panic came in wrenching gasps, clouding her vision, prickling her skin. *911.* She had to call 911 before the man came out and saw her.

Still gripping the rolling pin, she reached her other clammy hand into the market bag and fished for her cell phone.

The pantry door creaked, then cranked open all the way.

It was dark inside, but a man's silhouette stood under the doorjamb. A large man. Tall, broad shoulders. The hood of a black sweatshirt obscured his face.

"Freeze, dirtbag!" Arm stiff with fear, Ruby held out the rolling pin, brandishing it as if it was a gun.

"What the hell?" The man took a step toward her.

"I said freeze," she squeaked, because technically, there wasn't much she could do if he decided not to obey.

"Easy," the guy murmured in a patronizing voice, like he was trying to lure a scared puppy or something.

"You hold it right there, asshole!" She waved the rolling pin again. "I'm calling nine-one-one."

"Take it easy." Slowly, the man held up one hand while the other took down his hood. "It's me, Ruby," he said. But *me* who? All she could see were the bright lights of fear, shooting holes through her vision. Because she'd never been able to fight back. When Derek came at her, when he laced his fingers around her neck and reminded her he could squeeze the life out of her, she'd never been able to fight back...

Gasping for a breath, she realized her fingertips were tingling with numbness. *Oh god!* How would she fight back with a *rolling pin*?

"Ruby!" The man shuffled a step closer. "Lower the weapon."

How? Her arms seemed locked in place. Her lungs heaved and gasped. *No!* Not here! Not now! She hadn't had a panic attack since she'd come to the Walker Mountain Ranch. But sure enough, her heart pounded so hard her head got light. It felt like her lungs were filling with water. She had to fight for a breath.

"Hey." A hand enclosed hers.

Fire roared through her. "Don't touch me!" She ripped free and swung the rolling pin as hard as she could, feeling a thud as it collided with the man's body.

A winded groan punched out of his mouth and he sank slowly to the floor, clutching his groin.

"Holy Moses," she whimpered. She'd taken the guy down. What now? What the hell should she do now? Frozen, she stood over him, still clutching the rolling pin.

"You hit me with that again, I'm pretty sure I won't be able to walk for a week," the man said. "Kids'll probably be out of the question, too."

A joke? The perp was joking with her?

Ruby's vision cleared. She gazed down at him and stared into eyes so blue they put the Colorado sky to shame. "Sawyer," she panted. Realizing who he was didn't do much to curb the panic. Sawyer was Bryce's cousin! A cop! She'd nailed a cop in the balls with a marble rolling pin!

"I'm so sorry!" She dropped to her knees next to him. "Are you okay? I thought you were an intruder!"

"Obviously," he mumbled as he gingerly sat up and hunched over, resting his elbows on his knees. He shifted slightly with a wince.

"Why didn't you stop me?" Yes, it was perhaps a bit unsympathetic for her to ask that question when the man's voice was still cracking like a preteen's, but what the hell? With all of those bulging muscles of his, he could've immobilized her with one maneuver. He could've taken away the rolling pin and they wouldn't be in this situation, now, would they?

"Didn't want to scare you," Sawyer mumbled. "You already seemed pretty freaked out."

Humiliation soaked her face. This was not good, him seeing her have a panic attack. Really not good. Out of everyone here, she'd avoided Sawyer the most. He was a cop. A little research and the man could bring down her entire fabricated life...

"You want to tell me why you didn't recognize me?" His tenor had settled back into the deep, gravelly lovemaking voice she'd heard before. A tingle raced up her spine. It was like having a conversation with Keith Urban.

"Because you looked right at me," he continued, locking his gaze on hers.

Oh lordy, those eyes. So gorgeous. His face wasn't bad, either. Straight nose, strong, square jaw stubbled with a few days of growth. And there was an adorable faint line running down the center of his chin. Her heart started a traitorous flutter until she realized he was waiting for an answer, then the flutter turned violent.

"Um." She studied her hands, worry boiling up. "I saw you. Of course I *saw* you. I was just...a little panicked, that's all." If she told him the truth, that she couldn't control the panic, that it crashed over her and dragged her into a riptide of confusion, he'd start asking more questions.

"A *little* panicked?" Sawyer shot back.

"Well, can you blame me?" Her heart thumped in her

ears. "I mean, I wasn't expecting anyone to be hiding in the pantry—"

"Hiding?" Sawyer laughed. "Why would I be hiding in the pantry? Bryce asked me to fix the shelves while he was gone."

She shot to her feet. "At five o'clock in the morning?"

He was slower to get up but at least he wasn't grimacing anymore. "I'm on shift at eight."

Panic started to pump through her again, but this time it had nothing to do with fear and everything to do with the way he looked at her, the way his gaze drifted down her body. She crossed her arms so he couldn't guess her cup size. "How'd you get in here, anyway?"

Sawyer casually leaned against the kitchen counter, still looking her over like he appreciated what he saw. "I have a key. I'm staying here."

The room whirled. Not what she'd hoped to hear. That was bad. Very, very bad. It was hard enough to avoid him before, but if he stayed there, it'd be impossible! "I thought you were moving to Denver," she said, going for a casual, conversational tone. Damn the squeak of panic.

He shrugged. "The house sold faster than I thought. I still have a month left at work."

Fabulous. That was just her luck. The last thing she needed was a cop poking around the Walker Mountain Ranch.

"So what's with the panic attack?" he asked again, sounding more like a cop this time.

She busied herself with unpacking the rest of the kitchen utensils from her bag. "Whadda you mean?"

"You know what I mean. I know what a panic attack looks like, Ruby."

"It wasn't a panic attack," she insisted, then focused on lining up her measuring cups so he couldn't read the flush on her face. "I was surprised. That's all. No big deal." She peeked over at him.

His eyes were narrowed into skepticism. "Do you hyperventilate every time you're surprised?"

No. But she was about to hyperventilate right now. "Why do I feel like you're interrogating me?" she demanded in case he could see how weak she felt. Now that the adrenaline had drained away, her legs and arms felt unstable. The memories were closer, breathing down her neck. If she would've hit Derek with a rolling pin, he would've broken her jaw...

"Ruby? Is everything okay?" Sawyer asked quietly.

Crumpling the market bag in her shaky hands, she turned and smiled. "Everything's great." She'd learned how to lie, how to cover up the truth a smile. "I'm so sorry about your..." The blush made a strong comeback. "Um...do you want ice or anything?"

A smirk made him look less guarded. "Do I want to walk around with an icepack on my crotch? No thanks. I'll live."

"Okay." She sashayed past him like nothing had happened, like her stomach hadn't tightened into a painful knot. "I should get to work, then."

"You're sure everything's okay?" Sawyer called behind her.

"Of course." She unstacked the stainless mixing bowls from the shelf above the sink.

"All right, then. Guess I'll get back to work, too," he said slowly. The pantry door opened then clicked shut.

But something told her that wasn't the end of the conversation.

Fall in Love with Forever Romance

EVERY LITTLE KISS
by Kim Amos

Casey Tanner, eternal good girl, is finally ready to have some fun. Step one: a fling with sexy firefighter Abe Cameron. But can Abe convince her that this fling is forever? Fans of Kristan Higgins, Jill Shalvis, and Lori Wilde will fall for Kim Amos's White Pine series!

HOPE SPRINGS
ON MAIN STREET
by Olivia Miles

Now that her cheating ex-husband has proposed to "the other woman," Jane Madison has moved on—to dinners of wine and candy, and to single motherhood. When her ex's sexy best friend Henry Birch comes back to town, their chemistry is undeniable. Can Henry convince Jane to love again? Find out in the latest in Olivia Miles's Briar Creek series!

Fall in Love with Forever Romance

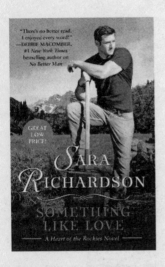

SOMETHING LIKE LOVE
by Sara Richardson

Ben Noble needs to do some damage control. His heart has always been in ranching, but there's no escaping the spotlight on his high-powered political family. The only thing that can restore his reputation is a getaway to the fresh air of Aspen, Colorado. Not to mention that the trip gives Ben a second chance to impress a certain gorgeous mountain guide. But Paige Harper is nothing like the shy girl he remembers...she's so much more.

WALK THROUGH FIRE
by Kristen Ashley

Millie Cross knows what it's like to burn for someone. She was young and wild, and he was fierce and wilder—a Chaos biker who made her heart pound. Twenty years later, Millie's chance run-in with her old flame sparks a desire she just can't ignore...Fans of Lori Foster will love the latest Chaos novel from *New York Times* bestselling author Kristen Ashley!

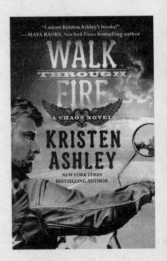

Fall in Love with Forever Romance

"A delightful new voice in historical romance!"
—Tessa Dare, *New York Times* bestselling author

ONE WILD WINTER'S EVE
by Anne Barton

Lady Rose Sherbourne never engages in unseemly behavior—except for the summer she spent in the arms of the handsome stable master Charles Holland years ago. So what's a proper lady to do when Charles, as devoted as ever, walks back into her life? Fans of Elizabeth Hoyt and Sarah MacLean will love this Regency-era romance by Anne Barton.